I0738867

大蛇の旗幟
Orochi no Kishi

by Itoshi

Art

cover by Aldaria
interiors by Lehanan Aida

The Hourglass comic
by Aldaria
story by Itoshi

For my fans.
Thank you for loving this world and people
as much as I do.

I promise many more adventures ahead.

- Itoshi

Chapter I

A Man Named Mouse

Blythe, Arizona (2071)

"Mouse!? Hey, Mouse? You out here?"

Mouse failed to hear his name. From where he lay under the dirt-clotted engine of the pick-up, the rattling fans and the blaring of the single speaker radio echoing off the metal walls of the garage made it nearly impossible to hear a thing.

The old man kicked his dolly. "Jesus' bloody corpse, kid, ain't you hearing me?"

Mouse dropped his socket wrench and swore, pulling himself out from under the rusted front-end bumper with an irritated yank. The right mount gave way and the aged chrome fell, swinging an inch off the floor. Mouse scrambled back just in time to escape castration. "Fuck! I'm working in here!!"

"Watch yer mouth boy, I got good cause. We've got company."

Mouse struggled to sit up, scrubbing the sweat from his forehead. He looked at the oily dirt streak it left on his arm and sighed, getting to his feet. "Customers?"

"Dunno, look like kids to me," Fred said, spitting on the concrete floor. He'd given up chew five years ago when the last of his front teeth fell out, but somehow the spitting had remained. He grinned ghoulishly. "But then, everybody looks like kids to me."

"Don't spit in my garage, Fred." Mouse pulled his sweat-soaked cap off, freeing his long damp hair as he stepped over tool chests and old tires, heading for the utility sink. He kicked on the faucet; the pipes groaned and came to life. The water was as hot as the tin roof of the garage. He stuck his hands and arms under it, wincing, grabbing for the soap. "Tell 'em I'll be out soon as I find a shirt!"

"You got it," the old man said, heading out the side door and back into the station shop where they sold a few cold drinks, first-aid supplies, canned goods and road maps for whatever people could pay.

Mouse was pulling a fairly smudge-free t-shirt over his head when Fred appeared at the garage door again, eyes big. "We got racers, Mouse! Sonofabitch!"

"Racers? Are you sure?" Mouse asked, winding his sink-wet hair into a coil that he piled atop his head and affixed with a mechanic's pencil.

"Yeah, they got them fancy street bikes and shit in their face and stuff!"

Mouse let out a sigh. It was the last thing he needed today. He shrugged, "Well, best not keep them waiting."

Fred got serious. "I'm locking the cash drawer!"

Mouse followed him out. "Why bother? It's not what they're after, anyway."

He let Fred fuss over whatever imagined safety precautions he could think of, and gathered himself for what waited on the other side of the shop's smeary front windows. Eight or nine of them it looked like – all on road bikes. They'd pulled into the pump stalls and were stripping off their outer gear and beating the red Arizona dust off of their limbs. Looked like they intended to stay a while. One of them was kicking at pump #5.

Mouse stepped out into the brick-oven afternoon heat. "We don't have any gas, here!" he yelled. "You'll have better luck in Bridesfall – about 30 miles north of here, back on the main highway."

The bikers didn't react to his helpful directions – just kept about their business – sorting packs, drinking from canteens and adjusting their leathers. Fred was right – they were young, and they did have shit in their face. A lot of shit: rings, bones, bits of ornately carved wood – all of it symbolic of something, pulled through the flesh of their ears, noses, lips and nipples. It made him shudder.

He noticed there were two others parked further out nose to nose, blocking the drive. They kept their gear on, goggles and scarves covering their faces, vigilant of something – what, he couldn't guess but it was his chief focus of concern. A pair of kids pushed past him and into the shop – one brushed his shoulder like he was a piece dust himself.

Mouse stuck his hands in his pockets and followed them back in, if nothing else to make sure Fred didn't try to pull something epically stupid.

He joined the old man behind the counter. Fred was rubbing a pocketknife between his palms like a string of prayer beads. Mouse hitched a leg up on a stool next to him to wait it out while the kids, now there were five of them, ransacked their meager wares.

Fred wore a drooping frown. He was muttering to himself as the punks ripped open packaging and toppled rows of baked beans onto the floor. One of them unzipped his jeans and proceeded to relieve himself on the Twinkies.

"If your father had lived to see this... "

But Mouse's father hadn't and for what it was worth, it honestly didn't matter. They'd gone from almost getting by, to having nothing, to having less than nothing so many fucking times it just didn't pack the same punch anymore. Racing gangs, gamblers, outlaws – same wolves in different clothing. Didn't matter where you lived, somebody would be there

aldaria

to lie, cheat or rob you out of whatever livelihood you'd managed to make for yourself. He'd pack up everything he owned in a rucksack and head north to cooler climes if the stories he'd heard about the overcrowded disease-ridden cities held a higher appeal. A loud crash brought Mouse back to the present. They'd just toppled the Coke machine.

"Hey!" It wasn't the loss of a few sodas that concerned him nearly as much as their one working cooling unit biting the linoleum floor. He leapt over the counter only to find himself grabbed hard by the arms and pinned against the empty beer case. The pencil fell out of his hair and the long strands tumbled over his eyes. He tossed his head and blew it aside. *Goddamned hair.*

"Where the fuck you going?" a voice hissed in his ear. The kid's foreign accent muddied the English he spat out. "We're just shopping here."

It occurred to him now that they were all Asian of some sort or another. Maybe all the same sort – who knew? Brotherhood was an identity some clans liked to claim even if their bloodlines shared only a tenuous connection. They wore their clan insignia proudly – sewn into their jackets, tattooed on their arms, or sprayed in stencil on their bikes. Theirs was some kind of Chinese script lettered in gold over a many-headed serpent. Mouse hadn't seen it before. His arms were cramping, it pissed him off.

"Shopping? Really? You remember to bring money?" His quip earned him a knee in the lower back. Mouse's legs crumpled and his palms hit the floor, catching himself in time to see the glint of a knife flash from his attacker's belt.

The kid laughed at him, twisting the game knife under his nose. "You like this, eh?"

With his focus firmly on the knife blade, Mouse was only dimly aware of a large black shape approaching the doorway. All commotion in the room stopped as the door swung open with the jingle of the overhead bells.

A man's voice shouted at the kids in a foreign tongue and they dropped whatever they were mangling and reluctantly slunk out. A large hand came into view and covered the fist of Mouse's assailant. It gripped the stubborn fingers until the knuckles popped and the kid yipped, dropping the knife. Mouse lunged for it, grabbed it and dove forward, rolling away from the pair who were now locked in an eye-to-eye battle. Curses were thrown, that much he could comprehend, and the kid soon backed down. With a toss of his partially shaved head, he strutted away, kicking over the last standing shelf before exiting.

The man watched him go before turning about slowly to survey the room through his dust-rimmed goggles. He'd been one of the two figures watching from the driveway.

Mouse scrambled to his feet and backed himself carefully up against a wall, knife poised. "Take whatever shit you want and get the fuck out!" he sneered, fighting against an unnatural fear of the imposing aura this figure commanded. The man wasn't very tall but he was broad-shouldered, built like a concrete wall Mouse didn't relish slamming into.

The man turned to him, but didn't approach. Instead he lifted his hands to flip up his goggles, revealing a pair of deep almond eyes. The bandana was next, pulled down over his nose to rest below the cropped beard that defined his chin. The face that looked down on him had unadorned, smooth skin. He wasn't old, but he didn't look young, either. The road had aged him – he carried it in his eyes.

"Are you the man they call Mouse?" he asked. His accent was the same as the boy's only less prominent. Mouse didn't know what to make of him, and squeezed the knife grip tighter.

"You might want to see to grandfather over there," the man suggested. "He's bleeding quite a lot."

Fred? He'd forgotten about him. Mouse gave the man a wide berth and ran to his friend. The old man had been slammed against the countertop by the looks of the red splatter. He'd ricocheted back and fell slumped against the wall. His lids were half-open while a river of red dripped from his nose. The unopened pocketknife was still in his palm. Mouse hadn't even seen Fred get pushed. He set the game knife down at his knees and grabbed an oil rag from behind the counter and held it against the old man's nose.

"Come on, Uncle Fred. Open your mouth. Breathe easy, buddy." Mouse hadn't called him 'uncle' since his father passed away a decade ago. It was a name he'd been asked to call his dad's best friend since he was a little kid. But there was no actual relation. Aside from his father, Mouse didn't have anyone else he could rightly call family.

"Motherrfuckerr," Fred mumbled. "You see me clock that sonof… " The blood made him choke and sputter. Mouse did his best to catch it in the rag but what for? The whole fucking store was a shithole to begin with.

"Can you stand a little? Let me get you to your cot so I can clean you up."

"Yeah, sure… no ballroom dancin' though." Mouse wrapped an arm around the old man and moved to stand him up gingerly.

"I hope you people are pleased with yourselves," Mouse growled, "Beating the shit outta an elderly – " he stopped.

The shop was empty. The roar of bike engines heading into the distance, the mess, and the two one-hundred dollar bills left on the counter were all that remained of their late afternoon customers.

Chapter II

Secrets

Mouse sat at the bar in the Iron Horse Saloon, fingering the game knife. It was expensive, looked custom-made and like the bikes they rode in on, was marked with their clan's symbol – a mythic creature with eight snake-like heads and as many tails. He nursed his warm beer and traced the golden characters carved beneath the creature's belly with his thumb. He was two rounds to the house in, and still nobody was talking – although he'd barely made a dent in the hundred he'd brought to town. Not that the locals *weren't* talking – talking was all they did – but they just weren't telling him anything he needed to know.

Yeah, they'd seen the gang come through – caused a fuss over at the general store, stole some supplies, but they soon rode right on out in a hail of dust. Only Mouse had the chance to share a brief face-to-face with any of the members – not that it had been enjoyable. He stretched his back. It still smarted from the kick. He winced and resumed his slouch.

"Aw, honey, you should just let it go," a familiar voice said. "Take that money they left you and use it to get out of town."

Mouse shrugged and dragged the end of the knife along the worn countertop. The bar dated back to the late 1800s and had the pockmarks and bullet holes to prove it. "Go where?" he said, looking at the barmaid who was stroking his arm with her bony hands.

She smiled and kept patting him idly, "Anywhere but here, darling. You've got your whole life ahead of you. Don't know why you keep wasting it rolling around in that dusty garage."

Mouse lifted his beer and suffered through another sip. Bland as it was, it was calming his nerves. "Need to look after Fred."

She grunted. "That old turd? He can look after himself just fine. I'll see to it, even if I have to do it myself."

"Thanks Gloria, but I'm just fine where I am… "

"Are you hon? You look a few shades pale. Why don't you come on in the back with me and have a nice lie-down? I'll put some color back in your cheeks."

Mouse grinned. "I thought you just told me to save my money?" Despite her age, the woman had determination. She propositioned him nearly every time he stopped into town, especially if he was carrying cash. She was old enough to be his mother. Maybe she was – or another one like her – scrambling to keep a roof over her head like the rest of them. All in all she hadn't done too bad for herself. There weren't a lot of women to be had in the Southwest. It wasn't the kind of place you wanted to raise daughters. It'd been years since Mouse had seen a woman under the age of fifty.

"Get your claws out of the boy, Gloria. Don't you have any decency? Man's just had his livelihood turned upside down and you're already trying to wring a few dollars out of him." Doc Meadows had emerged from the curtains at the rear of the house, wiping his freshly washed hands on a towel. "Besides, backroom's taken. I've got patients trying to get some rest."

Gloria leaned in close. "Offer's always open," she whispered and stepped away as Meadows took the stool next to him.

"Woman's like a damn horse fly," he said gesturing for a glass of beer himself. "No tellin' what kind of shit she's been into. Present company excluded, of course."

"Of course," Mouse nodded. "How's our patient?"

"Can't cure ornery, but he'll be fine. He's got few bruises is all. Took a hell of a wallop to the nose. I gave him something for pain – knocked him right out," Doc said and took his glass from the bartender graciously. Mouse dropped a few singles on the counter while Doc drank the glass down in long gulps. He paused to burp mid-way. "Thanks, that hit the spot."

"Hot day," Mouse said, taking another drink himself. His head was starting to float a little and the ache of his own injuries was at last beginning to numb. Alcohol was what the doctor had ordered – due to a general lack of supplies. The government hadn't made a decent aid drop in about six months. What little medical equipment and pharmaceuticals Blythe had were reserved for only the most serious cases. Last summer's tornadoes had torn up the north end of town, forcing Doc to move his makeshift hospital to the saloon's former bordello suites – much to Gloria's chagrin.

"Yeah it was hot alright," Doc agreed, raising a glass to the setting sun through the window slats. "Tomorrow will be hotter still. And the day after that. Gloria's got some sense left. You should think about her offer."

Mouse coughed. "Excuse me?"

"Heaven's boy, not *that* offer, I mean the one about pulling up stakes. Hardly nobody uses that highway route anymore. I don't think your father would have held out half as long as you. This town's dead as a mayfly on a windscreen. Get out while you can. Take that blood money and buy yourself a decent life. I know I would were I half my age again."

Mouse spread his bills out on the counter. $73.00. That plus the other $100 hidden back at the station would certainly buy him a bus ticket to somewhere. Question was where? The leaving he could picture clearly, the arriving was much more murky.

"Why do you suppose they came through this way?" Mouse asked. "We haven't had any races out this way for a decade."

Doc shrugged. "Maybe they got lost. I heard Dry Lakes still holds a competition or two. They could have been on their way out those parts."

Mouse passed Doc the knife. "They left me a token," he said.

Doc fished around in his shirt pocket for his reading glasses and took a closer look at the handle. "Hmm... some kind of Chinese writing. Can't rightly tell what it says. Not my area of study."

"They were Asian," Mouse said. "One of them asked for me."

"Huh? They looking for a mechanic?"

Mouse shrugged. "This stern looking guy – their leader I guess – asked me if I was 'the man they called Mouse' as if he'd been asking around about me."

Doc wrinkled his brow and inspected the knife again. "Could be it's one of these bike gangs out of the Pacific Rim. I heard on the radio sometime ago they were having a problem with illegal immigrants coming in through Baja as part of the gambling rings. Thing of it is a lot of those island countries are under water and good flat land's scarce. They come over here now where they can tear up the wasteland with their tire tracks. Some make a pretty good penny for it, so I hear. Still, doesn't answer the question of why they'd be asking for you. Any of 'em have a flat?"

Mouse shook his head and took the knife back. "Seemed to me they were only interested in letting off some steam. Most of them were kids: 16, 18 ... hard to tell the way they were pierced up. Their English wasn't very good. Definitely not local."

"Well, I think it's best if you lay low for a bit. No telling what they're after. I know nobody around here would wish you or Fred any trouble, so somebody must have sent them your way. My old leg's telling me, they'll be back."

"Your leg predicts rain, not bikers."

Doc waggled his brows and returned to his beer.

Mouse considered his options. Driving back to the station to face the mess wasn't something he was ready to deal with just yet. Earlier, after the bleeding slowed, he'd laid Fred down on his cot while he took a sledgehammer to the front bumper of the pickup. Once it was off and the wheels had clearance, he got Fred up in the truck and hot-wired the ignition. A few mild shocks and curses later, the old engine turned over. Soon they were kicking dust up the frontage road into town. Mouse knew the saloon had a short-wave radio and it didn't take long for Doc to show up with his black leather bag. He knew Fred wasn't seriously injured but at his age, any punch to the right place could prove to be his last – though the old man always said he wanted to go out in a fight.

Sorry, buddy. Not on my watch.

"Maybe you're right. I should stay in town tonight."

"Good call," Doc said, setting his empty glass down and getting up. "Grab a bed in the back. I'll keep Gloria off you."

Mouse grabbed a chair instead and pulled it next to Fred's bedside. The old coot was snoring up a storm in an opiated dreamland. Despite the outer frailty of his thinning body, his heart was still strong and would likely last him several more years. Like a 100-year-old saguaro cactus – this hot dry land suited Fred. He'd grown up in it and lived his life simply and honestly.

Although they'd been constant companions since childhood, Mouse's father hadn't fared so well. He enjoyed his smokes and whiskey – lived a little on the edge, with a run-in or two with the law when this town still had laws. Despite his restlessness he was good man at heart. He raised him right. "Don't do like your old man, Son," he'd say, after coming home a little bruised and tipsy from a night on the town. "Stay away from women and dice and you'll do fine in life." Mouse took the advice his father couldn't. But despite his reputation for brawling, the man did good with his hands and folks around town knew he was the one to call on whenever a tractor snapped a driveshaft or a fuse blew on an electrical box. He always brought Mouse around on his stops. As a kid, the women would coo and stuff him with cookies but as he got older, he preferred being keeper of the tools: holding the spare nuts and bolts, sorting them carefully and having them ready when Dad called for them. His father recognized his natural aptitude and encouraged it, taught him all the maintenance basics.

They'd make weekly trips out to the junkyard to see Barney and his pack of nasty dogs. Mouse always remembered to bring bacon for them.

"One man's trash is another man's treasure. You see treasure here, son? It's all around you. Nothin's ever too far gone to be done with." It was a philosophy essential for carving a foothold in a world without catalogs or shopping malls. "If you need it, you'd best go find it or make it – cause it ain't coming in the mail."

His dad taught him what to look for and what to avoid when picking through discarded household items, or rusted heaps of crumpled vehicles for useful bits and pieces. Mouse became especially fond of piecing together discarded motorbikes – as they proved to be the most efficient method of navigating the debris-ridden country roads. That, and they were fast. He liked riding out into the open desert as long as they could spare the gas for it.

Mouse remembered his father hitching them a ride on a 18-wheeler to Phoenix to buy him a decent welding torch for his 14th birthday. They bounced around with a cargo of stinking chickens for 12 hours in the heat and his father was never the same after it. He'd developed a cough that only grew worse as the months passed. He blamed the damn poultry flu for it but Doc Meadows didn't buy it. It was likely something much more serious that he no longer had the means or equipment to cure.

Mouse and Fred looked after him, kept him cool and comfortable through the wasting illness. By the following spring he was gone and everything the man had owned in the world – the gas station, the old pickup, and a hell of a lot of tools – became his. They buried his Dad at the foot of Salvation Hill with the rest of the former townsfolk under a pile of red and gray rocks. The Preacher had come down from Bridesfall and said a few words over his Bible but they gave Mouse little comfort. He remembered Fred at his side during the service, in an ill-fitting black suit, his face stern and hard as if he was holding back a storm of emotion. Mouse felt he had a responsibility to keep his chin up for him. He didn't want to know what was behind that hard face. He'd already had a few months to get used to the idea of being an orphan – the funeral was just one more thing he had to get through. When the Preacher finished he felt Doc Meadow's hand on his shoulder.

"Don't worry, boy. In this town, we look after our own."

His father may be long gone, but the torch and the gear that the man had scraped, saved and sat in chicken shit for still hung in the station garage.

We look after our own.

Mouse stood up and threw the curtain back. Back in the bar area he found Gloria fanning herself by the windows as the last of the daylight gave out. He reached in his pocket, grabbed the remainder of the cash and dropped it on the table on front of her. Her eyes got big.

"Lordy, be!"

"See to it the old man wakes up with a smile on his face," he said, and strode out of the saloon for the last time in his life.

"Shit... " Mouse gripped the steering wheel and pressed his forehead into his knuckles. He stopped the pickup, idling at the top of the hill. Below, a tenth mile down the slow grade was the station. It was basked in the red taillights of a flatbed truck that had been backed into the drive. The flatbed was covered in canvas and at the head of it were a trio of street bikes – halogen headlights casting the red dust in eerie shadows. His guests were back.

Mouse raised his head, thinking. Clearly they had returned to get something they wanted and it wasn't roadmaps. His plan to get out of town, such as it was, had now taken an unexpected turn. The money he needed was locked up in the one place he couldn't get to unseen. The whole business was pissing him off. He pulled the truck into gear and sped down the slope straight up to the garage like he'd been expecting them. He left his headlights on as he jumped out to unlock the bay door.

"Garage's closed!" he hollered over the groan of the flatbed engine. It was a heavy hauler, burdened with a load hidden under the canvas. He couldn't even guess what all that shit was about. There were four men present. One was sitting up in the truck, the other three had come in on bikes. He was sure he'd recognized two of the men from before. Mouse turned his back to them and worked the combination lock.

"We have urgent business that requires your assistance." The one who'd spoken to him before, the apparent leader, stepped forward casually, removing his riding gloves. "We have been patiently waiting for you to return. You owe us the same courtesy."

Mouse lifted the garage door and rolled it up in no great hurry. "I respond in kind, gentlemen. So considering what happened earlier today, I'd say I owe you jack shit."

A second man stepped forward aggressively but the first one stopped him with a word. There was a brief exchange between them – clearly there was a difference of opinion between them on how to handle this.

The leader seemed unfazed. "You've been compensated for your troubles. Perhaps not adequately enough?"

Mouse turned about sharply and met his eyes. "I don't want your money. Take your urgent business elsewhere." The man stood just a few inches taller than himself, but he looked like he was built from iron.

"Why don't we go inside and have a talk?" the leader suggested. "I think you will be interested in what I have to say."

Mouse took a step closer. "Maybe you're having trouble with my English. I said take your goons and get the hell off my property."

The man's eyes narrowed as if he were mildly amused by Mouse's brazen actions. He smiled. "This piece of dirt, it means that much to you?"

Mouse didn't blink. "Yes." He walked away from them and got back up in the pickup. His hand shook a little as he shifted into drive to bring it in. Adrenaline was pumping through him. One minute he was ready to put this shithole a hundred miles behind him, in the next he was willing to get his ass royally kicked to defend it. *Calm down, dipshit. Play this one smart.*

By the time he parked the truck and shut off the engine, the men had invited themselves into his garage and were seating themselves around a card table he kept in the corner. There were only two folding chairs. The leader took one and his sidekick sat in the second. The younger man was nosing about his machinist's chest. Mouse flicked on the garage lights to keep a better eye on them but the sun had long set and all he could get from the solar reserve batteries was a dull brownish light. He wasn't going to waste generator fuel on this.

"Please," the leader gestured at a short stepladder, which he'd pulled up to the table as a third chair. "Let's sit and have a civilized discussion."

"I'll stand, thanks," Mouse said. There was no way he was going to be able to avoid this conversation it appeared. He took a calm confident stance but his mind was racing to recall where he'd left the hunting rifle and ammo. He saw that three of his guests carried sheathed knives.

"As you will," the leader said, removing the rest of his headgear and setting it on the table. His hair was dark and swept back. The man to his right wore his in long tight braids — the left side of his face was tattooed and the right lower lip was adorned with three small silver rings. "We should make introductions. I am called Sadao Koga. This is my Captain, Ichiro Tagata. We manage a high-tier racing team for the Northwest Division stakeholders."

The man called Sadao paused as if this pronouncement was supposed to impress him. Mouse crossed his arms and sighed.

"I'll get to my point. I'm looking for a mechanic."

"Ah... sorry. Can't help you. Terribly busy."

Sadao exchanged a look with his captain.

"More specifically, one intimately familiar with 21st Century Japanese engineering. I was told to find a man called Mouse."

"Don't know him, sorry. Best be on your way, I have a shop to clean up."

Mouse walked away from them and was heading for the inner office door when a shout from the younger man and the sound of a heavy tarp being pulled off whipped him back around. "Hey! Don't touch that!"

Sadao and his men were on their feet surrounding the object their younger counterpart had uncovered. All three were talking rapidly in ... Japanese it would seem.

"Hey! Back off!" Mouse yelled, pushing through them. He tried to gather the cover back up off the ground as if it were possible to hide what was already plainly revealed even in the dim light. "Don't touch it."

"Titanium. Impressive. Very hard to come by in this country," Sadao said, as his fingers traced the partially assembled frame carefully line for line. The kid noticed something in the rear of the object and pointed it out to his elders. The men looked closely, nodding and talking swiftly. Sadao stood, "Your braking system's Ducati. I'll have to forgive you for that. It takes a fine hand to reassemble a Ninja 650 from spare parts."

Mouse shrugged. "It's a hobby."

"Hobby, indeed. Your welds are nearly flawless. There are men who would pay a very high price for this hobby of yours... Mr. Mouse."

"Are you trying to flatter me?" Mouse said, pulling the cover back over the ¾ assembled street racer. All told, it represented the past nine years of his life: selling, trading and scavenging for extremely rare parts.

Sadao looked him straight on. "I need a mechanic I can trust."

Mouse laughed. "Ah, and so to build the foundations of this trust, you send your punks in to trash the shit out of my shop. Smart plan."

Sadao smiled like a proud father. "They're just 'high-spirited.' Where they came from no one taught them manners. What you could earn in one year would buy you a whole new shop and a new town to go with it."

Mouse laid the cover back over the bike reverently, smoothing out the wrinkles. He didn't answer.

"At the very least, I can give you the parts to finish your bike."

Mouse considered it for a moment, and then returned to reality. "I'm assuming you're not known for your charity... "

"I have something I want you to look at," Sadao said, resuming his business manner. He nodded toward the flatbed in the driveway.

"What's on it?"

"Why don't you go have a look?"

Sadao shouted to his driver and his two men set about untying the canvas. When it was rolled off the side and into the dust, Mouse was invited to climb up onto the bed. A mechanical massacre was the best he could describe it. He stepped over the twisted metal and smashed safety glass among the remains of tortured Kawasakis, Hondas and off-road ATVs. There was even a Sidewinder sand car among the casualties. He'd never seen so many racing class vehicles in one pile before. It made his mouth moisten.

"I hope you realize these are beyond repair," he yelled down. "Even if I had all the foreign parts. What the hell kind of competitions have you been in? Canyon jumping?"

Sadao and his men looked unamused. "We're not asking you to repair them. We're asking you to look at them."

Mouse jumped down. "For what, scrap value?"

Sadao made a small gap with his finger and thumb. "Secrets."

Secrets – whatever they may be – required proper light to see. So despite his reluctance to waste precious fuel, Mouse fired up the generator and set two of his flood lamps on either end of the garage. He blinked into their brilliance as Sadao's men struggled to drag some of the wreckage into the hastily cleared space. He told himself this wasn't about giving in, but rather allowing himself a rare chance to study the proper assemblage and fittings of classic Japanese models. The bikes were old, 60 years or more. They were on- and off-road racers with durable chassis and combustion engines no longer manufactured in Japan, the US, or much of any place anymore. Feather-light solar was king now, but it was shit for acceleration, speed and endurance. Mouse wouldn't get caught dead behind the wheel of one. And in a region where the roads were unkind and the weather changed so suddenly – goddamned dangerous.

He righted a Honda trail rider on a repair rack and adjusted his lamps to study the damage. It had been ridden hard over coarse gravel from the pockmarks he could see in the chrome. The front-end suspension was crushed, jamming the steering damper. A closer look at the shattered number plate revealed the black splatter of old blood. It looked like it had been driven straight off a cliff.

"Jesus... "

The smell of tobacco smoke arrested his attention. He turned around in time to catch Sadao and his captain sharing a light in the bay doorway. "Hey, are you insane?! This is a gas station!"

"Taga-kun, tell me what my old ears heard. This man said no gas, correct? Not for 30 miles?"

Tagata took a long drag from his cigarette and flicked bright sparks of ash onto the garage floor. "No gas," he repeated. "Boss-sama ears are good."

"Let's get one thing straight," Mouse said. "This is my garage. You want me to do you a favor – you can do me a favor and take your coffin-nails outside."

Tagata fingered the hilt of his knife and smiled. Sadao took another thoughtful drag then nudged the younger man's shoulder and passed his half-smoked cigarette to him. "*Ikinasai*," he said and Tagata bristled, but obeyed, sticking both smokes in his mouth and puffing heavily as he sauntered away.

"Thank you," Mouse said as Sadao approached him.

"Now you are free to finish your work. *Safely*," Sadao said, with caution to his tone.

"As safely as your men who rode these bikes?" he asked. "Were these suicide runs? There's DNA all over them."

"Casualties of war," Sadao replied, grimly. "My men know the stakes. Have you been to the races, Mr. Mouse?"

"It's Mouse. And yeah, my old man used to take me when I was a kid. Back when it was a legit sport."

Sadao shrugged. "Times change and we change with it. It's called evolution – necessary for survival."

"Not when you kill off your own kind."

Sadao's eyes narrowed. "Keep looking," he said and returned to his watchful post at the bay door.

Mouse looked over the rest of the mud and blood encrusted off-road bikes first, then a pair of high-speed Kawasaki street bikes. All had met one way or another with fatal rapid deceleration. And aside from his earlier comments, Sadao hadn't offered anything else. The mangled street racers were especially painful for Mouse to examine. He'd desired one for himself his whole life. His father used to take him to the street races each year in Phoenix starting when he was five or six years old. He'd fallen in love with their sleek powerful aerodynamic designs, and perhaps a little with the daring men who rode them at top speeds of 120 mph as they flew by in roaring streaks of color under the city lights. Races were a family affair back then. People would travel in from miles around and camp under the stars in caravans of Winnebagos and vans. Mouse used to sleep in a sleeping bag on a stack of blankets in the bed of the old pickup, counting shooting stars as fans partied late into the night around campfires. But at some point, as the economy and population dwindled, the events became more rare and the guests shifted from locals to out-of-towners with large bankrolls and much higher stakes. Gambling rings formed and grew influential and the men they financed became more ruthless and risky. Some of them did quite well for themselves, he'd heard. Others paid for their privileges with the ultimate sacrifice. It had been a decade since Mouse had attended an official race.

"Anything?" Sadao asked.

Mouse stood and stretched his back, hours had passed and Sadao and his men were getting restless. "Unless you're willing to give me some hints, my advice to your riders is: slow the fuck down."

Sadao chuckled and then shouted for his driver. There was an exchange of words but Sadao's men reluctantly – and with not a small amount of cursing – dragged, pushed and shoved the sand car into his crowded garage.

It was an old Sidewinder with a VW beam style suspension. The design was essential for controlling the pitches and shifting surfaces of sand racing. From what he knew about sand cars – the car drove you, not the other way around. The rear-end beam had snapped on this one, and from the scrapes and embedded sand in the interior, appeared to have pitched the car end over end, planting it firmly and fatally several feet deep in a dune.

Mouse tapped the broken beam with a hammer. Good solid steel – something about this one wasn't right. The breakpoint was not at the load-bearing joint as one would expect. It was a little off. His heart beat faster as he reached for his spotlight.

"Sadao, I think I found that secret you're looking for."

The younger one got in his face before he could blink and grabbed the back of his shirt collar. "You call him, 'Boss!'" he spat angrily. Evidently, first names were an offense.

"He's not my boss, asshole."

"Goro-kun, *hanase!*"

The kid shoved him down and backed off, keeping a leery eye on him. This kid was like a trained attack dog, only responding to his master's commands.

"Show me," Sadao said.

Mouse straightened his collar. "Hand me the spotlight."

Sadao squatted down as Mouse got on his back on the garage floor and lit the underside of the carriage. "This here, the break point? It's a clean break. Not the result of metal fatigue – pattern's not right. And yeah, as I suspected, there's a weld here that was placed over it. Weak metal alloy – not steel."

Sadao leaned in close – the spotlight illuminated his narrow eyes. "What are you telling me? Be precise."

"I'm telling you this was cut and welded back, half-assed. With the action this suspension's supposed to carry in an average race, it would snap and crack-up the whole car. Boom. Head in the sand."

Sadao stood slowly. Something in his expression told Mouse he wasn't surprised.

Mouse scrambled out from under the sand car. "This is what you were hoping I'd find, isn't it?"

"I told you I need a mechanic I can trust."

"Someone's sabotaging you, aren't they?"

Sadao didn't answer, he seemed deep in thought. The hardness of his expression gave Mouse the chills.

"Why trust me? I could be lying to you, too."

"But, you are not."

"How do you know?"

"You have nothing to gain by lying," he said and called to his men and they began the arduous task of dragging the sand car back out to the hauler.

Sadao stood just outside the bay door, eyeing the sabotaged vehicle with a decisive look. Mouse paced around anxiously, uncertain of what to do. Eventually, Sadao emerged from his private thoughts and re-entered the garage to gather his goggles and gloves from the card table.

"Mr. Mouse, my offer is good," he said, shoving his hands into the gloves. "If you work for me, I can pay you very well."

"No thanks. Not everything in life is about money. Around here we value an honest living – I still have to face myself in the mirror each morning."

"You really believe we are so… uncivilized?"

"Call it a gut feeling. I'd rather not be responsible for sending kids to an early grave."

"Do you think any of my boys would be alive today had I not made racers of them?" Sadao countered. "You Americans know so little of the rest of the world. Your pride is what makes you blind."

Mouse had enough. "Get the fuck out of my garage," he said quietly.

Sadao refreshed his grin. "I'm not accustomed to being dismissed, especially when I'm in a gracious mood."

"Then you'll have to get used to it."

"Very well. Keep the bikes if you like," he said, setting the goggle strap over his head. "You can salvage the parts and finish your Ninja."

An odd trickle of panic rose in Mouse's chest as he watched the man walk away. The hauler was loaded and the rest of Sadao's men were busy re-stringing the canvas.

"You're going to answer me a question first," Mouse shouted after him, stopping

Sadao just shy of the bay doors. He caught up to him. "How did you know my name?"

Sadao looked him over slowly, end to end. There was an intensity to his gaze that made Mouse want to punch him. "It's obvious, isn't it? The name suits you."

Mouse shifted his stance. The whole encounter was making his skin crawl. He wanted to throw something black and sticky at that smug grin.

"I imagine your mother saw something cunning in those cold blue eyes of yours. You keep yourself vigilant and wary of things that frighten you. The tail is a fine touch."

To his utter shock the man moved a quick hand to touch the end of his hair. But like his namesake, Mouse was faster and stepped out of reach.

"Excellent reflexes. I wonder what kind of racer you'd have made."

"I've got much better ways to waste my time."

"Hm, I imagine so. *Sayonara, Konezumi*," he said with a tight bow and walked out.

Mouse stood frozen, surrounded by the blood-christened casualties of steel and rubber. He watched the man mount his bike, gun the engine and ride away ahead of his men into the night.

Sometime after midnight found him steeped waist-deep in the large dented metal tub he kept in the garage. Under the blow of the fans, the water had cooled to tepid. Mouse laid his head back on a folded towel draped over the rim, eyes closed, listening to the hiss of the radio. Exhausted and unsettled by the day's events, he'd stowed the wrecks in the shed out back and locked them up tight, uncertain now of his plans. The salvaged parts were worth a few thousand alone. He'd take what he could for the Ninja and would sell the rest to Barney out at the junkyard. It'd fetch more than enough to set Fred up for a few years.

Wind was kicking up in bursts outside, blowing sand and pebbles into the tin walls while coyotes made their distant presence known in long howls. It was the quietest he'd ever known the place to be. Largely due to Fred's absence – no one muttering about the old days and could-have-been tales from before he was born. He welcomed it for once and let his mind wander on the edge of sleep. Half dream, half memory he saw the blue and grey Peterbilt stuck in a flood rut not far up the road. The man who'd come down – older, tall, with a slow smile – asked about getting some boards to set traction under the rear wheels. The cool rain was falling and with mud up to their knees – they'd eventually managed to get the 16 wheeler out. He'd been honest about offering the man a place to wash and a cup of coffee but once shirts were off and the tub was drug out – there was a look in the man's blue-gray eyes that he knew.

He'd been kissed first, that was a strange thing. No one had ever begun it that way before or since. He didn't know where to put his hands and just let them drop to his sides as he was taken up in that sturdy embrace. There was patience in those warm dry lips as he was kissed thoroughly, breaking only to let the tongue trace the cords of his neck with agonizing slowness. He breathed through it, at all costs fighting the urge to moan shamelessly, though his groin refused to stay still and pressed forward eagerly. Kisses rose softly to his ear: "What's your name, child?"

He'd lied, told him it was Aaron, Eric or something of that sound. He didn't want to be himself in that moment – he just wanted to be taken someplace else, be someone else. He was undressed and washed thoroughly in this tub. His hand now trailed the paths the man's hands had taken – down his belly and thighs. He could still feel the man sitting behind him, his erection probing his back as strong hands stroked and caressed. Mouse moaned into the grip of his fist. God, how he'd wanted it – but had to wait and wait, breathing into that tension until there was no breath left in him. He pleaded then, begged like a whore between each deep kiss. He wanted the sweet agony to end so he could begin to find himself again. On his knees in the water, at last the heat of the man's flesh pressed into his body, steady, unyielding, splitting him open. He gripped the metal rim as water sloshed across the floor with each thrust as he bit down to silence the screams.

"Shh... child, let it come... it'll be okay... "

Mouse groaned as hot ropes of cum shot over the surface of the water and dripped down his fist. He opened his eyes and watched it melt away into the water with the memories. He breathed deep and let it go. His limbs relaxed as he sank back into the water, for the moment mollified by the release. But whenever the rains fell he still found himself looking up the road for a gray and blue truck leaning into the ruts.

Chapter III

Open Desert

In his dream he smelled gasoline. For someone who lived in a service garage, this would not be strange. Except there wasn't a drop of fuel left in the storage tanks below the station. The provisional government had seized it years ago.

The scent of smoke was more troublesome. Generally not something one wanted to smell when sitting atop a half ton of petrol – had there been any. But Mouse could remember a time when there was, so even in the depths of an exhausted sleep he managed to drag himself toward wakefulness.

He forced his body to roll on the narrow cot. On his back he could just begin to detect a flicker of light from behind his eyelids. The flicker grew stronger and his eyes flew open.

Fire.

On his feet in the next second, Mouse jumped into his jeans and boots. Wide-eyed, he stared at the light emanating from the small window in the door that separated the office where he slept from the main garage. Hot red-orange flames shot angry flickers of light across the darkened room. The garage was on fire.

"Shit... shit, shit, shit... !"

Mouse grabbed the shop keys from the hook on the wall and ran to the front glass doors. He steadied the keys in his hands as best as he could to get the doors opened quickly.

Throwing the doors open, he ran out past the pumps to the front of the locked garage doors. One of them was open halfway. The lock was cut and lying broken on the ground. The fire now raged inside along the left and rear walls, burning up the wooden shelves and cabinets. Mouse ducked in under the door. He raised a hand against the heat and light. Dark black smoke rose in rolling clouds toward the tin ceiling. He could smell it – the telltale stench of burning gasoline.

He dropped to the floor and held a washrag over his nose, crawling forward cautiously. The heat was incredible and he couldn't see much past a yard ahead of him. Following the cracks and stains on the floor he knew like a roadmap, he inched forward through the smoke until his hand reached metal. It was still cool enough to touch. Smoke filled his eyes as he gripped the rear leg of the repair stand and pulled. The stand moved only an inch before his hand slipped and his lungs rebelled in a coughing fit. He stepped back out of the open door to catch his breath and try to think.

Chain, hook – they hung on a pole just inside the door. He took a few more giant gulps of air and wrapped the rag over his nose and mouth, tying it behind his head. He ducked back in and grabbed the chain he used to lift engines from the wall. It dropped in loops to the floor and he scrambled to find the end with the spring-lock hook. With the heavy clasp in hand, he dove back into the thick of the smoke and with a lunge to the floor, swung his arm and blindly latched it to the leg of the frame.

Mouse backed out fast. Sweat poured off him as the heat of the fire grew unbearable. The tin ceiling and walls were glowing. He made it to the opened door and swallowed great gulps of air, coughing hard as if he would retch. *Are you stupid? Run! Leave it for fuck's sake!*

Stubborn won over sense and he tightened the rag and gulped air until he thought he would faint and ducked back in far enough to grasp the end of the chain. He looped it around his arm and shoulder, got to his feet and pulled. Heat scorched his right arm as the fire lit up an old oil pan. But the rack moved and he threw his weight against the chain again and again until he was within a few steps of the open door. Which, to his smoke and panic filled eyes, appeared to be closing.

Mouse dropped the chain and ran to catch the end of the door as it sank. The once lightweight aluminum had gained several pounds of force. And legs. Someone was outside.

"Stop!!" Mouse screamed, confused. He flailed his hand through the narrowing gap. "I'm inside!!" he yelled, banging on the aluminum slats with his fist. A boot came up and kicked his hand off the lower lip of the door. He fell to the floor and tried to crawl under on his belly but it was too late and the door slammed down just missing his hands. Flames lapped closer as he tried again and again to lift the door. Now that the door was fully closed, the black smoke was trapped and sank lower and lower. On his belly, Mouse pressed his face to the small clearance between the base of the door and the concrete to try and breathe. "Let me out!!"

Please... please... God, no! I'm sorry! I'm sorry!

Sweat poured down his face as he struggled to breathe, coughing more out than he could take in. His head spun and his heart raced futilely as his lungs succumbed to the smoke and within seconds, everything went dark.

The wind was intense. It blew hard against him, blowing his hair around his face like tiny whips. It was hard to breathe. His lungs hurt terribly as he coughed against the dry roaring wind. He opened his eyes and encountered a view of blurred dark objects that moved away from his limited vision as fast as the air. His head spun and he coughed some more, trying to move a hand to hold his hair back from his eyes. His arms were unmovable. So were his legs. He was bound by nylon cords to a leather surface. He turned his head and looked down where he could see the running lights of the motorcycle illuminating the driver's boots – the same boots that had trapped him in the garage. He pulled at his bonds but his arms were tied firmly behind his back. He was mounted backwards on a touring bike in a kneeling position, with his calves strapped to either saddlebag and his chest tied around the backrest.

It all came together in that instant. *I'm being kidnapped! That asshole sent his punks out to kidnap me! Who does that?*

Mouse watched the road flying away behind him in the taillights, trying to pick up a discerning landmark. But it was a moonless night and they were moving too fast. Plus, riding backwards only allowed him the reverse side of any freeway signs and turning his head only gave him a view of his hair. He didn't even know which freeway they were on, or what direction they were traveling in or for how long. Tilting his head down and to the side allowed him to just make-out the shoulder and back of his driver. He knew he'd have to either jump the driver or disable the bike to get out of this one. And being all bound up and backwards riding at freeway speeds offered little chance of that.

Mouse closed his eyes and tried to use his other senses. Above the roar of the wind he could detect two other bike engines ahead of them. So there were three men at least. From the smell of the sage they were still somewhere in the midst of the northern desert plains – but that land went on for a hundred miles in every direction from Blythe. Limb by limb he felt his way through the wrapping of his bonds. Arms and legs were tied fast. Mouse arched his spine against the ropes that coiled around his back and fixed him to the leather backrest. He felt the ropes give a little and slip higher up the tapered backrest the more he wriggled. Careful not to move too suddenly to alert his driver, he kept flexing and arching until he recovered a reasonable amount of movement in his torso – just enough to tip the odds in his favor.

He closed his eyes and let his mind follow the vibrations and movement of the bike. They'd been on a straightaway for sometime but now the road was curving more and more to the left as they wound up a lazy grade. He bided his time, waiting for the drone of the leading bikes to fade away. He guessed correctly that the two-passenger bike he was on would slow on a grade and fall behind the others. He braced himself and waited for the next curve. As soon as the driver began to lean his weight into the turn, Mouse threw his own weight in the opposite direction. The loops of the rope slipped off the top of the backrest. The driver swore and tried to steady his bike. Mouse lunged again even harder and the rear wheels lost traction. The bike slid in the loose shoulder gravel, pitching forward into the ditch and throwing the driver off as the whole machine fell hard onto its side, dragging Mouse with it.

"Aaagh!!" Mouse screamed along with the scraping and sparking of the bike's tail-pipes as it ground to a halt in the belly of the ditch. He hadn't really thought about the end result of his plan. And it fucking hurt! The whole left side of his shoulder and chest felt as if it'd been sandpapered off. Fortunately, so where the ropes from around his chest and left leg. Thanks to his kneeling position, his leg wasn't crushed under the weight of the bike and the saddlebag absorbed most of the impact rather than his skull. He spit gravel out of his mouth and fought to free his right leg. His arms were still bound tightly behind him, prohibiting his plan to escape on the same bike he'd just crashed. He yanked at the right saddlebag until the bonds came loose and he was able to wriggle his calf and ankle free. On his feet, he took a quick look behind him. The driver was on his hands and knees in the middle of the lane some yards back, lifting off his helmet slowly to make sure he still had a head it seemed. Long rows of dark braids fell around his face. It was Tagata. Sadao's Captain.

Mouse yanked at his arm bonds again and again but it was no use. Tagata would regain his legs soon and come after him. And he couldn't steer with his toes. *Fuck, run!* This time Mouse listened to himself and set off into the desert on foot. He slid down the short hill on his backside to the basin floor where he gathered his legs and ran hard over the dry uneven ground, stumbling over the occasional rock and rabbit hole. At first all he heard was the pounding of his heart and the rasp of air in his lungs. But soon distant shouts carried out over the basin and the roar of bike engines grew louder. Faint lights flashed out across the landscape.

Tagata had alerted the cavalry and they must have doubled back and regrouped. Mouse ran hard but knew his smoke-damaged lungs and injured left side would give out long before their motorcycles ran out of gas. He had to hide and fast. The beams of the remaining two motorbikes granted him flashes of distant landmarks. No mesas in sight. He was running away from the only slope of hills. Everything ahead of him was flat as a sheet. Another pan of lights passed him and in that moment of illumination he saw a grove of tall saguaros standing off to his left. It was his only option. He made a final dash for them, but as he ran blindly his foot caught on something and he fell hard on his wounded side. "Nngh!!"

Mouse rolled and looked over at what he'd tripped on. It was a fallen saguaro skeleton, over six feet long and a few feet around. Mouse crawled to it on his belly and chipped at the side of it with his boot toe. The dried bone-like ribs fell away forming a sort of sleeve half-buried in the dirt. He could hear the engines drawing closer and wriggled like a giant earthworm into the carcass as best as he could and lay like the dead.

On his stomach in the dirt, Mouse fought the urge to cough his guts out and tried to calm his frantic breathing and heartbeat. He'd never heard his heart pound so force-fully – it felt like it was going to explode through his ribs. Nevermind the fact he'd just shoved himself into a favorite home of rattlesnakes and scorpions to boot. Headlights and engines became louder and brighter and there were several moments where he was certain they'd spotted him, but then all he heard was an increased amount of arguing and wheels spinning in the dust. At last the shouts and lights faded as the search party moved deeper into the desert and faded completely.

In the darkness, Mouse rolled painfully to his back and sat up slowly, lifting his head out of the saguaro coffin. With his arms still tied behind him, he moved gingerly into a sitting position. Nothing had bit him but his whole left side burned with pain and felt damp. He couldn't see very well but the smell of blood was apparent. At first he thought he should try to make it back to the road to flag someone down for help. But since the hunters had moved on, he hadn't seen any new lights or engine sounds. Perhaps it was a closed highway. There were many that crisscrossed Arizona, no longer maintained by the government – the seasonal storm floods had made them impassable to long-distance trucks. And the wastelands weren't exactly a favorite vacation spot.

Without a populated highway to ferry him back to safety, Mouse looked to the stars. It was a clear moonless night and the North Star was easy to identify. He could use it to guide him, if he knew what direction to head in. Whatever direction he chose, he had to make it quickly so he could be well on his way before the morning sun climbed too high and the desert heat spelled out his death sentence.

Mouse got up and began to walk, but now the going was much more difficult. Without the reserve adrenaline to force his body to action, he now felt every inch of his injuries and his legs moved unsteadily over the ground. Even if northeast proved to be a wise guess, he just wasn't moving fast enough to cover enough ground to make a difference.

Doc Meadows had said he thought racers might be moving to the Dry Lakes region which was southwest of Blythe, roughly. But from here – if he had deducted where "here" was correctly – that could mean a 40 mile walk. So despite his exhaustion, Mouse forced his legs to keep moving.

Dawn came a few hours later. As soon as light provided him with a better view, Mouse thought he could just make out a far line of familiar mesas off to the East and headed for them. He allowed himself a short break to sit by the edge of a large stone to work the loops of his wrist cords against a rough edge. By the time he snapped the cord and got his hands free, it was getting warm. Sweat dotted his forehead and he wiped it on his shirt collar. The blood that had seeped from his left side had dried and his partially shredded T-shirt was stuck to it, effectively making a bandage. Peering under his collar it looked like a very bad scrape, nothing more. But the loss of moisture was doing nothing for his thirst. He'd kill for a bad Iron Horse beer about now. *So much for leaving town.*

With nothing to keep him company but the ever-rising sun and his own footfalls – Mouse mused over the events that had brought him to this predicament. His decision to leave town had been the right one, he felt. But where he went wrong was not leaving fast enough. *Should have just grabbed the money and ran.* But he hadn't. Instead, he'd entertained Sadao and his bullshit, then opted for a bath and bed in order to get a fresh start in the morning. He'd intended to drive out to Bridesfall in the morning where he'd send a letter to Fred explaining his plans. Then fill up on gas and take the main highway to Phoenix. From there he could trade in the pick-up and buy a bus ticket to Montana or Vancouver and learn how to live in the "real world." Even fancy city folk needed things repaired once in awhile, didn't they?

What you could earn in a year would buy you a whole new garage and town to go with it, that smug sonofabitch had said. *Should have punched him when you had the chance.* Still, the offer had tempted him even if he didn't like to admit it. The chance to work on top class racing vehicles would be the answer to a long-sought dream. Just not with the kidnapping and stuck in the desert part of it. From what Mouse knew of biker gangs, they were in it for themselves and be damned if you got in their way. This was the direct result of his non-compliance. Sadao though, had come to him seeking answers to a riddle he already knew the answer to so what more did he want from him?

By the time the sun reached its zenith, waves of heat rose from the rocky dusty ground. Mouse had made a crude hat out of folded yucca leaves and plucked a few of the last of the season's prickly pears to moisten his mouth – but the heat in this part of the desert rarely peaked at under 120 degrees. He had to find shade and fast. The mesas were still at least ten miles distant so Mouse found himself a friendly circle of sagebrush and huddled under it, sucking the last of his prickly pears. The meager shade of the brush did little to staunch the oven-like heat.

Thirst filled his every thought. Once, when he was a reckless teen, Mouse had run out of gas on one of his off-road excursions and faced a long hot 18-hour walk back to town. He had good desert sense and could find what nibbles of edible plants he could. But on that occasion he'd carried a full canteen. And he knew which direction to go to get back to town.

Mouse swallowed painfully around his swollen tongue and squinted through the liquid heat at the mesas. He wasn't sure anymore if they were the landmasses he'd originally taken them for. But they'd served as a beacon of sorts to keep him heading straight through the day. Straight into nowhere perhaps. Straight into his own grave.

He'd been told once the worst way to die was at sea, in a desert of endless water without a drop to drink. But at least at sea he thought, that water would be cool and a means of keeping the flesh from cooking right off your bones. And also, in the bitter end, a means of escape. He'd stopped sweating hours ago and it was not yet 2 pm. If he made it past 4 he might live. He pressed his forehead into his knees and fought for each breath.

Four o'clock came and went. Mouse lay flat in the dirt under the sagebrush as the sun gradually sank. The temperature was falling but his breath was shallow and weak. Consciousness rose and faded in waves. Delirium was all that filled the gaps in his broken timeline. In the fading moments he knew himself, he only wanted to know one thing. *Was it enough?*

He sat in a desert garden under the shade of a wigwam. The sun was bright over-head but the heat no longer touched him. At his feet was a still pond – no ripple disturbed its calm surface. It seemed he had sat here for many long days and had no desire to move from this simple place until the sun faded, blocked by a cloud of darkness. He watched as the pond lay helpless to the pattering of the falling rain. He stood then, turning his face into the cool soothing rainfall. Water fell over his skin: his chest, legs and arms. And under the roar of the rain thrummed the beating of his heart.

Chapter IV

A Barrell of Sake

He was lying on a soft surface under a warm breeze. The moving air felt good against his aching skin and carried the scent of drying hay. His head was pillowed gently as he passed in and out of wakefulness. His limbs felt heavy and his body wasn't coated in dust and grime. In fact, he felt clean and … naked? Mouse struggled to open his eyes. In the dim light he could just see the outline of his legs under a thin cotton sheet – the only piece of cloth he was wearing, it seemed. It was early morning and already beginning to get a little warm.

Great, I've died and it's still hot.

He gave into the heaviness of his eyes and drifted back to sleep.

A door opened and there were footfalls across a wooden floor. He woke again and it was much brighter, but his eyes stayed shut. He heard water pouring and the click and flare of a pilot light. Pots banged together and drawers moved. Someone was cooking. He realized he was hungry and thirsty. Very thirsty. *Hope God makes good coffee,* he thought and moved to sit up. Arms wouldn't move. He opened an eye and looked down. Legs moved under the sheets okay. Arms – no go. He turned his head. His left wrist was bound with rope. So was his right. Both were tied to opposite ends of the same short rope strung through the sturdy wooden slats of an antique headboard.

It's hot, I'm naked... and tied to a bed. This can't be good.

Fully awake now, he tried to yell but his throat was too dry to make more than a croak. Footsteps approached and he struggled to move but the shortness of the rope kept him on his back.

"Good, you're alive." Sadao entered, holding a wooden spoon. "You'll need to keep drinking," he said, setting the spoon aside and fetching a water bottle from the bedside table. He sat on the edge of the high bedframe and helped Mouse lift his head to drink. The water was cool as he gulped it down his throat.

"I found a sack of oats," Sadao said. "For horses I think, but they'll cook soft. You need to eat, too – your body is very weak."

Mouse finished off most of the bottle and lay back panting. The effort to drink had made him dizzy. "Tied up... why?"

"Because you like to walk in the desert with no direction. Very foolish."

At once, the memories of the fire, the midnight ride and the blistering sun came back to him. He closed his eyes, trying to make an account of time in this long, confusing nightmare. "Where am I?"

"Farmhouse. West of the desert."

Mouse blinked and took in the room. It was clean and decorated in white frilly lace and rose patterns. "Whose?"

"Can't say. Recently abandoned, perhaps. Water and gas supply are still good. Maybe they'll be back soon," Sadao said, reaching for a jar of salve. He unscrewed it and dipped a finger in. "Hold still," he said as Mouse tried to turn his face away. "You have scrapes from your fall and burns from too much sun."

"Untie me," Mouse said, wincing from the cool spread of the cream. His neck and shoulders ached and felt hot. Sadao ignored his protests and spread the medicinal-smelling stuff over his damaged skin. Then he pulled the sheet down to expose his chest. "Hey!"

There was an angry red scrape along his left side, ending in a bandage. Sadao worked the numbing cream into it, easing the pain. "Where are my clothes?"

"Stop moving. Your jeans are drying on the fence outside."

"Drying?"

"I cleaned them. Your clothes were a little dusty and stank of smoke."

Despite his weak state, Mouse jerked Sadao's hand away with a twist of his hips.

"You sonofabitch, you burned my home down."

Sadao sighed and wiped his hand on the sheet. "Unfortunate circumstance. The fire was not part of my orders. Taga is… overzealous sometimes. He's been reprimanded."

"Reprimanded?" Mouse couldn't believe what he was hearing. "With what? A spanking over your knee?"

Sadao grinned. "Something like that."

"I almost died in that fire! Everything I had was in that fire and you sit there like it's some kind of goddamn joke?"

Sadao patiently screwed the cap back on the salve and set it aside. He got up. "You need to rest. Heatstroke is not something to take lightly. It kills men stronger than you. I've seen it."

Mouse turned his head away. Hot tears of anger and frustration were gathering in his eyes and he didn't want Sadao to see it.

"I'll bring you food soon," his captor said and left the room.

Sadao returned later with a bowl of steaming oatmeal and a pile of scrambled eggs. "We have chickens," he said.

Although it was embarrassing as hell to be fed by your enemy, Mouse's hunger was stronger and he accepted a mouthful of eggs – a little salty but good. He chewed and swallowed. "Don't talk like we live here," he said, irritated.

Sadao looked around the room. "Too pink, maybe? But not so bad. You complain a lot, Mr. Mouse."

"I said, it's Mouse."

"Very well... *Mouse.* I know you are bitter about losing your home. But let's not pretend you weren't planning to leave it."

"What the hell are you talking about?"

"The money I left you, the motorcycles. They were tickets I offered you for your freedom. Careful with this, it's hot," he said spooning a dripping mouthful of oats and honey into his patient's mouth. "I intended to let you leave on your own. I had my men watching you, but I ran out of time," he said.

"You don't know what I was thinking. You don't know shit about me."

"You are... how old? Twenty-four, maybe?"

Mouse accepted another bite of eggs. "Twenty-six."

"Older than I thought. Time to leave the nest. When I first came to your little town I spoke with a man at the junkyard – the one with all the nasty dogs."

"Barney," Mouse breathed. Now it made sense.

"This is a friend of yours? He tells me about a young man who has been visiting his yard for many years, hunting and bargaining for foreign parts. Japanese engineering preferred – good taste. This, I tell myself, is a young man I need to find."

"You mean kidnap. It's a federal offense."

Sadao laughed and fed him another bite. "Your government is lacking in consistency. I have no issue with them. They stay out of my way; I stay out of theirs."

"You pay them off."

"In a sense. But the authorities are not my concern. My problems are much closer to your own – day to day survival. In this part of the world, money doesn't buy as much as the right connections. My boys and I struggle as much as you, my friend."

"I'm not your friend. And I don't understand how you think tying me up and dragging me along with you is going to gain my cooperation."

"Like I said, I did not have time to convince you. And your 'stunt' cost me a cruiser plus an extra two days to drag your dying flesh out of the desert and bring it back to life. I'm a busy man with a schedule to keep."

"So you just stole me, like you steal everything else."

Sadao blew on a particularly steamy lump of oatmeal and popped it into his mouth.

"I see it as a scavenging tactic. We all have hungry mouths to feed."

"You're nothing more than a gang of thieves."

Sadao scooped up a dribble of oats that fell from his lips with the spoon. "Don't talk so much. You need to eat."

Mouse turned his face away. He was still hungry, but was not about to be fed like a toddler for another minute. Sadao gave in. He set the spoon down and picked up the dishes.

"*Douitashimashite*," he said, getting up.

"What... ?"

"It means, 'You are welcome.'"

Mouse dozed throughout the afternoon as Sadao moved about the house and yard. It was getting uncomfortable lying with his hands up over his head and as the hours passed he became aware of another, more urgent discomfort that only grew the longer he tried to ignore it. He squirmed and tugged at his bonds. *Dammit!*

Sadao eyed him from where he was sitting at a table by the window, enjoying a smoke and an old newspaper. "You awake? You slept most of the day away." He crushed out his cigarette on a saucer and came closer. "You should drink... "

Mouse ignored him and yanked at the rope. Sadao looked him over. Understanding soon came into his eyes. "I'll get you something for that," he said and stepped into the kitchen briefly to retrieve a discarded water bottle.

"Fuck – no! Untie me."

Sadao uncapped the bottle and sat at the edge of the bed. Mouse glared at him. "Untie me! I'm not pissing in that!"

"You are an exceptionally stubborn man. If it's modesty that concerns you, be assured there is no part of you I have not already seen," Sadao said, throwing back the thin sheet.

Mouse rolled away from him in shock. His face burned with more than sun exposure.

"I want to use the toilet."

"No."

"You're a sick bastard, aren't you?"

"So I've been told," Sadao said, pinning him by the hip and fitting the end of the bottle over his embarrassingly stiff penis. Truth was, at this point his need was beyond modesty.

Mouse squeezed his eyes shut for a few moments, then let out a breath. "I can't," he gasped.

"Why not? We're both men."

Mouse glared up at him. "Because I can't fucking pee lying down, okay?!"

Sadao broke into laughter.

Mouse looked away. "It's not funny."

Sadao removed the bottle and tossed it aside. He wiped at the corner of his eye. "The face you are making is very cute… " he managed to say.

"Screw you."

"*Oi, Konezumi*, what am I going to do with you?" He unsheathed his knife and reached above Mouse's head and with one stroke, cut the rope in two.

The bonds fell away from his wrists and Mouse sat up, grabbing the sheet back around him. He stood too quickly, and the room began to swim. Sadao caught his arm before he fell and steadied him, guiding him the few steps to the bathroom.

Mouse grabbed the door frame. "I got it. Let go! I *got* it!"

"Are you sure you won't need me to hold your cock?"

Mouse wrenched himself free and slammed the door in Sadao's smug face with the last ounce of strength he had.

The face in the mirror looked ghastly. Mouse collapsed on the toilet, stuck his hand between his legs and pissed like a girl. It felt so good he started to weep, and then laughed. *This is a fine fucked-up mess you've gotten yourself into.*

He flushed and laid his pounding head on the cool countertop to think. *If he wanted you dead, he would have left your sorry ass in the desert. Man's got plans for you. Question is, can you trust him?*

He lifted his head weakly and looked at the crumpled sheet caught in the door – half in and out of the bathroom. "I want my pants!" he yelled.

There was a return shout but he couldn't make it out. Gripping the counter, he stood slowly and stared at the mess of himself in the mirror. Sadao's sponge bath had gotten the grime off but not the bruising across his left cheek or the angry rim of red around his neck where the sun had gotten between his makeshift hat and shirt. His hands shook as he turned on the sink and splashed water on his face.

There was a polite knock on the door. He opened it a crack and his more tattered than usual jeans greeted him along with a fresh T-shirt. "Thanks," he said and pulled them in, shutting the door again. He had to sit down for a moment to gather the strength to put them on. He was as weak as a kitten. There would be no walking away from this situation. He finished dressing slowly and opened the door.

Sadao was at the table reading again. Tired of lying down, Mouse decided to join him and took a chair opposite. He sat down heavily and reached for a glass of water, gulping it down.

"What does this word mean?" Sadao asked, pointing at a line in an article.

Mouse squinted at the newspaper. It was faded and old. The headline was dated twenty-seven years ago. "Where did you find this?"

"There was a stack of papers in the shed outside. I helped you use the toilet – you can help me with my English."

"Which word?" he asked.

"This one," Sadao said, turning the paper towards Mouse.

"Precipitation," he read.

Sadao shook his head, not comprehending.

"It means rainfall or snowfall," he said. "It's an article about the 100-year drought."

Sadao grunted approvingly.

"Where did you learn English?" Mouse asked, curious.

"In school, of course. Required language."

"I didn't," Mouse said. "Learn in a school, I mean. Tornado took out the schoolhouse when I was three."

Sadao raised his eyes from the paper and Mouse continued. "It was Widow Baker who taught me how to read. Mostly from the Bible and some old children's moral tales. I caught on pretty fast, but my father didn't appreciate me addressing people as 'thee' and 'thou' and got me books about trucks and trains instead. I liked those better and so did he. He couldn't read, you see."

Now it was Sadao's turn to be curious. "He was illiterate? I didn't think that happened anymore."

Mouse nodded. "Oh, it can happen. Most of the town I grew up in had barely more than a 4th grade education. When the government pulled out, so did the schools. I got lucky – there were still older women around willing to teach a growing boy his letters in exchange for house repairs. My father couldn't read, but he was good with a hammer and soldering iron, so we got by."

"Sounds like a good man, your father."

"Aside from a few vices, yeah, he was."

"Was... ?"

Mouse nodded at Sadao's cigarette case. "Lung cancer."

Sadao picked up the shiny black case and tucked it in his rear pocket. "A curable disease."

"Not out here in the sticks. Natural causes rarely makes the coroner's report. Life expectancy is a game of chance. Disease, radiation, starvation – we all know the stakes. We're all living examples of Job in a way – if you know your Christian Bible."

"A little. Are you a religious man, Mouse?"

He thought about it – he certainly was in the fire. "I suppose so, yes. In a spiritual way. Not in a 'tornadoes are a finger of God' way. God doesn't make bad shit happen,

He just... I don't know … helps us deal with it."

Sadao was quiet for a moment. "Where I came from we did not have much time for religion. But we carried with us our superstitions and rituals. Our cultural practices are what kept us sane."

"Japan, right? Where you're from?"

Sadao nodded. "Mie prefecture on the Ise Peninsula by the ocean. Famous for pearls. My family raised *kaki* – oysters. Very beautiful place. My classmates and I used to chase monkeys through the bamboo forests. Before the start of the Civil War, of course. Then we chased each other, with guns."

"How old were you... " Mouse tried to do the math in his head and failed. The Japanese Civil War, if he recalled the date correctly, began about 25 years ago.

It looked like Sadao was having trouble with the math, too. "11, 12, maybe," he said at length.

"How did you wind up in the US?"

"I was orphaned during the war. My uncle sold me to a merchant from Chiba for 35 American dollars and a barrel of sake. Eventually, I got away and hid aboard a ship heading to Baja."

They were quiet for a while, watching the wind blow outside across the dying hay fields.

"Was it good sake?" Mouse asked.

Sadao nodded. "Imperial label."

Mouse shook his head. "I can't believe I'm talking casually with my kidnapper about God, all the while wondering if you're going to tie me up to the bed again."

"I won't. You're in no shape to run."

Odd memories were coming back to him from his trial in the desert. *Is it enough?* That's what he remembered asking himself. "How on earth did you find me out there?"

"Instinct, and a good eye for tracks. You didn't hide yours very well."

"Wasn't the first thing I thought of. I just wanted to get away."

"That is your first instinct. And not a very wise one."

Mouse nodded in agreement. His stomach grumbled. "What's for dinner?" he asked.

Sadao folded his paper. "I'll go look."

When Mouse awoke next it was late in the night. After sleeping for 18 hours the day before, he couldn't sleep anymore and lay on his back in the darkness, thinking. During their dinner of dug-up potatoes, carrots and more eggs, Sadao explained that if Mouse was strong enough in the morning, they'd ride out to catch up with the Team which had already broken camp and was moving to a proving ground 60 miles south in the heart of the Sonora Desert. He needed vehicles repaired and primed for timed trials the following week. Hence, his need for haste in securing a new mechanic.

Mouse had listened and nodded amicably. Honestly, it had sounded exciting – traveling with a professional racing team across the wastelands. But after taking in a full meal and re-gathering his strength, he had doubts. Serious ones.

He rolled over slowly to watch the man sleeping beside him. Sadao lay on his back, one arm behind his head and the other at his side near his knife and the short chain that held the key to the bike parked outside the front door. Mouse debated in his head what to do. For some odd reason Sadao appeared to trust him. In his arrogant manner he'd assumed a great deal about Mouse, his position in life and his character – most of it correct. But not all. True, Mouse had never killed a man, never carried a loaded weapon into the wild intending to shoot anything bigger than a rabbit – but his instincts for self-preservation and a general mistrust of the unknown were weighing heavy on him as he peered through the darkness at his captor.

You'll only have one chance to make this move. Make it count.

Long silent minutes passed. Mouse watched the slow rise and fall of Sadao's chest as he worked through scenarios in his head. He wasn't stronger than Sadao, but he was faster. More than the new life Sadao had promised him, he didn't want the people of Blythe to think he was dead. He saw Fred dressed in his rumpled black suit as the townsfolk piled rocks next to his father's grave over an empty hole. Slowly and silently, he reached across Sadao's chest for the knife.

"Aah!" The grip that caught his hand was vice-like and the pain that shot up his arm made him cry out. He remembered now how that same grip had saved him from the blade of the game knife the first day they'd met. "Aaaghh... !" the grip rotated slowly and his wrist popped loudly.

Sadao pulled him by his twisted hand closer until he could see his eyes. There was no mirth in them. "Did you think I would lie here and let you cut my throat?" he said quietly. His arm continued to twist until Mouse crumpled forward onto his chest, trembling with pain.

"I wasn't ..."

Sadao's mouth was very close to his ear now. "I will tell you this only once. And you will listen and remember my words: I am not a common thief. I am not your countryman. I am neither your father nor your priest. I do not answer to your laws, your government, or your god. I am Sadao Koga and if you ever raise a hand in threat to me again, I will peel the skin from your limbs and drag your screaming corpse into the desert and leave it for the wild dogs."

Sadao loosed his grip and Mouse drew back, clutching his arm in pain. The nerves throbbed all the way up his spine.

Sadao relaxed and adjusted his pillow. "We roll at dawn," he said, closing his eyes. "If you feel well enough to grab my knife, you are well enough to clean the kitchen."

Mouse rubbed his arm and swore as he stumbled off in the dark to find a dishrag and soap.

Chapter V

The Orochi Banner

They rode out at first light. Mouse promised not to cause any trouble and was allowed to ride passenger facing forward this time with his hands and legs untied. It was soon made clear to him why they had to wait for light – the roadways Sadao followed weren't found on any maps. Most were unpaved and none were marked with any kind of signs. The occasional hill or mesa passed in and out of view, but for the most part there weren't any landmarks this deep in the uninhabited desert. Aside from the general knowledge that they were heading South, Mouse had no idea where they were.

Sadao's touring bike was a big heavy machine built in the early 2000s perhaps, and refitted with a double gas tank for covering long distances. It was custom painted in metallic slate blue with rolling clouds of grey and black. Smoke was the intended effect. He supposed it suited him – like the dragon of the desert.

They stopped only once to gulp water and stretch their legs. It was a utility shack of sorts, abandoned now and crumbling. It looked like it had once served as a pumping station for an underground well, long gone to rust. Only one human item remained – a workman's glove, remarkably well preserved, was lying in the dust in the middle of the rotting floor. It felt good to remove his helmet and let the breeze dry his hair in the shade of the slanted roof. Outside, Sadao was barking orders in Japanese to various people on his CB radio. The man had been preoccupied all morning by some matter back at camp and had hardly spoken two words to him.

"Let's go!" he shouted. "Or the sun will rise too high to make it to camp."

Mouse didn't want to raid another farmhouse for lodgings and obeyed, walking back out into the fierce sunlight. "I take it there aren't many trees where we're going?"

Sadao started his engine, unamused. "Have you ever hit a tree cornering a turn at 160 kilometers per hour?"

Mouse shook his head and donned his helmet. Point taken. He climbed aboard and they pulled back out into the dust.

Despite their speed, it was growing unbearably hot in the helmet and riding jacket

Sadao had loaned him. Mouse wanted to shift out of the jacket but then the sun would cook his already reddened skin. It was well on noon, approaching 1pm by the height of the sun. By 2pm they'd have to find shelter. And from what he could see through the sunshade, there wasn't any for miles in any direction.

The land they roared across was flat and bone-colored – a long dead lake bed. Even the sagebrush failed to take root in this hard cracked ground. They'd left the faint tracks of the roadways completely. Sadao was tapping a compass on this dash, checking and rechecking their direction. And like himself, mindful of the sun.

Sadao increased speed to cross the dry lake swiftly and far ahead on the horizon, Mouse thought he could make out small grey shapes, floating above the ripples of heat. He tapped Sadao's shoulder and the man nodded, pointing in the same direction. Mouse relaxed, grateful he'd be able to get out of the sun before he collapsed again.

The grey shapes grew and became a wide spread of tents, trailers, vans, RVs and trucks. They slowed as they pulled into the mass of vehicles – a hundred or more with only a few humans in sight, walking purposefully between shelters, heads and eyes shaded from the painful sun.

Sadao drove through the maze until they passed under a wide banner stretched across two massive haulers, loaded with gear. It bore the sign of the 8-headed snake, their emblem. No sooner had they crossed under it when a pair of young boys shot out from behind storage barrels and rushed the slowing bike.

"Boss! Boss!" they yelled, running beside them as Sadao slowed to a stop.

"Boss!" One of them shouted, trying to climb up into Sadao's lap as he shut off the engine and removed his goggles.

"*Abunai-yo!*" Sadao said with a laugh, picking the kid up by the back of his pants and laying him over his shoulder as he dismounted. The second one, even younger – five maybe, reached up with plump arms, hopping with excitement. Sadao bent and tucked the boy up under his arm like a sack of flour.

"My boys!" he said with a glance back at Mouse who was still slowly removing his helmet, dumbfounded. "They get very excited."

"Why are you not at *hiru ne?*" he asked the kids, bouncing them as they shrieked. "Your little heads will pop in the sun."

"You have kids... ?" Mouse asked, dubious. Although Japanese, neither kid looked much like Sadao.

Sadao smiled proudly as he was pelted by elbows and knees. "They are all my kids. The little ones, the big ones – all my many sons. *Ore no Musukora, ne?*" He was answered by a swift kick to the gut. "*Itai, itai! Yasashi yaro!*"

"You take them this young?" Mouse asked, getting off the bike and shrugging out of the jacket. "Where are their parents?"

"Parents? You think these boys have parents?" Sadao said as a means of explanation.

"Leave the gear – I want all of you out of the sun!"

They walked a short distance through the camp to a long trailer. Sadao, loaded with the young boys, kicked at the back door. It didn't open. "Take this one," he said to Mouse, passing him the five year old so he could free a hand to work the door latch. The kid touched Mouse's face. "You ugly," he said.

"Takeshi-kun! That is not a proper way to greet our guest. Use good English."

"You... *are* ugly!" the kid said, beaming at Sadao's approving nod. Maybe he was his son after all.

Sadao got the door open and all of them were hit with a heavenly blast of cool air. Inside were rows and rows of bunks fitted to each wall of what was once a large horse trailer. There were a dozen or more young men inside, sleeping on the beds under two roof coolers. Sadao unloaded his kid and reached for the one insulting Mouse and tossed him up into a bunk.

"Lie down," he said to their sleepy protests. "We'll have dinner when you wake up."

Mouse suddenly realized he was starving. They hadn't eaten that morning in order to get an early start. He was tired too, and a bit shaky from the ride and his recent ordeal. He was about to say as much when Sadao bent to the lower bunks to punch a sleeping teenager in the shoulder. "Lupe! *Okinasai!*"

"Eh... ?" the kid rolled over, rubbing his arm. He was Latino. He blinked up at Sadao, yawning hugely. "Boss, you're back."

"Yes, I'm back in time to find my boys running around in the midday sun!"

"Eh... ?" he sat up and Sadao lifted him to his feet by the collar of his shirt. "Boss!"

"Two of them this time. And you are lying here dreaming?!"

"Sorry, Boss, I ... hey, where'd you pick up the gringo?"

Lupe shrugged Sadao off unfazed and took a closer look at Mouse. "He looks like shit, Boss," he said, poking Mouse in the chest.

"Sadao?" Mouse covered his belly where the kid poked him. "Who's this kid?"

"This is Lupe, our artist," Sadao said. "Lupe, this is Mouse, our new mechanic."

Lupe wrinkled his nose. "This guy? This is the new guy? You find him wandering the desert or something? He doesn't look like he knows shit."

Sadao gave him a shove. "Take him to see Sensei and then to the mess hall. They will complain, but see that he gets something to eat and drink. My orders."

Lupe shrugged, "Okay, Gringo, let's go... ow!" Sadao smacked the back of his head.

"That's for letting my little ones get out."

"What the fuck?" Lupe said, rubbing his head and opening the door to let himself and Mouse out.

"Lupe!" Sadao called after them from the doorway. "Has General Shiratori reported in?"

Lupe shook his head. "No, Boss. He's still out of range."

Sadao didn't look happy with this news. "Wake up Kei, send him over to look after the kids. When you're done feeding Mouse take him to my trailer until I can find a spot for him. Don't let him out of your sight!"

"Why do I always get stuck with babysitting?"

"Because you're so *dependable*. He's your new boss Lupe. Be respectful, or he can smack you too," Sadao said, shutting the door.

"*Hai, hai...* " Lupe said, gesturing Mouse to follow him. "Why's Boss such an asshole today, eh? You piss him off?"

"Maybe," Mouse said. "You mean there's days when he's not?"

Lupe laughed. "Oh, Boss, he's okay. You just got to get to know him. General Shiratori though, he's the real prick. You got to learn to put up with him, though. He's in charge of tactical – so that means he's in charge of equipment, too. And the garage. There's no getting around him, he's like a stone fucking wall. With a chip in it. Trust me – you really don't want to piss him off. But then he's always pissed off. So it's hopeless. He'll get right in your face man, scream for 20 minutes at you in Japanese. You speak Japanese?"

"Uh, no... "

"Good for you, then. You won't know what he's saying. But of course, that will just piss him off even more. It's why we can't keep mechanics around for very long. Sooner or later they just pull a knife on him and that's the end of it."

"Knife... ?"

"Yeah, but don't worry. They don't let the staff carry weapons anymore. Too many fights. Only racers carry them, like samurai or some shit. They're all very traditional – you'll get used to it. Oh, and another thing," Lupe took a breath in his stream of dialog to look Mouse in the eye.

"Don't ever call Boss by his first name. They'll slit your throat."

"Why, Sadao is... "

"Shhhh... !" Lupe threw a hand over Mouse's mouth. "*Gringo pendejo!* They won't let you get away with that shit here. It's like you crossed borders when you crossed under that banner," he said, pointing to the camp insignia. "You are *gaijin*, now. You call him 'Boss.'"

"*Gaijin...* ?"

"Foreigner."

"We're in the middle of Arizona. I was born here."

Lupe shook his head. "Don't matter. You are *gaijin* and you will always be *gaijin*. You and I, Gringo. We are not one of them. So don't ever act like it. If you want to keep your tongue in your mouth you call Boss, 'Boss' and everyone else by their last name with -san. Speaking of which, let's go eat... I don't want to wake up Sensei on his siesta. That old man is a prick, too. Oh and you call Sensei, 'Sensei' Or 'Yamagawa-Sensei.' And when you introduce yourself, only use your last name."

"I don't have a last name."

Lupe giggled. "That's really gonna fuck with them."

"What do I call you?"

Lupe smiled. "Whatever you want, Gringo. I'm easy."

Lupe led him to a long wide tent set at what appeared to be the center-most part of the sprawling camp. They ducked inside and caught the breeze of a half-dozen large fans, rattling in their cages. Rows of bench tables filled the enclosure with a large concession truck parked alongside one end. The windows on it were mostly pulled closed, but people could be seen moving about behind them along with a clatter of dishes.

"They're cleaning up, but take no shit from them. They got food back there," Lupe said, strolling up and banging on the aluminum siding with a fist. "Open up Cook-san! We got a late-comer."

An elderly Japanese man appeared, peeping under the half-shut window. He made an 'X' with his hands. "*Dame, dame!* Closed now! Closed!"

Lupe peeped right back. "No *dame* me! Boss sent me. He'll *dame* you if you don't feed this guy."

The cook's eyes fell on Mouse and widened. "*Nan da?! Gaijin da?!*"

"*Hai!* Cook-san! Boss's *gaijin*. New *gaijin* needs food. Serve it up!"

The cook disappeared a moment and came back lifting the window and opening a steamer of white rice. "*Gaijin* like *katsu-don?*"

Lupe shrugged. "I dunno. Gringo, you eat curry?"

Mouse shrugged back.

"Yeah, *gaijin* love curry! Pour on that shit and get me a bowl too!"

Mouse supposed he would have liked the breaded pork curry better if he wasn't trying to suffer his way through eating it with chopsticks. This kind of food needed a big ass spoon to enjoy properly. And Blythe wasn't known for its Eastern cuisine. Mouse soon gave up on the idea of picking anything up with the worthless sticks and just used the end of one to shovel bites up the lip of the bowl and into his mouth. Lupe didn't seem to notice his plight and just kept right on talking between expertly manipulated bites of pork and rice like they'd known each other for years.

"So get this, when I was 12 I was living in San Diego, you know? I had all these brothers and sisters all over the place. So my mother, she didn't really watch over us much. I was street trash, like a gangster – always running from border cops. So one day I'm down near the docks and I see this row of big expensive rides. So I think, I show these assholes whose town this is, right? I go get my cans and come back to the docks when it gets dark. Those bikes are still there. So I run over and start to do my thing. Next thing I know this guy has me by the throat. He picked me right up off the ground. I just about pissed my pants, man. Cause this guy's got a knife in my face and he says he's gonna cut my hands off. So I kick this asshole in the *huevos* and as I'm about to run, this second guy grabs me from behind and pins my arms back. I hear him in my ear asking if I'm the little shit who tagged his bike. And I say 'Yeah, so the fuck what?' And he says, 'Nice job. How about you come work for me?'"

Mouse choked on a lump of rice and downed a quick glass of cold tea to clear his mouth.

"You gotta be shitting me. You tagged S-- that guy's bike and he let you off?"

"Yeah, man. Boss liked the work. He saw talent in me. Could have just dumped me off the pier."

"What were they doing in San Diego?"

"They go down that way and wait for the ships to come in every year or so."

"Ships?"

"From Asia, man. They get recruits. Fresh blood."

"So... you were recruited? At 12? Did your parents know?"

Lupe shrugged. "Eh, they wouldn't miss me. Probably haven't noticed yet that I'm not around for dinner," he laughed.

"I take it there's no age limits in racing? That guy's got a whole trailer full of tots."

"No, there's a limit – a regulation limit. Boss can't race a recruit until they've been trained for at least 18 months. And they have to be 16 when they start training. Of course these guys all lie about their ages and shit. Racers, good ones, make some serious money," Lupe said with a wink. "I keep begging Boss to let me train but he says he don't want me messing up my hands. Wants me on bodywork, you know. But if I keep bugging him, he'll give in."

"But why does he take them all so young?"

Lupe shrugged. "He doesn't always... but these kids come off those boats in pretty bad shape, all dirty and bony. War refugees, you know. He don't look it, but he's got a big heart, Boss does. Especially for those tiny ones. General Shiratori screams at him every time he brings another brat home."

"Not much of a parenting type, this Shiratori guy?"

"No way. He says this camp is run like a fucking kindergarten. But he's got no say in it. Boss, he's in charge of personnel. He decides who does what jobs around here. Shiratori-san, he just does numbers and counts everything. Better keep track of your bolts and nuts, 'cause he'll get in your face if you let something go missing."

"Which one is in charge?"

"That's just it. Both of them are. Shiratori-san was leader of a rival clan, the white bird clan. That's what his name means – white bird. They had their own banner and everything. Then a freak dust storm came in and broke some wires. His camp went up in smoke so fast it blew their fuel truck all to shit, killed half his team. It was really, really bad. He almost died too, but Boss called in the medic chopper and they got him out and to a fancy hospital up north. They gave him a new arm and everything. When he came back Boss had merged the teams and Shiratori-san with them. They know each other somehow – back in Japan during the war. But neither of them likes to talk about it. They just kind of put up with each other."

"I don't think I'm looking forward to meeting this guy."

"He won't like you. But then he doesn't like anybody, really. So don't take it personal. He's just a little what we say… *loco*. Runs around in all that samurai bullshit with swords and everything. Like it's still ancient Japan or Halloween or something.Hey, there goes Tagata-san!" Lupe spotted Sadao's right-hand man passing the tent opening outside. "We need him to open the garage truck, hang on!"

Mouse stiffened as Lupe jumped up and raced out of the tent flaps. Tagata was the last person he wanted to run into in camp. At least not without Sadao around.

Does that sound logical to you? Which one's worse? The guy who nearly cooked you to death or the guy who gave him the orders?

For some odd reason Mouse felt he could trust Sadao – at least as much as he didn't want him reduced to a pile of ashes.

"Mouse!! Get out here, man!"

Mouse sighed and got up, leaving his dishes for Cook-san who gave him a polite bow as he headed out into the heat after the kid.

Tagata was already walking purposefully toward the garage and Lupe was rushing to keep up. Mouse had to break into a jog himself to catch them before they disappeared between the rows upon rows of trailers. He wondered if there was any logic to the layout. The camp looked big enough to require addresses just to know where your buddies were parked. At last they came to a massive custom black 18-wheeler with rear and side ramp entrances, sealed up and locked tight with an ID lock.

Tagata gave Mouse a cold glance before entering a series of numbers into the keypad, then leaned into an eyepiece that emitted a flash of red – retina scan. The screen turned green and Tagata was able to engage the ramp mechanism. The whole back-end of the truck opened up and under the guide of hydraulics, laid out flat to the ground creating a wide ramp. The interior lights flickered on and Mouse stood in awe of the layout inside.

"Boss said to show you," Tagata said bluntly. "Look quick." He stepped aside and assumed a watchful stance at the end of the ramp.

Lupe nudged Mouse in the back. "Go on, go in. It's okay. They just want to guard it. Once they trust you, they'll give you access so you can get in and set up."

Mouse climbed up the ramp and went in, heart racing like it used to when he'd find an abandoned trailer at the junkyard – except this wasn't junk. It was state of the art. There were two levels to the garage. The split upper floor held rows of heavy cabinets and floor anchors for light vehicle transport accessible by a lift. The main floor was fitted with more anchors as well as winch straps, repair frames and large and small cabinets filled with labeled tools and parts. Mouse opened a few of them delicately to peer inside – afraid of somehow disturbing the grandeur of the well designed space. He took it all in, noting various tools and parts stowed along the walls or hanging from the ceiling. On the top floor near the front of the trailer was a small pull-down bunk and just below it on the bottom floor was a wash area with lockers.

"Jesus… "

"It's cool, man, right? They got good stuff here. During competitions the whole left side opens up and they put up this tent and tile flooring out to the side so you can fit 20 bikes or more in here."

"I can see why they keep it locked up," Mouse remarked, peeking in more cabinets and drawers. "These foreign parts are worth a small fortune – "

Lupe shrugged. "It's not our people we worry about."

Mouse closed the shelves he was nosing through. "What's that?"

"They keep it locked up so the competition won't sneak in and mess shit up."

Mouse looked at him, confused. "You mean they just come in and knock holes in stuff?"

Lupe looked nervous, like he'd said too much. "Security is a big problem in this scene – teams backstabbing other teams. Not all of them play fair, you know. See that safe over there?" Lupe pointed to a heavy box bolted to the wall.

Mouse hadn't noticed it until now. "What do they keep in there?"

Lupe took a quick glance toward the open ramp door to check on Tagata. The Captain had his back to them both. "Keys. They don't want anyone having access to the prepped vehicles before a race. There's a reason Boss is anxious to hear from Shiratori-san. He's on a special mission."

"What kind of mission?"

Lupe leaned in closer. "Manhunt," he said and stepped away, whistling.

Manhunt? Mouse caught the kid's shoulder and turned him around. "Is this about the sand car your Boss brought me to check out?"

Lupe's eyes got a little bigger. Then he shrugged like it was nothing. "Gotta ask Boss about that. I don't know nothing about that."

"Why can't you tell me? Is it a secret? I already know somebody was messing with your gear."

"*Hiyai shite yo!*" Tagata yelled out.

"We gotta go," Lupe said and started to walk out.

"Hey! What? Wait!"

Mouse shut the drawers he'd opened and hurried out after him.

Sensei was a man of indeterminable age, but Mouse was betting around 120. He'd heard that the Japanese were a long-lived people but this guy looked as if he was going for the record books. The old guy had about the same number of hairs as he had teeth. His hands were like cold twisted sticks but surprisingly steady as he ripped off Mouse's bandages and poked at the scabs.

"Ow – ! Does he have to do that?" Mouse asked. Lupe raised his hands in hopelessness. Sensei did as Sensei wanted and that was it. The old man stopped his prodding and motioned for Mouse to put his shirt back on while he rattled about the rows of storage trunks in the medic tent. They were brimming with supplies, all likely stolen from the pharmacies of Blythe and neighboring towns. He wondered if the old man could even read the labels. He didn't appear to know a word of English. Soon, he found a bottle he was looking for and shook out some pills into his hand. He brought them to Mouse with a Dixie cup of water.

"*Yonde kudasai*," he said, presenting them to Mouse.

"What the hell is it?" he asked, peeking in the cup. Looked like antibiotics of some kind, three of them. Sensei mumbled something in Japanese and Mouse shook his head. "I don't understand."

Lupe rescued him. "He says take one now, one tonight and the other tomorrow morning. I'd do it if I were you. Old man knows his shit. I've seen him bring people back from the dead."

Mouse took his word for it and swallowed the first pill, pocketing the other two. The old man sent him off with a tube of ointment for the worst of the scrapes with instructions to keep the area clean and wear loose fitting clothing. Funny, because all the clothes he now owned in the world were on his body at the moment. One doesn't usually pack for a kidnapping.

Last stop of the afternoon was Sadao's trailer. It was hard to miss. It was a 50 foot long silver and black motor coach with an attached living space that was in turn hooked up to a massive gooseneck equipment trailer. Lupe knocked on the side door of the living compartment before circling around to check the locks on the cab. He peered in the windows carefully before fishing in his pocket for a set of keys.

"Boss must be out," he said and chose the right key among a half dozen and returned to the side door to open it. He got it unlocked and popped his head in, "*Ojamashi-masu!!*"

He waited a beat then let them both in, switching on the lights. Mouse shut the door behind him, then gasped in awe for the second time that day. The inside living space was bigger than the house he'd grown up in as a kid.

The wall opposite was an expansion section that pushed out to double the floor space when the vehicle was parked. He stood in the kitchen mid-trailer with the cab to his right, a vinyl pull out couch and dinette U-shaped seating area in front of him and a bedroom and bath off to the left at the end of a short hall.

"The gas mileage on this thing must be shit," he said, taking it all in. Lupe had already helped himself to a beer from Sadao's fridge and plopped himself down on the soft vinyl lounge at the table.

"Yeah, Boss has it pretty good," Lupe said, stretching out his legs and picking up a remote to click on the air cooler and large glass plate TV. Some old comedy show was on which seemed to amuse Lupe greatly.

Mouse's curiosity was more compelling than television, and since Lupe didn't seem to care what the hell he did, he took his time looking around the place. There were a lot of shelves and cupboards filled with books and small hand-carved wooden figures propped up here and there among them. Although the interior furnishings were could be easily identified as Modern Bachelor the place was kept remarkably in order. But then perhaps that was necessary for a home that needed to withstand freeway speeds and unpaved roads.

There was a display shelf up above the sofa-bed with a collection of medals and banners, faded with age. Among the forgotten trinkets was a framed photo. Mouse put a leg up on the couch to reach up and take it down. He blew a light coating of dust from it. It was a media shot of an awards ceremony dated 2052 for an overland competition. The MC was presenting a very young beardless Sadao with a ribboned medal.

"Boss was 17 in that shot. Can you believe it? Youngest overland racing champion in the history of the sport – holds the record to this day."

"I thought racers couldn't be activated until age 17?"

"They can't. That's why it was such a big upset. A lot of bookies went home happy that day. Nobody ever expected a rookie to make pole position. But he did and left them all in the dust. Was a hell of a race. He's got a recording of it somewhere. I've seen it. It's fucking brilliant. But he won't show it unless he's really drunk. Claims he had a great mechanic."

Mouse chuckled to himself as he placed the photo back on the shelf. *Did he?* Mouse inspected the book selection next. It was puzzling. The bindings were all written in different languages. Some he vaguely recognized. Others he had no clue – the characters were foreign to him. He pulled one out and flipped through it. It appeared to be a biography – there was a lot of handwriting in the margins in Japanese characters. "What's with all the books?"

"Huh? What do you mean? Just books. Boss likes to read... and smoke."

"I've noticed that about him," Mouse said, putting the first book back and selecting another – same thing, lots of tiny notes in the margins. "Can he read all these languages?"

"Oh that... yeah, he likes studying foreign languages. Knows quite a few, I guess."

"Really, does he speak them?"

Lupe seemed bored with this topic – probably because it had nothing to do with things on wheels. "Uh, yeah I've heard him speak Chinese and stuff. When there's foreign teams around. He's the one who's gotta go talk to them about territory land use and stuff. So I guess it's a good thing he knows how to speak to them. His Spanish is kind of funny but he gets by with it in Mexico."

"I was lucky to learn English," Mouse mumbled.

"What's that?"

"Nothing... "

A perusal of the remaining shelves only revealed the typical items one would expect to find in a racing trailer: maps, manuals, guides, long distance scopes and binoculars, and a heavy duty phone attached to a charging unit with a lot of dials and flashing lights.

"What's this?" he asked.

"Oh! Don't mess with that! That's Boss' satellite phone. Works anywhere on the planet he says. It's what he uses to talk to *his* boss."

"Your boss has a boss?"

"Yeah, the stakeholders vote each year on a Chairman. That's the guy or gal Boss answers too. The money-holders. If he doesn't do what they like, they can axe him. Or so I've been told. So he's under pressure of his own. That's why he can be a dick sometimes."

"Makes sense. Hey, is this a radio?" Mouse flipped it on and a comforting hiss of random static issued from the speakers. Lupe gave him a weird look. It was making it difficult to hear the TV. But when it came to background noise, radio hiss was like a lullaby to Mouse who was accustomed to only watching TV in bars.

"Yeah, man, but it's short-range. You won't get no music or nothin'. It picks up radio transmissions in the camp. Sometimes Boss likes to listen in on what's going on, you know. Stops a lot of fights before they begin that way."

A conversion started coming through just as Lupe finished speaking. In Japanese of course, but something in the transmission made Lupe turn down the annoying laugh track on the sitcom he was watching. Two men, then three broke into the line popping and talking over each other. Lupe sat up and came closer to the speaker. "Turn it up... "

Mouse adjusted the dial. "What is it?"

Lupe held up his hand and listened hard. "It's Tagata, he's asking his team to call in

… it's something big… I don't…" Lupe's eyes got bigger. "Oh, fuck!" he broke into a smile. "Fuck yeah! General Shiratori's called in!" He jumped up then, clambered over the table and ran for the door, stopping for a moment when he remembered Mouse was still in the trailer.

"Hey man, I gotta go! It's something big. But Boss wants you to wait here, okay? So just wait, eh? I don't need Boss smacking me twice today, okay?"

Mouse shrugged. "Okay, but what's… "

Lupe was out the door and gone before he finished his thought, leaving him standing confused in the lap of Sadao's luxury.

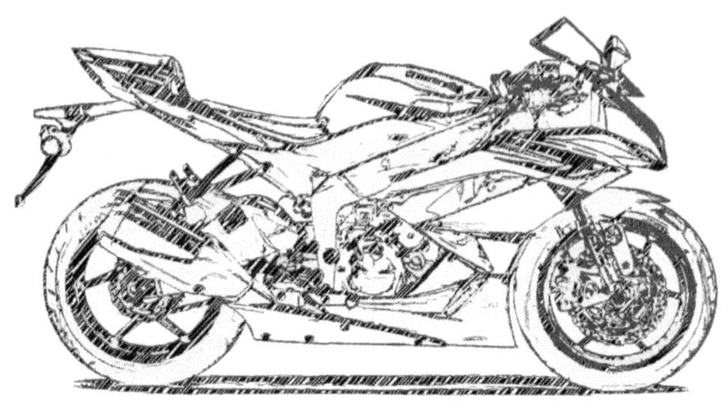

Chapter VI

The Serpent's Lair

Mouse sat for a while at Sadao's table listening to the radio. It had spoken volumes to Lupe yet said nothing to him except for occasional shouts and quick exchanges of foreign babble. Whatever the fuss had been about, it appeared to be abating. He got bored and shut it off.

He tried the TV for a while, but soon grew tired of that too and got up. The door to Sadao's bedroom was open slightly. Now here was a private space to entertain his curiosity. He went to it and pushed the door open.

Slipping into the Boss' lair felt criminal, but there was nothing particularly unusual about the space from what he could see. There were more drawers of this and that, more books and a closet of clothes well suited for racing and hot weather. Mounted to the wall next to the closet was a long steel gun case. Mouse tried the door on it but it didn't budge. Locked tight. He wondered if Sadao shot game. The mental picture he conjured of Sadao coming home with a jackrabbit over his shoulder was highly amusing to him.

Beside the gun case was a narrow table and chair. On it were various chunks of partially-carved wood, a magnification lamp and a tray of small sharp knives and a diamond hone. He picked up a piece of wood and rolled it around in his palm. It looked like a small totem – a bird of prey with a human face and a long tail that narrowed to a point. It looked like an ear plug. Perhaps he carved these for his men as ornaments.

The rest of the room's interior furnishings were similar to the rest of the trailer. The bed was rather nice – it had a big comfortable mattress with proper sheets and pillows for burrowing in. Mouse sat on the edge of it and bounced. *Must be nice*, he thought. His whole life he'd slept on an army surplus cot or in the cab of various trucks and cars. This life maybe wasn't half bad if one had access to air conditioning and... a shower!

He hopped off the bed and continued his snooping in the bathroom. Inside was a remarkably clean shower and toilet combo – not a stray hair or forgotten pair of undershorts in sight. Maybe Sadao had a maid. That was the only explanation he could think of. He had, after all, ordered Mouse do the dishes at the farmhouse.

The medicine cabinet held typical hygiene items, over-the-counter medicines and a beard trimmer with a few dark brown flecks of stubble. Mouse scrubbed his chin. A shower and a shave sounded good so he locked the door behind him, stripped and helped himself to the amenities.

The cool water flowing over his body felt heavenly, quite a change from the garage sink and old metal tub he called his bathroom back in Blythe. A pang of regret flashed through him as he washed. The old sink was full of ashes now, he supposed. It hurt that he hadn't been able to say goodbye. Maybe he could talk Sadao into letting him send a radio message to the Iron Horse, if the camp had long range capabilities. They had a satellite phone for chrissakes. He made a promise to himself that he'd ask about it. No, he'd insist. They were asking him to do them a favor, after all.

Clean, shaven and dry, Mouse emerged carefully – not wanting to burst out to find Sadao standing in his bedroom, arms crossed and glowering. But the man hadn't returned and the sun was falling fast outside.

Not wanting to put his dirty clothes back on, Mouse flipped on the bedroom lights and snooped around for something to wear. He tried the closet first but lost his nerve putting on something meant for competitions. Drawers next: T-shirts, jeans, more t-shirts… and hang on… he pulled out a long dark cloth robe. Of all the things he'd observed in Sadao's bedroom, this was the only item that looked Japanese. It wasn't fancy, the pattern was simple black and dark blue with silver trim, and he wouldn't have to feel weird about going commando in it. Sadao's underwear drawer was the one place he hadn't desired to dig around in.

Mouse put it on and tied up the sash. The robe ran a little long on him, but it would do. He didn't see how Sadao could object. It was better than going naked. He grabbed a comb from the dresser and returned to the main room to do battle with his hair and wait.

At some point Mouse fell dead asleep on the couch to the hiss of the radio – which now, long after dark, had come back to life. The sounds of motorcycles cruising around the campsite outside entered his dreams and he thought he was being chased through the desert again. The trailer door banged open and he blinked awake in time to see Sadao march right past him into the bedroom. Mouse sat up, straightening the robe and rubbing his eyes. Through the shades he could see other men outside on motorcycles, waiting.

"Hey!" he called out. No reply. He got up. *Rude not to greet a guest*, he thought. He stopped at the threshold of Sadao's bedroom. The man was in there, goggles atop his head and hair all wind-blown, unlocking the gun case. It looked like he'd been out on a long ride. Mouse yawned. "I hope you don't mind, I borrowed your shower and some clothes."

Sadao didn't respond. He opened the case to reveal a collection of long Japanese swords and knives – the kind you see in old samurai films. Sadao selected one and unsheathed it, turning the blade about in the lamplight.

"I used up the rest of your shampoo, too. The minty stuff... "

Sadao snapped the sword back into its scabbard, re-hung it and selected another one.

"And I promise I won't tell anyone about the dildos I found in your sock drawer... "

Sadao inspected the blade of this one too, flicking the edge carefully with his thumb.

"Or the inflatable cow... "

WHAM!!

Mouse nearly pissed himself. Sadao had gone ninja on one of his little carvings, cleaving it cleanly in two and taking a chunk out of the table underneath. He inspected it, pleased with the mini sacrifice. He sheathed the sword and slung the strap over his shoulder, shutting the gun case.

"Jesus Christ!" Mouse gasped. "Warn a guy, will you?!"

Only now did Sadao seem to realize he had a guest in the trailer. His eyes immediately focused on Mouse's choice of evening wear. "Where did you find that?" he asked, sternly.

Mouse shrugged. "I don't know... in a drawer." *Shit, did it belong to his grandfather or something?*

Sadao crooked a finger at him. "Come here."

Mouse looked nervously at the figurine lying decapitated on the floor. "Um... "

Sadao came to him instead and pulled the sash loose with rough yank. He threw the robe open exposing Mouse head to toe.

"Hey – !"

Sadao rearranged the layering of the front panels – left over right – and wrapped the sash from the front crossing it at the back and then tying it with a simple knot again at the front, tucking in the ends. "This is how you wear *yukata!*" he said, with a finger in his face.

"Huh?"

Sadao dismissed him and hurried out. "You were wearing it the way we dress the dead!" he shouted, opening his front door. "Very bad luck!"

"Geez, sorry!"

The bossy finger was aimed at him again. "Do not leave this trailer! Not for any reason!"

"What's going on? Who are those men?"

"Stay!" Sadao ordered, slamming the door and locking it behind him.

Stay? What am I, a dog? A proper yukata-wearing dog?

Mouse peered out the window blinds. Sadao and his blade were ready to ride and so were the men who had accompanied him. Tagata was among them. Their bikes roared and drove off out of sight. Something was clearly up. Mouse tried the door. It was locked fast of course. But no amount of working the bolts from the inside released it. *The hell?*

That bastard locked me in here! Fuck this!

He kicked at Sadao's door and winced when his toe hit metal. He tried the trap down to the cab but it was locked from the cabside as well. The windows were all fastened tight and if they opened, they were designed to open only a few inches to keep kidlets from rolling out onto the freeway when the vehicle was in motion. This left... the shower. He remembered it having a fairly wide vent.

Mouse invaded Sadao's lair again and slipped into the shower. The vent was unusually large – likely to keep moisture from warping the trailer wall paneling. He tugged on it. The fan cover was bolted in four places. Mouse went back into the main room and opened and shut drawers until he found a multi-tool with adjustable screw heads. Then he grabbed the chair from Sadao's carving table and set it in the shower to get himself closer to the ceiling. Fans had been his thing as a kid and he disassembled this one in record time, setting the housing and blades down carefully. He didn't want to break anything unnecessarily.

Once the whole fixture was removed, he was able to get both hands and arms up and through it, feeling around the roof for a place to grip. There was an equipment rack of some sort and after adjusting the chair position and adding a tall stack of books to the seat, he was able to lift himself up by the outer rack, leg up onto the stack of books and pop up out of the hole and onto the roof. He sat there in the dark for a moment, getting his bearings. The land was very flat and barren and only a half moon was lighting the eastern sky. Sadao had the privilege of owning one of the taller cabs so Mouse was able to climb up and get a good view over most of the vehicles.

There was something big going on to the west outside of camp about a mile or so out in the desert. He could see the lights of several bikes circling and distant shouts. Torchlight too, very odd. He wanted a better look. Mouse scrambled back down the way he had come up and returned to the roof with a pair of long-distance binoculars around his neck. There was indeed a group of about 20 men or so with torches and flashlights in a circle around a bonfire.

Mouse lay down flat against the roof of the cab to steady his view. It was hard to track the men as they moved in and out of the frame. Some were carrying chains. Some of these chains appeared to be hooked to some of the bikes. Then a distant cheer went up and he saw something really bizarre – a man dressed in some kind of antiquated Japanese armor, dragging another man behind him with a sack roped to his head. Mouse raised his eyes from the binoculars. Was this a ceremony? Some fucked up samurai tradition he wasn't supposed to witness? Sadao had ordered him to *Stay!*

and technically he was still on the trailer, if not in – but he needed a closer look. Just one good look and then he'd scramble back and pretend he was repairing the fan like a good house guest.

Mouse forgot he wasn't wearing any shoes when his bare feet connected with the hard lake bed earth. Too late for a change of clothes, he heard voices coming up the line of vehicles. Mouse ran between the trucks and trailers in starts and dashes, staying away from the voices and out of view. He stopped as he neared the farthest edge of camp. Keeping a mental picture in his head of how to retrace his path, Mouse crouched low and ran into the open desert. It was dark enough he didn't think anyone would see him. He didn't carry any lights and used the binoculars' night vision settings to see where he was going. He slowed when he got a quarter mile or so from the bonfire. Here he ducked down behind a rare boulder and balanced his viewer against the stone.

What he saw now made his bones shiver. If this was a hazing ceremony, he hoped to god it wasn't required of mechanics. The man with the bagged head was lying on the ground on his back with his limbs spread out. Each wrist and each ankle were clamped to a chain, the opposite ends of which were attached to four separate motorcycles with riders upon them. Engines running, the men were poised ready to hit the throttles in four separate directions. Someone was speaking, orating in Japanese. He couldn't understand it but it sounded like a proclamation of sorts. It seemed to be coming from the man in the armor.

Heart pounding, Mouse scanned the crowd over and over for Sadao. Was he in on this shit? He had to be. But the racers all dressed alike more or less and in the dark... There was a shout like a battle cry and the bike engines revved and their wheels began to spin in the dust. Their victim screamed as the dust rose and through it came Sadao, sword overhead, glinting in the firelight. His blow fell in a flash of steel, cutting off the horrible scream clean through the throat. The bagged head rolled away as the bikes throttled up, ripping and snapping the limbs and clothing apart in an explosion of blood and flesh.

Mouse's *katsu-don* came exploding out as well onto the dirt beside him. He clamped a hand over his mouth to stifle the scream that wanted to come out next, but it didn't have the chance because he was dragged back by the neck of the *yukata* across the flat earth as a new shout went up now to his immediate right. There were shadows of young men in the dark, likely with the same notion as himself – sneaking out to watch the spectacle themselves.

Mouse scrambled to get purchase on the ground with his heels but he was being dragged too fast. Then other hands were on him, shouting and laughing, grabbing his arms and legs and lifting him, running him now through the dark away from the bonfire.

"Let me go!" he screamed! "Let go! Sadao – !!"

As if that name was going to save him. Mouse gathered all the air he could into his lungs and screamed it again and again until he was thrown to the ground, pinned and gagged by the sash that once held the robe closed. Now it was all he could do to breathe. His hands were bound too behind him with bootlaces and the men, maybe five of them, picked him up and carried him back toward the dark end of camp like a trophy.

When he hit ground again, he was between the towering cylinders of the Orochi fuel storage tanks. It was an uninhabited end of camp, hidden in the darkness. The *yukata* was thrown open and his bare flesh was kicked and toed at by heavy boots. The young men were snickering to themselves, trying to keep their voices down to not be discovered. One of them came forward, pushing the rest aside. He motioned for some of the others to hold Mouse's legs wide apart while he went for his side knife.

"Remember me?" the voice asked, turning the blade in the feeble moonlight. "You took my knife. Now I show you my new one," he said proudly, lowering it to run the point down Mouse's chest to his groin. Mouse screamed into his gag and stiffened. He couldn't move with them sitting on his legs and shut his eyes tight as his balls were lifted and the tip of the blade ran cold underneath. "Maybe you pay me back, eh?" The knife point dug in slowly under his scrotum, pushing up the contracted flesh. "Trade?"

There was another scream, louder than the one in his head, and a whoooosh of something long and fast swung over him. The boy and the knife blade in his nuts were both knocked away with a whump! Mouse opened his eyes in time to see the armored man from the bonfire leap over his head and onto his attacker, thwapping him this way and that with a… fake sword? The other young men had scrambled every which way into the darkness while this one took his lumps and then some.

At last, the armored vigilante kicked the kid one final time in the ass and let him scramble up and away. Then he lifted his rather lame sword up in the air and shouted some chant to the moon, punching the sky with his metal arms and *fuck* this had better be a nightmare —

The nightmare samurai finished his chat with the moon and bowed deeply at Mouse who lay exposed and gagged in the dirt. The figure lifted his helmet to reveal a stunningly beautiful, if not wholly insane man with a big smile and one white eye under a shock of black hair. *"Shiratori, Kyouji tomoushimasu! Hajimemashite!"*

"Gmmmffhp," said Mouse.

"Aa, gomen." The samurai bent to one knee gallantly and removed Mouse's gag and cut his hands free. Mouse scrambled to his feet, covering himself. Then he beat the dust from the trashed *yukata* and coughed.

General Shiratori, he presumed, took a step closer, squinting at Mouse in the darkness with his one good eye. He took a handful of Mouse's hair in his metal hand and sniffed it before taking a step back. "Who fuck are you?"

"What do you mean who the fuck am I? I'm Mouse!"

"Mouse-su? Nan da? Mouse-su? Dou iu koto da?"

Mouse was getting pissed now. "I'm the mechanic! I work for Sadao!"

Mouse felt metal fingers at his throat and before he knew it the full metal arm produced some kind of locking chain and he was cuffed and attached to this idiot. "Don't ever use Boss's first name." *Thanks Lupe,* he thought, as the little man shouted at him in Japanese and proceeded to drag him like a second trophy through the camp.

General Shiratori knocked on Sadao's trailer door. When there was no immediate response, he drew his bamboo sword and attacked it, leaving dents.

The door flew open to a hail of curses – Sadao's and Shiratori's both. Apparently, it all had something to do with him. Mouse yanked at his bonds. His wrists were chained together and another ran down to one ankle. He just wanted to crawl in a hole.

"Get him in here!" Sadao growled and stepped aside so Shiratori would have the honor of tugging him over the threshold like a roped calf.

Once inside, Shiratori kicked at the back of his knees and Mouse fell to the floor in the middle of Sadao's kitchen – the floor of which was spotted in blood. His eyes tracked the dotted pattern up the leg of Sadao's pants to his blood splattered shirt and neck. Sadao's katana was stuck upright in the sink, the naked blade still slicked with gore. It made Mouse want to vomit again and he squirmed to get as far from it as Shiratori would let him.

"Chain him to the table," Sadao ordered, throwing a hand towel on the floor and pushing it around with his boot to soak up the drips.

Shiratori released the clamp on his metal arm and swung the chain under the table so it locked around the steel pipe that held up the dinette, securing him fast.

"Fucking murderers!" Mouse cursed between his teeth.

"*Urusai yo!*" Shiratori bent and yelled in his face, one brown eye flashing.

"Quiet down," Sadao said to both of them, removing his shirt and tossing it in the sink. He leaned in, knocking the faucet on with his elbow. Across his back was the most elaborate tattoo Mouse had ever seen—it was of a snake with several heads and tails clutching a giant black pearl. It writhed and coiled around the muscles of Sadao's back as if it were alive as he washed the blood from his arms and shoulders. *Who the hell are these people?*

Mouse looked to Shiratori who had taken a triumphant seat at the end of the lounge.

"Is this how you two get off? Chopping off heads?!"

Shiratori found this question hilarious. He began to chatter jovially at Sadao who was now dunking his entire head under the spray. He didn't answer the General, just kept to his grim task. When he was done, and his blade cleaned and sheathed, Sadao shut off the water and shook his wet hair out like a dog. He grabbed the weapon and

went into his bedroom to work the combo on the gun safe, opened it and put his sword away carefully.

Shiratori was still laughing and having a one-sided conversation with himself when Sadao returned and in no uncertain terms, was told by Sadao to leave. The General jumped to his feet, rattling his armor and bowed stiffly, "*Shitsurei, Boss-sama!*" he said, theatrically before making an exit worthy of an emperor.

Sadao locked his door after him and grabbed a fresh towel, drying his hair and chest. He dragged out a chair and sat in front of Mouse who was huddled on the floor. Sadao eyed him like the inked snakehead that wrapped around the front of his left bicep. "I gave you very simple instructions," he said coldly, tossing the towel aside with a *fwap*. "Do you know what it means to build trust?"

Mouse felt his face redden. He hated being talked down to. So he talked back. "*Do you?*"

Sadao sat staring at him, fury threatening to break loose at any moment. "I don't think you understand how much I have riding on you."

"That's not my problem."

Sadao leaned in closer. "It becomes your problem when you ignore my orders and run out of here half-naked like a piece of desert trash. You're lucky to still have your balls!"

Mouse spit directly into Sadao's left eye. Before he could blink, the man's hand came down across his face with a thundering smack, knocking him over. Mouse covered his cheek, blinking the stars from his eyes as he struggled to right himself. He hadn't expected that.

"Fuck you! If you brought me here to murder me, then get it the fuck over with!"

Sadao wiped the spit from his eye with the back of his hand. His leg bounced a moment, then he got up, knocking the chair over. "*Kuso!*" He kicked it out of his way as he went for the freezer. He dug into it with his hand and wrapped the ice he pulled out of it into his last clean kitchen towel.

He tossed it at Mouse, who failed to catch it, letting the ice shoot across the floor. Sadao slammed the freezer shut. Mouse stared numbly at the peace offering scattered on the linoleum while Sadao stared at the far wall as if his gaze could burn through it and provide an escape for them both.

"That *kusoyaro*, he killed two of my men. My sons! What you witnessed wasn't murder," he said lowering his eyes. "It was justice."

Mouse gathered up the ice and pressed the towel to his cheek. It stung like a sonofabitch. "How merciful of you."

"I was merciful. I took off his head. There are worse ways to die in the desert as you know. While I was tracking you across the desert, Shiratori-san was tracking *him* — your predecessor. He disappeared from camp the same day I ordered the wrecks driven out to your garage for inspection."

"My predecessor? Is this why you can't keep a mechanic around!? You behead them if a bike cracks up?! Who the fuck do you think you are? Judge, jury and executioner?"

"There is no one else," he said. "This is my clan. My decisions. My rules."

"I don't want any part of your decisions or rules."

"It's too late. You sealed his fate and your own the night I came to your little garage."

Mouse was stunned. How dare he? "Don't put that shit on me! I gave you what I would give anyone – a fair evaluation. I didn't think you would turn around and make coyote food out of someone!"

Sadao righted his chair and sat back down, reaching for his smokes on the table. He took his time lighting one and calmed himself over a few slow drags. The smoke rose in swirling clouds to the ceiling where the air vent caught it and sucked it outside. Mouse wondered if he could fit through that hole too.

"We are 85 miles from the nearest inhabited town," Sadao said, flicking his cigarette at the ashtray on the table. "There are no marked roads or outside radio signals. The stakeholders choose these areas carefully. The garage is under constant guard and the keys are kept locked away. Even if in time you gain access to these, you will not be permitted a ration of fuel sufficient to cross the desert. You will stall and die in the sun."

Mouse's heart pounded in his chest. *85 miles?*

"Lupe gave you a good tour today, I hear. You've seen my people. They have a good life here. The decisions I make are for their protection. We have four days to prepare for our next competition. We have a new Chairman and our performance will be under his evaluation. If you can look into your short-sighted mind and grasp what I am saying to you, you'll realize their fate is not in a small part dependent upon what decisions you make over the next few days."

Mouse adjusted the ice on his cheek and stared at the chain around his wrists and ankle.

"Unlock me."

"No."

Mouse laughed sickly. "I think you've made an enormous mistake. I'm not who you think I am."

"I don't make those kinds of mistakes."

Mouse looked up but the gaze Sadao was laying on him was too hard. *What the fuck is up with this guy? He doesn't know me!*

"I don't put faith where it's not warranted. It's time for you to grow up, *Konezumi*," he said and got to his feet, crushing out his cigarette. "I'd offer you my shower, but it's broken at the moment. Your chain will reach the couch and the fridge. You can piss in the sink. I don't care."

And with that, he slapped off the light panel and went to his room, shutting the door and leaving Mouse in the darkness under the table to think.

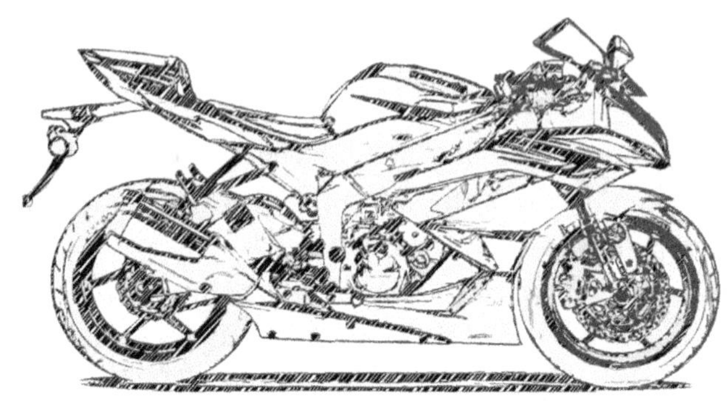

Chapter VII
Bad Gas

The kid had him dead to rights. Gun pointed squarely at his temple, Mouse was boxed in between the garage truck wall and the workbench. There was nothing left to do but surrender. He put up his hands.

"*Hizei! Hizei!* On knees!"

Mouse did as he was told, keeping an eye-lock on the kid. No false moves. The kid inched closer with a squint of retribution in his cold brown eyes. Mouse waited for the right moment to strike.

"Got you!" he said, grabbing the half-pint and rendering him helpless with a barrage of tickles.

"*Hanashite! Hana--!*"

"Say, 'let me go.'"

"Me let go!"

"Close enough," Mouse said, tousling the kid's dusty hair and giving him a whap on the tush. The kid squirmed away, grabbed his wood-carved weapon and scampered off squealing.

"*Nani o shiteiru n da?*"

Crap. Mouse tried to stay hidden behind the workbench but it was no good. Shiratori was after all a manhunter … and a general, accountant, samurai, village lunatic and regrettably, his boss.

"Just… having a little fun."

"Fun?! You have time for fun?! I not work you hard enough?!"

And from there he lapsed into a tirade of Japanese. Mouse stood and took it like a man, watching the clock on the wall behind the mini shogun, hoping to God Lupe would get back soon from lunch and put an end to it. It really was a good thing Mouse wasn't armed. But – and this really sucked – he was still chained. By only one ankle to a support strut in the middle of the dual level garage, free to move about and get work done, but chained nevertheless. Boss' orders. For the last two nights he had slept on Sadao's sofa tethered by the same ankle to his dinette. This at least allowed him to drag his shame with him as far as the repaired shower and back, scuffing the floor as he went.

Still, it beats having to work outside.

The garage was well air-conditioned and had two big ass ceiling fans. They had opened up the side walls and set up the tent and portable flooring outside for lining up the bikes for servicing. Mouse had been up since 4am adjusting throttles, brakes, lubricating shocks, changing tires, plugs, oil and fuel filters. There was a line of prepped vehicles that Lupe had been touching up with his airbrush outside in the tent, where the temp now peaked at 110° degrees. They had to take a break or else die trying to live up to Shiratori's expectations.

Outside, Sadao's team was running clocked speed and performance trials across the dry lake bed that was marked out with flags and checkpoint banners. Mouse couldn't really see them from inside the truck, but he could hear them roaring off and roaring back. The machines were sounding good – tip-top shape. But Shiratori was not pleased. As was evident by his now… 10 minute tirade.

A bike roared into the tent outside. The rider dismounted and pushed the high-suspension offroad vehicle up into the truck, throwing the stand and flinging his smothering helmet to the ground. Great, it was Mouse's second-favorite person – Tagata.

Tagata pointed at the bike, then at Mouse and joined Shiratori in screaming at him in Japanese.

Mouse yawned. "Y'all gotta start drawing pictures or something because *I can't understand a fucking word you're saying!*"

"Hey, hey, hey, Gringo! Settle down. Show respect, man." Lupe had just popped back in from his visit to the lunch trucks.

"I'd show respect if they'd grab a clue and use English!"

Shiratori puffed up and rattled his day armor – yes, he wore it 24/7 – but this set was notably lighter than his evening wear of heavy leather and polished metal.

"English is disgusting language," he said. "Only good for swearing: Fuck! Piss! Shitball!"

Mouse started to crack up.

Tagata's hand went for the hilt of his knife. "*Bakayaro!!*"

"Okay, now that word I know. It means dumbass, right?"

"Good Gringo, see he's learning!" Lupe slipped into Japanese and at last everyone began to calm down a bit. He listened, asked questions and nodded. Then he turned back to Mouse.

"Okay, so this is the problem. Bikes are good, run good. Then after three or four trials, they slow down."

"Slow down? Slow down how?"

Lupe addressed the issue some more between Tagata and Shiratori.

"I dunno, man. Tagata-san says you need to look at his bike. It's shit, he says."

Mouse kicked at his chain. "Gee, I'd love to take it for a test drive around the trailer but …"

Tagata threw his keys at him.

"Ow! Geeze… Okay, I'll start it up at least."

Mouse rattled his chain across the corrugated flooring and threw his free leg over the seat, inserted the key and pressed the start. The engine caught immediately and at first sounded good. He kept the bike in neutral and throttled up slowly, watching the tachometer – the engine gained RPMs appropriately. He throttled back down and let it idle a minute and then cranked the throttle up hard. There it was, a choke. He powered it down and did it again – same thing. Weird, he'd tuned these all this morning. Mouse shut it off.

"Okay, I can see what they're saying. Bring me another bike, one that's been out in the sun for a while. These Honda 450s have flat slide carbs you know, they don't like extreme heat!"

Tagata and some of his men rolled in three bikes, all of which exhibited similar issues with inconsistent throttle up, which led Mouse to assume one common element – fuel injection. But these Hondas were famous for holding up well offroad, provided they were kept tuned properly. The fuel injection systems were new – custom engineered for the team like all their foreign parts and imported from overseas at a tremendous cost. These babies were not cheap by any means.

Mouse had two of the men lift the worst of the bikes up onto a repair frame. Donning a pair of insulated gloves to prevent his fingers from cooking, Mouse pumped out the tank and then proceeded to take the fuel system apart. The obvious place to start was the filter. After unscrewing the gas tank and exposing the hoses, the filter cap came out easy – he'd just put it in that morning, but he wasn't prepared for what came out with it – a dribble of black ooze.

"Lupe! Had me a tub, will you?"

Lupe brought him a flat-bottomed container and Mouse knocked the gunk out into the bottom of it. He got up and took it to the workbench, shining a light on it. He took his gloves off and pushed it around with his finger, giving it a sniff. "That's not good," he said.

"Was is it?"

"I'm not sure. I need to check the other filters."

Mouse did the same on the other bikes and found the same evidence more or less – varying degrees of black gunk in the filters. Mouse eyed Shiratori and Tagata who had been observing his inspection with suspicious frowns.

"I hate to tell you this gentlemen, but it looks like you both have a case of bad gas."

Both men looked confused at Lupe who quickly explained, resulting in a reprise of "blame the mechanic."

Shiratori got in his face. "Gas is good! Very good! Very best we buy!"

Mouse crossed his arms. "You buy from government agents?"

"Eh?"

"Where do you buy your gas? Because if it's that government-issue shit, you're just setting dollars on fire."

"I get very best!" Shiratori insisted.

Mouse leaned over the workbench at him. "Look, I'm sure they tell you it's the very best. But I was raised in a gas station. If there's one thing I know, it's the fuel trade. And unless you're a total ass, you don't buy from the government!"

"Gas is good!" Shiratori snorted indignantly and turned on his heel, marching out.

Mouse shook his head. Tagata leaned over the mucky tub and sniffed it himself. He seemed more convinced.

He looked up at Mouse with a glimmer of belief in his eyes. "I go get Boss," he said in confidence and followed Shiratori out.

Mouse went to the utility sink and cooled down his head while he had the chance. He was not looking forward to changing two dozen fuel filters after every race. He really needed a team of assistants. Lupe was pretty good with a wrench on the basics, but when it came down to it, he just needed more hands on these machines. According to Lupe, the last guy – the guy who was currently attracting flies and being pecked at by vultures – didn't like a lot of extra people in his garage.

Mouse shut off the water and twisted his hair dry. "Lupe! Grab some buckets! We've got tanks to drain!"

"You know, I could teach you some Japanese, if you want," Lupe said, holding up the freshly drained, half-detached gas tank so Mouse could change the filters faster and get them wheeled back into the "done" line just outside.

"Yeah? What's 'fuck off'?"

Lupe laughed. "Japanese isn't like English or Spanish, you know. You got levels of respect you need to use when you address your superiors."

"Great, I think I'll pass on the lessons. The less I know the more I can speak my mind."

"*Shi-ne*, is 'fuck off,' but it really means 'die.'"

Mouse snorted. "Die? That's the best they got? Your Boss is always kicking things saying... what is it – ?"

"*Kuso?*"

"Yeah, what's that?"

"It's like 'damn' but literally it means 'shit.'"

"Suits him, I suppose," Mouse said, resetting a fuel hose clamp. "Also... there's this word he always calls me... "

"A word? Like *baka*, 'cause that's 'idiot.'"

"No, I know that one. It's something like nez-mi or ..."

"*Nezumi?*"

"Yeah, but there's a k-sound, too. Um... ko-nezumi I think."

Lupe was instantly taken by a fit of giggles. He dropped the end of the empty gas tank onto Mouse's finger.

"Ow – !"

"Oops, sorry but that's so funny!!"

"What? Does it mean 'dipshit' or something?" Mouse said, waving the pain from his smashed finger.

It took Lupe a moment to catch his breath and re-lift the tank. "No, no. Nothing like that. It's very cute. *Nezumi* by itself is 'mouse' but with ko- it's like he's calling you baby or kid – 'little mouse' is what he is saying. So cute."

Mouse rolled his eyes. "Oh, God."

"I think Boss liiikes youuu," Lupe sang as the man in question entered in through the tent flaps.

"What does Boss like?" Sadao demanded, stomping up the ramp. "Because I'll tell you what he doesn't like – getting pulled off the track in the middle of trials to come settle fights in the garage!"

Mouse took a moment to regain his bearings and stood up. "Look," he said, nodding toward the workbench. "Over here."

Sadao met him at the table as Mouse flicked on the lamp. "See this shit here, coming out of the filters?"

"Yes. That's why we change them."

"I changed them this morning. This built up after a few runs apparently."

Sadao picked up one of the filters, peering inside. "Are you sure? These look old."

"I'm certain these were changed. I changed all of them – I kept a log if you don't believe me."

Sadao put the cap back in the tub with the other two. "So, Taga says it's the fuel."

"It is. Shiratori got screwed trying to save a buck, I think."

Sadao sighed. "That doesn't surprise me. So what do we do? We don't have time for a fuel order. Takes weeks. We're too far from a depot. Can we filter the supply?"

"Your storage tanks are another problem. I got a pretty good look at the underside of them while I was having my balls shaved by your nice men the other night. Flat-bottomed tanks. This black ooze is probably organic material – it needs to settle into a wedge without being driven around on country roads everyday."

Sadao shook his head. "You can't drive a seven-ton truck with an uneven liquid weight. Goes right over. We'll have to filter on draw."

Mouse threw up his hands. "Sure, we can try to filter it until the cows come home but what you have left is still old gas with a lot of microscopic engine-killing shit in it. And unless you want to find me 20 men who understand English and cram them in here during competition to change fuel filters every ten minutes, we've got a problem!"

Sadao wiped the sweat from his forehead in frustration. "Okay, so we're fucked. Is that what you want to tell me?"

Mouse thought about it a minute. "Not completely fucked... I have a possible solution."

"*I-tai! Nani no koto ita no ka?* When were you going to tell me this?"

"Only after I got you so flustered you forgot your English. I need maps to explain. Lots of maps."

"I have maps! In my trailer. What kind, treasure maps?" Sadao started to turn to head out.

"Something like that. Uh, the chain... "

Sadao stopped, got out his keys and crouched down to untether Mouse, tossing the unlocked cuff across the room.

Mouse looked smugly down at him. "So, if I get you out of this mess, no more ball and chain BS, deal?"

Sadao stood and brushed off his hand, taking Mouse's in a firm shake. "Deal."

Mouse pushed past him in his new found freedom. "Come on, let's go find treasure!"

Sadao cleared the table with one long sweep of his arm and dumped rolls of area maps and land surveys on it. "The whole Sonora Desert is here. What do you need? Topography? Roads? *Dochi?*"

Mouse was looking at him. It was fun to watch the Big Boss scramble for a change.

"You have something to show me or not?" he said, annoyed.

"Yeah, let's start with where we are. Give me landmarks: canyons, mesas, hills... "

Sadao rolled the maps around and selected two. He popped the rubber bands off and laid them out one partially over the other. "We're here," he said, pointing to the exact middle of nowhere.

"Okay now show me the road we came in on before we hit the lakes region."

Sadao eyed him. "Is there a point to these specifics other than planning a possible escape route?"

Mouse snorted. "Still don't trust me, huh? Look, I'm trying to retrace our path during the ride in from the farmhouse to I can extrapolate the location of the shed we stopped in to cool down."

"The shed? Why?"

"It's not the shed itself but something I remember seeing in it. A workman's glove. It looked too new to be lying there."

"Are we hunting trespassers? For fuel?"

"They're not trespassers. They're rangers. They maintain silos and depots for the provisional government all over the wastelands."

"So they stash fuel in these sheds?"

"Sometimes. If that shed is what I think it is there should be a trapdoor or hidden wall somewhere. I used to raid these kinds of places when I was a reckless youth."

"So you stole gas? That's interesting... "

"They stole it from us first! Pumped out all the underground tanks – a legal seizure supposedly for our own good. And to goad us hangers-on into getting the hell out of town."

"How well are these deposits maintained? Gas gets old fast."

"I know, but they stabilize it and keep it sealed. It holds up really well. I used it for years to power my truck and generators. Good clean fuel. What I don't know is how active this site may be. If it is a site. We'll need to scout it."

"And if it isn't an active site?"

"How well do you know this territory?" he asked Sadao, spreading the maps out even wider.

Sadao shrugged, "I know the good level ground areas. I don't pay too much attention to crumbling buildings."

"Can you think of any odd structures? Something that seems out of place?" Mouse drew a line with his finger from where they were located to the route back to the main highway.

"Radio... "

"Huh?"

Sadao pointed to an area ten or so miles north of the approximate location of the shed. "There's a radio station tower. It's up here to the north past Beggars Canyon. But I've never caught a signal from it, yet I've seen vehicles parked inside its gates. Very high gates for a radio station."

Mouse felt his blood pumping with excitement. "Feel like joining me in a raid?" He hadn't broken into a government facility since his teens.

"I'll get a pair of bikes ready. Draw up an equipment list. We'll leave at sundown."

The waning moon had fallen below the horizon as they rode out over the dry lakes under the brilliant stretch of the Milky Way. Mouse hadn't noticed earlier that other teams were beginning to roll in at some miles distant from the Orochi camp, setting up their own banners and flags in the cracked dirt. But he didn't have time to squint at their lights in the distance now, it took all his concentration to keep up with Sadao whose tail lights kept gaining distance on him.

"You ride like my *Obaasan*," he'd said on one of the occasions he'd had to slow to allow Mouse to catch him. But Mouse was fairly certain Sadao's grandmother had never owned a Kawasaki KLR – a sturdy offroader ideal for tackling a variety of unknown terrain with room for an equipment rack over the rear fender. Aside from some simple dirt bikes, most of the motorcycles Mouse had come in contact with during his life had been in pieces. And with the scarcity of gas, speeding across the open ground for miles after miles wasn't something he'd had the opportunity to do very often. Still, it was embarrassing as fuck to get left in the dust.

Mouse saw Sadao's lights flicker as he expertly drifted into a stop. *Show off.* Mouse caught up to him and came to an idle beside him. Sadao was holding a penlight in his teeth, inspecting the map and compass coordinates. After a moment, he took the light out of his mouth and looked at Mouse.

"Still fighting that clutch?" he asked, impatiently.

"I'm fine!"

Sadao shook his head. "We're still on the flats, too. From here we have to leave the lakes and head north over uneven ground to the shed if we can spot it. I'm going to lose you. You'd better go ahead."

Mouse was irritated. "I can keep up! Just slow the hell down a little."

"Sadao Koga slows for no one," he said, rolling up the map.

Mouse responded by cranking his throttle, spinning his rear wheel, and for once leaving Sadao in a hail of dust. Mouse had to admit to himself, as he watched the man scramble to stow his map as he sped away in the side mirror, he was beginning to enjoy his kidnapping quite a lot. Once he'd decided to 'roll with it' the benefits were far outweighing the drawbacks. Sure, he still had to deal with assholes, but tonight with the wind in his hair and the stars burning up the endless desert sky, it was well worth the trouble.

They found the shed – perhaps more by dumb luck than anything else. The night was near perfect darkness but somehow Mouse's headlights managed to glance upon the edge of the structure in the distance. Sadao was right behind him and they both stopped together just in front of the broken gate that surrounded the failing building.

"See," Mouse said as they dismounted. "Looks like a pumping station, right? But what is it pumping? This area's been bone dry for decades."

"I hope you're right," Sadao said. "Shiratori will have words to share with me if we come up empty."

"Why do you let that guy scream at you like that?"

Sadao fetched a pair of flashlights from his pack and tossed one to Mouse. "Because he is a genius. You will see. One day he will impress you."

"Well he's gotta try a lot harder than he has," Mouse said, clicking on the light. "Right now he comes across as having the IQ of a sofa. Shall we?"

The inside of the leaning structure looked exactly the same as when they'd last visited some days earlier, except for one notable difference. Mouse shined his light on the dusty floor. "Glove's gone, see?"

Sadao inspected the area himself with his beam. "Coyotes could have taken it. There are prints around."

"They hunt mice, not gloves," Mouse stated. "Old buildings like this are a rodent's haven. Aaaand scorpions." A pair of small red pinchers backed out of Mouse's spotlight. "Great, the red ones – they're the kind that can kill you."

"Any idea what we should be looking for? There's not much here."

Mouse nudged at the loose flooring with his toe. "Not sure, maybe a panel or … rock."

"A rock?"

Just outside the broken exit door, Mouse's torchlight caught the shape and color of a granite stone that had no business being anywhere in the state of Arizona. He went to it and toed it with his boot. A couple of scorpions ran out and he gave them a good lead before he lifted the edge of the very hollow stone to reveal a small cranking system hidden underneath.

"What's that?" Sadao asked.

"Let's find out." Mouse crouched down and inserted the pipe into the crank and gave it a turn. It stuck at first, but after a kick or two he got it going. A loud creak came from within the shed. "Go look," he told Sadao and kept turning the pipe.

"Part of the flooring is coming up," Sadao called out. "Give it a few more turns … one more… hold!"

Mouse grabbed his flashlight and joined him. A trap door entrance about three feet square had opened up in the center of the floor. "Bingo," he said and joined Sadao in peering through the gap at the darkness below.

"I think I can fit down there," Mouse said. "Can you lower me?"

Sadao knelt in the dirt and held out both arms. Mouse grabbed his forearms and swung his legs over the opening into empty darkness. Sadao lowered him carefully, dangling Mouse in mid-air.

"It's okay. You can let go, I see floor!" Mouse said. Sadao let him slip out from his grip and he dropped another foot or so to the ground. Mouse took the flashlight from his back pocket and shone it around. The dirt basement was home to five large rectangular fuel containers. He whistled.

"What is it?" Sadao asked.

"It's a fuel cache! Not sure what kind yet," he shouted up. "I'm checking the gauges!"

"How much?"

Mouse focused his beam on the level gauge. The first tank read empty. *Crap*. He tried the second. It was empty as well. The third and fourth indicted full levels and the fifth half a tank.

"It looks like 40, maybe 60 gallons!"

"That's not a lot!"

"I know!" Mouse tried to loosen the seal on one of the full tanks but it held fast. "Sadao! Run out and bring me a large wrench from my equipment bag!"

"Okay!" He was back a minute later. "I'm dropping this down, stay clear!"

Mouse heard the wrench hit the dirt and went and fetched it. He tightened it around the sealed cap and pulled with all his weight. The cap made a satisfying pop! and came loose. Mouse unscrewed it the rest of the way and pulled out the chain, letting the cap dangle so he could peek in with his light. It was gasoline all right, he knew by the scent of the fumes. Fresh too. The light revealed a slight reddish tint to the fuel. It had been well maintained with stabilizer. No sediments at the bottom to speak of. *Excellent*. He screwed the cap back on and checked the others. He verified there were indeed two full and one half-filled tanks of liquid gold.

He went back to the opening and shouted up to Sadao. "It's all good. Grade A shit. I told you!"

"Good! Very good! I'll radio these coordinates to my men and have them come out with a truck and fuel cans. Do you think we can siphon it?"

"Shouldn't be a problem! Now get me out of here before I get stung!"

Sadao hauled him out by rope and made sure they put the trapdoor back the way they found it. Although, by all appearances this location wasn't under any kind of guard. But then, there hadn't been a whole lot of gas to protect.

"Do you think it's enough?" Mouse asked as he donned his eye-shield to begin the ride back.

Sadao had just finished communicating his orders back to the camp on his CB. "Forty gallons at worst you think? No, it won't be enough for all heats but it will give us an advantage... " his voice trailed off in thought.

"Are you thinking about the radio tower?"

Sadao nodded. "If we are right and it's another depot. It could be guarded. Our presence would trigger an alarm."

"I thought you weren't afraid of the government?" Mouse said.

"I did not say I was."

"Then let's get moving, Cowboy," Mouse said and started his engine.

Navigating Beggars Canyon proved to be more of a challenge than Mouse was prepared for. The canyon mouth had been nice and wide going in but midway the walls heightened and narrowed considerably. The dirt road was choked with dead trees, boulders and shifting gravel. Sadao once again held every advantage as former overland champion with an uncanny sense for navigating dicey ground even in the dark. He'd instructed Mouse to follow his lead precisely, but Mouse inevitably kept sinking behind. He would lose the path and get his ass stuck between rocks and logs, and had to dismount to walk his bike back out again and again.

Sadao, to his credit, didn't nag as much and even tried to give some helpful instruction. But Mouse was losing his patience with the whole affair. His arms and legs were getting sore and he was growing tired and cranky as the night wore on.

"How much further?" he pestered, trying to yank his front wheel out of a mass of sagebrush.

Sadao had his knife out and was trying to hack him loose. "How did you manage to get this badly stuck?"

"This fucking bike doesn't turn worth shit."

"It's not the bike," Sadao grumbled.

"Okay, so I suck every kind of ass there is! Is that what you wanted to hear?"

Sadao hacked the remainder of the bush loose, freeing the spokes. "I didn't hire you to be a racer. It takes training and skill. My boys practice for years under better conditions than this. Maybe we should turn back, it's getting late."

"No! I got it, okay? Stop coddling me."

Sadao looked confused. "What's coddling about speaking the truth? You are complaining a lot, *Konezumi*."

"Don't call me that!"

"Call you what?" Sadao asked, sheathing his knife.

"That stupid nickname."

"*Konezumi?* Ah, you know what it means."

"Yeah, I know what it means and it's insulting."

"I do not say it as an insult."

"I don't care. It's embarrassing, okay?"

"To be embarrassing, others would need to hear it. I only say it to you."

"Well, I don't like it. My name is Mouse. Not Mr., not some cutesy pet name, just Mouse."

Sadao brushed the dust off his jeans. "Are we done here, *Mouse?* Or do you want to argue names all night?"

"While we're on the subject, why don't you care if I call you Sadao?"

"Am I supposed to care? It's my name," he said, joining Mouse in pushing the bike back onto the path.

"Your men care."

"They are Japanese. We have rules of respect you don't comprehend."

"Then you don't care that I don't call you, Boss?"

"I like the way you say my name. Your American accent is very cute," he said with a grin. "Perhaps I should teach you some Japanese."

Mouse got on his bike and started it up. "Fuck, Japanese. Let's move."

It wasn't much longer before they reached the north end. From their vantage in the belly of the canyon, Mouse could just make out the lights of the last 50 feet or so of the radio tower up above the lip of the crumbling shale walls. It was all lit up and blinking against the night sky.

Sadao was fiddling with his CB, trying to catch a signal. There was a great deal of noisy chatter. The hiss and pops sounded odd to Mouse who was a connoisseur of static. It wasn't empty air; there was structure to it.

"Are you getting a signal from that thing?" he asked.

Sadao frowned and adjusted his dials again. "It is something. But I can't seem to find the right band."

"Then it's broadcasting. Maybe Freud was wrong and it is just a tower."

"Eh..?"

"Nevermind. Let's go have a look."

Sadao's eyes scanned the cliff above them. "We'll have to stow the bikes and climb."

"Night's not getting any younger!" Mouse walked his bike off the path and hid it behind a thick tangle of brush. Sadao did the same close by. He threw a tarp over his gear to further camouflage it and met Mouse with the flashlights at the base of the canyon wall directly below the tower.

Mouse took his and shined it up the layered rocky shelf. "Hmm, not a beginner's climb. What do we have, rope?"

"Rope and clamps for hauling and securing, not rock climbing."

Mouse didn't want to entertain the idea of riding any further up canyon and kept scanning the wall for possibilities. One eventually produced itself in the form of a drainage pipe some 30 feet up.

"Sadao, hold my light. Keep it on me." Sadao took the flashlight and shone it on the rock face above Mouse while he made a leap upwards and grabbed a bit of rock shelf by his fingertips. He quickly swung his leg out and caught a foothold on a narrow protrusion.

"Careful!" Sadao called up. "I don't want to drag your corpse back out of this hole."

"Don't worry," Mouse said between his teeth as he climbed by the skin of them one tiny ledge at a time. His handgrip was good but the round thick toes of his boots kept crumbling the delicate formations. "Rock climbing was my second-favorite pastime as a kid." His foot lost purchase as he was pulling himself up and for a moment he was dangling in space.

"*Abunai!*" Sadao shouted and dropped the flashlight in a lunge to get under him.

"No need to catch me," Mouse said gasping, hanging on by his fingers. He swung a leg up and out again, connecting with a solid shelf. "I'm not up that high!"

"We'll see who catches you when your head cracks in half on the ground!" Sadao said angrily, recovering the light and guiding his way again. "You're no use to me in pieces!"

"Thanks! Hey... I got it!" Mouse gripped the end of the drainage pipe and pulled himself up onto it. There were cables here to grip that held the heavy pipe in place. He looked down over his shoulder at Sadao and the light. *Whoo*, it was farther up than he thought. "Throw me a rope. I'll tie it on here and you can climb up!"

If Mouse had been a pain in the ass about the canyon ride, Sadao was twice the ass when it came to climbing. He got up to the pipe after kicking out most of the loose rocks in the cliffside with a hand-over-hand rope climb. Now, as they inched their way up the pipe, he was complaining about the cables messing up his fancy racing gloves.

"These were a gift – Italian leather, too. In shreds for what? You owe me new gloves and a *yukata*!"

"Shh... we're at the top," Mouse said, waving at him to shut the hell up. He crawled up onto an asphalt surface and motioned Sadao to join him quickly. In the dark they were near invisible and kept their lights off as they crossed the road to the edge of the complex. There was a set of dumpsters just inside the locked perimeter gates and they used them as a shield to peer between.

"What the hell is this?" Mouse whispered. Through the fence were three long pre-fabricated single-story buildings set out around the base of the radio tower. Inside, the buildings were a buzz of activity. Several men moved past the partially shuttered windows hurriedly. Some looked like they were carrying heavy boxes or equipment. There were several vehicles in the lot: delivery trucks, cars, and moving vans.

Sadao shook his head. "I have no idea. There are too many here for a radio station."

"It looks like a makeshift control center," Mouse whispered. "But for what? Let's find o... aahgk!"

Sadao caught him by the back of his shirt collar before he could climb the fence. "You're not going in there. I don't need my mechanic in lock-up the day of the race!"

Mouse tried to shake free. "That's all you care about? The race?"

Sadao eyed him coldly. "Yes."

"But we could be onto something here. Something the government doesn't want us poor desert saps to know about. I've never seen a set-up like this before."

Sadao brought Mouse's face closer to his own. "This does not concern us. I don't risk my neck for useless reasons."

"Then I'll... "

"Or those of my crew."

"Let go!" Mouse tried to wriggle out of his grasp, but Sadao held the front of his shirt tight. In the distance there was a flash followed soon after by a rolling boom. Both men froze. "Did you see that?" Mouse asked.

Sadao's hand released him as an afterthought. "Yes. We need to leave – get back to the bikes quickly."

Mouse nodded. For once they were in agreement – their worst foe in this scenario was a sudden storm. So he left the tower mystery behind and joined Sadao in a hasty climb back down the pipe to the ground. Mouse only stopped once his feet hit the canyon floor to try and yank the rope free.

"Leave it!" Sadao ordered as he uncovered their bikes. There was another flash. "It's still far to the north. We have time, but we have to move!"

"I know, I know!" Mouse said, shoving on his headgear and backing the bike out.

"We follow our tracks out!" Sadao said, starting his engine. "Keep your eye on the canyon floor! Do *not* lose me!"

"I won't!"

Adrenaline made the soreness in his limbs vanish as Mouse kept a fixed eye on Sadao's rear wheel, following the bike's twists and turns back through the debris. Sadao was moving fast but keeping no more than a few feet distance between them. There was a flash again, then another. The booms were growing louder and closer together.

The wind was picking up and whipping through the canyon, making a hollow moaning sound. Dawn was still some hours off.

Soon they reached the canyon's narrow midpoint and the dead bushes and fallen logs grew thicker again. Sadao was slowing down – taking it notably easier than earlier. Mouse felt shame that it was due to his lack of ability that they were being slowly overtaken by the approaching storm.

"Don't slow down!" he yelled over the wind that suddenly whipped around them, swallowing his voice. He didn't think Sadao could possibly hear him, it had gotten so wild and loud. But then he saw Sadao's head turn a moment to look back at a sound that just now caught Mouse's ears and stopped his heart. A roar – not wind, not thunder...

"Ride!!" Sadao yelled and his bike leapt forward into the night.

Mouse buried his throttle as the ground shook and the wind screamed. Behind him in his side mirrors Mouse could see the dry canyon walls turn to black curtains of raging, crashing chaos. *Oh, God!* In the next second he was flying, tumbling, crashing, the bike lifted away like paper from beneath him. Water, mud, rocks in his nose, eyes, choking, gasping, arms grabbing at air and water. For endless moments there was nothing but tumbling, groundless cold pain and the desperate need to breathe.

And then it stopped. A sudden force took him in, wedged him between hard and rough objects while the rage of the sudden river poured over his shoulders and head. *Air!* He took a gasp, coughed and gasped again. His lungs were burning. His leg was trapped under him, caught in the debris. A log had stopped him. His chest was pressed to it so hard he had to push against the flow with all his might just to fill his lungs before the next crash of floodwater soaked his head.

This is what it feels like to drown.

It was too much – the water, the force, the cold and pain. Mouse was detaching from it. His mind grew oddly calm. His body refused to give up the fight to push against this terrible crushing pressure to suck another few gasps of air into his lungs. Cough and push again. Each time he drew farther away from himself – just watching the flow and ebb in the darkness.

"Mouse!! Don't let go!!"

In the voice was an urgency he didn't feel anymore.

Who's coming for me? The devil? Jesus? Aunt Elma?

"*Konezumi!!*"

Great, it's that guy.

He was being lifted. The water was at his waist and then his shoe gave way and he came up out of it. By the hair!

Ow!!

When Mouse found his body again it was hanging upside down over Sadao's back, puking muddy water. They were moving up an uneven slope in the darkness. Rocks were rolling and breaking. He got the sensation of falling or sliding once or twice but held on. Then he was set down on a boulder and someone was yelling at him.

He coughed.

"I said stay here! Do not move for anything! I'm going for my pack!"

It was dark again. He was being shaken. There was a sting across his face. *Am I getting bitch-slapped again? Did I forget to 'stay?'*

Mouse opened his eyes. Sadao's eyes were searching his, white with panic.

"Okay," Mouse mumbled and a palm cupped his cheek where it still stung for a moment and then was gone.

Mouse sat coughing and shivering until he saw a large tarp floating up from below with a light.

"Hold this," the tarp said and only now did Mouse realize it was starting to rain hard. The pack and tarp were being slung around him and then all of them together were being lifted and carried again.

All Mouse could see was darkness and rocks and the smell and sound of rushing water and rain. Then it faded and all around was a hollow echo. He was set down on a dry rock and a flashlight was placed in his trembling hand. He'd never felt so cold.

Sadao shook out the tarp. It appeared to be reasonably dry. Unlike 99% of Mouse's everything.

"Get out of those clothes," Sadao ordered.

Mouse stared up at him blankly, shivering. *Is this a cave?*

"I don't want you going into shock."

"I'll b-be okay."

Sadao kicked the bones aside from an old coyote kill and spread the tarp out over the sandy bowl of the cave.

"Strip, or I'll cut the clothes off you!"

Mouse got to his unsteady legs and pulled his shirt off and undid the button and zipper of his jeans. He had to hold onto the crumbly cave wall for balance to pull them down and off each leg. The soaked material stuck to his reddened skin. Socks and his one shoe went next with shaking fingers, then...

Sadao reached out a hand to steady him as he removed his undershorts. Cotton soaked up the river more than anything.

"Come," Sadao said when he was done, shriveled and shaking. "Sit down before you fall down."

Mouse took his hand and stepped over the loose rocks to the tarp. Sadao followed him and together they sat down in the middle of it. "Come here. Sit back against me," he said. He pulled up the edges as best as he could with a cover that was meant for a single motorcycle, not two men. Sadao wrapped an arm around his middle and pulled him back into his lap. Mouse gasped at how warm he was.

"If the rain stops I'll go back out for the jacket."

Mouse gripped Sadao's arm tight with his cold fingers. "No... I don't want you..t-to do that. It's too dark."

"Your skin is like ice." Sadao's beard brushed the back of Mouse's shoulder as he settled and tucked the tarp around them both. Soon he was held fast in both of Sadao's arms, his frigid skin melting into that incredible warmth. Mouse closed his eyes and held on to him, almost as tightly as he had to the log in the water. He couldn't stop shaking.

Sadao settled in even closer, laying his cheek against Mouse's shoulder to warm it. "It's okay," he whispered, as if to a child.

"Mmnn--" For some reason the shaking was getting worse but not from cold. He panicked.

"Shhh... " Sadao rubbed his palms over Mouse's chest and arms to warm him faster. "Relax. It's shock. Your body will adjust... "

Mouse realized he was crying and dipped his head to hide it under his mass of damp hair. Sadao pressed his lips to his neck and the warm breath of his whispered comforts slowly rode out his convulsions of relief.

Minutes passed and the heat from Sadao's body sunk in deeper. Muscle by muscle, Mouse slowly unwound and relaxed. His breathing eased and his eyes grew heavy. Sadao laid him down gently, spooning him and pillowing Mouse's head on his arm. "Sleep if you can," he said. "I've got you."

Mouse sighed in his exhaustion and closed his eyes, letting himself be held.

Chapter VIII

Pale Shelter

Mouse awoke with his nose in the dirt. He sneezed and shook his head, sitting up slowly. For some reason he appeared to be wearing a motorcycle cover... and nothing else. Every inch of his body ached as the jumbled memories of the night before flashed through his head. Sunlight poured in from the wide mouth of the cave where Sadao sat on a rock, eating something from a wad of plastic wrap.

Why was it whenever he was with this guy, sooner or later he wound up naked?

Mouse got up and wrapped the tarp more securely around his waist and shuffled on bare feet over the rocky rubble toward the morning sun.

Sadao turned as he approached. "Feeling better?" he asked.

Mouse sneezed. "I smell mud every time I breathe in, is that normal?"

"Normal for you. You rode out a flash wave last night. And not very well."

Mouse gave his back a stretch, hearing several bones crack back into place. "I think it was the Flintstone mattress that really did me in. Is that food?"

Sadao produced a wrapped rice ball from his pack. "I saved you one," he said, tossing it to him.

Mouse caught it, sat on a nearby rock and sniffed the wrapping. "This one isn't that corpse flavor is it?"

"If you mean *natto*, no. It's *ume*... plum."

Mouse undid the wrapper and took a bite. He was starved but the flavor that assaulted his tongue did its best to prevent the contents from making it to his stomach. Mouse swallowed hard and made a frantic gesture for the canteen. Sadao smiled and handed it over.

Mouse took several long gulps. River water. *Uck.* "Blah, plum my ass! This shit tastes like sour fruity corpse!"

"It's an acquired taste," Sadao admitted. "But you need food in you. *Ganbatte.*"

Mouse tried not to think of the dead while he did his best to keep down the *nigiri*.

"Do you remember what happened?" Sadao asked after Mouse had succeeded in finishing it.

Mouse took a long drink from the canteen and thought it over. The prior night's adventures were coming back to him more or less in the order they occurred in. "Yeah, I think so. We rode in. Climbed some rocks. Saw a tower. There was thunder, then a lot of water. It took the bike right out from under me. Then I got trapped by a log and Jesus came and pulled me out."

Sadao laughed. "I don't think it was your savior. But it did take a miracle to find you. I thought that wave would have taken you halfway to Mexico. Fortunately for us both, you don't sink very fast."

"Fred always said I was full of hot air." The mention of his old friend brought with it a different kind of wave. Mouse was quiet for a moment. "Can I ask you a favor?"

Sadao looked at him. "Haven't I done you enough? Rescuing you is getting to be a habit I'd like us both to quit. One of these times I'm not going to be fast enough to catch you."

"Yeah, this almost dying thing is getting pretty old," Mouse admitted as the memories resurfaced of being carried from the water and then held in strong warm arms as he slept. Sadao had proven to be surprisingly generous when it came to sharing body heat. It made his mind wander into places it shouldn't when one is only wearing a tarp.

"What is the favor?" Sadao asked.

"I'd like to get some kind of message back to Blythe. My old friends must be worried sick about me. Maybe even looking for me. Or mourning me. I want to put their minds at ease."

"And tell them you were taken by thieves?"

Mouse regarded him a moment. "A few days ago, yeah, I might have said that."

Sadao searched his expression. He seemed pleased with what he saw. "I can send a runner if you like. Write something down so they will know it's from you. I can send it anytime."

Mouse smiled to himself and nodded. "Thank you. I'll do that. But maybe first we should think about how to get out of here?"

"While you were sleeping I radioed camp. My men have already been at the shack, collecting the fuel. I told them we'd ride out after sunrise and hopefully beat the sun."

Mouse stood and looked down over the cliff at the trickle of a river below. "Where's your bike? I thought it was lost, too."

Sadao stood up and pointed to a spot not far downstream. There was a rise in the rockbed and Sadao's bike was perched atop behind some brush. The area appeared to have been just high enough to miss the deluge.

"How'd you get the bike up there?" Mouse asked, amazed.

"Practice," Sadao said smugly and tossed Mouse his jeans which had been laying out in the sun. "I think those are dry enough to wear. There's a jacket still in the saddlebag. But, I'm afraid you're down to only one shoe. River took the other."

"And the other bike... " Mouse said, eyeing the riverbed.

"We can ride together, but we have to leave now. Sun is rising. Get those on. Let's go!"

Although it was designed with multi-purpose terrain in mind, the KLR was not designed for multi-passengers. Even with the rear equipment rack removed, it was a tight fit that pitched Mouse forward and snug up against Sadao's ass. In this position there was only one reasonable way to hold on as they rode over the uneven ground of the canyon, and that was wrapping his arms tightly about the man's waist. On the one hand, it allowed Mouse a chance to observe up close how an expert driver handled the clutch and braking. On the other hand, it also allowed him first-hand knowledge of the form and feel of every muscle across the man's back and abdomen. As well as a rather intimate understanding of the way those muscles worked together to flex and pump to operate the vehicle with fine-tuned precision.

Mouse had to admit – Sadao was easy on the eyes. A little too easy. The vibrations of the motorbike weren't doing him any favors either. Before he knew it, he had one hell of a hard-on.

Shit, what am I, 18?

"Hold onto me, or you're going to fall off into the water again!" Sadao shouted over the roar of the engine. He was navigating the widest part of the stream now. There was no dry land where the canyon flattened out as they approached the mouth not more than a mile ahead. Water was splashing up and behind them, soaking them both from the knees down. But the sky overhead was clear and the day was already growing hot. They had to hurry and that meant Sadao had to drive as fast as possible. Mouse swallowed his pride and squeezed up against the man's nice tight muscular buttocks with his nice tight happy-to-see-you crotch. Had the situation not been so pathetic on his part, Mouse might have considered it a "date." He pressed his cheek to Sadao's shoulder, tightened his arms around him and decided to just enjoy it.

As soon as they rode out of the canyon, Sadao redlined the tachometer to make a dash for the Dry Lakes. An hour later, just as they were about to hit the bone-colored earth, Sadao slowed the bike to a stop.

"Get off," he said abruptly. Mouse dismounted and pulled the flaps of Sadao's borrowed racing jacket across his bare chest. It hung just low enough to hide his little problem, thank god.

"What's wrong?" he asked. *Please don't say, "I'm tired of your dick poking me – walk home!"*

Sadao shut off the engine and dug around for his maps in the saddlebag. He unrolled one and checked his compass.

"Are we lost? Because I think this looks like the way we came in?" Mouse offered.

Sadao shook his head and lifted off his goggles. "That's not the problem. It's fuel. We're using too much with two passengers. We'll run dry if we try to cross the flats before high noon."

"Oh." Okay, that wasn't good. "What do you suppose we do?"

Sadao squinted back the way they came. "We need to get back to the hillsides. Find shelter. I'll radio for one of my best riders to bring out a spare can of fuel. We're losing a lot of time out here."

"How long do you think until they can reach us?"

Sadao held a hand up to block the sun. "I can't ask them to leave camp until after 5 and it's a few hour's ride at least."

"If you want to, you could leave me here and go back alone and send a... "

"No!" Sadao said, rolling up the map. "We stay together."

Mouse felt oddly glad to hear that. "Okay, then. Let's go find shelter."

The shelter they found must have been a hay shed in its former life. Now, it was an abandoned relic without much of a roof left to speak of.

"Well," Sadao said, knocking on one of the shelter's three remaining roof beams. "It's not ideal but it will get us out of the sun."

"Yeah, I guess." Mouse took a drink out of the canteen and sat awkwardly on an old hay bale before he passed it back to Sadao.

He watched as Sadao took his drink, fascinated by the way his throat moved, the way the sweat ran down along the tendons of his neck and pooled at the base. He dragged his eyes away. *Jesus, Mouse, get it together.*

But his eyes were right back on the man in the next moment when Sadao stripped his shirt clean off and proceeded to wipe at the sweat pool with it as well as the droplets that glazed the well-muscled contours of his chest and belly. Now there was no denying the heat inside this shed.

Mouse looked at his shoe while Sadao dug around in his pack for his cigarettes. He didn't find them, and after a patting down of his jeans and a second check of the pack, he scrubbed at his hair in frustration. "Smokes are gone," he said with a sigh.

"Sorry," Mouse said. "Maybe they fell in the river?"

"*Kuso...* " He kicked at the hay bale and sat down heavily next to Mouse who stiffened.

Sadao looked at him. "Are you okay?"

He nodded.

"If you want to lie down, go ahead. I can stand."

"No – ! I mean... "

"I don't want your body getting stressed again. We have a competition in two days."

"I'm fine! I'm…"

"Still hard?"

"What!?!"

"Sorry... when we were riding, I noticed."

Mouse could feel every drop of blood that wasn't already in his pants shoot straight to his cheeks. He couldn't even begin to speak.

"It's all right. I just thought if you wanted to take care of it, we have time to kill... "

Mouse wanted to say something, anything that would save him from this situation but there was nothing. All of the cognitive power he possessed was firmly jammed in his crotch.

Sadao looked back at him, amused. "You are impossible, *Konezumi*." He made a spinning motion with his finger. "Turn around."

"Uh... what?" There, some words made it off his tongue.

"I know you haven't had any privacy lately and that is largely my fault. So let's set a few things right."

Mouse was still… still.

"Your mouth is going to catch flies. Turn around or I'll move you around."

Mouse moved and sat even more stiffly, straddling the bale. The shift and situation were unbearable – in more ways than one. "I'm not going to... not in front of you... oh!"

Sadao had assumed the same position and was now up against his ass. His hands rested on his thighs gently. His lips were at his ear. "I didn't say *you* had to do a thing."

"Huh? ...ahh!!"

The man's hand was cupping him, examining the situation, making an introduction. Mouse surrendered to his lust and let his head drop back against Sadao's bare chest.

"*Hisashiburi, ne?*" he said, rubbing him in slow circles through his jeans. "It's been a while."

Mouse, eyes closed, just nodded while his back arched, easing himself into his teasing caress. It already felt so good he just didn't give a fuck.

"Undo your fly," Sadao whispered, moving his hand up to stroke the sensitive skin of his abdomen. "I promise you, I'll make it good."

Mouse unbuttoned and unzipped as Sadao's hand slid down and in, giving his swollen cock a nice squeeze.

"Ahhh – !"

"Feel good?"

Mouse answered him with an impatient grind of his hips.

Sadao pulled him out and began to stroke him fully from balls to tip, nice and slow. Mouse dug his fingers into Sadao's arms, moaning, rotating his hips into each pull of his fist. Soon he was spreading his legs wider, just so he could get more of it, more pleasure – *more... yes god, please...*

"Settle down, no need to rush." Sadao paused, squeezed the base of his cock, feeling the deep pulse there, then drew his fingers up in agonizing slowness, pushing out the moisture so it ran from the flushed tip in a hot cascade.

"Haaaaahhhh!!"

"Good... that's what I was waiting for." Sadao caught it in his fingers and spread the slickness low down over his balls, massaging them, rolling them in his palm. Mouse lost all remaining sense of composure and grinded himself into his hand, reveling in it. "Mmm, that's nice. Show me how you want it... "

Sadao moved his grip back up his shaft holding steady so Mouse could fuck his hand, thrust into it at just the right angle and speed. Mouse moaned, gripping hard on Sadao's arms, using them to push up with. He got so into it, his ass wasn't even on the bale anymore. He was breathing fast now – thrusting and grinding, wanting desperately to make this last and yet unable to stop his body from seeking more and more of it.

Sadao's hand moved with him now, matching his pace and squeezing just a little harder on each upstroke, twisting him, increasing the friction. Mouse opened his eyes and looked down, not quite believing what was happening. Sadao was working his cock with the same sure grip that had taken off a man's head and it was so...

so...

"Aaaaaaaghh!!"

Sadao jerked him fast to bring it on, then held him tight through the contractions one and another and another and yes... one more... a little more... *so good so good so good...*

Mouse collapsed boneless into Sadao's arms, panting wildly.

"Good boy," Sadao said, stroking his sweaty hair back from his face and kissing his temple. "You really needed to come. I think you hit the wall over there."

"Huh – ?" Mouse blinked up at him, blurry with release. *Did he kiss me? Oh shit... my junk's hanging out.* He struggled on weak arms to sit up.

"Easy, easy... I think you should lie down for a while. Here, let me help you with that."

Mouse tried to protest to being put back but at this point, after stripping naked for him last night and getting jerked off in a shed today, it just didn't matter a whole lot who zipped him up. He was so wrung out he didn't think he could manage a zipper properly anyway.

Sadao patted his thigh. "Let me up, I think I remember stowing an extra smoke or two in my vest pocket."

Mouse elbowed himself up and watched the man who had just pleasured him brainless dig around his motorcycle compartments for a four-inch tube of tobacco like his life depended on it. Mouse lay back on the hay bale and covered his eyes.

I really need to think about a career change.

Mouse supposed he must have fallen asleep when he awoke to the roar of an engine approaching. It was Tagata. He'd come across the desert in the midday heat, despite Sadao's orders to wait until the sun was lower. Either way, both Mouse and Sadao were relieved to see him appear so soon with a collapsible fuel can strapped to the back of his bike. He also brought fresh canteens of cool water and *blech*, more corpse balls.

Sadao nudged Tagata not long after he dismounted. "*Tobacco wa?*" The captain pulled out a pack from his riding jacket. Sadao looked as if he'd just found a lost kitten. He tapped one out and leaned into Tagata's lighter. He took a few hard drags and shook his head, looking at the little flaming bit of paper between his fingers. "Terrible fucking habit." He shared some words with Tagata and soon the captain was fueling up the KLR while Sadao caught up with his nicotine deficiency at a safe distance.

Sadao decided they should leave around 4pm so Mouse kept to the inside shade while the two men huddled down in the growing shadow of the slanting roof outside. It felt odd now to Mouse to be disconnected from Sadao. They'd spent the last two days alone and in relative comradery, but the arrival of Tagata meant the arrival of Japanese and the language barrier closed its door tightly around the two men outside. Mouse felt like a dog left out in the yard while the family got on with the better part of their lives. He sighed, managed to swallow more icky *ume* and tried to doze off on the hay bale again when a faint whipping sound caught the attention of all three men.

Back in the sun, they all looked to the northern sky. Sadao muttered a curse and grabbed a small pair of viewers from his gear bag. He looked and handed the binoculars to Tagata. They discussed between themselves a moment and Sadao nodded. Then he spoke to Mouse for the first time in hours.

"We need to leave now," he said. "Our hosts are beginning to arrive early. It will be very rude if we are not there to meet them."

"What hosts? Who's coming?" Mouse asked and was subsequently ignored as the men fell back into their native tongue as they readied to depart.

Back at camp, Sadao delivered Mouse to his trailer and told him to go in and clean up. They would be expected at some sort of dinner soon. Mouse was relieved because he was close to starving. So starved in fact, he raided Sadao's fridge the second he entered the trailer but his choices were beer or more beer. Something was going down. Helicopters like the one they heard earlier were beginning to whirl about overhead and the whole camp was astir.

By the time Mouse got out of the shower, Sadao had returned with a big box of clothes, which he set on the bed.

"Go through these, see if something will fit you," he said, stripping out of his shirt and moving toward the shower. "Pick out something decent, this is a formal event." The door shut and the shower started up.

Formal? How formal? Mouse didn't have any real experience with that word. He'd been to a wedding once. He wore a long sleeved shirt to that. With buttons.

He dug around in the box. It looked like a lost and found assortment. Nothing really matched anything else. He dumped the contents out on the bed and started making a pile of stuff he wouldn't be caught dead in. There was a lot of racing wear – pants and jackets. He pulled out a nice tapered pair of white and grey pants with red accents. He tried them on and they seemed to fit decently. Finding a shirt that didn't look ridiculous with those pants proved to be more difficult but near the bottom of the pile he found a long-sleeved tight-fit pullover of a similar grey tone. It fit well but the sleeves were a little long so he bunched them. Sadao had thrown in some boots too. They were higher than he liked with a thick sole, but they fit. He pulled the pants down over them. He hoped they had air conditioning where they were going because he was going to get hot as hell in this get-up.

Sadao emerged from the shower, towel about his waist and Mouse moved to step out of the room.

"Wait," Sadao commanded.

After what had happened earlier that day, Mouse didn't want to wait around too long in a bedroom with a mostly naked Sadao. The pants he had on were rather fitting. Mouse turned to him and tried not to stare too obviously at the man's chest, which was still a bit damp from the shower. Sadao took him by the shoulders, sizing him up. "Not bad," he commented. "You'll need a jacket."

"Really? Are we going to the North Pole? It's 110 degrees in the shade."

Sadao opened his closet and began flipping through it. "I'm sure it will be very comfortable. The Chairman spares no expenses, or so I've heard," Sadao said, selecting a red and white racing jacket. He passed it to Mouse. "Try this."

Mouse put it on. Sadao looked at the arm-fit carefully and nodded. "It's good. Now, the hair... "

Mouse put a hand to the back of his head. "What about my hair?"

Sadao made a face. "Can you do... something with it?"

Mouse frowned. "Define 'something.'"

"Mouse, this is a very important event. All the racing team leaders will be there. I have not yet met this Chairman in person. But I have heard he likes a certain level of class."

Mouse crossed his arms. "Well if my hair isn't classy enough for him, I'll stay here. Screw him."

"He asked to meet you, specifically."

"Huh?"

Sadao handed him a comb and pushed him gently out of the room. "Work with me."

Sadao shut his door and Mouse stuck the comb in his fashionable rat's nest. It went about halfway and became hopelessly lodged. This is why he rarely did "something" with it. He pulled the comb out and looked around. A container of chopsticks caught his eye on the kitchen counter. He put the end of one in his mouth, and watching his reflection in the microwave door, rolled up the whole wad in a messy bun and stabbed it in place. He selected a second and stabbed it in at another angle just to be "classy."

Done.

Sadao emerged soon after in a dark long-sleeved shirt with a black leather vest and jacket combo, complete with laced riding chaps over jeans. A biker fetishist's wet dream.

Mouse swallowed.

"Looks good," Sadao said, attaching his key chain to his belt.

"Huh?"

Sadao pointed to his head. "The hair. Are those my *ohashi?*"

Mouse just nodded mutely as his eyes soaked in the leathered Sadao. He noticed the man was wearing his knife, too.

"You're armed?"

Sadao smiled, patting the scabbard. "Ceremonial. I don't feel like taking the katana tonight."

Mouse followed him out the trailer door to his waiting cruiser. It had been cleaned and polished. Lupe really put some elbow grease into it. Jesus, this was beginning to look like fucking prom night. Except the girl had already been felt up. Or down, as was the case when there wasn't a girl. Mouse covered a snort of laughter.

"What's funny?" Sadao asked, shoving his gloves on.

Mouse shook his head. "Nothing."

"Then get on," he said, mounting the bike. Mouse hopped on behind him, relieved to be back on a two-seater. He noticed the back of Sadao's jacket bore the Orochi clan symbol in intricate embroidery. As soon as they started to roll out, two other bikes rounded the corner to join them. Tagata was on a spit-polished black Ninja wearing a similar clan jacket to Sadao's but in red. And... Shiratori rode on a brilliant white classic cruiser painted in long flowing feathers. The General himself was resplendent in what appeared to be gold-plated armor with matching katanas. His hair was up high in a warrior ponytail and he gave a wild shriek as they took off across the open desert.

Chapter IX

Heritage

The sun was setting into the western horizon as the three bikes crossed the desert toward a giant glowing white tent in the distance. As they approached, Mouse could see three enormous triple blade helicopters parked on the flat dirt surrounding the tent. Hundreds of people were moving about. In front of the tent were several rows of parked motorcycles and other offroad vehicles.

An attendant flagged them as they drove up and sent them to the proper row to dismount. As Mouse got off he could see the various team insignia on the machines.

"How many teams are here?" he asked.

"Forty or more. Soon the empty lakebeds will fill with spectator camps as well. These are our VIP guests," Sadao said, indicating the helicopters. Another was just arriving, whipping the air with its giant rotors. "High rollers, I think you could call them. They are our primary investors and stakeholders. Be nice, they pay my bills."

Mouse kept his eye on the landing behemoth as he followed Sadao, Shiratori and Tagata toward the main entrance. A door opened on the side of the craft as it settled to the ground and its blades slowed. A ramp was deployed and men and women dressed in finery began to descend the ramp. These were city people Mouse realized. He'd never met more than a few of them in his life. They looked clean. Important. Expensive. Mouse hated them already.

They were stopped by a guard near the entrance who motioned them to a long line to the right of the main pavilion. The line was for a security entrance with a metal detector. Mouse, who was officially starting to die of hunger, groaned aloud when he saw the pat down the racers were getting before being allowed entrance. Giant crates of swords, spears, and other weapons the event staff had been removing from them were quickly piling up. From the looks of their progress, this was going to take the rest of his adult life.

He nudged Sadao who was in mid-argument with his men, both of whom were armed to the teeth.

"Can I just meet you hooligans in there? I wasn't stupid enough to bring knives."

Sadao leaned into his ear. "You won't get in without me. This is something new. We've always come with our weapons."

Mouse sighed. "I'm hungry."

Sadao ignored him and went back to arguing with Shiratori about his ceremonial swords.

The other team leaders were all in the same boat it seemed and having their own arguments in myriad languages. Most of them looked Asian, Black or Hispanic. There was even a Native American team, but one thing was clear – the white people were all taking the metal detector-free entrance.

It was another 20 minutes before Tagata got the first crack at the machine. He'd already turned over his bowie knife and a small switchblade. Even so, the detector gate lit up and beeped in terror. He got pulled aside and run over with the whoop-whoop wand. His braided head set off a tone of complaint from the device and Mouse stood mouth open as he proceeded to pull five small throwing knives from his hairdo.

Next was Sadao. He handed his hip scabbard over then bent down and lifted his leather chap to reveal a calf-strap with another short knife stowed in it. The guard motioned him forward and the machine gave a weak blip. They backed him up and gave him a second run at it. Same thing, a little blip.

"It's probably the belt," the whoop guard said and motioned him aside. He ran the wand over Sadao's belt and sure enough there was a chirp. But as he waved it lower over his crotch the damn thing chirped again. The guard stared at him a moment, then tried it once more. Chirp, right over his package.

Sadao crossed his arms. "Do you want to frisk me?"

The guard nervously gave Sadao's groin a half-assed pat and swiftly waved him through.

Mouse who was next, sailed through. He was dying to ask Sadao what the heck his chirpy crotch was all about when Shiratori marched himself through the machine gateway. Shiratori, who had failed to surrender any of his accessories, nearly broke the damn thing as the warning panel lit up like a Christmas tree. Five armed guards immediately surrounded him.

"Nan desu ka?"

"Sir, step back and surrender your weapons!"

Shiratori only answered them in Japanese. When that had succeeded in only more guns getting shoved in his face, Sadao tried to intervene and was similarly surrounded.

"No English. No English!" Shiratori pleaded, which of course was a total lie.

"Look," Sadao said. "These are ceremonial weapons. He can not surrender them."

A guard stepped forward and pulled the longer of the two swords from Shiratori's cloth belt. He extracted it from the sheath.

"What's this?" he demanded.

"Bokken dake ii deshou ka?"

"What is he saying?" The head guard now addressed Sadao who was allowed to come forward.

"These are *bokken*," Sadao said, pointing to the wooden blade. "Practice swords. Harmless. They are for show."

"He has to surrender all weapons!"

Shiratori planted himself firmly.

"He will be greatly dishonored," Sadao said. "Samurai do not surrender their swords to commoners."

Samurai my ass, Mouse thought. *Crap, this was going to take all night.*

The whoop master came forward and wanded the swords. No chirps – only the hilts were gold plated.

Next, he tackled Shiratori's armor. It sent up a chorus of chatters from the device. Gold plate, every inch of it, in intricate layers of fitted panels.

"Armor is not permitted," the guard said.

"Do you really want to see what a Samurai wears underneath?" Sadao asked.

The security officials discussed among themselves a moment and deemed the armor permissive.

"These arms, are they dangerous?" the guard asked, inspecting the mechanical ingenuity of Shiratori's robotic arm and gloved hand.

"They are his *arms*," Sadao explained.

Shiratori spoke to Sadao as the men inspected his mechanical limbs. The whooper complained bitterly as it was waved over each one. Sadao frowned and argued with his General, then at Shiratori's insistence, spoke.

"Okay, he says he will gladly give up the arms if you will allow him the honor of keeping his swords."

"These come off?" the guard asked.

"Yes," Sadao said. "Give him a moment."

The guards took a step back and Shiratori grinned, first detaching the metal fingered glove from his left hand. Underneath were the remains of his damaged hand – one and a half fingers and his thumb were all that had survived. He wiggled them like a crab. Next he held out his full metal arm to Sadao, who was allowed to take it in his hands while Shiratori pressed a series of buttons at the top where it met his upper arm. There was a click and the whole arm went dead in Sadao's grip with a rattle as it separated from Shiratori's body. Sadao handed it off to the security staff carefully while Shiratori waved his stub at the men.

"Okay, no bad arm. Good now?" Shiratori asked.

Sadao took the fake katana back and tucked it back into Shiratori's belt. The General made a show of how impossible it was for him to draw his bamboo swords left-handed with only two and a half digits. The guards were appeased and at last, they were allowed to proceed onto the main tent.

Once inside, the pavilion was much larger than Mouse had thought. The peaks of the tent went up over two floors high and were lit by huge hovering globes of inert gas. Mouse felt dizzy looking up at them as he followed Sadao and his men through the crowd of guests. At the back of the tent was a long raised stage with a panel screen emblazoned with the Northwest Division's logo superimposed over a slideshow of historic racing photos from the last 30 years. To either side of the stage were roulette, craps and blackjack tables – already busily relieving guests of their extra cash.

Fancy cloth covered tables with candles and fine china and crystal were dispersed around the middle of the enclosure and guests were mingling around them, carrying cocktails and nibbling on finger foods served from platters by the bow-tied staff. Mouse made a beeline for the closest platter and saved the waiter a lot of trouble by robbing him of the whole tray. Asparagus wrapped in bacon. *Fuck yeah, bacon!*

He'd devoured six or seven of them by the time Sadao caught him and yanked him along by the arm, taking away his tray and returning it to a beleaguered staff-person's arms.

"Those aren't single servings," he said, angrily. "I know you're from a small town, but try to act half your age at least!"

Mouse trotted to keep up with his pulling, licking the last of the delicious bacony goodness from his fingertips. "It's not my fault you forgot to feed the prisoner!"

Sadao pulled him up short. "Listen, tonight is very important. We have an impression to make. I explained this to you."

Mouse yanked his arm loose. "Okay, okay! I get it. Fuck. At least I won't pass out now."

"Watch your mouth, too. Our hosts don't appreciate vulgarity."

Mouse rolled his eyes. "Can I swear in Japanese?"

Sadao looked defeated. "Fine."

"*Bakayaro!*" Mouse sneered.

This only made Sadao smile. "Your Japanese 'r' is terrible."

The lights flickered and guests looked up at the floating globes.

"Come, we need to get to our table. Or they might not feed you, either!"

Mouse followed him to a table with a mini Orochi flag stuck into a vase of fresh flowers. He took a seat between Sadao and Tagata with Shiratori across from him, armless and pushing his utensils around with his thumb. The stage lit up and music played a welcoming salute to the hodge podge of mismatched guests. An MC appeared, made a bunch of pompous statements about the glory of the Division yada yada... Mouse was far more interested in the wine selection at the table and poured himself a glass of white whatever and gulped it down. Mouse was on his third glass by the time all the various whoever-they-weres had finished explaining their significance. His eyes only tracked back to the stage when the Chairman was announced.

"It gives me great pleasure to introduce our Guest of Honor. His family name has been a part of the racing tradition since the '30s. Join me in raising a glass to our new Chairman, Marcus Getty!"

Applause went up, lights spun and a reasonably attractive, tall young man with short light brown curly hair waved to the audience from the trappings of a tie-less well-fit suit. His no-nonsense manner as he approached the mic took Mouse by surprise. He didn't look as aloof and snotty as most of the other guests.

"Welcome everyone – team leads and valued patrons. It's a great honor for me to be here. As you know, the Gettys have been active in the racing scene since my father was a young boy, traveling by bus hundreds of miles with my grandfather to follow all his favorite champions in race after race over the expanse of these great desert lands. It's a tradition I want to bring back – that hometown feel of community as we share our love for this exciting sport with each other.

"My father told me, there is no greater glory than that of a good clean win. That's the spirit I want this Division to embrace again. So let's not delay dinner anymore and raise our glasses to glory well won!"

Mouse raised his glass while Sadao, Shiratori and Tagata all exchanged 'what-the-fuck' glances. Mouse downed his glass and reached for the wine bottle as Sadao slid it out of his reach.

Mouse sighed and rested his dizzy head in his palm, watching the light balls float around. The smell of food soon stirred his woozy senses. A small army of servers flowed in the side doors with hundreds of hot trays. His plate barely made touchdown with the tablecloth before Mouse was carving and stabbing the food into his mouth as fast as his ability to chew and swallow would allow. *Mmmm prime rib and potatoes.*

The Japanese were not amused with his gluttony. Tagata looked disgusted, while Sadao sighed. Shiratori attempted to pick up his fork with his pinky finger and thumb, dropping it with a clatter on his plate.

"You need me to cut that?" Sadao asked the General.

He smiled brilliantly and bowed his head. "*Onegai shimasu, Boss-sama.*"

Sadao moved the digitally challenged man's plate closer and went at it with the steak knife and fork. Mouse had to admit, he really didn't get those two. One moment they were screaming at each other like bitter enemies, in the next it looked like they'd walk across a bed of cactus barefoot to say hello. Mouse wanted to ask them about it, what it was like back in Japan before the country went to shit, but his mouth was too busy filling his stomach.

Sadao finished preparing Shiratori's plate for him before he started in on his own. Shiratori rolled his steak bits in the sauce and potatoes and lifted them one by one to his mouth between his thumb and little finger with surprising grace.

"Now what is this I see here? Shiratori-san, where are your hands?"

Mouse sat up and wiped the sauce from his chin. The Chairman had arrived at their table with his small entourage.

"Bad man took arm," Shiratori said in fake broken English, poking his thumb at the Chairman's main bodyguard.

The Chairman turned on his guard with a look of deep concern. "Is this true?" The guard started to stammer out an excuse – something about potential threat to the safety of his person.

"That's nonsense! You must restore the man's hands, how is he supposed to eat? We do not shame our guests! Especially one as esteemed as General Shiratori!"

Shiratori stood and bowed deeply. From his good side the man was stunningly beautiful. Too bad he was also bug-nuts. The Chairman bowed in turn and said something polite in Japanese. Sadao and Tagata also stood and did the same.

"Tagata-san, Koga-san, *hajimemashite*," he said, shaking their hands warmly. "I am greatly honored to meet the leaders of the Orochi Team face to face. I've been a fan for years!"

Koga-san? It was utterly bizarre for Mouse to hear someone use Sadao's last name.

"And correct me if I am mistaken, but is this Mouse?"

Mouse looked up from his plate, surprised. For the first time in over a week someone got his name right on the first try. He was too surprised to even stand up and took the Chairman's hand from his chair.

"I've been anxious to meet Koga-san's secret weapon."

"He has a secret weapon?" Mouse asked, getting late to his feet. *Oh, wait, he means you, dumb-dumb.*

The Chairman smiled broadly. He really wasn't all that old, 30 tops maybe. But his casual open manner had yet to put Mouse completely at ease.

"I'm quite excited to see what you're capable of. Koga-san told me he found you smack in the middle of nowhere."

"Blythe," Mouse corrected.

"Oh, Blythe! On the California border? Off I-10?"

Mouse nodded. The guy had heard of the place. Interesting.

"You were working in a small station there yet you had antique Japanese motorsport expertise. What an uncanny coincidence."

"Yeah... it was pretty weird, I guess."

"Well it was a happy accident. I was concerned to hear the Orochi team had lost their chief mechanic so soon before competition. The bond of trust between a racing team and their mechanic is a very special one. But from what he's told me about you, I'm confident he made a fine choice in securing you."

"Yeah, he secured me all right, with chains – ow!"

Sadao had kicked his ankle from under the tablecloth.

"Mouse has already proven to be an indispensable asset to the team," Sadao intervened. "We are honored to have him among us."

Honored, isn't a word I'd use...

"Sir, Mr. Chairman!" It was the tool from security. "We have released the gentleman's gauntlet. It appears to carry no threat. But I'm afraid Sir, I cannot approve the arm. At least not until we can determine what it does."

"*Te dake de mo ii desu,*" Shiratori said, bowing deeply and re-attaching his heavy metal glove.

"What does he say?" the Chairman asked Sadao.

"He said, 'Just the hand is enough.'"

"*Sore ja, taberaremasu,*" Shiratori continued, flexing his metal hand. "*Arigatou gozaimasu.*"

"Thanks, he can eat now," Sadao confirmed.

Mouse wondered why in the heck Sadao played this bad English game with Shiratori. Both of them knew he could speak fairly decent English and understood it perfectly when spoken to him. Irritating was all this was. As irritating as his sightless white eye, which Lupe told him could have been replaced with a mechanical one but Shiratori preferred to keep it a blank white hunk of glass. Without an iris it was hard to read his expression most of the time, or tell exactly where he was looking.

With Shiratori no longer helpless, the Chairman moved on to other guests. Mouse sat and kept his mind on his food while the men around him ate and chatted in Japanese. They seemed concerned about something, but as usual weren't explaining anything to him.

Mouse was thoroughly enjoying the chocolate souffle and coffee service when the stage came to life again. It was a short retrospective film of the last 30 years in racing. Mouse perked up at this because for the most part, it was the racing experience he remembered as a kid. Families in minivans and trucks traveling after their favorite teams: Onroad, offroad, closed and open course – the film featured vintage footage and modern clips of riders on and off the racecourse interspersed with music. A short clip of a teenaged Sadao flashed across the stage at one point – holding up his cup and waving, covered in mud.

Mouse giggled and glanced at the man seated to his left. Sadao ran a hand over his face. "Ancient history," he said.

Mouse leaned in closer. "Not so ancient. You beat a flood out of a canyon last night, remember?"

Sadao held a finger to his own lips. "Don't tell."

The film ended in applause and the lights came back up. The Chairman retook the stage and resumed his speech about returning 'glory' to the grand old traditions, etc. Then a topographic map of Utah stretched across the screen behind him with dotted lines marked out across most of the abandoned state – canyonlands to salt flats, dunes to Rocky Mountain peaks.

"To commemorate this new direction, I have proposed a special challenge for our teams. I have spoken to the other Division directors and we are in agreement. The Overland competition needs to return to the season schedule with a three-day race across the great state of Utah. A multi-vehicle relay covering hundreds of miles that will test not only our machines but our men as well."

Sadao sat up and exchanged a quick look with his men. Mouse couldn't decide if they looked enthused or horrified. A similar grumble could be heard throughout the tent. Nobody, it seemed, had expected this.

"Street, sand, dirt, canyon and mountain will all be covered. Vehicle choice is up to each team but one of each category much be featured: bike, car, ATV and buggy."

"*Kuruma? Nan da?!*" Shiratori and Sadao now both exchanged quick tight words.

Kuruma must mean 'car' because as far as Mouse had seen, the Orochi Team did not race autos.

"We know this announcement will spin some heads, but I've come to learn over the years a great team comes prepared for anything! And along those lines, I have something new to show you – "

Overhead, the hovering globes parted and a basketball-sized round translucent black object descended. The head and base swiveled independently 360 degrees as it zipped down and over the guests. The Chairman waved for the device to fly closer to him and at once his face filled the stage screen from its video feed.

"These are our new camera drones. One of the main shortcomings of the Overland was lack of good camera coverage. So our teams had to be limited to specific checkpoints and roadways. Our drones are programmed to follow the vehicle they are assigned to and cover it from every possible angle during a race – in all conditions and at all speeds. The Getty Corporation has invested billions in this new technology in hopes of bringing the thrill of racing home to our residents up north. This unprecedented streaming coverage will reintroduce the cities to the sport I loved so dearly in my youth – without having to leave the comfort of home."

Assigned to a vehicle? By whom? Was there going to be a swarm of these things hovering around the garage? Mouse didn't like this plan one bit. Racing was a wasteland sport for those willing to brave the climate – or else those who had the means to provide their own air conditioned portable environments. Cushy Northerners living their crowded expensive lives need not butt their noses into it. Mouse didn't believe this guy for a minute. *Tradition his nutsac*, this guy wanted more of the Northern deep pockets dumping out gambling dollars into his wallet. Extensive, exclusive coverage on paid network channels would certainly encourage that.

Surprise announcements and dinner now over with, the evening entertainment got underway. A jazz band populated the stage and a sultry singer with a mane of tight brown curls stepped up to the mic in a silky black dress and began to sing in French.

The men of the Orochi Team took no notice as they set glasses and flower arrangements aside to draw imaginary plans on the tablecloth with the remaining utensils. Mouse watched them for a while but the lines they were drawing didn't make sense.

He raised his hand. "Can the mechanic ask a question?"

Sadao looked at him. "What?" he asked tersely.

"Sorry, I just wanted to ask... what are we doing about a racecar?"

Sadao shook his head. "I have no idea. I can't pull a million from my back pocket overnight."

"I could make one," Mouse suggested. "Well, rebuild one. If you can get all the parts – hit up all the right junk dealers. It's not impossible."

Tagata spoke for once. "We are Orochi! We do not race junk!"

Sadao waved him down. "We only need it for one leg of the race," he pointed out. "The bigger problem is, who will drive it? I have no men trained in auto racing. It's not what we do."

"Can you opt out?" Mouse asked.

Sadao shook his head. "All Division teams are required to enter. If he means to run it the way we used to, this will be an unlimited multi-division race. There are no course limits. Each team will devise their own navigation. We did not plan for this."

"Did anyone else plan for this?"

Shiratori recovered from his English amnesia. "All teams send strongest man to race best for him. Many do not qualify for races they are not strong in. Orochi Team does not race auto in road race. Our street bike go faster than car. No need. Now rules change. We must have car. Very good car!"

"So it sounds to me like everyone is going to take a hit on this one, am I right?" Mouse asked.

Sadao agreed. "Yes, but we still need to finish ahead of them if we all want food in our bellies and fuel in our bikes!"

"Sell kid," Shiratori suggested. "You have too many not old enough to race! Eat all the food! Always big problem!"

Sadao grabbed his steak knife and slammed it into the table, rattling the crystal. "I do *not* sell children!"

Mouse got up.

"Where are you going?" Sadao barked.

"I need to piss and I'd rather not get in the middle of a table duel."

"Tagata, take him."

"Oh, for fuck's sake – I can pee by myself!"

Sadao held up a finger. "Do not leave this tent!"

"Fine, I'll take a leak in a vase and go spin the roulette while you all bicker in Japanese. Gimmie some money."

Sadao glared at him, then caved and dug around in his pockets, slapping a $50 in his open palm.

"That's it? Some salary."

"Win me a purse, then we will talk salary!"

Mouse pretended to be grateful and after a good long pee in the men's room and a few hands of blackjack, he was already out. He was about to vacate the stool when Sadao appeared, taking the seat to his left and placing a stack of chips in front of them both. He motioned to the dealer to deal them both in.

"You lose my money already?" he asked.

"Yeah, I suck at gambling." Mouse said, eyeing him. The man looked calmer, resigned. He snuck a look at his cards and scraped the table for a hit. The dealer had 19 showing. Mouse requested another card as well – a king. He was instantly busted. Sadao doubled down and tapped for another hit.

"What do you need to build this car?" Sadao asked.

Mouse shrugged. "It depends. Good solid chassis, clean engine, decent fuel injection and steering system. I guess we can go cheap on the body. Aside from the roll bar of course."

"How well do you know Classics?"

"Classics? You mean Mustangs? Pontiacs? I grew up working on those rides. '70s American muscle cars were the shit."

Sadao nodded. "I was thinking American." He turned over his cards, 21 on the nose – the dealer had 20. The man just made his money back with one hand. Sadao gathered his chips and walked away.

Mouse scrambled off the stool and followed him to the cashier where he changed it back into a $50 and put it back in his pocket. "That was a headlight," he said. "How much time will you need?"

"I don't know, exactly. Six weeks maybe, with assistance."

Sadao shook his head. "You'll have four and we need to relocate the camp."

"I'm going to need more men!"

"Train some of the younger ones – get Shiratori off my back about useless orphans."

"Sadao, *mon cheri*, where have you been hiding?" the French jazz singer came up from behind and wrapped her thin white fingers around Sadao's arm. She nuzzled his cheek and gave him a soft kiss. Clearly, they knew each other.

"*Bonsoir*, Gisette. You sounded lovely tonight, as always," Sadao said, returning the kiss to the side of her painted red lips.

Mouse felt his dinner rise in his gut. Is this what Sadao went for? This bony chick? She wore a hell of a rock on her left hand. He hoped to Christ it wasn't from him.

"Who is this? He is new, no?" she asked coyly.

Sadao squeezed her hand. "This is Mouse, my new mechanic. He's going to maneuver us through this latest twist in the Chairman's plans."

"Is he? He's cute, too. Where did you find him?" She asked, looking Mouse over.

"He found me in Blythe," Mouse said, annoyed. He hated being talked about as if he wasn't standing right there in front of her.

"Hmm... " she cooed in Sadao's ear. "I've never heard of it."

"That doesn't surprise me." Mouse grumbled.

"He looks tense, doesn't he? Shall we bring him along?" she asked, nibbling on Sadao's ear.

Sadao smiled and touched her cheek. "Gisette, what would your husband say to such a proposal?"

"He'd say, 'Thank goodness. She'll stay satisfied for a while,'" she laughed.

"I'll pass, thanks," Mouse said bluntly. "I like cock."

Gisette smiled. "Excellent choice." She tugged at Sadao's arm but he didn't move. Her smile faded.

"*Je suis désolé*, Gisette," he said, regarding her fondly as he unwound her arms from his and kissed her hands. "I promised the men I'd return for campfire tonight."

Her lovely mouth dropped open in disbelief. Mouse beamed.

"Perhaps some other time."

"You are always so devoted, my Sadao," she sighed. "A pity not more so to me."

A pity for your husband, lady.

She gave one last forlorn look at Sadao before she slinked back into the swarm of guests and was soon nuzzling up to someone on the Korean team.

"Really?" Mouse asked as they worked their way back to the table. "You stick your dick in that woman?"

Sadao laughed. "How do you think I got my trailer?"

Back at the Orochi table Tagata was nowhere to be seen but Shiratori was entertaining two blonde Swedish twins in matching silver sequined gowns. With Shiratori's armor between them they looked like a lounge act. The ladies were twittering at him in Swedish and pawing at his glove and stub.

"Where is your arm, Shiratori-san?" one asked in English.

"Mean guardman took arm," Shiratori said as she played with his ponytail. She reached down and pulled his sword. The twin across from her took the other. And rising together, all three set off to do battle with the Chairman's forces of evil.

Mouse looked to Sadao. "Who are all these women?"

"Loyal patrons," Sadao said, gathering his jacket. "Tagata was snared by a brunette tonight. You could do worse, you know. Despite your preferences, many of these women hold very large bank accounts."

"Of their husbands' money," Mouse said pointedly.

"I'm not particular," Sadao said with a shrug.

"Apparently... " Mouse muttered under his breath.

"What?"

"I'm tired, I said. I slept in a cave last night, let's go back."

Campfire was held not far from Sadao's trailer in the center of camp. Although he was exhausted, Mouse was slow to leave Sadao's side and followed him to it. Sadao's men greeted him with shouts as they blasted loud music and set off small firecrackers and sparklers in the flickering light. Many of them had been drinking it appeared and were staging sloppy wrestling matches in the dirt.

Mouse sat on an overturned bucket somewhat outside of the circle while Sadao relaxed in a folding chair closer to the fire, smoking and watching the spectacle with pride. One of his little ones wandered into the fray, holding a blanket. He looked like a refugee of the kid trailer. He wandered a bit until he saw Sadao. His pudgy face lit up and he ran to him, grabbing his leg and gibbering in high-pitched Japanese.

Sadao crushed out his cigarette in the dirt and patted his knee. "*Oiede*, Ta-kun!" The kid scrambled up into his lap and nestled against his chest as Sadao wrapped the blanket around him. The little guy popped his thumb into his mouth and closed his eyes. Sadao ruffled his hair and in a matter of moments the kid was sound asleep.

These really were his children, his family. It was not hard to see he loved them all deeply, even the troubled ones. And they loved him just as much, each in their own way.

Mouse felt a warm ache pulling at his chest. He realized he wanted that same kind of deep connection with a man. He desired desperately to be beloved to someone like Sadao. Someone fearless and strong in soul and body; someone who would not hesitate to open his arms to keep him warm at night. He envied that little boy who could just walk up and ask for his affection openly.

Jealous of a five year old, Mouse? How sad. What are you going to do? Throw yourself in another river just so he'll put his arms around you again?

Mouse got up and left the campfire to head back to the trailer for the night, alone. Sadao did not notice.

Chapter X

Duty

Sometime after midnight Mouse woke from a dead sleep to the headache-inducing sound of Shiratori in full bitchout. Thinking he'd fallen asleep at work, Mouse sat straight up on the sofa bed to get an eyeful of Sadao and Shiratori at the table. They were hollering at each other in their native tongue among a pile of maps, rosters and equipment lists. It seemed the Swedes had done nothing to take Shiratori's edge off.

He was still in his golden armor, face-to-face with Sadao, ponytail bouncing, livid about something. Likely money. There were invoices spilled out over the table too. It seemed to be their number-one topic of contention. It was no joke according to Lupe that Shiratori valued equipment far above men and as far as he was concerned, Sadao had too many for what the team actually required.

"For the love of God! What the hell are you two yelling about?! Some of us need to get up for qualifiers tomorrow!"

Sadao's fist came down hard on the table. He was furious. "Go lie down in the back!" he yelled, pointing to his bedroom.

Mouse got up and stumbled past them to the rear bedroom and slammed the door shut. He hit the lights and collapsed into Sadao's bed, pulling the sheets over himself, asleep in seconds.

Mouse awoke to sunlight passing through the slits in the blinds of Sadao's bedroom window. That, and a tapping sound.

taptaptap... taptaptap

He closed his eyes and rolled over away from the window. His forehead came up against something hard and cold. He opened his eyes and gasped. Shiratori's metal arm was poking him in the face. He sat up, pushing it away. The disembodied arm flopped up against Sadao's bare back, side, and holy mother-of-god, bare ass.

taptaptap... "*Shitsurei shimasu*, Boss-sama... "

Mouse tore his eyes away from the ass and leapt out of the bed, checking himself. He had clothes on still. He looked at Sadao who was facedown in a pillow, dressed in his birthday suit, dead to the world. A towel that looked like it may have tried to cover his hips at one point had given up and was now dangling from a thigh on its way to the floor. The room stank of sake. No, sniff, sniff, Sadao stank of sake.

taptaptap...

Shit! Mouse tiptoed around his comatose bedfellow and opened the door a crack.

Shiratori, breastplate hanging by a thread, ponytail askew and face ashen, greeted him in the gap with his good eye. "*Ude kudasai?*" he asked with a gravelly voice.

"*Ude... ?* Oh, arm!"

"Yes... arm. Please." He held out his gloved metal hand in waiting.

"Please tell me you two weren't playing strip poker last night." Mouse held up a hand before Shiratori could answer. "No, don't speak. I don't want to know! Just... wait a minute... "

He shut the door quietly and locked it against a narrowed solitary brown eye.

Mouse wasn't sure if he should giggle or barf. Sadao hadn't moved an inch. The arm was leaning up against his ass, palm up as if it were begging to be rescued. Barf seemed appropriate.

Mouse reached over Sadao's back and lifted the arm up by the thumb. The whole thing was limp as a dead fish and rattled loudly. He checked Sadao. Not a twitch. *Maybe he's dead.* Mouse poked Sadao in the hip with the end of the arm. Nothing, except the slow rise and fall of his breathing. *This could be fun!*

taptaptap...

Mouse reopened the door, wider this time and slipped out into the shitstorm that was once Sadao's uber clean kitchen and lounge area. It looked like a Kirin Ichiban tornado had hit followed by a sake flood. Half of Sadao's carving knife collection was scattered about along with random items of clothing, chopped bits of fruit, stray noodles and chopsticks. The other half of the knives appeared to be stuck in the walls and one in the ceiling.

"*Ude kaeshite kudasai.*"

Mouse turned to the likely culprit. "Did you do this? What do you think this is? A frat house?"

Shiratori was tired of asking politely and snatched his arm back, sniffing the fingers suspiciously. "Did he fuck you with it?"

"What... ?! Gross! No! We don't ... not with a ... aaagh! Leave!"

Shiratori reaffixed his arm and the dead weight came back to life, lifting to brush its master's hair back from his hungover face. It truly was an amazing device. Shiratori smiled. "Boss-sama cheats at arm-wrestling."

"I said I didn't want to know! Out! Before I throw you out!"

Shiratori narrowed his eye. "I would like to see you try, *Okusama*," he said with a bow, and proceeded to let himself out – minus a critical part of his costume.

Mouse picked it up and shook the soba off. "Uh, General, your ass-plate?"

Shiratori's metal arm went for his backside and patted around. Nothing but a piece of air-thin cotton was blowing back there. Shiratori whipped about, grabbed the armor piece and held it in place. "Nobody must know what happened here!"

"Uh, you don't need to tell me that," Mouse said looking around.

Shiratori bowed. "*Yoroshiku.*"

Mouse did the same and waved as he let him out. "Bye bye... "

Mouse locked the door and picked his way back across the noodly floor and slipped into the bedroom. Sadao still lay there like a giant slug – a giant hot-as-fuck naked slug.

Mouse slid back in bed beside him and watched his face. He was breathing, deep and slow, mouth slack and eyelids shut like they weighed forty pounds each. Mouse poked him in the nose. Nothing. Mouse opened one of his eyelids and waved. Still nothing. Damned cute to witness the ever-alert Sadao in full shutdown.

Mouse sat up and rotated the window shades open just enough to let the sunlight reach Sadao's back and the tattoo lit up in a blaze of rich blue, purple, red and gold. Mouse was in awe. Until now he'd only been able to catch a glance or two at it. It was a masterful work of the eight sinuous heads and tails of the Orochi, all twisting and coiling around each other – doubling back, diving, rising, biting and hissing. It must have taken months to complete.

The topmost dragon-like snakehead draped over Sadao's left shoulder and the lowermost tail curved along the muscle of his right ass cheek. Mouse smiled, he'd had no idea it went that low. He wondered how long Sadao had worn it. And who the artist had been, that lucky sonofabitch who had the chance to work with such a worthy canvas of hard muscle and bone.

In the middle of it all at Sadao's lower back was a large black shimmering pearl, held securely in the coil of one of the Orochi's tails. Pearl farming he'd said was his family's occupation back in Japan before the war when... Mouse saw something odd as the sun slowly rose and caught Sadao's back at an angle. There were lines of slightly raised skin under the brilliant colors of the tattoo. Mouse lowered his head so the light caught them just right. Lines and more lines of scars – old ones that had faded and flattened out with time? No, with age. These were a child's scars. So many. The man who was that child had done well to hide them. "*I was sold to a man in Chiba for 35 American dollars and a barrel of sake,*" he'd said.

Is this why you have so many sons?

Mouse reached out with the tips of his fingers to try and trace the paths of the hidden wounds. They were thick on one end and thin on the other. Whiplashes. He wanted to rub them away, one by one with his finger...

Sadao snorted and came to life. Mouse dropped down and played dead. He cautiously opened an eye. Sadao's left hand made a half-hearted attempt to scratch where Mouse had evidently tickled him. But it gave up, plopped back down on the mattress and in one heaving move, the man flipped over onto his back – eyes closed, head turned away, dead once more.

Mouse's heart was pounding. He could see the Orochi head that snaked around Sadao's shoulder. It was taunting him. "Come-on," it said. "You know you wanna look."

Mouse waited a few breaths until Sadao started snoring softly and eased himself up on his elbow. With the man's arms limp at his sides and towel long gone, Mouse at last was treated to the full glory of Sadao Koga. His eyes followed the cut of the man's hipbones down to the straight black tuft of silky fur crowning the best snake of all. It was as limp as the rest of him, but that did nothing to hide its magnificence. A rather impressive piece of thick flesh slept coiled against a sumptuous sac of manhood.

Mouse was dizzy. God, it was beautiful! His own dick throbbed and grew hard, tenting his shorts. His mouth ran with saliva. He wanted nothing more in the world just then than to lick and kiss and suck... Hang on, there was something else. Something dark and round was poking out from under the deep rosy skin of the well-defined head.

The fuck is that?

Mouse had to know. And to know he had to get the serpent to show its underbelly. That would require... chopsticks! There were the two left over from last night's hairdo resting on Sadao's headboard shelf. Mouse reached up slowly and brought them down. He moved lower on the bed, ready to go opossum at the slightest sign of movement. The last thing he needed was for Sadao to open an eye and find him staring at him with lust-blurred eyes and a monster boner. But then, maybe he'd get another hand job out of the deal. Or maybe he'd be really generous and offer him a good long suck... *shit* he had to stop thinking or he was gonna starch his shorts.

Mouse leaned in and with utmost care, gave the flesh a little lift-up. Pearls, black ones, capped the ends of a half-ring of metal, strung through the sensitive ridge of skin just under the head.

Goddamn, the man had a pierced cock. No wonder the metal detector had gone off.

Bang! Bang! Bang! "Put Boss-sama penis down and get to work!" Shiratori was at the window, peering in, looking furious. Mouse tossed the chopsticks across the room and leapt out of bed throwing the sheet over Sadao.

"Okay, okay! You don't have to bang!" he said. Mouse clutched his chest, certain he'd just had a mini-heart attack.

Shiratori peered at him through the slats. "I don't pay you to play with Boss-sama like piece of sashimi. Garage, now!"

Mouse hid his crotch but Shiratori was already marching away. In either case, he needed a shower, and quickly.

It was hot as hell in the garage tent, even with the blowers going full blast. The truck had been moved to the track-side in the Orochi marked staging area between the various competition rings for the morning's qualifying heats. The event was a full desert motocross with drag strips, circuits and short tracks for motorcycle and ATV competitions. Eight different events in all, and the Orochi team was competing in all of them with a complement of 30 registered racers – the most registrants of any representing the Northwestern Division. Sadao knew how to pick men and Shiratori new how to pick machines. Too bad they had such a hard time picking mechanics. By 10am Mouse and Lupe were in way over their heads.

Although they'd had time in the prior weeks to get the vehicles ready, the nature of hard offroad track racing often resulted in bent or damaged fenders, wheels, handlebars and the like. Mouse couldn't tell if he was a mechanic or an assembly worker. He was wiping sweat from his face and shouting at Lupe every 20 seconds to rush this or that part to him as fast as he could work a wrench. Still, it didn't help that Mouse was distracted.

He'd banged one out in the shower before leaving the trailer by 7 that morning following Shiratori's wakeup call. But the vision of Sadao laid out in the flesh kept flashing through his head. *You haven't had sex in forever, is your problem,* he kept telling himself. But Mouse still couldn't keep his thoughts from straying from the task at hand to the tactile memory of being in that man's arms. Riding up against him, his hand going down his pants, stroking him. *Jesus,* he wasn't going to get a damn thing done right today. And there was so much to do!

The rains had left pockets of mud along the circuit tracks and tires needed to be changed out to accommodate. Shiratori had left a laundry list a mile long of vehicle prep orders and adjustments for the evening heats. He and Lupe were on it, but with all the incoming repairs, it would take a cloning machine to finish everything in time. Outside, motorcycle engines roared and fans cheered and shouted. But Mouse hadn't had more than two seconds to actually see any of the live runs. He was only granted a moment to marvel at the miles upon miles of nomadic racing fans' traveling convoys dotting the distant desert vista.

Mouse had left a quick note taped to Sadao's chest before he left that morning. It was his letter to Fred, addressed to the Iron Horse Saloon in Blythe, Arizona. He hoped Sadao's men could find it on a map. He didn't write a whole lot as he sat with a pen at the dinette table sticky with sake and lemon rinds, but he did tell the old man

that he thought maybe he had found his place in the world. An unlikely place, but a place where he 'fit'. Despite his trials in getting here, Mouse felt like he'd done more living in the last week than he had in all 26 years of his life. That was something he didn't want to give up. If he could prove himself to Sadao and his team, maybe this would become a place he could call home. He hoped the old man would understand.

It was after 10:30 am when Sadao finally made an appearance at the garage. Mouse was repairing a flat on an ATV and tried to act as nonchalant as possible. *Nose buried in task, yessir.*

"Mouse! Put the tire down and come here," Sadao ordered from the outside ramp. Boss mode had resumed.

"It'd better be good! I've got a shitload of work here!"

"You hurry and go, man," Lupe said. "Boss sounds pissed."

Mouse locked eyes with Lupe. "He's hungover."

Lupe's expression lit up. "No shit?"

"Am I speaking English?" Sadao bellowed. "Now!"

Mouse handed the wheel off to Lupe and sauntered down the rear ramp, wiping grease from his hands into a rag. "How's your head?"

Sadao gave him a "don't ask" look as he stood at the rear security panel, punching buttons. He was wearing a cap low over his eyes. "I need to give you access," he said, evading the question. "Tomorrow we'll be in nearly every heat back to back. Shiratori, Tagata and I won't be able to let you in and out. Tagata's competing and Shiratori and I will be on the observation deck with the Chairman. You'll need to close up during the midday break and reopen in the evening."

"I see, so... you trust me now?"

Sadao glanced at him and kept pushing buttons until the panel flashed yellow. "I have to. Come here and look at the center dot with your right eye. Don't blink."

Mouse stepped forward and the panel flashed faster until there was a pan of thin red light and Mouse could see the back of his eye for a second. *Whoa.* The panel beeped, flashed green and shut off. "Did I blink?" he asked.

"No, we got it. When you open up or close the ramps this scanner will request authorization. All you do is look in it when it flashes yellow and the control panel will respond to your selection. Go ahead and try it."

Mouse pressed the rear ramp "close" button and the panel flashed, scanned his eye and with a clank and whine, the rear ramp began to lift. *Cool.*

"This authorization panel only works on the outside. There's an escape switch near the utility sink if you or someone else gets stuck inside."

Mouse nodded. "I've seen it."

"Good. Now you know we keep a pair of guards at night on this truck. Make sure you notify whoever is on watch when you plan to lock up. Ask Shiratori if you are not certain. He handles the rotation. With all the people running around the area during this event, I want to be absolutely sure no one gets in here who doesn't belong."

"Are you still worried about sabotage?"

Sadao meet his eyes. "Always. One more thing... " Sadao reached for his keychain and unfastened a small cluster. He handed it to Mouse. "This is a spare set of keys to my personal trailers. I just had the equipment section moved to the staging area behind us here. Our 'special fuel' is stored in it. Shiratori and I agree it should be reserved for the finals tomorrow, especially the drag races. I don't want it moved to the garage until tomorrow, understand? I don't want the other teams knowing about it until it's too late for them to try to steal it."

Mouse nodded and accepted the keys which he stowed in his rear pocket. "Thanks," he said. "Thanks for having some faith in me."

Sadao managed a grin although it clearly pained him. "Despite my better judgment, I do. So don't disappoint me!"

It was 2pm, hours after the qualifying heats had ended, before Mouse got a chance to try out his new access and shut down the garage for lunch. He was starved. The teams had broken up and had gone back to camp to rest, eat, catch a nap and escape the blistering heat of midday in the Dry Lakes. Mouse showered the sweat and grease off in the garage facility and put on some fresh clothes before riding back with Lupe to camp.

They had a late lunch in the mess hall together before Mouse decided he'd like to catch a snooze in the comfort of Sadao's well air-conditioned trailer before the evening qualifiers got underway. When he got to the trailer, no one answered his knocks. Not surprising, really. He still had Sadao's equipment keys on him and wondered if one of them would open his trailer door, too. After he tried a few he found one that unlocked the front cab door, so he crawled in that way and up through the trap into the main living space. The place had been thoroughly cleaned. The air was on as were some of the lights.

"Hello... ?" he called out. Sadao's bedroom door was closed. Was he here? Sleeping? Mouse went closer to the door and put his ear to it. He heard something and was about to knock when he realized what the sounds were. His heart went still and he stepped back. Someone was moaning in that room and it wasn't Sadao. Mouse stood still, both wanting to listen and wanting to run. *Did that French bitch come calling?*

Mouse knew he should leave, that he had no rights to be here right now, but envy burned in his chest and he had to know who? A special patron? Were there many? Or just her? He didn't know which would be worse. He pressed his ear to the door again and breathed shallow over the furious pounding of his heart. He could hear Sadao speaking softly in Japanese and the other… sounded as if they were in the final throes of ecstasy. He realized then that the high-pitched cries weren't that of a woman. Mouse stepped back from the door in shock. *No, no, no this isn't happening. He wouldn't…*

Soon the sounds stopped and he could hear Sadao speaking in hushed Japanese – that soothing mesmeric mumble of his. Mouse fought every urge not to break the door down.

Instead it opened and Sadao stepped out casually, fully clothed. "Oh, it's you. I thought I heard someone come in," he said, closing the door carefully behind him. He went to his fridge and pulled out a water bottle. He held one up, "Want one?"

Mouse shook his head, beyond shocked.

In another minute Goro came out, head down, eyes hidden by his long bangs. Mouse had seen this kid skulking about his garage once or twice and shooed him out. He was in training so that made him… 16, 17 maybe? Sadao patted his shoulder and kissed the boy's head. He said a few more words to him quietly before the young man hurried out. Mouse watched the kid go as Sadao went back into his bedroom, unfazed.

Mouse got his feet to work and followed him. Sadao was seated at his carving table gulping water and preparing to work on a small wooden gun under his maglight.

"What the hell was that?!" Mouse demanded.

Sadao spoke with his back to him. "This? It's a gun. My kids love them. But they keep losing them so I'm thinking of hiring elves to keep up with demand."

"I'm not talking about toy guns!"

Sadao glanced over his shoulder quizzically. "You mean Goro? You've met him. I've brought him to your garage before. I think he wants to be a mechanic. He's not proven to be much of a racer yet, I'm afraid." He turned back to his work.

Mouse crossed the room to stand next to his table.

"I know who he is. What the hell were you doing to him?!"

Sadao glanced up and took another drink. "If I have to explain it, it's been too long for you, *Konezumi.*"

"Don't *Konezumi*, me! I fucking hate that!"

Sadao ignored him and resumed carving.

"What kind of sick monster are you? You start with little toys and a warm lap then graduate them to what? Blow-jobs and pearl necklaces?"

Sadao stuck his knife in the table and swiveled to face him. "I am not a predator! Goru is not a child! If my boys come to me for comfort, I offer it. I do not exploit it! Believe me, I know the difference. Your Christian sexual taboos do not interest me!"

"So that's what that was," Mouse said nodding to the bed. "Comfort?"

Sadao shook his fury off and picked up the little gun, smoothing it with a bit of sandpaper. "Goro is of racing age. He's not like the other boys. He's alone. No parents, no brothers, no friends – who is he supposed to turn to that would satisfy your morals? We have no women here. The older boys will eat him alive. I'm honored that he comes to me. I don't fuck him; I keep him safe. I keep all my boys safe."

"And when they start coming around every night?"

"I don't pick favorites," he said, giving Mouse a look. "I can not afford to. Goro understands this. You, apparently do not."

Mouse felt like his stomach just hit the floor but he kept his face up.

"So I'm just another one of your 'boys,' is that it?"

Sadao glanced up at him again, irritated. Still, it took him a moment to answer. "You're different," he said. "But if you think a handjob in a barn equals a romantic relationship, your life has been a sorrier one than I thought!"

Mouse turned Sadao's chair toward him and leaned into his face. "Fuck you!" he screamed. "Don't you *ever* put your hands on me again!!"

Sadao stood up and grabbed him by the shoulders, shoving him back onto the bed with a whump! He climbed up over him, pinning Mouse's arms and legs. His eyes were flashing with anger. "Is this what you think I do?! You think I just take what I want?!" he pinned both of Mouse's wrists in one hand and grabbed his chin by the other as if he were about to kiss him.

Mouse struggled but couldn't move. He couldn't speak either by the way his chin was being crushed in the man's grip. "Nnnmgh."

Sadao brushed his lips across Mouse's for a moment, then trailed up to his ear and whispered. "If I wanted gratification, I could take it. From anyone, anytime. There is no man in this camp who could best me. I have no need for passive innocent boys!"

Mouse wriggled. "Stop... get off... "

Sadao kept his lips at his ear. "I touched you because I wanted to. And because you needed me to. Don't flatter yourself into thinking it was anything else!" And with that he let him go and stood up.

Mouse got up more slowly, adjusting his clothes and nursing his wounded pride and ugh, feelings. Why did he have to have those now?

"Get out of my trailer," Sadao said and returned to his carvings like there was no one else in the room.

Mouse got up and slunk back into the main room, rubbing his wrists. He felt sick and confused. *Fuck* the last thing he wanted to do was get emotional, but if he didn't get out of here now that's exactly what was going to happen. He went out the door into the late afternoon and ran smack into Shiratori.

"Leaving?" Shiratori smirked.

"Leave me alone," Mouse said morosely, trying to get past him but Shiratori jumped right back in front of him.

He cocked his head, looking Mouse over. "Oh, you and Boss-sama have big fight, eh? Poor Mouse-san."

"Fuck off." Mouse said, brushing past him.

"You will come to understand soon, I think, why Boss-sama lives alone!"

Mouse walked away, showing Shiratori his middle finger over his head as he went.

Shiratori cackled. "You will be back! I will see you soon, ne?"

Mouse lay on his back in the garage on the upper floor cot, trying to regain a hold on himself. *Slow deep breaths*, he told himself. *Don't be an idiot. He ain't worth half this misery. You just met the guy what, just over a week ago? You don't know anything about him – other than he looks like a fucking Asian god in the boo.*

But there had to be more to it than that. Mouse had plenty of well-built men pass in and out of his life. There was something else less tangible than a cock with a hole in it and a sweet ass. Of course there was more to Sadao. It was what had made him chase after that man as he started to leave his garage the night he found the bad weld in the sand car. *How did you know my name?*

Truth was he didn't care how Sadao knew his name. He just couldn't stand the thought of never seeing his face again for the rest of his life. Whatever it was that drew him to Sadao, it was beyond his ability to control.

But realize, if you want him, you'll have to share him. With everyone -

Mouse didn't think he could handle that. He was too selfish, he supposed. The degree of his want was too big for occasional unexpected diversions to satisfy him. What little they had shared, and yes it was sad and pathetic to think of a "handjob in a barn" that way, but it had touched him far deeper than his belt line. Mouse just wanted him – in a bottomless gut-pulling way.

He wanted Sadao's hands on him – his sweat and muscle up against him. He wanted that grip around his body, his mouth feeding on his with thick powerful kisses: Biting, sucking, marking his flesh. More than anything he wanted that man's cock, hot and ready, seeking release from his mouth, hands, ass – hell, Sadao could fuck his armpit, he just didn't care.

All the unrequited lust that had been building up inside Mouse was pounding his blood and filling his cock, trapping it in an angry bulge in his jeans. Christ, he'd already let it out that morning but the fight with Sadao had only made it rise right back up again with a vengeance. He unzipped to ease it.

Could I go to him? He wondered. If he apologized and asked nicely, took him by the hand into the bedroom with a smile and lay down beside him – would he do for him again what he did for his boys? *You're different*, he'd said. Did that mean he'd take him, pin him down and spread his legs wide apart and seek that gratification he otherwise denied himself? Would Sadao use his body to unleash the torrent of restraint, even if it didn't mean anything more than a release of semen into a warm, willing place?

"Aaaaahh!!" Mouse's cock unloaded over the railing onto the lower deck. The orgasm was sudden and powerful, the cum as thick and copious as his desire. He lay back panting, wiping the sweat from his brow. Shit, he'd just gone and fucked himself without his own consent.

You have to get out of here. Go find a man who has room for you in his life. But the thought of doing that depressed him even more. He simply didn't want anyone else.

Fuck, fuck, fuck...

The release relaxed Mouse just enough that he was able to drift off into a light sleep. But the recharge he needed was interrupted by someone engaging the ramps. Mouse opened his eyes and lay still. Shiratori marched in the back ramp and proceeded to fuss about with the equipment. Probably counting supplies again. He was a rabid counter of things. No... not this time. Shiratori worked his way to the section of the garage that was directly below Mouse. He went to the key safe and spun the combo lock. Mouse, soundlessly lowered his head to get a better look. Through the grating of the upper floor he could just make out the numbers: 25 – 33 – 15 – 7? Was that it? Mouse closed his eyes and repeated the numbers in his head a few times.

Shiratori exchanged some keys and shut the safe, spinning the dial. He took a step and paused, looking around as if he sensed something amiss. Mouse moved his head back so he lay perfectly flat against the cot. If the General looked straight up he would not be able to see him. Mouse could hear a sniffing sound. Could he smell him? Or his missing jizz? It'd gone down there somewhere. Ah, god this day was sucking ass. Mouse held dead still until he heard Shiratori curse under his breath before marching himself back out and closing up the ramps again.

Certain the coast was now clear, Mouse dropped down to the lower floor and tried the combo. It took a few spins and an adjustment of numbers, but on the third try, the safe opened. Inside were rows and rows of keys – all labeled carefully in... *crap*, Japanese. Mouse was never allowed unsupervised access to keys until now. He ran his hand through them where they hung on little hooks until a set of random characters caught his eye. They looked familiar. If he wasn't mistaken, he'd seen the same characters etched into the back of Sadao's little carvings. It was his name: 古賀貞雄.

Mouse lifted the key off and added it to the set of Sadao's trailer keys he'd been loaned earlier. Mouse shut the safe and spun the dial. Time to go inspect the equipment trailer.

Sadao's personal equipment trailer wasn't far away – only a few rows back from the garage truck. From the angle of the sun, Mouse knew he only had about an hour before the camps would stir and come back to life. He took out Sadao's spare keys and opened the trailer door, letting himself in. Inside were Sadao's babies – his street bikes lined the far wall. There were three of them, rare and expensive custom rebuilt sport Kawasaki's. Along the opposite wall was his workhorse, the old smoky painted cruiser he hauled Mouse around on – the one with the double gastank. Mouse theorized that perhaps Sadao had loaned Lupe the spare key so he could polish up his ride before the Chairman's dinner last night and tried it in the machine. The key fit and turned with a click. For once, something was starting to go his way because at his feet and all around the spare areas of the floor of the garage were collapsible gas cans, filled with liquid gold.

Chapter XI

Winners Circle

The morning of the Dry Lake Races main events dawned with heavy showers and periodic lightning. Fans that had traveled from hundreds of miles around were unfazed and filled the grandstands and packed the tracksides to cheer their favorites on huddled under multi-colored umbrellas and scraps of plastic. The betting stalls were crowded with soaked patrons, flapping bills and shouting to get their bets in before the next gun. Meanwhile, the Northerners – unwilling to let their fine clothes get smudged – kept to the enclosed private boxes, lording over the spectacle from the comfort of their elevated lounges. And to capture it all were the Chairman's creepy little camera drones, whizzing about overhead, swooping down now and again to catch a splash of mud fan-tailing off a racer's wheels in the heat of the action.

Mouse and Lupe stood in the rain by the edge of the main motocross circuit track and watched the teams line up behind the starting gate. The gun fired and the rails dropped. Bikes leapt onto the track, roaring around the earthen course, slick with mud and dotted with growing puddles. The bulldozed jumps and turns had become mudfalls in the downpour. No matter who took the lead, there was little telling which rider would make it to the finish without spinning out into a splatter of mud and disgrace. So much for training – Mother Nature had scrambled the odds for everyone. Bookies were running about frantically, betting slips falling out of their pockets. To-day, those who won or lost were at the mercy of chance.

Soaked to the skin and mud up to his ankles, Mouse found the whole event thrilling. He was sore and exhausted from the morning's prep and continuous repairs. But now that the first half finals were nearing completion, he and Lupe had found a moment to sneak out of the garage to enjoy some of the excitement. The Orochi Team was well represented in the Winners Circle despite the weather, particularly in the speed and distance races. He'd heard there was grumbling amongst the other teams as to what was giving them an advantage when the environment was so unpredictable, and maybe there was more to it than just superior fuel.

If he squinted through the rain, Mouse thought now and again he could catch the outline of Sadao up in the windows of the private boxes, binoculars to his eyes. No doubt he was enjoying his champagne and caviar with the better half. Mouse vastly preferred the mud. Too bad this was going to be his last day living in it. Although the perfect escape had been granted to him, he'd decided in the end to man-up and see this final day through. At least then he would have a suitable climax to this whole sordid tale. Granted, not the one he'd hoped for, but something to brag about. That, and he couldn't let down Lupe or the men who had put their best skills forward, counting on solid engineering under their command.

Mouse had filled Sadao's double tanks and hid an extra full can of fuel in the back of the garage where he knew even Shiratori wouldn't notice it. Tonight, after the conclusion of the evening finals, during whatever drunken revelry was certain to commence, he'd sneak away out over the damp desert wasteland, making for the main highway and whatever new adventures lay beyond. He only wished it hadn't come to this so quickly.

Mud was everywhere in the garage. Busted machines had been loaded in coated with sticky gooey earth all over their popped chains and broken spokes. Most of the repairs would be set aside for another race and another mechanic, Mouse supposed, as he hosed off the deck. High noon had come, and with it, the sun reappeared from behind the clouds, drying the puddles and raising the outside temperature well past 100 degrees in a matter of hours.

Mouse had sent Lupe off for lunch and a shower while he closed things up until the evening finals got underway. Despite the heat, there was still a lot of activity going on around outside. Shiratori's ever-present guards were keeping eye on the garage perimeter so Mouse felt it was safe enough to strip off his own muddy clothes and give himself a hose-bath over the utility sink. He had just finished rinsing the soap off his back and out of his hair when he got the distinct crawly feeling he was being watched.

Mouse whipped around. Sitting up on the workbench at the opposite wall of the garage was Chairman Marcus Getty, swinging his legs and smiling. Mouse dropped the hose, still running, and wrapped the towel he kept by the sink around his waist.

"Chairman?"

"Sorry," the man said, hopping down. "Let me get that for you."

The Chairman came forward and shut off the hose, looping it back into the storage bracket. Mouse covered his chest with his arms, not sure what to do.

"Sorry for the intrusion, but I wanted to catch you before you left for lunch," the man said with a friendly tone, as if they'd watched each other showering naked for years.

"When did you come in?" Mouse asked, opening a locker and taking out a clean shirt.

"Oh, just a moment or two ago. I didn't mean to startle you."

Mouse pulled the shirt on over his head and reached for some clean work pants. The Chairman didn't look as if he was going to turn away and grant him any privacy, so Mouse pulled the pants on up under the towel. To hell with undershorts – he wasn't planning on giving this guy an encore to the peepshow he'd already enjoyed.

"Is there something I can do for you, Chairman?" Mouse asked, bending to slip on fresh socks and stepping into his hosed-off boots.

"Yes you can," he said, smiling brightly. "You could honor me with your company at lunch."

Mouse looked around nervously. "I was heading to the mess hall," Mouse said. "I need to close up here and get back in time for the evening prep."

"Oh, I won't keep you long, I promise. Just a quick lunch and I'll have you on your way."

It didn't look like he was going to take any answers other than yes, so Mouse decided why not? Chairman food was probably better than what Cook-san had been boiling the shit out of all morning.

"Yeah, all right. But I can't stay all day."

The Chairman had a driver waiting outside in an SUV with multi-weather tires. Mouse secured the ramps and locked up the garage before joining the Chairman in the backseat. The interior was all fine black leather with polished chrome fittings. Dude had money alright.

"Where are we going?" Mouse asked, looking out the windows at the rows and rows of racing trailers as they drove off.

"My private helicopter."

Mouse's blood went cold – he was terrified of flying. The Chairman laughed at what must have been his very pale expression.

"Don't worry, we'll stay grounded. It's my home away from home. It has everything – office, living room, bedroom, kitchen, bar … you could even take a rest if you'd like after your meal, there are plenty of lounges."

Mouse eyed him cautiously. It didn't take a rocket scientist to figure out the man wanted something from him and it wasn't just conversation. "I told you, I need to get back."

The Chairman just kept right on smiling. "Yes, of course."

The Chairman's helicopter was a refurbished double-blade military transport ship. The rear ramp descended and the SUV drove them right on up into it. Mouse felt trapped and uneasy as he got out of the vehicle. But once they'd entered the main cabin, unless you knew you were in a helicopter, it looked just like a long narrow studio apartment with all the comforts of home. As one would guess, the walls and tables were decorated with racing banners, photographs and Division awards. A small dining table was set up near the window with a view of the sprawling desert, dotted with fans' campers and tents.

The Chairman invited Mouse to sit at one of the two chairs set up at the table. Mouse sat and looked at all the silverware. Why on earth would anyone need three glasses, three spoons, two forks and a knife? The Chairman sat across from him and clinked his wine glass. A waiter popped out of a rear compartment door pushing a dinner cart with covered entrees and bottles of wine.

"I hope you're not allergic to seafood," the Chairman said as they were served a hot soup and mixed green salad with fresh sliced baguettes and butter. "Lobster Bisque. I had it flown in from Washington."

Mouse shook his head. "No allergies," he said, picking up his biggest spoon and diving in for a steamy bite. A buttery delicious hunk of pink and white lobster fell apart on his tongue. Ohh it was good, especially after a week of nothing but shit dumped over rice. If he never ate Japanese food again it would be too soon.

"Sir, our two wine selections today are – "

Mouse grabbed both glasses and held them up. "Both," he said, happily.

The waiter paused, but the Chairman just nodded and Mouse got his wish. He gulped half of one glass down. Then he grabbed a baguette and dunked it into his soup, stirring it around and ravenously devouring the end. The waiter backed away with an uneasy nod. "Enjoy, sirs."

The Chairman waved his servant off and after carefully placing his napkin in his lap, began to nibble at his salad while watching Mouse shovel in his $275 plate lunch like it was a state fair chili-dog eating contest.

"I'm glad you are enjoying the soup," he commented amicably.

"Mmm... ohmigod... mmm... is there more of this?" Mouse managed over his indulgence.

"I'm sure there is. Please eat your fill."

The Chairman let Mouse polish off his first bowl and called the server for a refill before he started in with the conversation.

"So tell me, what is it like working for Koga-san?"

"Mmmn... " Mouse swallowed another mouthful of soup-soaked bread with a few gulps of wine before he spoke. "Fine, I guess. I dunno, I've never worked for anyone but my father before this."

"Is that so? I didn't realize that. Koga-san must indeed have as good an eye for talent as I've been told. I'll admit I was skeptical about your acquisition at first. It's exceedingly rare for clan bosses to hire mechanics outside of their immediate circle. Indeed, it's a first for the Orochi Team, but evidently a successful one. The Orochi's have had an excellent showing in the final events so far today. Certainly an improvement from prior years."

Mouse watched the Chairman's face, wondering if he was making idle conversation or fishing for inside information. "I'm a good mechanic," Mouse said simply, stabbing at his salad. Fresh greens were a rarity this deep in the wastelands.

The Chairman laughed. "And an honest one. I can appreciate that."

Mouse munched on his veggies. "I didn't know the Orochi Team was struggling," Mouse said, doing some data mining of his own.

The Chairman thought it over. "I wouldn't say struggling per se, but certainly fading a bit. Their core team has been stagnant for some years and they have been going through a lot of changes in the garage staffing of late. It was a concern to me. But I'm happy to know they've found someone solid at last. And Koga-san did approve five new young racers this year for the roster, all of whom have been performing well."

"He has a lot of young men in training," Mouse added in Sadao's defense. "They all work very hard."

The Chairman nodded. "I'm certain they do. Koga-san has been training racers for decades. Did you know he is the longest-reigning clan boss in Division history?"

Mouse raised a brow. "Really?"

"Yes, 12 years now, I believe. Very uncommon. Although the merge with the Whitebird Clan four years ago did mix things up a bit. Tell me, what do you think of General Shiratori?"

Mouse chewed on a hunk of bread for a moment. "He's a royal pain in the butt and a complete lunatic. But other than that, he does know good wheels when he sees them. The Team has grade-A gear. It's been fun working on the machines – top of the line."

"Yes," the Chairman agreed. "Shiratori-san has always put his trust into steel over muscle. I suppose it's why he works so well with Koga-san who has such talent choosing recruits. Tell me, how many non-racers does he have in camp now?"

Mouse stalled on this question. He honestly didn't want to answer it. No matter how pissed Mouse was with Sadao right now, he certainly sympathized with his desire to rescue starving orphans from the streets. "Hard to say," Mouse answered. "He finds work for all of them around camp. They run messages, handle laundry, take turns watching the younger ones – that kind of thing."

The Chairman looked impressed. "Is that right? Well, excellent. Let me ask you then about Ichiro Tagata. He's certainly been Koga-san's brightest star for the last few years. How well do you think he performs as a Captain?"

Mouse shrugged. "I can't really say. He doesn't speak much English and I'm not a racer so I don't come in contact with him often. I know Sa-... *Koga*-san relies on him a lot. They're joined at the hip most of the time. The men seem to respect him, if that's what you want to hear."

The Chairman took a drink of his wine. "Just curious to hear another perspective on the inner workings of one of my favorite teams. My relationship with the Orochi Clan has been mostly through statistics and via broadcast."

"You speak to Koga-san on that super satellite phone, don't you? You should really be running these kinds of questions by him. I've only been with them a little over a week. I don't know the whole score."

The Chairman dipped his spoon at last in the soup and blew on it. "Of course. Certainly, I will follow up with him directly. But I didn't want to pass up the opportunity to get an insider's perspective. Thank you for your candid replies."

Mouse took advantage of the break in questioning to focus on his meal while the Chairman rambled on about his own childhood love-affair with racing, many aspects of which mirrored Mouse's own – right down to sleeping in the backs of vans and pickups like the swarm of fans down on the desert flats below. By the time the Chairman had finished eating, Mouse had finished off four glasses of wine, three bowls of soup and all of the baguettes. Stuffed to the gills, he was more than happy to retire to the lounge area in front of the Chairman's enormous glass plate TV.

He sank back into the feather-soft leather overstuffed cushions and belched, putting his booted feet up on the coffee table. He could smell coffee brewing. He was supposed to stay alert long enough to watch some presentation. Yeah yeah... god, a nap sounded delicious right now. His eyes started to close.

"Mouse, if I could trouble you a moment."

Mouse shook his head and blinked himself more awake.

"I know this is your rest period, so I promise to keep this brief. Afterwards, you may relax here as long as you like and my driver will see you back to the garage promptly at your word."

"Yeah," Mouse yawned. "Gotta get back by 4."

The Chairman relaxed in the lounge adjacent to Mouse and similarly kicked his heels up on the glass coffee table. He held out a remote and clicked the screen on. The glass display lit up and a vintage Division logo splashed across the screen with similar 20-30 year-old footage that had run at the reception dinner.

"I saw this," Mouse said and accepted his cup and saucer of Italian Roast and madeleines from the manservant.

"Watch carefully," the Chairman said and pointed to the screen.

Mouse blew on his coffee and watched. The film was old but still clear. The camera panned over a raceway and Mouse was struck with an eerie sense of deja vu. He set his cup and saucer down absently, dribbling some of it as he realized why. It was the Phoenix Grand Motorsport Raceway – the exact raceway his father took him to as a kid. A narrator was rambling something about the 2050 commemorative event. "It was a time of big dreams... "

The camera clips showed bits of footage of people standing and shouting from the grandstands. The pan stopped and the camera seemed to blur and refocus, slowing to zoom in on a particular pair of racing fanatics moving in slow motion. Mouse's heart stopped. He was watching himself – age five, atop his father's shoulders, smiling and waving a flag. "A time when every young boy dreamed of what the future might hold..."

The image of himself and his father slowed, froze a moment then faded.

Dad – ?

The screen faded in with footage of himself from earlier that day, just a few hours ago standing with Lupe in the rain, watching the circuit finals. It was shot from somewhere across the track so the riders flew by in a blur in front of his wet, excited face. "Today that dream has been realized... "

From there the footage shifted to him sweating in the heat outside the garage tent, giving a thumbs up to the riders as they tore off on his freshly tuned machines. Then there were shots of himself coated with grease, hands in the toolbox, tuning an engine, gunning a throttle – footage so close and clear you could see the sweat dripping between his collarbones. He hadn't even noticed a single camera.

Mouse stood up abruptly, knocking his shin into the coffee table and dumping coffee across the pristine polished surface.

"What the fuck is this?! You've been spying on me?"

The Chairman sat up, shutting off the screen. "No, no... not at all. This is merely a promotional reel. A test reel."

"My father... *How?*"

The Chairman beamed. "Impressive bit of software scanning technology, isn't it? I had my production staff log our archival footage into a database by year. We had a bone structure map created of your face and ran a regression simulator backwards year by year until we found a match. The whole process took only 12 hours or so."

"How did you know I would be in the audience? There were dozens of races near where I grew up – you knew that too! You knew which highways led to Blythe! How the fuck do you know so much about me?!"

The Chairman shrugged. "It's not that hard, I asked Koga-san a few basic background questions about you and the rest was simple. I knew you would be the perfect subject for my new marketing campaign. Starry-eyed small town child grows up to become a mechanic discovered by a top-tier racing team and brings them back to glory. It's the perfect fairytale, don't you see?"

Mouse shook his head. "No, I don't see. And excuse me, but for a man who has every bit of secret camera spy bullshit at his fingertips, you sure got the plot of the story dead wrong! Driver! Get me the fuck back to the garage, now!"

The Chairman rose fast, blocking Mouse's exit. He wasn't a terribly strong man, but he was taller than Mouse.

He held up his palms in a calming gesture. "Please, Mouse. Hear me out."

Mouse crossed his arms and glared up into his pleading blue eyes. "You have 60 seconds before I throw you into your fancy glass TV."

"Fair enough. Just... realize for some time now racing has been losing favor among the middle class in the cities. The demographic feels, and rightfully so, that it's a gamblers' racket – something very low class and seedy. Hardly any desert race footage airs on public networks anymore. Only closed circuit feeds in dingy city gambling halls and bars. That's not the future I want for this sport and I don't think you want it either."

"No... but I don't see what the fuck plastering my face across the TV screens is gonna do to change it? I'm not even a racer! You want a story, focus on some hard luck kid from Mexico or some of these poor refugee kids from fucked-up flooded countries who have made the winners circle today. That's the story you want!"

The Chairman sighed, "I would love that. But I have to be honest with myself and with you. Northerners will not connect with foreigners as well as they will connect with you."

Something clicked in Mouse's head. "It's because I'm white, isn't it?"

The Chairman nodded solemnly. "Yes."

Mouse was appalled. "And you think that's going to make me feel good about it?"

"All I'm asking you to do is to think of the sport. Think back to those times you shared with your father, like I shared with mine when I was a little boy and ask yourself if those memories are worth fighting for. We can discuss terms. I've even taken the liberty to draw up a tentative contract; if you agree to sign it you'll become the spokesman of the common man. We'll chronicle your daily activities with the team, showing the upper states this is still a noble sport."

Mouse stared up into the man's eyes. Everything about this guy's demeanor said, "You can trust me," but it was the last thing Mouse wanted to do. *Never trust the rich,* his father had said. *They don't need you.*

Think about the sport.

Mouse did think about it. And when he thought about it he also thought about the extra tank of gas waiting for him and Sadao's spare keys in his back pocket. There was indeed so much more to this story than the Chairman could ever guess. He was a day behind and a dollar too late.

"I'll think better back on the desert floor," Mouse said and the Chairman had to reluctantly let him go.

Lupe accosted Mouse the moment he exited the Chairman's SUV as it pulled up at the garage trailer.

"Hey, Gringo! Where you been? Boss has been by three times looking for you."

"He has?"

"Yeah, I told him the guards said you were invited to lunch with Big Boss. He said to send you to him as soon as you got back."

"What's the emergency?" Mouse asked, stepping up to the access panel and activating the garage ramps with his eyeball.

Lupe shrugged. "He didn't say but he was one jumpy dude, man. He said he was going to lunch with Captain Tagata. I think they're still in the mess hall."

Mouse sighed and after getting Lupe started, made his way to the dining tent. It was beginning to clear out inside so it was easy to spot Sadao and Tagata bent over bowls of cold udon in the last row of tables.

Sadao noticed him immediately and motioned him over. Mouse applied his poker face and sauntered in his general direction.

"Where were you last night?" Sadao asked sharply, slurping his noodles. Both men were eating fast.

"Around."

"Where did you sleep?"

"I found a hole in the ground. What does it matter to you? You threw my ass out."

"Not permanently! I don't like you wandering about by yourself at night."

"Maybe I was out making my life 'less pathetic,'" he snapped.

Sadao gave him a long critical stare while he chewed. "I heard you were entertained by the Chairman today."

"Yeah, he had wine and lobster waiting just for me. I was getting sick of noodles."

"I don't care what you ate. I care about what you discussed."

Sadao's tense questioning made Mouse realize he really had no idea what the Chairman was up to. The luncheon had been a surprise to them both. Mouse decided it really didn't matter to him if Sadao knew the details or not. Right now he just wanted to throw a pitch back into his face.

"It looks like he's taken a special interest in me," Mouse said with a sly smile.

Sadao's brows narrowed as he slurped noodles. Why did the Japanese always eat so loud?

"Be specific," Sadao ordered.

"Specific how? If I have to explain it to you, maybe it's been too -"

Sadao grabbed his wrist and literally twisted his arm.

"Ow! Fuck!" Mouse crumpled against the table in pain. The racers around them took notice.

"I don't have time for games! Answer me!"

"Okay! Jesus! Fuck that *hurts!*" Mouse yanked his wrist free and shook out the pain.

Sadao's eyes were on him. *Don't fuck with me,* they said.

Mouse straightened himself. "He wants me to be his poster boy for small town virtue."

Tagata snorted into his noodles.

Mouse shot a scowl at him. "He wants me to sign some contract so he can use me in his marketing schemes. Use my 'story' he says – small town boy makes it to the big leagues or some shit like that. Like some reality TV star."

Sadao looked Mouse over as he shoveled in more noodles, like he was trying to decide if Mouse was telling him the whole truth or not. "Did you sign it?"

"Fuck, no! I didn't sign it. I don't want those damn floating camera balls following me around everywhere!"

"Sign it," Sadao ordered. "I'll tell him you agree."

Mouse shook his head. "Over my fucking dead body! I'm not agreeing to that bullshit!"

Sadao slammed his chopsticks down and wiped the soup drops from his beard. "For the last two days I have been thinking day and night how the fuck I'm going to get you from relay station to relay station fast enough during the Overland race. I don't have four mechanics! If you sign, we have helicopter support, can't you see that?"

"Helicopters? I'm not flying around in one of those death traps, forget it."

Sadao lowered his voice. "I don't care what you think. You will do as I say."

Mouse leaned in. "I don't have to do shit for you. You don't own me."

Tagata laughed, mocking his proclamation.

Mouse whirled on him. "You know what? You can shut the fuck up!"

Tagata got up, towering over him, fists at his sides. Men sitting nearby grabbed their bowls and shuffled off to give them room.

"You gonna come at me? Huh?!" Mouse was so fucking angry he'd lost all fear.

Tagata's reach was longer than he estimated and he grabbed Mouse by the collar, pulling him. Mouse dove forward and nailed Tagata in the gut with his head. Regurgitated noodles went flying as the two of them hit the floor, fists swinging. Mouse's aim wasn't very good, but he was fast and dodged Tagata's blows which went wild. They rolled, crashing into empty chairs, kicking and grappling. Tagata grabbed Mouse by his belt and held him down, laying a left hook straight across his chin. Mouse went limp, stunned by the pain and the sudden appearance of thousands of tiny shimmering stars.

"*Yamero!*" Sadao shouted, pushing Tagata off of him. Concern had washed over the anger in his face as he lifted Mouse up across his knees, brushing his hair back from his face.

"Look at me, *Konezumi.*"

The way he said his nickname just then made Mouse want to try, but he just couldn't get a focus on the world – it was spinning too fast. *He's holding me again. So good.* Mouse closed his eyes and let his reality melt into the arms circling his body.

Although dazed, Mouse was conscious enough to protest Sadao's carrying of him over his shoulder to the medical tent where he was prescribed rest and an ice pack.

"I'm fine," Mouse insisted, laying back on one of the several dozen futons on the floor of the medic hall, most of which were occupied. "There are other men here with serious injuries."

Sadao stood over him, stonefaced. "I don't want you to leave this tent until 4pm. I'm posting a guard out front who will escort you directly to the garage."

Mouse started to sit up, but Sadao put a firm hand to his chest. "Tagata got out of line. But I have warned you in the past, I will not tolerate any mistrust between us."

"Mistrust?! All I did was go to lunch! The guy showed up in the garage while I was buck-naked and lured me away in his fancy SUV. I hardly call that a betrayal! What did you think he was going to do, bribe me?"

Sadao's eyes flashed. "Did he?"

Mouse was utterly confused. Wasn't this supposed to be *his* boss? "No, unless phony TV stardom counts as a bribe." Mouse lowered his voice. "Wait, is this what happened to you before? Is that why you lost your other mechanics? They were bought by previous Chairmen?"

Sadao didn't answer.

"You think I'd whore myself that easily? That I'd risk your men like that?" Mouse looked around at the snapped collarbones and broken wrists surrounding him. "This sport is dangerous enough… "

"I told you, I don't know this Chairman. I don't know what he's capable of. And, I remind myself, I don't know you, either."

Mouse looked up at the man judging him as he held the stinging icepack to his jaw. It hurt to know he could be so mistrusted so soon. "Fine, you don't want to believe me? Go fuck yourself… "

Mouse closed his eyes and rolled over to rest. Sadao stood over him for another minute and then left without another word.

The sky had gone crystal clear with a high full moon as the last half of the main events got underway. With only seven of their racers left to compete in the last runs of the motocross, Mouse and Lupe made a night of it. They closed the garage, grabbed some hot dogs and beer and ran up into the stands overlooking the three main arenas and cheered the Orochis on like noobs.

The drag races were especially exciting for Mouse who had tuned the shit out of the Hondas' carburetors for maximum fuel load coupled with the best of the secret cache pumped into their tanks. Bikes, painted with the Orochi emblem, tore out several feet ahead of the others on green and there was no chance of catching them now that the lakebeds had dried out. It was one event clearly dominated by the eight-headed snake.

Lupe jumped up and down, tossing popcorn all over Mouse as the digital boards read out the final times and standings. "Did you see that shit, man? Damn! We did that shit! Me and you, Gringo!"

Mouse smiled and picked popcorn out of his hair, throwing it back at Lupe who ducked, spilling beer on his shoes. *Fuck*, he was going to miss this kid.

Tagata was one of the top contenders entering the 3 lap multi-cross final in the center ring. A strong technical rider – jumps, turns and maneuvers were his speciality. Mouse had taken special care in adjusting his private Suzuki's suspension and steering. Dubious of his abilities from the start, the Captain's showing in the qualifiers had earned Mouse a kernel of the man's trust as he now headed into the line-up against the finalists from 9 other teams. Most of the track mud had been filled in during the break by bulldozers giving the racers a more skills-based advantage.

The gun fired and Lupe stood on his bench, eyes wide, straining to catch every second. Tagata was first into the turns, but his competitor from the Taiwanese team took advantage of a soft spot in a rut on the downhill and cut him off on the third turn.

"Jeezus! You see that?" Lupe asked, nudging Mouse.

"Yeah, lucky slip," Mouse said. "He'll make it back on the straightaway, watch."

He was right. Tagata gunned it on the flats coming out of the hill jumps and returned the maneuver, undercutting the Taiwanese rider on the inside on the left, regaining the lead which he held onto just barely until the final flag.

Lupe let out a *whoop* and the remains of his popcorn rained down on the people seated below them. With the points he gained from earning first in the multi-cross, Tagata narrowly scored the victor in the best all-around category. The digital displays flashed the announcement and congratulations were broadcast out across the Dry Lakes. Fans on the lower benches threw desert flowers at Tagata's mud and dirt-splattered form as he dismounted and removed his helmet, waving at the cheering crowd as he went to ascend the steps to the awards platform.

The Chairman, Shiratori and Sadao exited the observation deck and walked down to join him on the platform. The Chairman gave a short speech only half-heard under the din of the crowd, something about Tagata and the Orochi Team being a supreme example of an honorable hard-working racing heritage.

Tagata accepted his trophy gratefully and the $150,000 prize money that came with it. Over all, the Orochi Team with all of their collected wins looked to take in about $300,000 from this event. Not a bad showing by any means – orphans could sleep easy tonight.

The awards ceremony moved on to honor other finalists from other teams. Mouse, Lupe and the throng of thousands began to get up and move down to the field. There was a lot of pushing and shoving to get near the stage for photo ops and autographs. Mouse felt this was it – the perfect time to slip away without being noticed by anyone, not even Lupe who was floating away from him in the sea of heads, waiving a pen and a program. *Goodbye, bud. It's been one hell of a race.*

Fireworks lit up the night sky from the arena as Mouse weaved himself out of the celebratory crowds and slipped through the dancing shadowy rows of camp vehicles to the Orochi Team garage. He used his eye to open a small side door. Once in, he dug the stowed gas can out of the back where he'd hidden it and locked the place back up without alerting any of Sadao's men in sight. With competition now over, the need for double security had worn off. Most of the team would be getting a headstart on frolicking drunk around a campfire by now.

Mouse moved on alone, can in hand to Sadao's equipment trailer. He unlocked the side door, grateful that in their final arguments, Sadao had not thought to ask for his keys back. Mouse re-locked the door behind him. Sadao's gassed-up cruiser awaited him as planned but for some reason, Mouse loathed to approach it.

Face it, you don't belong here. You never did. Get the fuck out while you can. But... where... And to what?

Mouse sank to the floor by the wall and laid his head on his knees. He was as depressed as he could ever remember being since his father's funeral. The chance he'd been given to do the work he loved on the equipment he loved was a gift he wouldn't get twice. But that gift had come with so many complications – not the least of which was the betrayal of his own heart.

Your name suits you. You stay vigilant and run from things that frighten you. Dammit, why did that man always have to peg him so well? Why did he have to care so much whether or not Sadao gave a fuck about him? Why not just keep the life and forget the man?

So Mouse, are you going to live up to your name now and scram?

Mouse got slowly to his feet and hit the overhead lights. As the interior fluorescents flickered on, he saw it. His eyes blinked twice, not quite understanding what they were viewing. At the back of the trailer was a covered shape he knew all too well – better than any covered hunk of half-assembled metal he'd ever owned.

Mouse set down the gas can and went to it, throwing off the cover. It was his Ninja – the one he almost burned to death trying to save. It was scored here and there with carbon from the flames but other than that, it was all here in one relative piece. Mouse ran his hands over the titanium frame in awe. There was something tucked into the fuel cap, a slip of paper. He pulled it out. It was a hand-drawn note:

Jesus H Christ, kid! We was so worried about you. But this feller here done brought us your note and now we all can all sleep well again. It looked like that bunch gone and stole you from us but it sound to me like you got yourself a new fancy garage! Good for you, boy! A real racing team! Gloria and I will hitch on out and see you when your team comes to Phoenix. The feller here says you been missing your favorite toy. I guess you must have asked him to come fetch it, so I had him load it up in his truck to bring back to you. Whew, that was some fire. Glad you weren't in it. Take care of yourself. Make your papa proud! --Uncle Fred

Mouse read the letter twice before folding it up carefully and sticking it in his pocket. He hadn't asked about the Ninja. But apparently Sadao had, and kept his word to send a runner to Blythe. Mouse's head spun and his eyes swam with unexpected emotion. He had no idea what to do now.

His indecision was soon interrupted by the sound of the sidedoor being released and the timely appearance of Sadao, disheveled and out of breath. So he *had* noticed his departure, for once.

"What are you doing?" he gasped, catching his breath. "Kei radioed and said you'd gone to the garage and then come in here. Why - ?" Sadao was taking in the whole of the scene: Mouse, the Ninja, the extra can of gas and the spare key to his cruiser dangling from the chain in Mouse's hand. His eyes grew wide as it all added up. "You were *leaving?*"

Mouse swallowed, tears dripped down his face as he gestured to the Ninja. "Did you do this – ?"

For a minute of silence Sadao just stood there in disbelief. For once the look of uncertainty was his. It was a match point for certain and Mouse was too enthralled by it to speak.

In another blink Sadao was at him, twisting his hand and snatching away the key ring, which he threw to the floor. Caught by the shoulders, Mouse was pushed back against the trailer wall and pinned between the thighs by the man's leg. Sadao braced his arm against the wall and tipped Mouse's chin up. "I don't pick favorites," he said, and kissed him hard.

Mouse's senses reeled. Of all the punishments he expected to receive – a blinding kiss was the last on his list. But, it had been on the list... *God, yes...*

Mouse slumped back against the wall, grabbing Sadao's shirt in his fist to hold on. Sadao's fingers tangled in his hair, tightening his hold on him while his tongue plunged in from one angle then another – again and again. It was like being eaten – and fuck, was it good.

Mouse's cock went rock solid in his jeans and he struggled to shift his hips for some relief only to brush against an equally solid mound.

Mouse broke from the kiss with a shout and pushed Sadao off, dropping to his knees. On the cool floor of the trailer the last fringe of his sanity snapped as he grabbed and squeezed at the hardness under the fabric. The belt tongue came free first, then he ripped open the zippered fly with a tug. Sadao's studded cock leapt out into his face and with a long lick that coaxed a groan from its owner, Mouse swallowed him up whole.

It had been forever since he'd had a man and the scent and taste of Sadao's groin was making him lose it. He jacked him, licked him, flicked and bit his stud and took him down as far into his throat as he could stand it. Sadao's pre-cum tasted warm and sweet. He squeezed him for more, licking and sucking the tip over and again for it, delighting in the feel of it slickening his lips and chin.

It wasn't long before Sadao made a noise deep in his throat and shot into his mouth, holding the back of his head while he thrusted through his climax. Mouse drank him down greedily, savoring each burst with a moan and sucking the exhausted tip for more.

Sadao hissed and pulled back, freeing himself. He had a curiously pleased look on his face.

"*Yabai*... what a hungry little thing," he said between breaths, running his fingers over Mouse's wet lips. "I'll feed you more... but not here. Get up."

Mouse got unsteadily to his feet. He wasn't sure he could stand properly and put a hand to the wall behind him. "Where?" he demanded, sucking the salt-sour taste from his teeth. He did want more of it.

"Go back to my trailer and wait," Sadao said, tucking himself back into his jeans. "Calm yourself. I'm not interested in another race. I have others to deal with tonight first."

Mouse laughed in his frustration. He was so aroused he couldn't stand it. "Of course you do... "

Sadao grabbed Mouse by the arm and pulled him into a rough kiss, sucking his tongue. "Once I begin, I don't care to be interrupted," he said, giving Mouse a shove. "*Ikeyo!*"

Mouse wiped the spit from his mouth and obeyed.

Chapter XII

The Bell Tower

Although the water coming out of Sadao's showerhead was cool, it was doing nothing to adjust the temperature of his body. Mouse stood, both hands on the wall, letting the water pelt the top of his head and flow over his shoulders and back. His breathing was rough and uneven. Images of what had happened in the equipment trailer kept flashing through his head, making his groin throb. Mouse wondered idly if it was possible to get a hard-on so stiff it'd get stuck that way. He let go of the wall and squeezed it. *Yep, this baby isn't gonna come down for nothin'.* Not after he'd tasted that man's beautiful thick cock with its glinting ornament. He was so turned on he was ready to fuck the walls.

This was a degree of arousal he knew only the deepest penetration could satisfy. He was desperate to know what that little piece of jewelry would feel like drilled up in his ass. He moaned as his hand moved slowly up and down his drenched dick. Just a little bit couldn't hurt… just a little… take the edge off… ahh…

Fuck him, if he doesn't get his ass over here in time, his loss.

The shower door popped open and Mouse dropped his cock – although "dropped" wasn't the best way to describe something that was clearly levitating all on its own.

"Didn't I tell you to calm down and wait?" Sadao said, catching Mouse by his wrists and stepping in under the spray. Fully clothed, door open, Sadao lifted Mouse's arms up over his head and pushed him up against the shower wall. He feasted on his mouth before Mouse could form a single word other than "mmnnnn… "

Sadao pressed Mouse's hand to his belt. "Take it off," he growled as he took his chin and continued to kiss the hell out of him. Mouse fumbled blindly for the belt he had expertly removed only 30 minutes ago, and the flesh he had sucked dry made a second, glorious appearance. He grabbed Sadao's cock and pressed it up against his own, letting the "boys" get acquainted.

Sadao rubbed his erection against Mouse's, dueling with him. "That's nice… " he said, dipping to indulge in Mouse's neck. "Get my shirt off."

Mouse, whose neck was famously sensitive, tried his best to gather up Sadao's shirt

as the man sucked and bit his throat, coaxing out louder and louder moans. "Please...
I can't... aaahh!"

Sadao tilted his head back by a fistful of hair. "Can't what?"

Reality hit: Sadao was there with him in the shower, thrusting their cocks together,
shirt up, chest exposed, pants half down, dripping wet, watching Mouse's face change
with fascination. "You want to come?"

Mouse squeezed his eyes shut, the vision and the friction were too much, too good.
"I can't... stand... oh *shit!*"

A primal sound burst out of this throat in time with the first hard pump of his climax, splattering across Sadao's belly. The man's grip caught him fast and squeezed the
head tight, stoppering the rest. Mouse wailed and shook as the second more violent
orgasm rocked through his hips. In a second, Sadao was down on his knees, tongue
replacing fist, as he licked out the second, third and fourth shots that spurted in his
mouth and dripped down his beard.

Goddamn, it was the single sexiest thing Mouse had ever witnessed in his life.

Sadao stood and wrapped him up in a long satisfying cum-flavored kiss. Mouse
clung to him, pleasure assaulting his nerves with each breath. "I want... " he panted
between kisses.

"Want? Did I forget something?" Sadao said smugly, rubbing his ass.

Mouse licked a dribble of spooge from Sadao's beard while he took the man's hard
dick firmly in hand – *god*, it was like a tree trunk. "I want this in me."

"I can see that," Sadao said, looking down. "If you'll go wait for me on the bed, I'll
make good use of that."

Face down on the bed, ass in the air, Mouse was moaning into the pillows before
Sadao had a chance to finish showering off. He'd never wanted a fuck so bad in his life.
Posed like a damn cat in heat, he just didn't give a shit anymore how immodest he was.
He wanted no misunderstandings – it was time to get down to business.

The water shut off and Sadao stepped out, drying himself with a towel. "Nice view,"
he said, climbing up onto the bed behind him, rubbing the towel over Mouse's damp
ass and back. Mouse moaned and pushed his backside into the cloth.

"Looks like anyone could walk by and get a shot at you. Should I open the trailer
door and let them line up?"

"Shut the fuck up and stick it in," Mouse said between clenched teeth.

Sadao moved over him and rubbed his half erection over the crack of his ass. Mouse
bit the pillow and groaned as he felt the man stiffen. Sadao kissed the back of his neck.
"This is one occasion where I prefer not to rush. I like to enjoy my mates. You'll have

to learn patience."

"Nnngh!" Mouse didn't care for this announcement and bucked his hips angrily. This earned him a sharp crack of Sadao's palm across his left ass cheek. "Ahhh!"

"You seem to forget *Konezumi*, who exactly is on the bottom."

Mouse turned his head to glare at that smug sonofabitch. "Fine, you want to switch? I'll tear your ass up! Get down here!"

Sadao laughed and smacked his other ass cheek, giving it a nice hard squeeze. "That sounds tempting but I doubt you will enjoy it half as much. You seem to want punishment."

Smack! Smack! Smack!

Mouse buried his face in the pillows and moaned. Fuck, that man could hit! And he had no intentions of stopping him. "Aaauuuugh – !"

At some point the smacking stopped and warm lips and a soft beard soothed his inflamed skin with light kisses. Mouse was in heaven. He arched his back, encouraging the caresses. The vicious spanking had calmed him oddly enough. It made him want to bring it down and go slower.

"Mmn, nice pink skin. It takes pain well," Sadao noted, kissing his way across each globe, squeezing as he went. He ran his fingers down the crack and gave Mouse's dangling scrotum a nice satisfying tug.

Mouse lifted his head and cried out in pleasure.

"You're fun to play with, *Konezumi*," Sadao said, milking his balls. "The noises you like to make are very exciting." He dipped his head and gave Mouse's taint a slow wet lick, ending with a flick at his twitching hole.

"Aaahhh … please… "

"*Kawaii sou*. You want me to eat you?"

Mouse squirmed. If his hole could speak it would be ordering that tongue to stop talking and get lapping. Fortunately, it didn't have to break the language barrier for in another moment Sadao had his cheeks spread wide and his face planted firmly between them, feeding like he was half starved himself.

The man knew how to work an asshole. Slick firm strokes assaulted his most tender spot. Sadao licked, sucked and flicked Mouse's ass rim – teasing it and soothing it, then going in for a rough plunder. Sadao's beard tickled his balls as he was tongued good and deep. Mouse was moaning so much now he had to remind himself to breathe. When he was good and wet, Sadao introduced a thumb, just popping it in and out of the ring, followed by a nice slow stretch of the folds.

"Don't... have to be so careful … " Mouse panted. "I won't break."

"Who's being careful? I'm just enjoying you," Sadao said and plunged two fingers in, twisting as they went.

Mouse howled and bucked, begging for more. Sadao banged him hard, firing up the nerves along his tight inner walls. Pleasure shot through him from ass to cock, goading a surge of precum up and out of his dickhead. Sadao gave him one last thrust and reached forward to gather up the fluid on his fingers, squeezing Mouse's cock and forcing more out into his palm. Sadao braced a hand against his back and Mouse dipped his head to watch the man working the slippery goo over and around his thick rod. Sadao milked himself too, adding more lube of his own to the mix, making the pearls shine. Mouse wondered what it would taste like, the two of them mixed together. But that fantasy soon faded as Sadao hooked a thumb into his asshole and cock in hand, prepared to enter.

Slick velvet heat pressured his puckered hole. Although he'd been well prepped, Mouse's body still resisted the full of Sadao's aroused glans. They were so close he couldn't hold still and pumped his hips to try and force it in. Sadao gave him another playful smack. "Settle down. You're too excited, too tense. Relax, I don't want you pinching my dick off."

Mouse shook his lust-addled head and took some breaths. He tried not to remind himself how the man he wanted more than anything was burrowing his way inside him. There was pressure and the smart of pain. He relaxed into it, letting the delicious stretching sensations take over. He groaned with each inch as Sadao worked himself in deeper and deeper. God, there was nothing like it on earth – this feeling of being filled up with another man's desire. His ass felt so hot, so full and stretched. No question, Mouse loved cock.

Sadao made a sound of satisfaction and grinded around in there a bit, getting a feel for the space. He wasn't freakishly long but he was thick, like a wedge. Mouse preferred girth over reach – it made him feel more exposed, more gratified by the feel of his asshole muscle being pulled taut over hot greedy flesh. His moans were darker now, more guttural as Sadao nudged himself in deeper until hipbones hit pelvis.

"… it in… ?" Mouse panted.

"Definitely… " Sadao said softly as if he were deep in amazement. "You're a good fit, *Konezumi*," he said, giving Mouse another stir.

"Aaahhh! Move … please … just fuck me… "

Sadao suddenly pulled out all the way. Mouse gasped like his spleen was getting sucked out. The space the man left behind felt cavernous and he ached to have it back. "No – !" Mouse protested, and got another crack over his rosy ass. He hissed through his teeth.

He heard Sadao spit and the warmth ran over his tailbone, down his crack to his greedy rim where it was sucked in. Sadao plunged himself in after it. Mouse sobbed and braced himself as the assault at last got underway. Deep, deep, hard thrusts shook his bowels. Sadao's dick jewelry became apparent, raking across his prostate with each thrust as it was properly designed to do. The black pearls were working to loosen that hard little knot of frustration Mouse had been harboring for so long and was desperate to get fucked out of him.

Sadao had him by the hips – controlling him, angling him, giving it to him just how he wanted – responding to his cries of need and delight. Mouse was vocalizing so much he was drooling right along with his dick, forming puddles on the linen. The pleasure stirring up in him was so good, so intense, he reached a point where he stopped moaning altogether – mouth frozen in a silent scream. Christ, he couldn't breathe...

Crack! Sadao hit him again and Mouse took the first gasp of air he could manage in who knew how long, exhaling into a long rough wail.

"Don't fucking pass out on me!" Sadao ordered. He was single-mindedly focused on his task.

Mouse sobbed and dug his hands into the mattress, trying to gain purchase. He was getting nailed so hard, he'd been shoved inch by inch almost to the headboard now. Soon he'd be bashing into it with his lust-crazed skull. If they weren't careful he'd wind up in the medic tent again. He lifted a hand and grabbed the shelf over the bed and pushed back with all he had. "Nnnnngh!!"

Properly braced now, Mouse was able to tilt his ass up just a little more and snap his hips back on each plunge, driving that beautiful man's stud even harder into his angry little gland. *Ugh,* the feel of it was incredible, indescribably satisfying, something no sad-ass handjob could ever accomplish. This is what he'd been missing, this is what his body craved late in the night when he lay alone on his cot in the garage back in Blythe – merciless animalistic fucking.

"You ready?" Sadao asked, his voice sounding remarkably controlled for the brutal pounding he was giving him.

"Yeah. No, I... " Of course he was fucking ready. His rod was straight out, filled to the brim, dripping and ready to pop. But he just didn't want this end ... ever.

"Don't worry," Sadao said as if he had read his mind. "This is only the beginning."

"Aaahhhhh – !" Mouse's joy knew no bounds. *There's more? There's going to be more?*

And then all thoughts stopped. Sadao found an extra gear in his transmission and, pardon the obvious pun, floored it.

Mouse's knuckles went white. He sucked in his last breath and held it, because after this he'd probably never need to breathe again. He'd be dead of happiness. Sadao could fuck a brick wall to its knees with the torque he was driving into him now. Mind swept away in a flood of carnal madness, Mouse became aware only of the force coming at him – how it rattled his bones, burned up his ass, made his balls suck up tight, tighter – preparing for what was coming. Sweat poured off their skin, it was dripping off Sadao onto his back, down his limbs. Juice ran from the hole that joined them, running down the back of his balls – making the lewd sounds that much more audible as they collided sac to sac, hip to ass.

Mouse could feel the man getting close, in the way Sadao's grip on his hips grew painful, in the way his thrusts were beginning to go wild, losing rhythm. Sounds were slipping loose from his throat in choked growls. Sadao was losing himself inside him as his big thick gorgeous cock reached its bursting point.

He wants this as much as me.

That one thought was the tipping point. Pleasure flashed and bloomed deep inside him. An unbelievably hot melting feeling rushed through him. Mouse found his voice and for a moment wondered who had screamed. He'd never heard himself sound like that before – so raw and wild. Sadao answered him as if they were calling to each other over an abyss as the man's cock pounded and throbbed, finding release deep in his ass in a gush of heat. Mouse unloaded in their last gyrations of bliss and they crumbled together, falling onto each other, emptying, spurting sloppily all over the bed.

Heaven had caught them in the act and spit them out in an ungracious ball of sweat and spooge. Mouse thought Sadao had come in him but either it all came pouring right back out or the total limb failure they'd both suffered had jarred him loose. Either way, his inner thighs and belly were both sticky with spunk. Mouse had never had it so good, so crazyJesusfuckingChristballsout good. His cock ached, he'd come so hard. His ass was in a gnawing spasm of disbelief. *What the fuck was that?* It asked with each throb. *And when can I get some more?*

"More... ?" Mouse echoed weakly.

Sadao's belly shook in laughter where he lay flopped half over him. The man kissed his shoulder, rubbing the sweat from his nose. "You'll have to give me a minute. I'm older, you know."

"Not... too old to still fuck like hell … *damn* … are my legs still there?"

Sadao smacked the back of his thigh. "Hear that? Yes. You still have legs."

Mouse laughed despite the sting, rolling over to face his attacker. "You're always hitting me."

Sadao's face was so beautiful, so close – even if it was doused in smug self-satisfaction. "Only because you enjoy it so much," he said.

"Kiss me, you bastard."

Sadao held his face and pressed a soft kiss to his mouth. Mouse melted into it, tilting his head to encourage Sadao to do it again. He did, allowing them to share a simple touch that was somehow so much hotter than the tongue dueling he'd gotten earlier.

Mouse loved slow drowsy post-coital kisses. Men so rarely enjoyed kissing him this way. It was so warm and close – he could feel the soft contours of Sadao's lips slipping over his own, and thrilled at every tingling scrape of his beard. He'd never kissed a man with a beard before. It was amazing, so masculine and infused with the scent of their sex. It wasn't long before he was licking it, mouthing it, nibbling at the tiny prickly-soft hairs.

"Careful," Sadao said. "You'll eat it right off me."

"Mmm … I want to... " Mouse purred, licking his way under Sadao's chin.

Sadao chuckled softly, maybe from his words or maybe because Mouse was tickling him a bit, but the vibrations made Mouse shiver. He slid his arms around Sadao, feeling him, the hard muscles of his back and ass under his hands as he nuzzled his way along his neck to lick his throat. Sadao murmured encouragement, winding his fingers into Mouse's hair, letting him feed on whatever part of his body he desired.

Mouse nibbled and licked his way down Sadao's throat to his collarbone, tracing the line of it with his tongue. He paused to lap at the hollow in between – that place that had drawn his attention whenever sweat dripped down Sadao's beautiful almond skin. Everything about the man was beautiful, and he wanted to taste every inch of it while he had the chance. Mouse worked his way down Sadao's chest, below the Orochi head to a flat brown nipple, sucking it deep into his mouth.

Sadao grunted but didn't stop him, even as his tongue flicked the tiny tip over and over. So good, so perfect. He wanted to stay like this forever, entwined with this man, living off the sweetness of his skin. Mouse sucked and sucked like a hungry pup, until saliva was oozing down his chin.

Sadao made a sound and gripped his hair, pulling him off. "Too much," he said, but his eyes were soft.

"What is?" Mouse breathed.

"You," Sadao said and kissed him. He rolled Mouse under him, deepening the kisses, tightening his hold around him. His heavy thigh slipped between Mouse's and he could feel the man hard again against his balls. *Hooray.*

Mouse spread his thighs as they kissed to encourage Sadao to enter him again. But the man ignored the invitation and just continued to explore Mouse's lips and tongue – a deep thorough kissing with no particular aim. Mouse was powerless under him and whimpered into his mouth, opening his legs wider and coaxing the man's stiff jeweled penis with little lifts of his ass.

Sadao paused a moment and kissed Mouse on the nose. "Are you trying to tell me something?"

"Fuck yeah, I am – "

"Maybe I don't understand your language," Sadao teased, biting Mouse's lower lip. "Why don't you try it in mine?"

"Nngh, I don't speak Japanese," Mouse protested, wiggling his ass to try and get it into position, but Sadao kept himself just off the target.

"It's time you learned," Sadao said softly in his ear, sucking the lobe. "*Nihongo*, is a superior language for expression of desires."

Mouse panted under him, growing desperate. His cock was up and ready for more, so much more but all he could do from this position was bonk it lamely at Sadao's bellybutton. "Fine, how do I say, 'Fuck me?'"

"We don't use such vulgar words," he said, licking his way under Mouse's chin.

"How do you … nnngh … yeah – right, my neck... like that … aahh... "

"We use the verb "to embrace" to ask for sex: *daku.*"

"Mnn? *Daku?* Then *daku daku* already!"

Sadao laughed as he bit into the tender flesh of Mouse's neck, making him moan and jerk his hips up even more, spreading dick goo all over Sadao's abdomen. "You didn't conjugate it correctly."

"Damn straight I'm not conjugating correctly! I'm stuck fucking your navel because you're being a pretentious piece of Japanese … aaaaahhh!"

Sadao was working the tendons of Mouse's neck with his tongue, driving him bonkers. "Okay, okay. I'll listen … teach me."

Sadao raised his head and smiled down at him in his misery. "When you want to be embraced by a *nihonjin* you say, '*daite kure*,' very politely."

"Politely… ?" Mouse wasn't sure he could ask for a fuck that nicely. Sadao grew impatient with his silence and made another open-mouthed move for his neck. Mouse stopped him, holding the man's head a moment, gathering courage. Underneath, he slid himself lower and rotated his hips back, spreading wide so the head of Sadao's cock was poised perfectly.

Mouse brushed their noses together and whispered, "*Daite kure, Sadao.*"

Sadao groaned in approval and at last his cock began to burrow. Mouse arched his back and took him in slow and steady, not letting him stop until he hit bottom. Ah, that was so much better. He had the man again right where he wanted him, filling him up. Mouse wrapped his arms around Sadao's broad shoulders, encouraging him to come down and put the full of his weight against him, locking his ankles behind his back. Sadao slid his arms under him and relaxed with his nose buried in his hair, letting Mouse enjoy the fullest embrace they could manage.

Sadao's lips were at his ear. "Does this satisfy you?" he asked, softly.

Mouse nodded as he breathed under the amazing presence of Sadao – on him, in him, around him. Heaven was what this was and indeed, it was very, very satisfying. They lay for several moments in this fashion, nuzzling, before Mouse began to wriggle.

"Evidently not completely satisfied," Sadao mused as Mouse's hips began to instinctively buck under him.

"Not yet," Mouse gasped, urging the man to lift a little and move in him again. His ass was still slick with cum and the little glide he was able to manage in this fully joined position felt so good. "I need more… "

"I wonder," Sadao said, kissing his neck and shoulder, "If any man has ever truly satisfied you."

"No... no one... stuck around long enough to, oh!"

"Then I accept the challenge," Sadao said. He slipped an arm around Mouse's shoulders and with a hand under his knee, lifted his thigh up, creating the leverage he needed to begin to thrust in earnest.

Oh, god yes, please... please don't let this end...

Sadao delivered deep slow strokes that brought them as close as their bodies would allow. Mouse was adrift in the flood of sensations running through him, surrendering to the feel of being fucked – locked in Sadao's strong arms at the mercy of the powerful workings of his thighs and ass.

Mouse wished he could see it, those hard carved muscles and tendons working together to provide such intense thrusts. He ran his hands down Sadao's back, as low as he could grab, digging his fingertips into the tension and release of that beautiful ass.

"*Oshiri ga ii yo...* " Sadao groaned under his breath as he closed his eyes and began to drive into him at a quicker pace.

"Ahhhhh, what?"

"*Ii yo,*" Sadao repeated and leaned in for a kiss.

"English, please?" Mouse asked weakly between kisses. But whatever had prompted Sadao to voice his pleasure, he'd gone beyond it now and was fully engaged in working himself all around inside Mouse – grinding and thrusting, lifting his thigh higher, shifting the angle, enjoying the increase in pressure and friction.

It got Mouse hopelessly excited, watching Sadao's brow furrow and lips twist in concentration as this man used the warm depths of his body to seek his own satisfaction. Mouse went boneless and let himself be moved, folded and manipulated, melting into his rhythm.

Mouse always felt the notion of becoming 'one' with another person was a ridiculous concept best reserved for vapid Top 40 radio lyrics. But as he closed his eyes and let go of himself, let himself be fluid in this man's arms, he understood why the Japanese chose *daku* to express it.

"Aaaaaaaahhh... " The orgasm that took him was sweet, slow and serene, echoing all through him. His cock spit a few drizzles across his belly, slickening the space between them.

Sadao kissed him hard and pumped his hips more vigorously, coaxing more and more cries of delight from Mouse who dug his fingers into Sadao's ass muscles, urging him to go as deep and hard as he desired.

At last Sadao gave a shout and pulled up and out of him, grabbing his convulsing cock in his fist as it unloaded in bursts across Mouse's chest. Through heavy lids, Sadao admired his art, smearing it over Mouse's chest and belly with his fingers.

"You made a mess out of me," Mouse remarked when he could remember how to speak. His asshole ached and twitched, his cock was a little shriveled pink piece of exhaustion stuck to his thigh in a puddle of unwound pleasure.

"This is one mess I will enjoy cleaning," Sadao said as he dipped to taste where they had run together on Mouse's abdomen. He paid special attention to the fine line of belly hair, licking the fur clean where it ran from navel to cock. Sadao lacked such a marking Mouse realized. In fact, aside from his head, pits, groin and chin, the man was virtually hairless.

Sadao raised his head and licked his lips. "*Umai*," he said and got up.

"Huh – ? Where you going?" Mouse asked in a small panic.

Sadao grinned. "Towel – I can't get it all myself." He went into the bathroom briefly and emerged with a warm damp washcloth. He knelt beside Mouse on the bed and slowly, thoroughly, wiped him from belly to ass, spreading his legs to get at all the hidden places he'd soiled.

"Your skin is very light here," Sadao said, running his fingers along the inside of Mouse's thigh where he'd just cleaned him.

Mouse twitched. It ticked. "Am I your first white boy?" he teased.

Sadao gave him a look. "No."

Mouse couldn't help but feel glum about that. This produced a flicker of regret in Sadao's expression. He tossed the cloth away and lay down beside him, brushing the hair away from Mouse's eyes where it always fell in unruly tangles. Sadao's gaze softened. "First blue eyes," he said fondly, stroking Mouse's temple. "Very beautiful."

Mouse's breath hitched. "I'll accept that," he said softly and welcomed Sadao's kiss. The man could be both passionate and tender in turns. He'd never been with anyone like him before.

Christ, Mouse, don't fall in love with this guy. Hmm, probably too late for that advice!

Sadao broke away from the kisses and rolled onto his back. He reached above his head to the shelf for one of his cigarette packs. Mouse snuggled up against his side, running his palm over Sadao's chest while he lit up. He let the man get a few hits of nicotine in him before he spoke.

"I want to know something about you," he said. "I want to know something that no one else knows. Something you've never told anyone before."

Sadao raised an eyebrow. "I imagine there's a lot of things I've never told anyone. I don't feel the need to discuss my business all the time like some."

Mouse looked up at him. "That's not what I'm asking. I want to know something personal, a secret that you've decided to keep to yourself."

Sadao took a long drag. He was mulling it over. Mouse dropped his chin on his belly and made the "please face" that used to get anything he wanted out of his father.

Sadao laughed and pushed his face away. "Okay, okay. I'll think of something."

Mouse poked at Sadao's left nipple, still a little red and swollen from his earlier attempt to suck it off his body. "Make it a good one or I'll tell everyone who comes into the garage about your tickle spot."

"You wouldn't... "

"Try me." He said and let his finger slide toward the offending zone.

"*Oi! Mou ii!*" Sadao threw up both hands in surrender. "I will tell you something. Something I don't think even Shiratori knows. It happened before I knew him. When I was a little boy."

"You were a little boy? Somehow I can't picture that."

Sadao set his cigarette aside in the ashtray. "I was. We all were, once."

Mouse laid his head on Sadao's chest. "How little?"

Sadao thought it over as his fingers idly stroked Mouse's hair. "Six, I believe. Or seven. But that doesn't matter. I grew up in a small village, you know. On the Ise Coast where the mountain jungle meets the sea. In the center of town we had a temple, where everyone would gather for prayers and festivals – special occasions."

"Buddhist temple?" Mouse asked.

"Yes, but we only had one small *daibutsu* – ah, image of Buddha, you would say. No, what was special about our temple was the bell tower. It was solid wood built at four angles, like this." He made a square shape with his hands. "It was wide at the base and narrowed at the top. It was a very old structure. And the bell the monks rang at the top was older yet. My father told me it was a gift from the Emperor – over 1,000 years old. Very sacred. I wanted to go up the tower to see it, but my father said only the most pure and dedicated of monks were allowed to climb the tower and swing the hammer that rang that bell.

"I didn't like this answer, of course, so I made a plan to conquer the tower after nightfall. I snuck out of my room that I shared with my brothers and ran down the hill into the village. The temple was very dark. The lanterns were not lit that night so I ran across the stones to the base of the tower and started to climb up the outside."

"Wasn't there a ladder or something?" Mouse asked.

"There was, but only on the inside. And that door was locked at the base so I climbed the outside of the tower on the edge of the crossbeams. Had I been any older my hands would not have been able to grip the narrow edge. I went straight up to the top and crawled into the space under that giant black bell and for the first time since I began to plan this adventure, I became scared. This bell was so much bigger than I thought and so much older, and so dark. I sat under it and realized I had no business being up there. I became so frightened, I was too scared to climb back down. I huddled there under the bell for the rest of the night and part of the next day.

"It wasn't until the monk climbed up the inside ladder and unlocked the trapdoor to ring the bell for prayers that I was discovered. He couldn't imagine at first how I got up there and took me for a *saru maboroshi* – a monkey spirit. I told him my name and then he knew me. He said my parents were terribly worried, they had gone out with their nets with our neighbors to the oyster docks, thinking I had drowned. I said, 'No, I have been here since yesterday.'

'Why?' he asked.

I said, 'Because I could not figure out how to get down.'

'Then why,' he asked, 'didn't I ring the bell?'"

Sadao reached for the rest of his cigarette and waited for Mouse's reaction. Mouse thought it over and shrugged. "Yeah, why didn't you ring it? I would have."

Sadao smiled. "Think about it," he said, taking a final puff and crushing out his cigarette.

"I am thinking about it and I think you made that up, right now on the spot."

Sadao shook his head. "True story."

"I don't get it."

Sadao wrapped an arm around him and pulled him up close, kissing his nose. "That is because you are American."

"What does that have to do with common sense? If you're stuck in a tower with a big ass bell, you ring it. Done."

"Maybe someday when you are older you will think of this story and understand."

Mouse tried to push away from him but was held fast. "I'm not a child."

"No, you are not. Good thing, too. You wouldn't approve of that."

"Stop it. I hate it when you start this older, wiser bullshit with me."

"I can't help it. Your innocence is very compelling."

Mouse tried to wriggle free again.

"And your stubbornness."

"Stop!"

Sadao grabbed him and flipped him over on his back, pinning him down.

"So you did not like my bell tower story, eh?"

Mouse evaded his kiss. "No. It wasn't what I wanted."

"What if I told you another story instead about a little Mouse."

Mouse tried to hit him but his arms were trapped.

Sadao leaned in and put his full weight over him. "A little Mouse who wanted to play with a snake."

"Shut up!"

"So he kept coming a little closer and a little closer, frightened but determined to get the snake to play with him."

"Nnnngh! Let go!"

"He'd twitch his nose and flick his tail right in front of the snake's mouth."

"Stop."

"Do you know what happened to him? That cute little innocent mouse who only wanted to play?"

Mouse looked daggers at him. "He was eaten alive. Is that what you're going to say?"

"No, something much more sinister. His antics charmed the snake."

"Huh – ?"

"And the snake became his slave forever."

Mouse stopped struggling. This shit was making his brain hurt. "That's lamer than the bell story."

Sadao groaned and got off him. "I give up."

"Good," Mouse said, climbing over him, straddling his hips. "The Mouse wants the snake to shut the hell up and stick its tail in his ass again."

Sadao nodded. "The snake can do that."

And like his prediction, the Mouse who only wanted to play got a good part of himself devoured whole during the long night that followed, coiled in the arms of the Orochi.

Mouse sat on the toilet, head back against the bathroom wall, half awake, letting his body drain. He was delirious with exhaustion. He'd been taken that night harder, deeper and more relentlessly than he'd ever known. His ass ached and throbbed as the evidence of Sadao's satisfaction dripped slowly from him. It was a wonderful pain that left his body and mind drained and floating in a giddy stupor of release.

His head lolled and dropped toward his chest. Shit, he was gonna pass out on the toilet if he didn't get the fuck back in bed.

Mouse flushed, killed the lights and used the walls to guide his rubber legs back to Sadao's bed and within it, Sadao's motionless body. He was pretty sure the man was still alive – his body was still warm as he crawled up into the fresh sheets to flop down in the pillows beside him.

He'd never known himself to feel so utterly spent. It was amazing. He wanted to die like this – die of carnal sins shared with this man. As his eyes dropped closed Sadao stirred, mumbled something in Japanese and reached for him. Mouse inched closer into his arms with the last shred of energy he possessed to lie skin to skin against him.

Over the sounds of their quiet breathing, Mouse could still hear the distant shouts of revelers in the camp, dwindling sounds of celebration giving way to daylight and fatigue. Tomorrow as it could already be rightfully called, held no work for either of them. Mouse intended to sleep the whole damn day away. And he hoped Sadao did too, because although some knocks had come to his door during their couplings and after, Sadao had made no move to answer them. For now at least, within the walls of this trailer, Sadao Koga had become completely his.

Chapter XIII

Unspoiled

Mouse woke from the deepest sleep he could remember to Sadao poking him in the ass. Too sleepy to move, Mouse lay like the dead. But that didn't stop his necrophiliac lover from trying to raise him. Sadao slipped an arm around him, nuzzled his hair and pulled him close – ass to groin. Somebody was up.

Did he think that poking him with morning wood was going to work? poke... poke... Okay, maybe it was beginning to work.

"I don't know what you think is going to happen," Mouse said, yawning. "I was done hours ago."

"Mmm, you don't have to do anything, just let me move you."

The sexy raspy edge to Sadao's voice was making him wish he had a little energy left in reserve. But after *several* attempts to call it a night, night had rolled into day and night again. Mouse had no clue how long they'd been here fucking, kissing, sleeping and fucking again. They'd managed to eat a few times but after a few bites in, the table became a serving area for a different kind of delicacy. The shower – Mouse had given up on trying to stay clean. Even coated in soap, he'd managed to get himself befouled. Although his asshole was in strong disagreement, he couldn't say he'd regretted a moment of it. *God, I'm a slut.*

"Ahh, wait! Ow!"

Sadao kissed his cheek. "Sore?"

"Agh, little bit."

The man chuckled and kissed his shoulder. "I'll get something." He rolled over and got up, walking naked into his kitchen, cock pointing the way.

"Get something – ? You mean you *had* something all along?"

Sadao rummaged through his cupboards. "Maybe. You weren't complaining."

"I've seen the past due dates on some of the shit in your fridge. I don't want anything from your kitchen going in my ass!"

"Why not? Most everything else did," he said, selecting a jar of something white and viscous.

Mouse pulled the sheets up over his head.

Sadao slid back into bed next to him and tugged the bedding up, exposing his bottom. Mouse shivered while the man stroked his thighs, softly. "I promise, I'll be gentle this time."

Mouse groaned. "You've said that before. Aren't you supposed to be getting old?"

Sadao nibbled his ear through the sheet. "Never too old to fuck a fine piece of ass," he said with a squeeze. "You were the one who said that no one had ever satisfied you."

Mouse heard the lid being unscrewed. It smelled nice. "What is that?"

"Coconut oil. It's solid at room temperature, but we'll change that," Sadao said, taking a dip of it and slipping his fingers between Mouse's tender globes.

"Nngh... " Mouse tensed but Sadao's fingertips felt warm and slick. The thick salve was soothing as Sadao spread it around his hole, massaging it in. "Mmn... "

"Feel good?" he asked, dipping his fingers part-way in and out again, getting him nice and oiled.

"I'm feeling… satisfied," he said, burrowing deeper into the pillows.

He heard Sadao mess with the coconut jar some more before he felt the hot knob of his dick pressing against his asshole.

"There's other… sssssss… parts of my body you could fuck, you know. Aaaaahhh… "

"Hmm, not as fun. Your ass is perfect."

"Mmfph… "

Sadao took his hips and hitched him up against his groin so he could work himself in deeper.

"Thanks for using English for once."

"Hm? What do you mean? I always use English with you."

Mouse unburied his head to look at Sadao over his shoulder. "Not when you've gone crazy for it. You babble Japanese at me and I don't know what the fuck you're saying."

Sadao stared him down. "Not true."

Mouse smiled. "Very true. What does *oshiri* mean?"

Sadao smiled and ground his erection deeper into Mouse. "It means ass."

"How would I know that word if you weren't moaning it when you're about to explode in me? Aaahhh… Oh, that's good… "

Sadao was in full and wrapped a coconutty fist around Mouse's cock, stiffening it in the coaxing glide of his grip. "Guilty, I suppose – "

They lay on their sides, back to front, hips moving in unison. Mouse didn't care anymore if he came or not. Just the close feel of this man's body up against him, moving in him, was pleasure enough. At this point he'd probably just spooge air anyway.

The knock came about five minutes or so later, just as they were both really starting to get lost in it. Sadao ignored it as he had the last several hours? days? He rolled Mouse under him and spread his thighs wide so he could kneel behind him and get at him even more solidly.

Mouse moaned and moaned in a haze of aching pleasure. Somehow getting fucked by Sadao made the soreness of getting fucked by Sadao melt away. Maybe it was the coconut.

The knocks gave way to bangs as they thrust against each other harder – Sadao's fist was jacking his cock, promising to work up a load of something from the dark depths of his balls.

Bang! Bang! Bang! Bang! Rattle! Rattle! Creak!!

"Fuck!!" Sadao shouted and pulled out, standing up stark-ass naked and marching to his door and throwing the locks.

Shiratori stood on the opposite side, bokken in hand. He'd been trying to pry his way in.

"*Nan da yo!*" Sadao bellowed, furious. "*Ore no jikan da!*"

Shiratori was livid and yelled back at him, pointing down at his glistening hard-on. Mouse hid under the sheets as Shiratori directed his tirade at both of them in English.

"When was good time to knock? This trailer not stop moving for three days!" Shiratori marched himself in. "Whole place smell like asshole and beach party! I have garage to pack for move to Utah. No mechanic! You kill him with big stupid cock?! Mouse-san! Come out!"

Mouse swore and tried to hide in the big bed while the two had their row. Next thing he knew the sheets and pillows were being thrown off him by metal fingers. His ass was poked, and not in a good way.

"Work now! No pay for lazy men!" Shiratori snapped.

Mouse rolled over and pulled a pillow over his oily erection, looking to Sadao. "Seriously? You're just gonna stand there? Aren't you the damn boss?"

Sadao slammed his dented and now bent trailer door shut as passersby were beginning to try to get a peek in. He dismissed both Mouse and Shiratori with a swipe of his hand as he headed for the shower. "You work for Shiratori-san!" he yelled and yanked the bathroom door shut.

Shiratori smirked at Mouse in triumph. "Get pants on. Work time. No more fuck for you!"

Mouse grumbled all the way to the garage. He didn't even get a chance to clean up properly with Sadao shut in the bathroom and Shiratori barking orders and flinging clothes at him. His ass was slippery and his legs felt like they were no longer attached to his body. He had to look down from time to time to stop himself from tripping. 9am and it was already hot. Today was gonna suck.

"Gringo! Where the fuck you been, man? I thought you ran off with another team. You've been MIA for days."

"Yeah, yeah. I know. I already caught hell from Shiratori, thanks," Mouse said, shuffling into the garage and taking in the task at hand. Machines needed to be lifted and chained down to the upper level. Tools and repair frames needed to be stowed or locked down. And the work bench looked like a pack of javelinas had been through. Mouse limped to the table and grabbed the edge before he fell over his right leg that forgot to move.

Lupe was at his side. "Hey man, you okay?" he said, worried.

Mouse smiled at his little buddy. It made him very glad to know their garage adventures would continue. "I'm fine, just sore."

"You been in an accident or something?"

Mouse shook his head. "No, but I guess you could say there was a collision of sorts."

"Those punks get at you again?" Poor Lupe was genuinely worried and looked ready to go start something.

Mouse put a hand on his shoulder. "It's okay. I'm actually very happy."

Lupe stated at him in utter confusion. Then something in Mouse's incredulous expression triggered a lightbulb. "Oh! So that's it, eh? You got some tail!" Lupe punched him. "Good for you, Gringo! Boss won't be happy you ran off but then, he's been missing too -" Lupe stopped mid-sentence as his eyes got big. "No fucking way!"

Mouse shrugged in defeat.

"I told you, man! Boss likes you, remember?"

"I remember. I'm remembering right now every time I try to walk."

Lupe laughed hysterically. "Lucky for us, huh? Maybe you'll stop pissing Boss off now and put him in a better mood."

"I wouldn't put money on that. He was plenty pissed when I left. Shiratori busted his way into the trailer to split us up."

Lupe was weeping with hysterics. "He ... just walked in? I wanna picture of that!"

"Well you're going to have to paint it yourself because I don't care to recreate the scene. Highly embarrassing. Let's get this shit stowed before I drop."

They worked as fast and efficiently as possible. But nothing was never efficient enough for Shiratori who seemed hell bent on making his first day back at work one to remember. He wanted buckets stacked, rags folded, parts tagged, and keys counted. He made inquiries as to the location of Sadao's missing spare but Mouse played dumb. Shiratori rightfully didn't believe him and changed the combo on the safe.

By the time they were excused from duties, half the camp had cleared out. Mouse was permitted to get cleaned up at last and changed into a soft t-shirt and jeans, ready to sleep through the next 500 miles of desert highways.

Shiratori was locking up when Mouse and Lupe were startled by a truck horn blast. Sadao had pulled up in his trailer now reunited with its full equipment extension. It looked like a small passenger train on rubber wheels.

"My ride's here boys, gotta bail," Mouse said with a salute to Shiratori who frowned.

Lupe wrapped him up in an excited hug. "Take care of the old man for me, eh?"

Mouse hugged him back. "I'll see you in Salt Lake in three days."

Lupe would be joining Kei – another one of Sadao's teenaged orphans – in driving the mobile garage up the main highways to their staging area on the Utah Great Salt Desert Flats. It was a place Mouse had only ever seen pictures of – endless miles of hard white salt crust that held most of the world's land speed records for experimental vehicles. It's where the Overland starting line was marked. Most of the Orochi camp was convoying in waves up the I-15 but he, Sadao, Shiratori and Tagata would be taking a more circuitous route through the mountains. They would be heading up to Williams to visit a junk dealer Mouse knew Barney did a lot of good auto parts trades with – a man called "Joe." All four men were hoping he was still specializing in the Classics.

Mouse waved goodbye to Dry Lakes as he climbed up into Sadao's cab and took shotgun. He shut the door and collapsed into the cozy bucket seat.

Sadao smiled at him in his exhaustion. "You can climb on up into the back if you like. Sleep in the bed."

Mouse buckled himself in and shook his head lazily. "No thanks, the view's better up here," he said, grinning at the driver. "I like watching strong men drive trucks."

Sadao let go of the shift stick and brushed Mouse's cheek with the back of his finger. Mouse caught his hand in his and kissed it. "Let's go, Cowboy. The highway's calling."

Sadao chuckled, "That sounds like a bad country music song."

Mouse put his feet up on the hump and closed his eyes as Sadao released the brakes with a hiss and shifted into first gear, pulling out. Mouse didn't care how cheesy it sounded – if it meant he could be at this man's side, he'd ride with him to the edge of the earth.

Mouse slept most of the long highway hours away. He was intermittently aware of Sadao communicating on the truck's CB, checking in with various team leaders as they made their way north via various routes best suited for their vehicles.

Shiratori and Tagata were on and off frequently – somewhere behind them, hauling their own trailers across the desert. Mouse only roused himself when he felt a change in the roadway. The drone of the long flat asphalt had given way to a chorus of shifting gears and sloping turns that rocked his head side to side.

"You awake finally?" Sadao asked, turning down the crackling jabber of his CB.

Mouse stretched and rubbed his eyes. "I think so. Where are we?"

"Climbing toward Flagstaff," he said, downshifting. "Sun's going down, you missed the whole ride."

Mouse rolled his head and yawned. "You sound grumpy. You want me to drive?"

Sadao glanced uncertainly at him. "Have you driven this many wheels before?"

Mouse shrugged. "Give or take a dozen."

Sadao nodded. "That's what I was afraid of. This isn't a pickup truck."

"You don't trust me? That hurts."

"You see anyone else driving this rig? I don't trust anyone with my own wheels."

Mouse didn't fight it. Sadao would do as Sadao wanted. He was a bit relieved he'd been turned down – the approaching sunset was beautiful, casting long shadows through the ever thickening pine trees. Mouse hadn't seen evergreens since he was a kid and his dad had taken him up to Colorado for a race. He leaned forward to look up through the windshield.

"I can't believe how tall these trees get. They're amazing. Can we stop for a bit? Let you get some rest?"

Sadao was quiet and Mouse figured he'd just let him focus on his own thoughts, whatever they were. They were beginning to lose the daylight. Long forest highways were notoriously risky to travel by night due to the occasional tree and rockfalls from freak storms. Wasteland roads were no longer maintained by the government if they no longer served a useful purpose to them.

Sadao sighed and squinted into the sunset. He flicked on his radio and hailed Shiratori. There was an argument that followed, naturally, but they seemed to settle it by the time the sun dipped below the mountains.

"Okay," he said in a more amicable tone. "We'll find a spot to camp for tonight."

Mouse smiled. He'd gotten his way.

Mouse bounced out of the cab as soon as they pulled off onto a wide unmarked dirt road that dead-ended in a small meadow circled with pines.

The night sky had taken over. Mouse looked up into the brilliant ribbon of the Milky Way rimmed with trees. The air was cool and breezy. Mouse wandered about as Sadao set up his living space, engaging the extenders that pushed out his walls and widened his main flooring by several feet.

"Don't get lost!" Sadao called after him and opened an exterior compartment to start up his generators that ran the Motorcoach's electrical and plumbing facilities.

"I'm not twelve!" Mouse shouted back, wandering further through the meadow. It was filled with tall buffalo grass that came up to his knees. He ran his fingers over the tips, tickling his palms. Under the starlight the grass took on an eerie blue tone. He didn't really worry about how far out he was getting until he heard a noise in the treeline up ahead. Mouse stopped dead. Something had moved. He held his breath. Was it the wind?

"Mouse?!" Sadao's voice sounded very far now and tinged with worry. Whatever he had heard in the wood, it was bigger than a bird or deer. It moved again and Mouse saw a large shadow pass between the trunks of two trees about 50 feet ahead. His heart pounded and he turned to run back.

Crack!!!!

Rifle fire echoed across the shallow valley and Mouse dove into the grass, hiding.

Whatever it is, it can shoot!

Mouse lay low and still. The valley was silent now. When they'd seen the turn-out neither of them had thought who might have commissioned this road. Mouse had heard stories of mountain folk who took unkindly to strangers. And in order to make Williams in a timely manner, they had chosen to take a lesser-known route through the foothills.

Fuck, this wasn't good. And worse yet, Sadao was no longer calling for him. Unlike Mouse, he'd been standing in the exterior lights of his trailer rig and rifles were distance shooters. Tears of fright stung his eyes. He squeezed them shut and listened. Footfalls crunched through the grass, slow and heavy. Mouse lay as still and flat as possible, trusting the flowing blades to conceal him.

He didn't risk lifting his head until the footfalls had passed him and were moving away back toward the trailer. Mouse cautiously raised his head and peered through the tall grass.

It was a heavy set man moving slowly across the meadow, rifle at his shoulder aimed toward the trailer. Sadao was nowhere to be seen. Mouse waited until the strange man was some distance away before he got to his feet. He moved, hunched over, quickly through the grass to his left to try and catch the treeline before he was noticed. He rushed into the safety of the pines and peaked around a trunk.

The man was at the trailer now, circling it, gun at the ready. The generator was running and the lights were on, but no sign of Sadao was apparent. Mouse kept moving stealthily through the trees until he had circled back in front of the trailer, watching the man's movements. He was dark skinned, bearded and disheveled. He looked as if he'd been living in the mountains for a very long time. The pine needles crunched under his heavy feet with each step.

Crash!! The man smashed in a window with the tip of his rifle and pointed the barrel inside.

Blam! Blam! Blam! Hot flashes of gunpowder lit up the interior.

"Sadao!!" Mouse screamed and was immediately pulled back by the throat.

He hit the ground and was subdued by a boot to his neck. It was Tagata. He held a finger to his lips and pointed to his left. Unnoticed by him in the shadows of the trees was Shiratori, bow and arrow in hand, braced against a pine, poised to shoot. Mouse nodded understanding and Tagata let him up. The man with the gun had whirled around at Mouse's shout, retracting his rifle from the trailer window. He yanked the bolt and attempted to reload the magazine from ammo that spilled out of his trouser pockets.

Mouse caught a glint of movement and zzzing! Shiratori's arrow flew.

"Uugh!" was the man's last word as he dropped his firearm. His hands raked at the feathered end of the arrow at his throat, sticking out of his Adam's apple, gushing spurts of blood. He twitched violently and pitched forward, falling headfirst dead into the grass.

Sadao leapt out of the broken window, katana in hand and ran the corpse clean through with his blade for good measure. He stabbed him twice, kicking the filthy blood covered corpse in the head.

Shiratori let out a battle shriek and ran out of the line of trees to Sadao's side, joining him in the blood feast of revenge.

"Ugh," Mouse clenched his stomach and stood up with Tagata's help.

"*Daijobu?*"

Mouse nodded, moving forward slowly on his own. "I'm okay. Blood makes me nauseated."

"Mouse!" Sadao shouted, seeing him emerge. He dropped his katana and ran to him, clutching his shoulders painfully, eyes wild. "I thought he'd shot you!"

"Well, he missed," Mouse said, gripping his arms. "Sorry. I should have stayed near the trailer."

Sadao touched his face as if he needed extra evidence it was really there in his hands. "*Yokatta,*" he breathed, and wrapped him up in a hug.

With a foot on his dead back, Shiratori pulled his arrow from the man's body with a sick sucking sound and tossed it aside. He grumbled something in Japanese.

"*Ah, sou da,*" Sadao said, letting Mouse go. He looked at him solemnly. "There could be others. We need to go look. Can you shoot?"

Mouse looked confusedly up at him. "Yeah, why?"

Shiratori bent and retrieved the dead man's rifle, clipped in the magazine and cocked it. He held it out to Mouse.

"Birthday present," he said with a smile.

It was decided they split up to scope the surrounding forest. Sadao and Tagata took rear guard while Mouse and Shiratori took lead. He wanted to protest not being paired with Sadao. But Shiratori, ever the tactician, reasoned the distance weapons should maintain the frontline and melee pick up the defense. Both Sadao and Tagata were hand combat experts.

Mouse walked beside Shiratori with the dead man's loaded rifle at the ready.

"Who do you think he was?" Mouse whispered.

"Mountain man," Shiratori answered in a hushed voice. "They hide in forest like this. Shoot without asking. Very dangerous; they have many weapons but not brain. Very easy to kill."

"You've killed these men before?"

Shiratori motioned Mouse to keep his voice low.

"Yes. Mountain men sometime come to camp to steal from us. This is why we must have guard. They come from woods at night like bear."

"How many have you killed?" Mouse now wondered exactly how violent his current company was.

"A warrior does not share his score."

"Okay, then how many of these men has Sadao killed?"

"Five," Shiratori said without hesitation.

"Oh my god," Mouse said, feeling his gut tighten. "I've never seen someone killed in my whole life and I've seen two now in the last few weeks."

"Would you feel better if we let bear-man shoot your boyfriend?"

"No! That's not what I meant. I just... " *Boyfriend? Really, that's the most shocking thing you've heard Shiratori say tonight?*

"Boss-sama and I are warrior, not common town man. We are trained to kill and protect. Even when child we must protect village from many enemy."

"Is that how you know him? Were you and Sadao charged with guarding your village together in Japan?"

Shiratori blinked his dead eye at him. "No. Sadao-sama was enemy."

Mouse stopped in his tracks. *What?*

Shiratori turned his head. "Keep up!"

Mouse shook off his shock and hustled forward. "I don't understand. I thought you two were old friends?"

"No, not friends. Enemy. Sadao-sama people killed many in my village long time ago. I was there when his clan burned down my family home. And I was there when my clan shot his parents and brothers."

Mouse was horrified. "I don't think I want to know anymore about this. You were a part of that? The murder of his family? How?"

"His clan very bad people. They want to take important bridge to stop supplies. My clan would not let them have bridge our many grandfather built. So they shot arrow of fire on us. Burn everything. My mother and aunt both burn to bone for bridge? No. I was ten, already good fighter. I joined raid to destroy pearl farm. I was glad in my heart to see Sadao-sama weep for his dead family."

Mouse was struck dumb. How could any of this be possible? Who lost his arm in a wrestling match the other night and tossed noodles on the ceiling? Is this what blood enemies did? And yet Shiratori seemed unfazed by this thread of conversation. He noted the facts as casually as if he was talking about the weather. It made no sense.

"I... don't know how... " he began when Shiratori shushed him. Ahead through the trees was a flicker of firelight. They stayed low until Sadao and Tagata caught up with them. The men started to whisper a plan in Japanese but Sadao corrected them.

"English, or Mouse will not understand," he insisted.

Shiratori began his instructions over again without a beat. They were to each take a point north, south, east and west of the light. They would surround it and approach simultaneously. If they faced opposition from the source of the light, kill and ask questions later.

"I won't shoot a person!" Mouse insisted. "I've never killed anything bigger than a rabbit."

"Then think of enemy as big rabbit," Shiratori said and lead the ambush.

Mouse ran through the trees toward the east side of the light. He didn't want to admit it to the men, but even with a loaded gun and a half moon overhead to light his way, the forest was a terrifying place at night. Especially considering what had just happened. If Fred and Doc Meadows could see him now – clueless soldier of darkness running with a pack of trained killers. The trials he'd suffered during his day to day garage labor now seemed trivial. Could he kill a man? He honestly didn't know. And the man who he had been so eager to leap into bed with had offed five... ? No, six that he knew of. And who knew how many more he'd killed when he was a child warrior. Yes, it had been war, but how does one know when the war is over?

The light was now passing him on his left so Mouse slowed and turned, marching slowly toward it. It was the last thing he wanted to approach, but he was anxious to not be alone any longer than necessary, even if it meant facing a fire-fight. Getting holes blown through his chest by Bigfoot's cousin was not how he'd planned to go. The stars didn't look so pretty anymore. Damn, he'd give anything to be back in the trailer on Dry Lakes snug and safe in Sadao's arms.

The light was a cabin – small and crude with roughly nailed walls. A fire was going somewhere inside, projecting orange light through the dull windows and sending smoke up through the roof. Mouse got as close as he dared and set up position as instructed by the General at a stone's throw from the east side of the structure. He was to hold his shot until he heard one of two signals. Mouse found a secure pocket of pines so he knew his back was protected and set his rifle barrel on the edge of a felled log to wait.

He was relieved to see Sadao and Tagata each approach, blades drawn from the north and south of the structure. He knew Shiratori would be holding his loaded bow from the far side, out of his view. Sadao and Tagata backed themselves up and peered in the windows. He saw Sadao wave an "all clear" and Shiratori and himself came out of the trees to meet them.

"Looks like a 'shiners cabin," Sadao said, kicking in the front door. It blew over easily. Mouse followed him in while Tagata and Shiratori watched the trees. Inside were several apparatuses of seeping, stinking crude alcohol. Mason jars, some full, some empty were stacked up or rolling on their sides on the dirt floor surrounding a single filthy mattress of fleas.

"This is what he was willing to shoot us for?" Mouse said, holding a hand over his nose. It was shocking how some people lived. They did live like bears, although bears smelled a lot nicer.

Sadao toed at a still, spilling out some of the lethal fluid. "If he was drinking more than he traded, it's doubtful he had any human will left."

Mouse looked at Sadao. In the firelight he seemed like a beacon – the one place he could hold on to in this increasingly dangerous world he'd gotten himself into.

"I want to go back," he said weakly.

Sadao met his eyes and nodded. "Let me put out this fire."

Mouse climbed the ladder up to the roof of Sadao's trailer with a blanket on one shoulder and the rifle strap over the other to join him in taking first watch over the meadow. He knew Sadao hadn't slept much and he insisted on staying by his side with the gun while Shiratori and Tagata dragged the bloody corpse away to leave for the wolves. Afterwards, they would settle themselves in for some rest. They'd pulled their trailers into a circular formation like a wagon train of bygone days and shut off all extraneous lights.

On the trailer roof in the darkness under the stars, Mouse could just make out the silhouette of Sadao, sitting in a lounge chair he'd hauled up a few minutes earlier. He was smoking and staring up at the stars when Mouse crawled up to him and climbed into his lap with his loaded gun and blanky.

"Oomph, you are a big child," he said, crushing out his cigarette and taking the gun from Mouse, laying it beside them. He let Mouse get comfortable against his chest and then threw the blanket around them both, holding him close. He dropped his lips to the crown of Mouse's head, running warm soothing hands up the back of his shirt. "You okay?"

Mouse took in a deep breath and sighed. "I'm trying to be. There's a lot I still don't understand."

Sadao rubbed his back gently and Mouse sank further into his embrace. "What don't you understand?"

He didn't see the reason to harbor it anymore, what Shiratori had been so brutally frank about.

"Shiratori told me you were his sworn enemy."

"Ah, did he? That sounds like something he'd say, certainly. When was this?"

"While we were on point tonight. I asked him how many of these men you had killed. He said five."

"Hm, why? Does it bother you? We were soldiers in a terrible war. Protecting our clans is what we do."

Mouse slid his arms tighter around Sadao's waist, not wanting him to slip away. "He told me he was happy to see your family killed and you crying because of it."

Sadao chuckled low in his chest. "I doubt he saw me crying, although he's always claimed to have been there during the attack on our farms."

"How can you trust somebody like that? He just made it sound so black and white. You are his enemy from 25 years ago and always will be – even if you cut his steak and play fruit ninja in your kitchen together drunk off your asses."

Sadao laughed at this and hugged him tight. "Shiratori is a simple man. His history may be complex and his ability to reason an enigma, but there is one thing that will never waver in him. He will always choose the path with the greatest potential for success."

Mouse sat up to look at Sadao. "Is that how he sees you? A path for his success?"

Sadao frowned a moment. "I suppose that's one way of putting it. When his team was decimated in the fuel explosion and his limbs torn apart, he had to make what many considered to be a very difficult choice. But for him the decision to merge our teams was simple. The man has only one goal in life – to win."

Mouse shook his head. "I don't believe that. Life is about so much more than that."

"To you maybe," Sadao said, lifting his chin and brushing his lips with his thumb. "For you life is an adventure – a life of hope, joy and sorrow. You may not know it, but you are a very rare creature in this world, *Konezumi*."

"How am I rare? There's nothing remarkable about me other than some skills in the garage."

Sadao slid his fingers into his hair and kissed him with a soft tongue. "You are unspoiled," he said, when their lips parted. The illumination of the stars rimmed the outline of his face in the darkness. "Your soul is not broken. And I will go to any length to see that it remains so."

Mouse rested his head against his chest and let Sadao hold him like a child. Above the dark wild of the forest, he was safe for now to "just be."

Chapter XIV

Payout

The lead team convoy pulled into Williams around 11am the next morning. It was fortunate that they had planned to stay the night in the forest, despite random bear-man attacks because the high road into town was blocked in several places by trees and mudslides. Sadao's skill at the wheel of his trailer managed to cross the mud but two of the tree falls had to be cleared using pulleys, winches and good ol' Orochi Team bilingual cursing.

Williams itself had the typical look of a wasteland abandoned town, except that it wasn't truly abandoned, just fortified. The central colony was fenced off and Sadao, Shiratori and Tagata alike, had to suffer armed boarding and a search by redneck militia. The three men didn't haul any illegal contraband, but their weapons – the longer and sharper ones – and Mouse's newly acquired rifle, were seized for the duration of their stay. Shiratori's metal arms were once again held under suspicion, but this time left in place when the General made a big fuss about the possibility of bleeding out if the appendages were forcibly removed. Shiratori, Mouse learned, was one hell of an actor.

Thanks to a good deal of good ol' boy negotiating on Mouse's part, the three trailers were allowed to enter town. About four miles square in size, the condensed population of Williams, however remote, was dense enough to warrant a main street with general stores and services. Sadao pulled into a gas station to refuel while Mouse did his best to talk up the locals and find out of Joe still ran his junk outfit.

"Yeah, ol' Joe. He's still kickin'," the station attendant said. "He's out by Buffalo Crick. You take the road to the left up here at the feed store, and head for the tallest pines you can find, you'll see his place."

Mouse thanked him and rolled up his map while the attendant rang up his ham sandwiches and soda from the cooler. "Thanks for the directions. This guy coming in now will pay for this," he said with a smile at Sadao who had just entered.

"What am I paying for?"

"My lunch. I'll puke if I have to eat another cup of ramen." Mouse grabbed his bag of American gas station cuisine and headed back out to the trailer to chow while Shiratori and Tagata refueled. *Mmmm, thin sliced processed ham – just like home.*

Soon they were back on the road, turning left and heading into the trees. Here the road lost its pavement and became a narrow gravel drive, making it risky for the trucks to go in any further. They parked just off the road in the woods and continued the rest of the way on bikes.

Another mile or so up, they encountered another fence. This one was much higher and patrolled by a pack of nasty dogs that looked to be the same unfortunate breed of mutt Barney had reared. It seemed these men traded more than just car parts. Beyond the fence was a random selection of mobile homes and aluminum garages, filled with cars and motorbikes – some more assembled than others – heading far back into the trees.

Mouse and the rest of the men dismounted and walked up to the gate of snarling, frothing, barking beasts. Over the chained entrance was a huge cowbell with a sign: Ring for Service.

"Now what?" Sadao asked, looking around.

"I guess it's obvious," Mouse said, and swung the rope to ring the bell.

Dong! Dong! Dong!

A trailer door could be heard opening followed by a shout. Mouse turned to Sadao, smugly. "See, when there's a bell, you *ring* it."

"I guess so," Sadao said, looking over Mouse's shoulder and drawing a knife from somewhere underneath his riding jacket. "Especially when you want to summon an Indian chief with a shotgun."

Mouse whirled around. A grey-haired Native American in eagle-feathered braids and beaded buckskins was approaching with both barrels open.

"Get off my property before I blast holes in you!"

"Whoa!" Mouse shouted, holding up his hands in surrender. "Joe?! Don't shoot! Barney sent us!"

The Chief lowered his gun a little and squinted, shushing his dogs.

"Who sent you?"

"Barney, of Barney's Trash and Treasure. In Blythe? I'm Mouse. Mouse, remember? I placed a lot of orders from here over the past decade. Japanese motorbike parts?"

The Chief lowered his barrels and called his dogs back as he stepped closer. "Mouse. Yes, I do know you. Only very old friends call me Joe. Here, I am called Chief Laughing Elk."

"Chief, my uh... " *Friends? Kidnappers?* "... *associates* and I need your help with obtaining an auto for an upcoming race. Barney often told me about your private collection."

Laughing Elk looked over Mouse at the men behind him, all brandishing various knives. "Mouse, why are you traveling with thieves?"

Mouse looked over his shoulder. "Put your knives away, you dumb fucks. I'm working the problem, okay?" Tagata and Shiratori grumbled in Japanese and slowly lowered their blades but didn't put them entirely away.

"Chief," Sadao said, tucking his knife back in his jacket. "I am Sadao Koga, racing team boss for the Northwest Division. We are not here to raid you. We have come with cash and are willing to bargain."

Chief looked unconvinced but did drop his gun to his side, just to the right of his moccasined feet. "Mouse, tell me, why is that man dressed like a samurai?"

Mouse looked the 'Chief' up and down.

"Oh... that's a long story."

After some more talk and promises from Mouse that the knives would stay hidden, the dogs were chained and the four of them were allowed in.

Unlike Barney, Laughing Elk had some organization to his particular brand of junk. The carports and sheds in his auto section were filled with various makes and models collected by year. Some of them went as far back as the mid-20th century.

"I'd like something late 20th century. Lighter but still ass-kicking, you know?" Mouse explained.

The Chief nodded and shouted to someone in a workshed. The boy who emerged looked half Indian but wore more reasonable clothes. His eyes lit up when he saw the men Mouse was with.

"Orochis... " he whispered in amazement. Clearly a racing fan.

"My grandson, Sam," explained Laughing Elk. "He'll know what you need."

"We're outfitting an overland endurance race," Mouse explained. "I need a hot, tough American car. Something with balls that can tear up the offload, but accelerate like a bitch on grades."

Sam thought it over and looked to his grandfather. "The Obsidian?"

Laughing Elk frowned. "Not for sale."

"Come on, Pop, it's just gonna rust! These guys are pros! They need good wheels."

"Laughing Elk needs good wheels too."

"Pop, you haven't uncovered that car in ten years. She needs to be driven or her spirit will die!"

Laughing Elk sighed. "Okay, show them the car. Save a spirit; break my heart. She won't go cheap!"

"She" was tucked away lovingly in a locking shed with a sturdy leak-proof roof. Sam ran and got the keys and let the six of them in. He and his grandpop untied her wraps and threw back the coverings, exposing her hidden beauty. Mouse whistled. The perfectly kept 1968 rebuilt Mustang Obsidian was black as well ... *obsidian*, with bright silver chrome all polished to a mirror finish. The Orochi men filed in and took a walk around, speaking in hushed Japanese.

Sam beamed proudly – clearly he had been taking very good care of her for some years now. "She's got a rebuilt V8 800 horsepower racing engine," he said, popping the hood. "Probably put in around 60 years ago. Computerized fuel injection, stereo woofers, the works."

Mouse helped himself to a flashlight and beamed it into the inner bowels of the machine. Belts, hoses, intakes, and filters all looked to be in pretty good shape. Amazing for the car's age. Sure there were some signs of cracking and hardening, but no rust – whoever had owned her had loved her a great deal.

"How did you acquire her?" Sadao asked.

Laughing Elk scratched his head. "Mmm, estate sale, I reckon. Had her a long time like Sam said."

Mouse moved from the engine to the driver's side and tried the handle. The door came open with a creak. "Wasn't a real racer," he noted. "Doors aren't welded." He slipped in and shone the light around the interior, knocking on the roof for a feel of what was underneath. "She has what feels like a four-point roll bar, but I doubt her former owner ever took her over 75 mph."

"Collector car," Shiratori said in agreement. "Man with money. No racetrack. Does engine start?" he asked Sam.

The kid tossed Mouse the keys and ran to get a battery and some gas.

"How much?" Sadao asked, trepidatiously.

Laughing Elk thought hard for several moments, worrying his beaded tassels. "Won't let her go for under 300K, cash money."

Sadao blew out a lot of air. Shiratori snapped at him in Japanese and the two argued until Sam returned.

"First, engine must start," Shiratori said pointedly. "Won't buy empty shell for emperor ransom."

Sam hooked the battery up and poured in the fuel. He locked the gas cap and gave Mouse the thumbs up. Mouse stuck the key in and turned, the ignition lights came on, good sign. No need to pump this one, he cranked the starter and the old girl rumbled to life. Wow! He let her idle a while, listening to the purr of pure 20th century piston combustion vibrating under his ass. Shiratori cocked his head over the engine, signaling Mouse to give her more gas. He did and she roared in response. The car really did have spirit like the kid said.

Shiratori smiled as Mouse shut off the engine and climbed out the window for flair. Both of them approached Sadao in unison: "Pay him," they said.

In the end, Sadao got the price down to $280K and the promise to pay Sam a few hundred to replace his bear-man busted trailer window. Mouse rode with the kid in his truck back to the trailer for measurements and into town to get some glass custom cut to fit. Sam was full of excited questions. He wanted to know what it was like working for a real racing team. Traveling all over the deserts and backroads – getting in gunfights with mountain men that broke windows, etc.. Mouse had to admit, his new life beat the hell out of languishing in a bone-dry gas station. He was becoming a celebrity of sorts – even without the Chairman's interference.

After visiting the glass smith, he and Sam stopped in a bar and grill to get some cold drinks. They sat at a table under the fans, sipping root beer and talking about the day-to-day life of a racing team mechanic.

"You gotta get up at the ass crack every morning. That part sucks. If I don't, Shiratori bangs on my window and screams at me in Japanese."

"How'd you wind up with the Orochis? They're a badass team."

Mouse shrugged. "Destiny I guess. They just came upon me and took me with them."

"You must make good money, huh? I hear racing team mechanics get sweet pay-outs."

Mouse snorted into his straw. "Yeah, right. Haven't seen a dime of it yet, but I think –" Mouse stopped mid sentence. Behind Sam was a big TV panel mounted over the bar, plastering his face as part of the upcoming Utah Overland All-Division Challenge.

Sam tracked his eyes. "Whoa! Hey, that's you!"

Mouse shaded his eyes with his hands. "Fuck."

"What? Aren't you excited? There hasn't been an Overland Race in eight years."

"I know, but I never asked to be the spokesman for it. I turned the Chairman down – our boss' boss – but Sadao, he wants me to do it so we'll have access to helicopters."

"You mean you get to fly too!?"

Mouse wondered if he could use a body double for some of the stunts he was about to be asked to perform if this kid was so excited. "I don't want to!"

"Why not? I'd kill to get to fly someday."

Mouse let the mention of helicopters blow over as he watched the ten minute Overland preview ad. It promised "unprecedented coverage" with examples of action shots collected during the Dry Lakes Motocross. He admitted the action shots, especially the ones taken during the downpour, were exceptionally clear and exciting – blood and mud splashing the lens with each flip-out.

The waitress came to collect their bill and eyed Mouse strangely. Even a few second's glance on the TV was enough for people to start doing double takes at him. Mouse handed her a $5 from the cash Sadao had given him for the glass and got up to leave.

"You got a general store around here?" he asked Sam. "I want to pick up groceries before we head back to the trailer."

Mouse was eating a grilled cheese sandwich with zeal when Sadao returned from the junkyard. Sam had dropped Mouse off before heading back up the road to his workshop to fit the glass with window foam and brackets. The car sale papers would be approved by late afternoon, and The Obsidian driven out and loaded up in Sadao's equipment trailer before dusk so they could get an early start in the morning.

Sadao sniffed the kitchen suspiciously.

"What did you cook?"

"This? Ancient whiteman recipe. Cheddar. Bread. Heat. Eat."

Sadao looked at him funny and opened his fridge. It was full.

"That stuff I put in there," Mouse said. "It's called food."

Sadao grunted. "So it is. Make me one of those."

Mouse grinned as he ate. "Let me finish this one and I'll make us two. If I knew I could wean you off corpse balls sooner, I would have insisted we stop at a convenience store weeks ago."

Sadao came over to the table and tossed a fat brown package in front of Mouse.

"Reimbursement for your trouble," he said, picking up the other half of Mouse's sandwich and taking a bite.

"Hey! That was mine! What is this?"

"Open it," Sadao said, chewing.

Mouse tore the tape off the front of the package and inside was the thickest wad of Benjamins he'd ever seen. "Fuck me! What is all this?"

"Your salary," Sadao said, picking a cheese string out of his beard and flicking it aside. "Thirty-four thousand even. I rounded up."

Mouse was aghast. "I won something?"

"Not exactly, but those who did have asked me to give you their thanks – 10 percent of the total team winnings. Tagata, however, elected to give you 15."

Mouse fanned the $100s out on the table like playing cards. All the bills were crisp and new. Sniff. *Yep, new money smell. Incredible.* "I've never seen this much cash all at once before. Certainly not any of my cash. What do I do with it?"

Sadao smiled, finishing his last bite. "Whatever you like. Spend it. Save it. Bury it in the ground. It's yours."

"I guess I could buy a wallet," Mouse said, thoughtfully. "I never needed one before. Do they make them this big?"

Sadao laughed. "You are adorable. You can keep it in my gun safe for now if you like. I'll give you the combination."

Mouse looked at his haul. "I guess I could use some pants. Ones that actually fit me. And some shoes. I don't really like boots."

"You can find a decent number of shops in Salt Lake. I'll take you after we settle camp. You might find one or two things you could use."

Mouse shrugged. "I don't know what else. I have food, shelter, spark plugs, welding torch, radio, bed… and sex," he said with a smile.

Sadao returned it. "I may start charging you for that."

Mouse picked up a fistful of bills and waved it at him suggestively.

"But… actually, I'd like to send a chunk of it back to Blythe."

Sadao nodded. "You can wire it from the city."

Mouse fanned himself with the stiff wad of bills, thinking. "How much does a trailer go for?"

Sadao looked concerned. "Why? Not happy with our arrangement?"

"I didn't say it was for me. Been thinking about your kids in the horse trailer. They could do a little better, I think. At least get a locking rear door – they're always popping out of that thing."

Sadao looked pleased. "You'll need to save. Motorcoaches go for around a quarter million."

"Hm, I'll need to squirrel this, then. You can buy groceries from now on."

"Sure, but before I give you my safe combo, you owe me a whiteman sandwich."

Mouse hopped up and planted a smooch on Sadao's cheek as he made for the stove and set the pan on. "Coming right up!"

Sadao eased up behind him as he dropped four slices of bread in the pan with a quarter stick of butter. The man wrapped his arms around Mouse's waist and began kissing his neck.

"Hey! Ahh… that's not fair. Cooking takes focus," he laughed, slicing off big manly slabs of orange heaven. Local made, too.

Sadao didn't listen and tipped Mouse's chin back for a good full kiss. Mouse moaned into his mouth. It'd been nearly eight hours since they had last fucked and the way their bodies were responding to each other, they weren't going to make it much longer. The pan began to hiss. If they kept this up the cheese was certain to go up in flames.

"You're gonna, mmngh… make me wreck this… mmm… " Sadao had many talents but kissing was one of his finest. The way he held his face, curled his fingers in Mouse's impossible hair – tongue and lips warm and voluptuous, parting and merging with his own without being sloppy. Mouse swore he could subsist on Sadao kisses alone.

"Your butter is smoking," Sadao murmured, freeing Mouse's face long enough for the cook to reach out a frantic hand to turn down the heat. Mouse grabbed a spatula and flipped the bread, dropping the cheese on them.

"That was close... oh!" Sadao took Mouse by the hips and began to grind his bulge into his backside. Mouse tipped his head back against his chest and sighed.

"Still hungry?" Sadao asked, kissing his cheek softly, while his nob nudged not nearly so softly at his ass.

"Fucking starving... but... I wanna... *goddamn!*" Sadao bit him in the throat and shoved a determined palm straight down into the front of his jeans, rubbing him hard. Mouse took the last shred of logical thought he had left in his head and pushed the pan off the burner. He whipped around and threw his arms around his attacker, leaping up to wrap his legs around his waist. Sadao took two steps back and threw him onto the table, sending money flying.

They kissed like madmen – tongues and teeth. Sadao ripped open Mouse's pants and tore them clean off in one sweeping move. He took Mouse's cock firm in hand while he undid his own fly one-handed and jerked his jeans down revealing one helluva hard-on. He squeezed Mouse's oozing rod, swirling the slipperiness all over his fingers. Mouse whimpered and hitched his ass up and his thighs back as far as he could fold himself, begging for a heaping serving of rigid flesh.

Sadao might be pushing forty but he could certainly work up a full load on the spot. Sadao lubed up his dick where it jutted straight out from a thatch of soft straight hair. The tip was flushed a deep rosy brown over the lustre of the pearls. Shit, it looked so good.

Mouse didn't have another second to admire it as Sadao came down over him and let the phallus of holyfuckyeah wedge its way in. Mouse threw his head back and cried out in excitement. Money caught and curled in his hair where it fanned out across the table. His ass opened easier than before – it was getting trained to Sadao's girth. It didn't take much work to bottom him out now. Sadao pulled back slow all the way, and pushed in again. Mouse groaned encouragements.

Sadao wanted it and didn't wait long to drive into him hard, pushing the air out of his lungs with each thrust. Money stuck to his ass and arms, sliding around the table as Mouse tried to find a grip.

"I... really... ugh... think we need to... ahh... talk about our feelings," he gasped.

Sadao smiled lecherously, "I think I feel like making you scream right now."

"Those are... ahh... good feelings... oh, yeah... more!"

Sadao gave him more, fucked him good and solid until Mouse's happy little moans degraded into grunts of cold hard need. He wanted to come, like now.

Sadao pulled out and yanked Mouse to his feet, flipped him and pushed him back down over the table with his face pressed to the tabletop. He smeared Mouse's nose in the cash as he reinserted himself and resumed pile driving the living stuffing outta him.

Mouse cried out and blew money off his lips. By the way he was getting rammed, this must have been on Sadao's bucket list for some time: "Fuck mechanic raw over giant pile of winnings."

"Don't make me come on my money!" Mouse protested, trying to push the cash away and off the table. Sadao didn't like this and grabbed his hands, pinning them behind his back with one fearsome grip while he grabbed Mouse's dick with the other.

"You'll come when and where I say," he growled, stroking the hell out of him.

Mouse couldn't help himself, this macho shit turned him on. His dick went rock solid in Sadao's palm. Question wasn't whether or not he was going to come, but how much.

"Ahhhh fuck! Don't… please… *shiiiiiit!!*"

Sadao stood him up and pumped his cock and ass mercilessly, groaning with success as Mouse screamed and unloaded white spurts of jizz all over the nation's founding fathers.

Sadao pulled out and shot between his legs – not quite making the tabletop, but making a point to try.

Mouse gripped the edge of the table, panting and gasping as the wasted sperm melted into the crisp new bills. "It's my first paycheck, you asshole!"

Sadao laughed and smacked his ass. "Consider it a blessing. For good luck!"

Mouse turned to look at him, zipping up all casually like he'd just delivered the mail.

"What the fuck is it with you Japanese and your magical good luck spunk! I'm going to be passing sticky bills for the next two years!"

Sadao leaned in and kissed his forehead. "So cute when you're pissed. Clear the table, let's eat now."

Mouse was cleaning up the dishes and Sadao was seated at the table dipping $100 bills into a tub of warm soapy water and patting them dry with a dishtowel when Shiratori and Tagata let themselves in for a planned team strategy meeting.

Shiratori strode in purposefully with rolls of maps tucked under his arm. He stopped, staring at Sadao and his money dipping. "*Nani wo shiteru n da?*"

Sadao held up a finger. "You never saw this. Not another word."

Tagata snickered and took a seat. "*Okusama wa tegowai desu ne?*"

Shiratori drew his eyes to Mouse, who stood at the sink wiping his hands dry. "*Okusama wa totemo tegowai. Boss-sama, taihen deshou...* "

Sadao smacked the table top making the water dribble. "*Omae! Urusai!* English only from now on. Mouse must know what we are saying!"

Mouse tossed the rag in the sink and came over to the table. "Yeah, Mouse does need to know! What the fuck does *Okusama* mean? They keep calling me that," he asked Sadao.

Sadao didn't answer, just moved himself and his bowl of shame over to make more room.

"I can look it up, you know! I know where you keep your Japanese/English diction-ary."

Sadao rolled his eyes between Mouse and his overly amused men. "It means 'house-wife,'" he sighed, dumping another wad of stuck bills into the soap bowl.

Mouse turned up his nose at the insult and scooted in next to Sadao, giving his arm a squeeze. "Damn straight, I'm the housewife! Respect!"

"Fine. If housewife need respect and very clean money, Boss-sama can be his happy bitch!" Shiratori proclaimed, arranging his maps. He selected one and unrolled it, done with the affair. "This map very large, not many detail but will show whole race checkpoint and change station here in red and blue."

Mouse, Tagata and Sadao all observed the various stations and trails marked out in different colors.

"Race go three days — four men, four vehicles. No stop. No rest. Four time at change station Orochi team get new driver and new vehicle. Each driver must hit three checkpoint before he finish at next change station. Mechanic must be at all change station," he said looking at Mouse.

Staring at the map it now made sense why Sadao was so worried about air support. The Overland would cover 2/3 of the state of Utah, starting and ending at the Salt Flats and coursing through sand dunes, canyons, wetlands, mountains and highways. They needed him in four places nearly at once, each a hundred miles apart.

"Race start here," Shiratori indicated a place called Saltair, a small wetland jut at the edge of the wide salt flatlands. "Racer one will cross salt desert and go south over hills and down through wetland mud and rocks. Must be fast and much skill with offroad. Must be bike and driver must be Tagata-san."

Tagata nodded agreement.

"I agree," Sadao said. "Next is canyon, right?"

"Yes. Canyon narrow and slow. Some rock, some water and log. Must have strong four wheels, good for climbing. ATV is best and best driver for ATV is Murasaki-san."

The men also agreed to this.

Sadao turned the map closer to himself. "We're in the sand dunes for the third leg, so that will require sand buggy, naturally," he looked to Tagata. "We haven't raced sand in a long time, who do you think?"

"I think... Sato is best for sand," he said.

Shiratori shook his ponytail. "Not enough experience. Racer must be good with navigation. Make good decision quickly. Sato-san will be lost."

Sadao looked at Tagata. "Taga. What do you think of his navigation skills?"

"I think navigation, okay."

Shiratori rattled his armor in disagreement.

"Well," Sadao said, acknowledging his General's dissatisfaction. "Who then?"

"I think Kinjo-san is best," Shiratori said with conviction. "Good with sand, good with map and compass."

Sadao sat back and drummed his fingers on the tabletop. "Kinjo is a problem," he said flatly. Tagata was in silent agreement.

"Who's Kinjo? Have I met him?" Mouse didn't recall hearing the name before, but then he'd only worked closely with the bike racers thus far.

Shiratori smiled and looked to Sadao. "You were not introduced?"

Sadao shot Shiratori a disapproving look before he turned to Mouse. "You've met him twice, I'm afraid."

"Wait, this isn't the fuckhead with the knife is it? 'Cause I ain't working with that piece of shit!"

"No piece shit," Shiratori said. "Good sand racer."

"Yeah, and he's also good with sticking a knife in my balls!"

"Like I said," Sadao repeated for Shiratori's benefit. "Kinjo is a problem. I want Tagata to work with Sato, get him better trained in navigation. Kinjo, can be an alternate."

Mouse was pissed. Even more pissed that the guy hadn't been thrown out of camp on his ass.

Sadao tapped the map to move the conversation forward. "We end with auto I see. Not what I wanted but necessary due to the landscape."

"Yes, auto must finish race," Shiratori agreed. "Checkpoint is at top of Wasatch peak. Very steep. Can use highway to get to all checkpoint and back to salt flat for finish."

Sadao and Tagata nodded agreement. "We just need to find our driver," Sadao said.

Beep, beep, beep, beeeeeeep!!

The satellite phone lit up on the charger base at the end of the table by the window. Sadao reached for it and motioned everyone to clear out of his trailer. The Big Boss was on the phone. Mouse left the trailer with the other two men reluctantly. Since Sadao had to take the call in English, Mouse wasn't allowed to stick around.

Still, he hung close enough to the door and far enough away from Tagata and Shiratori's conversation to overhear a few words.

"He's agreed… Tomorrow afternoon no good… Delivery delay… Pick up point … bright angel…"

It didn't make a lot of sense but he didn't have long to wait, the call was soon over and Sadao came out of the trailer with his riding gloves, goggles and headgear for Mouse.

"We need to go," he said, tossing the helmet to Mouse. "I need to entrust the Obsidian delivery to you both," he said to Tagata and Shiratori as he led Mouse back toward his equipment trailer.

"Where are we going?" Mouse asked, excited.

Sadao smiled and lowered his goggles, mounting the cruiser that was parked at the rear. "Get on. It's a surprise."

Chapter XV

Webspinner

By the angle of the sun, Mouse guessed they'd been riding north for over an hour. They'd wound their way out of the forests and back out to the plains. Here the land was populated with cactus and blue-grey brush against a backdrop of multi layered mesas in rich red browns, dusted with beige sand. The land here was different from the desert he'd called home for so many years. The elevation was much higher and the colors of the sky and earth were more varied.

Mouse rode snuggled up against Sadao's back, holding him the way he'd held him before when they shared the KLR. Except this time he could feel him up all he wanted and not worry about the welcoming response from his groin. Sadao hadn't said where they were heading, but they'd left the main highway many miles back and were following a faint dirt track. It looked regularly used, but not by many. Flash flooding had washed out many sections but new wheels had run over them in twos and fours.

Soon Mouse began to see small shacks and huts dotting the distant vistas, followed by a truck or two moving in dusty plumes through the low brush and rocks. He lifted his head from Sadao's shoulder and tapped it, pointing out their growing company.

"Navajo!" Sadao shouted over the wind. "They reclaimed most of this land after the population moved north."

So Laughing Elk was no joke as Mouse had wrongly assumed. He didn't realize there were still Natives living out in the far reaches of Arizona.

"Are they dangerous?" he wanted to know. Their more damage-inducing weapons were still property of the Williams Militia. They'd left in such a rush they'd not had a chance to reclaim their guns and knives.

"Don't worry," Sadao said, squeezing his arm where it lay wrapped tight around his waist. "I have a way with people."

"I was afraid you'd say something like that!" Mouse shouted. "Why are we here?"

"There's something I want to show you. If I can find it."

"You mean you don't know where you're going?"

"It's hard to miss." Sadao pointed to his compass. North, dead on. Apparently that was supposed to answer all of his concerns.

In another mile or so the shacks and small pueblo homes increased and came closer to the road, which widened and became more distinct. Mouse could see people now, working in their meager gardens and heavily irrigated fields. What they could grow out here – besides cow dung and adobe – was anyone's guess.

Sadao slowed as they came to a low fence which was fencing off pretty much nothing. It was the thought that counted to denote a barrier. There was a sign: Now Entering Navajo Nation. Stop at Guard Station. They did so and an earth-faced man with long black hair stepped out of his lean-to with a shotgun to greet them.

"What is your business?" the man asked.

"We are requesting directions and access to the Bright Angel Trailhead."

"Trailhead is closed," the Navajo said grimly.

Sadao reached for his wallet and pulled out a wad of bills, flipping through it. "We are also interested in stopping at your trading post," he said, holding out a couple hundred.

The man took the bills and stashed them quickly in his vest. "Go in. You'll see a long low adobe building about two miles in. That is the trading post. Ask your directions there."

Sadao nodded and drove on in.

"Your way with people is with your wallet," Mouse commented.

Sadao smiled, "It worked with you."

"I was more interested in what was next to your wallet."

"Behave," Sadao warned. "We're not on U.S. soil anymore."

Mouse sighed happily and sat back into his seat.

The trading post was hard to miss. It had a big hand-painted sign posted over its rough hewn roof beams: Navajo Nation Trading Co. They parked the bike and walked in under the blow of rusty fans which sent the wind chimes for sale that hung from the ceiling beams tinkling in a raucous chorus.

An old Navajo woman wearing a hand-woven shawl sat behind the long counter. Her face was so wrinkled and aged by sun it was impossible to tell if she had eyes. Mouse had only ever seen people like her and Laughing Elk in movies. Sure Blythe had its share of Natives, but they were so interbred you couldn't tell them apart from anyone else. These people were the real deal.

Mouse gave her a nod and sauntered to the glass counters, peering in. Silver and turquoise etched jewelry and leather goods filled most of the display. But there were totems, straw bowls and weapons as well, all set in inlaid stones and jewels. He wondered who – besides himself and Sadao – ever came by this way to buy shit.

Sadao motioned to the old woman and pointed down at some silverwork designed for body piercings. He probably shopped here once a year for his men.

Mouse walked through the rows of coyote and rabbit pelts until he came to wall hangings and blankets. There was a heavy woolen blanket with a fascinating interwoven pattern spiraling out from the center and interconnected with silver threads. He pulled it out and held it up to see it more clearly.

"Webspinner."

"Eh?" Mouse whirled around. The ancient woman had spoken. "That blanket you hold. Webspinner. Spirit of great power and deception. Those who do not watch their step become trapped inside the web."

Sadao was having her wrap up his jewelry purchases when he took notice of what Mouse had in his hands.

"It's beautiful. We will buy the blanket, too."

Mouse lowered the blanket against his chest. It was surprisingly soft. "Thanks," he said and walked over to hand it to the old woman to add to their gift wrapping.

"Webspinner has kind face and words but always spins lies," she said without emotion. "Many eyes he sees with – some you can see, some you cannot see." Without visible eyes herself, it was hard to read any of her expressions. But her wrinkles did lift at the sight of Sadao's wallet. "Three hundred twenty-five," she said.

"Oh my god, Sadao, it's not that beautiful... " Mouse said, aghast.

Sadao waved him off. "It's time I bought you something nice," he said, laying the bills on the table.

Mouse didn't know what to say. No one he'd slept with had ever bought him anything other than a warm beer. The gesture, however casual to Sadao, made him perversely happy.

After emptying out half his wallet to the Navajo Nation, Sadao gained the information he sought from the old woman and a younger assistant of hers and got directions to the trail he was seeking. He was presented with a crude map and wire-cutters that he stowed in his bike bags along with Mouse's blanket, and soon they were driving out of the back end of town.

As the adobe homes disappeared, more trees reappeared and soon they were moving along through a sparse pine forest again. Not as thick as the one they'd left in Williams, but thick enough to make it hard to see what lay over the next rise. Sadao stopped the bike at a fence line, this one much higher and topped with barbed wire. It seemed to go on forever. No guard towers were to be seen, so he stowed his bike and went to his saddlebags to pull out the wire cutters and Mouse's three-hundred dollar Navajo blanket.

"Bring this," Sadao said as he held it out for him to carry. He then bent to clip out a hole in the fencing for them to slip through.

On the other side, Sadao took his hand and led him through the trees. Mouse blushed at the touch and felt ashamed to act like such a schoolgirl – but in many respects this was his first real romance. If you could call falling for one's kidnapper and clan overlord "romantic."

"Put the blanket over your eyes," the man in question said with a grin.

Mouse was entranced. "Why? Where are we going?"

Sadao pointed to his head. "Go ahead, put it on over your eyes."

Mouse shrugged and did so, reaching for Sadao's hand. "I can't see shit!"

"That's the idea," Sadao said, guiding him with an arm about his waist. "Don't worry, it's not much further."

Without his eyes, Mouse became aware of other things – the sounds of wind in the pines, birds calling overhead, the crunch of dried needles under their feet. And then the trees seemed to part and ahead, if his ears and sense of space were correct, the world abruptly ended.

Mouse's heart pounded. "What is it?" he breathed.

"Close your eyes, I'm taking the blanket off," Sadao said in his ear and the blanket dropped from his face. Sadao stood behind and wrapped his arms around him. "Hold on to me and open them."

At first glance Mouse thought he had been tricked. They weren't at the edge of a forest at all but in some kind of enormous theatre with painted walls a mile high. And very good lighting. But then the wind came and a hawk flew over their heads, diving down into the nothingness that stretched out below them for miles and miles to the edge of vision in every direction. Somehow here the unreal became real.

Mouse's eyes clouded and he blinked at them in the wind, clutching Sadao's arms.

"Do you know where you are?" Sadao asked, softly.

Mouse swallowed hard and nodded. "Yes, of course. But... why is it *here?*"

Sadao laughed softly and kissed his cheek. "I took a guess that you didn't realize how close we were."

"But... " Mouse didn't know why he felt the need to protest, but he did. The unreality of what his eyes were seeing was too much for his brain to accept. "They closed it fifty years ago... "

"It's hard for anyone, even the all-powerful American government, to close the entire Grand Canyon, don't you think?"

Across the vast space, layers of rock twisted and wound about in an endless labyrinth dotted here and there with tiny huts and a few wisps of smoke from campfires. Wild horses, small as ants, ran along the canyon floor.

"The Navajos... " Mouse breathed. "They've taken it back."

Sadao held Mouse to him, sharing his view on the wide ledge he'd lead them out to with a mile long drop into the chasm on either side of them. Far below, the thread-like blue of the Colorado River trickled at the very depths.

Mouse tore his eyes away from the impossible view to reward the man who had brought him here with a long sweet kiss at the exact place he had promised to follow him to – the end of the earth.

Mouse lifted his face to the sky and cried out as he climaxed, sending small animals scurrying for cover as his voice echoed far down over the lip of the canyon into the deep below. They'd moved back from the edge to assure safety during their throes of passion, yet kept close enough to still see all the way to the bottom.

Mouse moaned and grinded himself down on Sadao's cock – astride the man lying beneath him on the Navajo blanket, naked to the world. Sadao's eyes were on his alone as he held Mouse's ass in the sure grip of his hands, seeking his own relief in another kind of depth.

"*Ahh... mou ii!*" Sadao gasped, screwing his eyes shut and emptying into him in hot bursts of groaning ecstasy.

Mouse collapsed against Sadao's chest as he finished, breathing hard in the cool thin air. The sun was beginning to fall behind the west ridge of the canyon. In another hour they'd lose the view altogether.

Mouse closed his eyes and moaned happily into Sadao's neck, kissing him. He could feel the man's pulse pounding under his tongue as his spent cock grew soft in his ass.

"*Oi*, easy," Sadao said, tipping his chin up and kissing his mouth. Mouse could taste the salty sweat on his lower lip and licked it for more, lapping spit and sweat from all around his mouth and beard.

Sadao laughed and hugged him. "You kiss like a puppy."

"Mngh... not my fault, your skin tastes so good."

"*Itai!* Careful, it's sensitive tasty skin."

Mouse stretched his back and let Sadao slide out of him with a wet plop. Mouse plopped as well at Sadao's side, resting his chin on his chest to admire the view.

"Still looks fake," he said.

Sadao turned his head to look as well. "I wouldn't want to risk it by testing that theory with a jump. Before they closed it, visitors used to tumble off the edge every month of the year. The Devil's Cartwheel, it used to be called."

Mouse looked at him dubiously. "How do you know so much about this place?"

Sadao traced the length of Mouse's nose with his finger. "I read. Or at least I used to. Now I'm lucky if I get to sleep in my bed, let alone read in it."

Mouse pinched the man's nipple to make him wince in regret for that comment.

"Am I cramping your bachelor style? Your *Okusama?* What a ridiculous thing to call me."

Sadao nodded. "I'll ask them to stop. They're not used to it, you know. I don't normally take strays into my trailer for very long."

"You try to throw me out, I'll kick your ass!" Mouse laughed and play smacked him. Sadao caught his hand and kissed it, effectively derailing the squabble.

"Come here," he said and closed his eyes, inviting Mouse into another long delicious kiss that slowly eased into soft brushes of their lips. Mouse felt like he was going to float right off the edge into that cartwheel.

"You happy?" Sadao asked, touching his face with his fingertips. Mouse nodded, fighting back the surge of emotion that threatened to burst out of him.

"Insanely... " he said with effort and bent close for another kiss and another. What he couldn't say to Sadao in words he wanted to speak to him with his flesh. He gripped him and urged the man to roll over onto him, parting his legs under him to invite him in again. But Sadao stopped them mid-roll.

"Huh? Too soon?"

Sadao shook his head and smiled wistfully. "We can't again. We're out of time."

Mouse laughed, taking it for a joke. "Why? Do the Navajo turn the canyon off at sunset?"

Sadao stroked his hair. "No, but we have to say goodbye soon."

Mouse felt gravity return, hitting him right in the chest. He sat up. "What are you talking about?"

Sadao continued to stroke his arm. "*Gomen, Kozenumi.* I gave us as much time as I could. Your ride will be here soon to pick you up."

Mouse was utterly flummoxed. "What ride?! The only ride I'm getting on tonight is your dick!"

Sadao shook his head. "That call I took – the Chairman isn't happy I've been taking so long to bring you to him in Salt Lake. He can't wait any longer, he's sending a helicopter. He wants you to start filming first light tomorrow."

"He can film the back of my ass! I'm not going anywhere unless you're coming with me!"

Sadao sighed and sat up, reaching for his pants and belt. "I'm sorry," he said, shrugging them on, "I have to drive my rig out."

"Call him back and tell him to fuck off! We'll get there when we get there."

Sadao stood up and tossed Mouse his jeans. Mouse let them fall at his knees, staring up at Sadao in disbelief.

"I can't refuse him," Sadao said, pulling on his shirt. "He's the one person in all of this I cannot refuse! He alone has the power to throw me out. I can't put personal desires before the needs of my team."

"But... " Sure, Mouse knew this and wouldn't expect any less from Sadao but after today? "I don't want to leave you," he said pitifully, looking up at the man who had managed in a few short weeks to become just about everything in the world to him.

Sadao's eyes softened and he reached down, pulling Mouse to his feet and wrapping him in a hug. "I don't want to leave you, either. But understand, I have no choice. It's only for a few days."

Mouse clung to him and shut his eyes. "Okay," he said quietly.

Sadao relaxed against him. "Thank you," he said in relief.

Mouse lifted his head. "Wait, did you say he's sending a fucking *helicopter?!*"

In Mouse's mind, the perfect end to the perfect day they'd just shared involved a nighttime ride back through the forest. Then, followed by a soapy hot shower, some more grilled cheese sandwiches and a warm soft bed – curled up snug in each other's arms.

Instead, he was stuck in a fucking helicopter – a small one with nowhere to go sit alone to enjoy his fantasies in the privacy of his mind. He was strapped into the seat directly across from the Chairman who kept staring at him quizzically. "I had no idea you and Koga-san were so close," the Chairman said dumbly. It was obvious he was shocked by this revelation. Before stepping up into the craft, Mouse, in full view of Chairman and crew, had grabbed Sadao's vest and planted a big messy smooch on this mouth.

"We *were* close until you dragged me away," Mouse said and peered out the window, hugging the Navajo blanket to himself as the dark cracked outline of the canyon faded away with the lights of Sadao's bike into the night.

"Ah, cheer up," the Chairman said brightly at his misery. "We'll get you reunited with the Orochi Team in a day or two."

Mouse looked at him. "Have you ever wanted to be with someone so much that it made your spleen ache?"

"Uh, my spleen? No... "

"Then don't tell me how to feel right now," he said bitterly and stared dismally into the blackness that had been forced between them.

Forty minutes later they were landing at SLC. The International Airport was still in use, although only at a third of the capacity of its former years. A car awaited them on the tarmac, another expensive shiny black SUV, and soon they were speeding towards the lights of the city. Mouse, still sulky, huddled in his blanket and watched the buildings get bigger and closer. He'd never seen a proper city before. Unlike most of the desert states, Utah had maintained a decent population. The founding LDS Church fathers were unwilling to give up their sacred ground to a little global warming. In the distance behind the city skyscrapers ran the ragged black silhouette of the Wasatch Mountains. They seemed impossibly high compared to the wide flat basin the city was built upon, which long ago formed the basin of an enormous inland lake. Up in the peaks, Mouse could see the blinking lights of a huge radio tower hundreds of feet high.

The Chairman's driver delivered them to the entrance of the Grand America Hotel, a 30-floor European-style luxury hotel in the middle of downtown. A man in a red jacket with polished brass buttons opened Mouse's door in welcoming.

Mouse slid out of the car with his blanket wrapped around his shoulders and stared up at the glowing golden lights illuminating the structure.

"Sir, may I fetch you your bags?" the man asked.

Mouse blinked, "Huh?"

"Or your uh, blanket sir. May I... "

"Nobody's touching this fucking blanket, let's get that straight!" Mouse said, tightening his grip on the wool. The little man backed away in defeat. *That's right asshole, my boyfriend bought me this. Three-hundred dollars and we fucked on it, too!*

The Chairman came around from the opposite side of the car and gestured to the little man to look to the rear of the SUV for their bags where the driver was now opening the hatch.

"Shall we go in?" he asked brightly, still hoping to somehow change Mouse's mood with his ridiculously annoying upbeat manner.

"I guess," Mouse shrugged and lead the way in through the rotating doors.

The Chairman and the red suit guy went to the reception desk while Mouse explored the lobby, staring up at the crystal chandeliers hanging from the high arched ceiling. A bit dusty and grimy from his afternoon in the Navajo Nation – Mouse became gradually aware that the uptight guests were giving him horrified glances as his boots tracked dust prints across the Chinese rugs.

He smiled and nodded at them. *That's right, desert rat coming through. Deal.*

"Mouse? Mouse!"

Ugh, it was like having a father again. A sober one.

A couple of old ladies on a couch lifted their feet, thinking a rodent was running loose on the floor.

"What?" Mouse shouted.

The Chairman waved a code card at him. "I have our room!"

Room. *Not rooms? Oh, fuck. Gotta watch my ass tonight,* Mouse thought and reluctantly followed him into the elevator.

Their 'room' was more of a 'floor' – a Penthouse suite at the top of the hotel. To Mouse it looked like a small department store of overstuffed, overpriced furniture and fixtures. Mauve was the prevailing color. Yuck. Mouse realized he now thought fondly of the pink farmhouse – and being tied up by Sadao. *Mmm bondage...*

"Mouse?!"

Christ, he wasn't going to get two seconds of thought to himself. "What?!"

The Chairman blinked in surprise. "I'm sorry, I seem to be upsetting you. I don't mean to."

Mouse sighed. The last thing he wanted to do was to apologize to this creep. He was Sadao's boss after all. "No, I'm just hungry and there's nut butter oozing out of my ass. Can I take a shower?"

"I – guess so... I'll call room service for some dinner." The Chairman smiled uneasily and waved at the maids to clear out. "There's a jacuzzi tub off the master bedroom."

Mouse spun around, unsure what wing of the room was the master one.

"It's that way," the Chairman gestured. Mouse dropped his blanket on the couch, lifted off his T-shirt, toed off his boots and left them in the middle of the floor as he made for the correct doorway.

"Do you want anything in particular?" the Chairman asked as Mouse slid out of his jeans at the entry to the bathroom.

"Yeah, a beer and a cheeseburger! Make it two! I'm fucking starved," he called out and shut the door.

Mouse spent as long as he could in the solace of jets and bubbles before the smell of dinner became too much for his empty stomach to deny. Mouse pulled the drain and toweled off, tucking the long thick terry cloth around his waist.

He emerged to the Chairman waiting patiently for him at a set table by the giant windows looking down over the lights of the city. Mouse and his towel took the chair opposite and he lifted off the tray lids. Just as he requested, underneath were two fat burgers and thin cut fries with tubs of fry-sauce and plates gooey with cheese run-off. Mouse dove in with both hands and indulged in an enormous bite, dripping special sauce on his bare chest.

"You um – they have uh, robes in the closet," the Chairman said as Mouse wiped up the spill with his finger and licked it clean.

"What's the point?" Mouse asked. "It'll just get burger spooge on it. Hungry as a tick right now."

The Chairman sat a moment in stupor, staring at Mouse's bare skin, then shrugged and proceeded to dine on his halibut with proper utensils.

"So, how are you getting along with the rest of the team?" the Chairman asked after Mouse finished his first plate and was starting on the second.

"The rest? Okay, I guess. If their bikes work well they don't give a shit who tunes them."

"Have there been any... protests to your relationship with Koga-san?"

"No. Should there be? There's just this one punk who gives me shit but I haven't seen him around the garage lately."

"A punk? One of Koga-san's orphans?"

Mouse shook his head. "No. He's a racer. Kinjo-something. Fond of knives. They want to use him in the sand-leg. I'm not in favor of that. I told the team leaders I wouldn't work with him. But I guess it's still under debate."

"You make decisions for the team now?" the Chairman asked, with mild surprise.

Mouse dunked a heap of fries into the fry-sauce vat. "I give my opinion. I'm not really in any position to make demands. Bunking with Sadao doesn't give me any special privileges. They trust me because I got them to the Dry Lakes finish line."

The Chairman nodded in agreement and sipped his beer. He'd ordered one for himself as well as Mouse's two – which were already mostly gone. "I understand you are very resourceful. Koga-san told me you got them out of a tight spot with a hidden stash of gasoline?"

Now it was Mouse's turn to be surprised. "He told you about that?"

The Chairman nodded. "Oh yes, he tells me many things. I had heard a rumor the Orochi Team had a fuel advantage and I inquired for more details. I was very intrigued to learn you had led them to a government repository."

"Then, you don't care that we bent the rules?"

"Not particularly. Besides, it wasn't a rule break precisely – it was a... creative solution. All teams are responsible for providing their own men and equipment and fuel. I only demand adherence to the conditions and rules of the race itself. As long as those guidelines are followed, I'm satisfied."

Mouse shoved the wad of fries in his mouth and watched the Chairman nibble at his fish. It made him uneasy Sadao told this guy so much. Especially since he claimed he really didn't know him at all. To Mouse, despite his reasonably good looks and fine upbringing, the Chairman seemed a bit of a lost soul. Pathetic, in a way – like a nerd who wants to play ball with the cool kids but can't throw worth shit.

"Speaking of resources, I hear you've found a racing auto – a Mustang. Good choice – I have a small collection of vintage Mustangs back at my home garage in Seattle. What year?"

Mouse smiled. "She's a hot bitch. A '68. I'm glad we got her. She's gonna tear up the

Wasatch," he said with a nod to the window view. Outside, atop the black crags that marked the edge of the Rockies, the giant radio tower blinked proudly. "Hey, what the hell is that thing? The flashing thing?"

The Chairman leaned closer to the panes. "Oh, the broadcasting station? That's one of mine. I had them renovated for covering the Overland."

The pieces began to click in Mouse's mind. "Did you have one at the far end of Beggar's Canyon, too?"

The Chairman wiped his face. He looked uneasy for a moment. "Yes. I did. A test facility. We used it to command the cameras for the Dry Lakes Motocross. How did you know about that?"

"Saw it. Sadao and I both did. Looked like a huge operation."

The Chairman looked at his plate for a moment, then continued. "Well, we had a number of experiments to carry out during that race. We didn't want to make any mistakes with Overland coverage. We're going into 15 networks over most of the northern states and into Canada. It's very important we get the shots we need – with the right spokesperson," he said, nodding to Mouse.

"Huh, we'll see about that," Mouse said, finishing his last bite of burger and sip of beer. He tossed his napkin on the table and got up. He was so full he felt like he might pop. "I'm exhausted. Which is my bed?" he asked, looking around.

"Oh, you have the guest room which is –"

"Where's my blanket?" Mouse asked, rushing to the couch. He now noticed belatedly that it was cleared of both his clothes and his prize gift.

The Chairman got up and joined him, stopping Mouse from flipping all the cushions off onto the floor. "It's okay. I sent it off to be laundered."

Mouse whirled on him, towel flapping. "You what?!"

The Chairman held up his palms. "It's in very good care. I asked them to dry clean it even, extra special. I know it's handmade – it'll be back in the morning."

Mouse was furious, boss be damned. "I said, *nobody* touches my fucking blanket! I don't want it washed! I want it back, now!"

"But it was dusty... and smelled funny," the Chairman stammered in his defense.

Mouse rushed past him to head off in search of housekeeping in his towel. "It smelled like Sadao!" he said angrily, throwing open the door and stomping down the hall, leaving the Chairman standing stupidly in the middle of all that mauve.

Mouse sat in the hotel's salon chair in a cape staring at himself in the three angled mirror while the Chairman argued with the stylist over what the hell to do with his hair. The mass of wet dirty blond hair fell in its natural twisted mess from crown to shoulders and partway down his back. He supposed he could use a trim but he'd never had one before – wire cutters and an oily mirror did the job back home. He had no idea what he'd look like "styled."

"Well, I think you need to take care of the weight here in the back," the stylist said, tugging at his tresses. "If we trim it to the neck, then this on top here can come forward and give a very attractive flip."

"No, no, no. That won't do. You need to work with the length, just trim it a bit so it can flow... " The Chairman suggested with a sweep of his hands.

"I can't work with split ends! It must be cut at least four inches all around!"

"Hey! Hey! The hair owner is speaking here!" Mouse interrupted. "Nobody's cutting a damn thing. Just... I dunno, comb it or something. I'll be good to go."

The Chairman leaned in to speak quietly to Mouse like a small child. "You see, the tangles... they will need to be cut out and the back here is several different lengths."

Mouse looked at him with shallow patience. He was still pissed at the Chairman over last night's blanket laundering fiasco. He'd reclaimed his prize possession – after chasing maids down 30 floors – but when he got to the laundry room it was already pressed and folded, smelling of Woolite.

"Sadao likes it the way it is," he said through his teeth. "If my appearance doesn't suit the cameras, then pick another subject for your hometown storyline. I come the way I am."

The Chairman nodded slowly and stood up to face the stylist. "Just... comb it. I give up."

Twenty minutes and three combs and a bottle of detangler later, Mouse had shockingly straight hair – trimmed despite everyone's wishes to a more or less consistent length. Mouse hated it. His hair was crazy fine and without its filler of tangles it clung to his shoulders and face. Mouse thought his head had shrunk two sizes. *Fucking awful.*

Next, the Chairman subjected him to a tailoring shop near the salon. He was measured, poked and fussed about until a number of suit coats, designer t-shirts and jeans were selected by the man paying the tab for all this "civilizing" of the small town mechanic. The only thing Mouse appreciated were the shoes – nice leather heavy soled laced shoes he could wear in the garage, even if they were $200 a pair. Everything he was now dressed in was some luxury brand this or that he'd never heard of. The Chairman rattled off the names as if they were supposed to mean something to him.

From there, he was dragged into a jewelry shop where the Chairman had requested the jeweler prepare a number of watches and rings in sets for Mouse to choose from.

Mouse stared at the shimmering gold and jewels and shook his head. "It'd scare me to death to wear something that expensive. I work in oil all day, or didn't you know?"

The Chairman just smiled at him and lifted up a triple-dial golden Rolex and slipped it over Mouse's wrist, snapping it in place. Mouse felt like his hand just gained three pounds. He brought the watch up to his face and peered at it. "Are those… Wait, are these diamonds?"

"It looks good on you, don't you think?" the Chairman asked. "We'll take it; add it to my tab."

The jeweler nodded and proceeded to bag up the case.

"Wait… what?! You can't just buy me shit like that!"

The Chairman smiled. "It'll look good on camera."

"But… " Mouse looked in shock at the small fortune on his wrist as he was led out of the store by the man who had just spent $25K like it was chicken feed. "I… "

"You're welcome!" The Chairman said cheerily and guided him gently toward the main lobby.

Dressed, coiffed, Rolexed and looking nothing like himself, Mouse followed the Chairman out the front entrance to his waiting driver. Although overcast, the weather was exceptionally hot and the new clothes felt itchy next to his skin. They drove about five miles out onto the start of the salt flats where a small stage and lean-to had been constructed with a banner that read *2071 Overland All-Division Challenge*. Cameras and crew were waiting with lights, bikes and large breasted women in tight jumpsuits. Beyond, far off in the distance, Mouse could see the team camps assembling along with the first traveling caravans of fans – even though the race itself was still three weeks away.

Mouse sighed. *Let the circus begin*, he thought, and mounted the stage for his close-up.

The interviews went on for hours it felt. He talked about his childhood, his first motorbike, his father, adventures with the Orochis (the ones not likely to land half the team in jail, anyways) and lots of personal questions about himself, which seemed to be wholly unrelated to the art of racing maintenance. The interviewer was a perky blonde lady in a tight suit coat that kept popping open to expose her bra cup whenever she crossed or uncrossed her legs. Mouse knew it was for the benefit of the viewers – mostly men, but if they wanted to keep him from nodding off they could have aimed for someone a little more testosterone-fueled.

Eventually, the wind started to pick up and they had to move indoors to a nearby studio for a quick on-set lunch and the remainder of the shoot. Background character-building sound bites were what they were going for, the Chairman explained. But after hours of it, Mouse felt he'd exhausted every known fact about himself. And there weren't that many to begin with. Some he even made up, just to make peek-a-boo boob lady happy.

By early evening Mouse and the Chairman returned to the hotel to clean up for dinner. Mouse found his room filled with bags of clothing and shoes from the tailor and even some more jewelry boxes containing a ring and a matching chain. *Jesus, I don't even wear jewelry. This guy must wanna get laid bad.*

Mouse stripped out of his fancy suit coat and shoes and flopped down on the bed. He tossed the Rolex up on the nightstand and grabbed his neatly folded Navajo blanket. He curled up in it, trying in vain to find a trace of Sadao still clinging to the hand-woven patterns. Scenes from the Canyon's edge flashed through his mind and he wanted desperately to talk to Sadao. He should be rolling in by now, albeit at the opposite end of the salt desert.

Knock, knock, knock.

Shit, not a moment of peace.

"Go away!" Mouse shouted. "I'm tired and I have nothing more to say!"

"Would you have something to say to Koga-san? He's on the satellite phone asking for you."

The door was open in two seconds. Mouse grabbed the phone from the Chairman's hand, said a quick, "Thanks," and shut and locked the door.

Mouse jumped up onto the bed. "Hello?"

"How's our team star?" Sadao asked, his voice cracking slightly over the connection.

"Fine. Tired of this bullshit, actually. Where are you?"

"We're just settling in, about two miles west of Saltair. Good wide space out here. No one should give our camp any trouble."

"I wanna come home," Mouse whined. "Can you come pick me up?"

"Is the Chairman done with you? He mentioned something about a garage shoot. He wants to get you with the equipment. Demos or something."

"What? No, I'm done with interviewing. Done, tired and he keeps buying me shit. Expensive shit. I think he wants me to suck his dick or something."

Sadao laughed on the other end. "No doubt he likes you, but I don't think you're meant to pay him back. At least not that way."

Mouse cuddled the blanket to his chest. "I want to see you. Can't I come back for the night at least?"

Sadao paused. "It's not up to me. I'm sorry, the Chairman has asked if I can spare you another two days."

"Oh, fuck no! I told you, I'm done! Come get me or I'll hitch a ride!"

"No need to do that. I'll be out all night, settling camp. Shiratori wants to start scouting navigation points at first light. I wouldn't have time for you for a while anyway."

Mouse sulked even though he knew Sadao couldn't see his expression.

"Mouse... ?"

"... yeah?"

"I can hear you sulking. Cheer up. You'll be back soon. There's a Mustang here that misses you."

Mouse perked up. "She make the trip okay?"

"She's snug in my trailer, waiting for you."

Mouse smiled. "Okay. I'll see you, huh?"

"*Oyasumi, Konezumi.*"

"Goodnight... " the line went dead. Mouse turned off the phone and curled up in the blanket. Thoughts of Sadao filled his head and he soon fell asleep, too tired to answer the Chairman's knocks for dinner.

Mouse suffered through the next two days and the constant persistent presence of the Chairman as best he could. He man seemed utterly unfazed by his inability to make an impression on Mouse. There were more unnecessary trips to city department stores, more fancy dinners in candlelight, and more idle chat that bored Mouse to tears. After the third day's shoot was called short due to a violent thunderstorm, Mouse arrived back at the hotel room ready to walk home, lightning be damned.

"Mouse, have some sense," the Chairman begged. "I don't want you or my driver heading out across the flats in this weather. You must stay until it clears. It's unsafe."

"What's unsafe is keeping me here another night!" Mouse snapped. "I have a car to remodel and I'm already three days behind because of this bullshit! You've got your shots! I'll call my own driver if you won't call yours."

"Mouse, please don't be unreasonable," the Chairman said, following him about the room as Mouse picked through the bags of finery for the scant few items he actually wanted to keep: the shoes, t-shirts and jeans. Expensive, but unlike the Orochi's hand-me-downs, they fit. Mouse threw them all into a Coach bag and grabbed his blanket, making to leave.

The Chairman trotted helplessly behind him across the polished floors of the suite they'd shared for three days. "But Mouse, the rest of your things... I insist."

Mouse turned on him. "You think I want those *things?*" he asked.

The chairman blinked in shock. "I – I don't know. I understood Koga-san pays you rather well," he said in defense, as if that made him equal in Mouse's favor or something.

Mouse took a step to bring them close, right under the man's nose. "Let's get one thing crystal clear between us, huh? I don't suck Sadao's dick for tips. I suck his dick because opening his pants is like fucking Christmas, Easter and my goddamn birthday all wrapped up in one. I want that big beautiful hunk of meat all the way up in my ass every minute of every day and if I wasn't stuck here with you, that's *exactly* where my ass would be!"

The Chairman stood there stupidly as Mouse turned away and opened the door to leave. "Mouse, if I may add... "

Mouse bristled and paused.

"A day may come when you will be in need of one of my gifts," he said.

Something premonitory his voice made Mouse look back.

The chairman continued, "And I hope you will understand, that my offer is always good, but not always free."

It was late morning the following day when Mouse actually made it back to camp. The Chairman had been right, no one would drive a disgruntled spokesman out across the flats in a full electrical storm. Instead, he'd spent the night in the lobby on one of the fine couches under his blanket. Mouse left the hotel at first light on foot until he came to a car dealership where he traded the Rolex for a Jeep and drove his own ass back to the camps.

Mouse puttered around the Orochi camp until he spotted Sadao's trailer. He parked the Jeep nearby, took a moment to bundle his too smooth hair back with a rubber band he'd found in the glove compartment, and hopped out to surprise his lover. Sadao's front door was unlocked and he let himself in.

"Honey, I'm home!" Mouse called out, as he made straight for Sadao's bedroom.

"Ah, you're back," Sadao said, a bit surprised and rose from the carving bench where he'd been working to welcome him in a hug.

"You miss me?" Mouse asked, running his hands up and down the man's strong wide back.

Sadao kissed his cheek. "Of course." He pulled back to look him over a moment. "You do something to your hair?"

Mouse shook his head. "Not really," he said happily and tilted his head up for a smooch. Sadao's arms tightened around him and drew him in for a slow deep welcoming kiss. Mmmm Sadao scent – shampoo and smoky leather. Mouse's dick grew thick in his pants.

Sadao's beard brushed his chin enticingly and Mouse moved to run his lips over all that wonderful soft ticking hair. Sadao's beard smelled of fresh soap and... something else. Something it took Mouse a moment to place.

Mouse jerked back, pushing Sadao away in shock.

Sadao was confused. "What is it?"

Mouse wiped his lips and spit on the floor. "Your beard smells like cunt, you asshole!"

Sadao cupped his own chin and sniffed. "It does? Huh... "

Mouse pushed past him to the freshly made bed, tearing the cover back and lifting a pillow to his nose. The sheets were fresh but the faint scent of perfume lingered near the bed. Mouse turned and threw the pillow at Sadao in anger. It hit him in the face, mussing his hair.

"How dare you! The second I leave for a few nights you replace me with some slut?!"

Sadao brushed his bangs back from his face in quiet resignation. "Not exactly."

Mouse took two steps forward and hit him, right across the jaw. Sadao rebounded slowly with narrowed eyes and caught Mouse's wrist when he moved to try it again.

"Enough!" Sadao ordered. "This is not your concern."

"Like hell it's not! Who was it, huh?! That French bitch? Or someone new?!"

Sadao just stared sternly at him as if he were waiting for a child to finish a tantrum.

"Fucking answer me!"

Sadao's voice was even and calm. "You know who I am. What I do."

"Yeah, you're a pretentious piece of shit who thinks he can fuck whoever he wants! I'm not one of your whores!" Mouse tried to jerk his wrist free. "Let go of me!"

Sadao kept his grip on him. "Calm yourself, *Konezumi*."

"I'm not your stupid little mouse! Did you think you could eat some bitch's pussy in our bed and I wouldn't notice?!"

Sadao raised an eyebrow. "Our bed?"

Mouse stopped. His blood was seething but it slowed suddenly, thickened like Jello in his veins. "What do you mean by that?" he asked.

Sadao let him go. "Nothing," he said, leaving the room.

Mouse marched after him. Sadao was pushing papers around on his table, looking for cigarettes. He found one, stuck it in his mouth and grabbed his lighter out of his back pocket. Mouse stood frozen in fury while he lit it, hitching a leg up onto the table, facing him. "What do you want me to say?"

Mouse shook his head. "I can't believe you're going to stand there and blow smoke in my face, literally!"

Sadao took a drag and folded his arms. "You know I have responsibilities," he said as if that justified everything.

"Aaand... I'm supposed to what? Check some kind of schedule to find out what day you you're free to park your dick in me?"

Sadao held up a hand. "Don't be ridiculous. I've been scheduling my appointments around *you*."

Mouse's mouth dropped open. "Appointments as in plural – ? You've never stopped, have you? Is that how it's been? You fuck my ass raw and then go out trolling for more?"

Sadao's eyes glanced heavenward. "Of course not. I don't do this for my own pleasure. I have you for that."

Mouse looked down and swallowed painfully. He didn't want to hear anymore. Somehow he'd been foolish enough to believe that he'd been enough. That Sadao had just overnight broken every heart in four states just to be with him in this little trailer. Their love nest? What a sick fucking joke. It occurred to him he really didn't know this man at all. He'd painted him how he wanted to see him and nothing more.

Mouse pulled his key ring out of his pocket and unhooked the spare to the trailer. "Here," he said, throwing it at him but not meeting his eyes. It bounced off Sadao's thigh and hit the floor. "That should help with your scheduling," he said bitterly and headed out the door, leaving Sadao to reclaim his own space.

Chapter XVI

Betrayal

The long hot days continued, heating up the salt flats and creating a constant permeating smell of rotten pretzels. Thankfully, the nights were somewhat cooler but windless. Working late, Mouse had left the garage ramps engaged. Shiratori's guards were outside sitting on overturned buckets, playing poker under a swirling mass of kelp flies in the lamp light. Mouse could only hear them intermittently as he ran the steel saw. Daytime was too hot for welding gear, so he took a longer nap than usual, ate dinner for lunch and set up his lights – prepared to work until dawn. Lupe promised he'd join him after his babysitting shift, or see if he could get a night off to do something he was better trained for.

Under the welder's helmet with one leg in and out of the rear of the Mustang, Mouse only saw the sparks that flew from the rim of the saw. He had plugs in his ears to prevent his ear drums from shattering. The diamond-edged saw made a sound not unlike fingernails on pottery times 500. It was shit work but the backseat had to go and sawing through the supports was the only way to do it. Besides, the unholy sound assured no one would come in to bother him. Especially Sadao.

Mouse had been living in the garage truck now for five days and Sadao hadn't made an appearance once. Logically, Mouse knew he had a ton of shit to do all over the camp and beyond, scouting roadways and setting up maintenance stations. If they hadn't split up, things might not be that different. Still, it hurt. For five days everything had hurt. His head pounded and his gut felt like it had been turned inside out. The hard burn of anger had given way to the miserable ache of loneliness. The fireworks spinning off the saw blurred and he had to stop. He set the saw down on the backseat cushion and wiped at his eyes for the umpteenth time.

Fucking get over it! He's not the only man in the damn world!

Mouse didn't know who he was more pissed at – Sadao, or himself. If he wanted somebody this much, then he needed to save those feelings for somebody who actually had room for him in his life.

Face it, Mouse. You were a cute piece of tail. An amusement. He wasn't going to give up one shred of himself to you. Except his cock! Ha! There you go, don't even start thinking about his fucking cock again!

He couldn't help it, though. As sad and angry as he was, he knew he'd never had sex half that good before in his life. And likely never would again.

Isn't that why it tastes so sweet? The cucumber you can't have all to yourself? Cucumber? Fuck, I need therapy.

He lowered the helmet and was about to switch the saw back on when he heard somebody coming up the ramp. Hoping it was Lupe come to liven up his pity party, Mouse extracted himself from the car.

It was Sadao.

Mouse's heart did a backflip. He'd been out riding, it looked – most likely most of the day. His skin had darkened around the line of his absent goggles, giving him a slight raccoon look. His hair was windblown all to fuck and he walked with a gait that intimated he'd been straddling a hot piece of vibrating steel all day. *God*, he was sexy.

"Oh, it's you," Mouse said and lowered his helmet. Leaning back into the car, he gave the rear support leg hell. *Good, make him deaf. That'll help.*

He was aware of a banging somewhere between the decibels of the saw. He ignored it. It got louder. *Shit, he's gonna break something and you'll have to fix it.* Mouse shut off the saw and threw it onto the backseat, sending stuffing flying as its rotations ebbed. He lifted his helmet and yanked out his earpieces. "What?!"

Sadao was angry. *Surprise!* "I need to talk to you!" he shouted over what was likely the ringing in his own ears.

"Yeah, well I'm busy. Got a car to make over."

"I know that!"

"You don't need to shout at me."

Sadao wiggled a finger in his ear. "Can't fucking hear with you running that saw! It's 11pm, half the camp is complaining!"

Mouse tucked his helmet under his arm defiantly. "It's gotta get done somehow, doesn't it? I can't wear this shit midday. I'll fucking pass out and run the saw through my leg."

"Okay, okay!" Sadao said, trying to gather his wits. "Shiratori says you're making adjustments to the interior seating."

"Yeah, backseat's gotta go. If I don't move the driver's seat back at least two feet the balance is off. Car will spin right out on the turns. This was a collector's car not a pro racer's."

"I understand that, but if you're making over the whole damn chassis, we might as well just buy a different vehicle and start over."

"I don't want to start over. This is the car I picked."

"It isn't about preference, it's about time. If you insist on this one, I can handle an unbalanced car."

"Yeah, I'm sure you can, but your driver-" Mouse stopped himself.

Sadao raised his chin.

"You're not seriously thinking you're gonna race this thing yourself are you? You can't, can you?"

"Last I checked, I was a member of the Orochi Team in good standing."

"But... you're the Boss – you're retired for chrissakes!"

"I'm not dead. I can still drive a car."

"Have you told Shiratori this?"

"Shiratori suggested it. We can't train a man in time."

"Then, tell *him* to drive it! You... "

Sadao smiled a little. "Afraid I might crack up? Are you that uncertain of your skills? Shiratori can't race legally with mechanized prosthetics."

Mouse's chest was pounding with concern. What the hell was he doing? Was he suddenly terrified this guy who dumped his ass was gonna hit a tree?

He had to cover himself fast, with a layer of attitude. "The car will be sound. And we'll make it in time."

"Good. I'll rely on you." Sadao nodded and started to turn to leave. He stopped himself after a step, looking back. "Shiratori says you've been sleeping in the garage here."

"Yeah, so? It's got everything I need. Bed, sink, oil pans... "

Sadao looked up at the bunk on the second floor. "I don't like you in here alone."

"What makes you think I'm alone?" Mouse shot back.

Sadao looked at him, pensive. "It's dangerous. Garages are the first place other teams raid. I'll assign you to a better living space."

"I said I'm fine where I am. I grew up in a fucking garage, remember?"

Sadao's brow gathered. "You'll stay where I tell you to stay."

"Hm... as long as it's faaar away from you!"

Sadao's forced calm cracked and he kicked the closest object with a classic *kuso*!

"How the fuck am I supposed to talk to you?"

"I don't know! Why don't you tell me? Maybe you should have thought about that before you stuck your dick in me!"

Sadao's eyes flashed with anger. "I told you the moment I kissed you how things were going to be!"

Mouse rolled his eyes and laughed sickly. "Ohh! That's right! You, the high and mighty Boss-man doesn't pick favorites! What a joke!"

"I have responsibilities!"

"You have excuses!"

Sadao paced, pointing at himself. "I am the one who holds this team together! No one else!"

"And fucking rich whores is the key to your success?!" His anger was rolling off the chart and he just didn't care. "Brilliant plan!"

"Patronage plays an essential part in the financial stability of this team!"

"So you charge them by the hour? Or by service? Do they get to pick from a menu?!"

Sadao's face flushed in fury. "I do *not* tolerate this level of disrespect from my men!"

Mouse threw the helmet down and got right up in his face. "What are you going to do? Tie me up? Hit me? Spank me? You've tried all of that. Didn't work. You know why? I'm not your man. I never was. You didn't raise me from a pup. I don't idolize you. I see right through you. You can't stand that, can you?"

Smack! Sadao cracked him across the face. Not his hardest hit, though. Mouse had him.

"Go ahead, hit me! Knock me down! Maybe then you'll feel like a Boss!" He shoved Sadao in the chest and his wrists were caught in Sadao's grasp – but not with the force he had used before. He held Mouse a moment and released him.

"I said hit me! Hit me, goddamn you!" Mouse's hands turned into fists and he pounded on Sadao's chest, shoving him back a step and another, yelling, shoving and punching. "Hit me, you sonofabitch!" Sadao didn't react to him, just took the blows. His eyes lost their heat and softened into sorrow.

Mouse was losing steam, hitting a brick chest like Sadao's was not only exhausting but painful, he was only hurting himself. Sadao no longer made a grab to slow his hands, just held both palms out like he wanted to catch him. Mouse wasn't yelling anymore, he was crying – tears, snot, the whole nine yards – and he hated it.

His hands stilled on Sadao's chest and he pressed his forehead to them, sobbing. "I hate you. I hate you," he said over and over. Sadao's arms caught him as he slumped against him, shaking and crying, sucking in breaths. "I hate you so much... "

Sadao lowered his head and his arms circled around him gently, holding him. "I'm sorry," he said softly. His nose brushed his cheek. "I miss you and I want you to come home."

"I don't have a home," Mouse sniveled. "You burned it down."

Sadao took a deep breath and let it out. "I know. I've made nothing but mistakes since the day I met you." His palm moved in circles over his back while Mouse's sobs slowed and quieted.

Mouse snuffled. "Y-you missed me?"

Sadao smiled against his hair. "Yes. I woke up this morning to an ashtray full of butts and said, 'What the fuck am I doing?'"

Mouse wiped his nose on Sadao's shirt. "You shouldn't smoke in bed, dumbass."

Sadao tipped his chin up, brushing his tears away with his thumb. "Who said anything about the bed? I fell asleep with my face on the table. Haven't slept in the bed since you left. Haven't slept much at all."

Mouse felt new tears brimming in his eyes, sweet ones. "Me neither. That damn cot's hard as a rock."

Sadao smiled sadly and kissed Mouse's forehead. "Let's go to bed, *Konezumi*. It's late."

Mouse felt like his legs had melted out from under him. "Okay," he said, weakly.

The guards outside looked like they'd given up their game quite a while ago, standing beside the buckets dumbfounded as Mouse and Sadao emerged, arms about each other, to lock up the rear of the truck.

"Uh, everything okay, Boss?"

Sadao nodded, punching the buttons and scanning his eye. "Yes, why?"

"Uh... "

The truck shuddered and the ramps closed. Mouse kept his face hidden under his hair as he clung to Sadao's side as they walked away.

Back in the trailer, Sadao started the shower and got them both undressed and washed for bed. They touched and kissed softly as the soap bubbled between their bodies, but neither of them made a move to take it further. Sadao turned the sheets down and dried Mouse's hair as best as he could with the towel. Mouse nearly nodded off under the soft circular caresses. Sadao shut off the lights and the moon cast the room in a dull glow. He lay back with arms warm and open and Mouse went to him and nestled at his side, head against his shoulder. Sadao pulled the sheet over them, nose dropping to his hair, and in the span of a few breaths they were asleep.

They slept late. It would have been even later if Mouse hadn't woken to a brick of a hard-on – two of them. Half awake and eyes still closed, he shimmied down Sadao's sleeping body and latched onto his dick. He sucked it softly, licked the stiff flesh all over, root to head. Sadao didn't move even as he worried the pearls and sipped up the sweet pre-cum that pooled at the tip.

Mouse savored him until he'd worked up a good mouthful of spit then scooted lower under the sheet to nuzzle the soft puddle of balls lolling between Sadao's thighs. He sucked a nut up into his mouth and rolled it gently on his tongue, moistening it, letting drool drip over his chin and on to the bed.

Sadao moaned a little in his sleep – eyes jerking about under his lids. Was Sadao dreaming of this, dreaming of him? The notion made Mouse's cock jerk and ooze out a dollop of goop. He released the captive gonad and went in for the second. Despite his rugged appearance, Sadao's privates were remarkably smooth. Sadao's pubes grew straight and soft as silk in a neat patch under his belly – and nearly nowhere else. Mouse licked all around the root of Sadao's cock – running his nose all through the hairs, inhaling the wonderful masculine scent that concentrated there.

"You can lick my ass too, if you want," Sadao murmured, voice all hoarse from sleep. *Faker, he's awake.*

Mouse lifted the sheet away, exposing him fully. "Really? You don't mind?"

Sadao smiled under heavy lids. "I'm too sleepy to fuck. Have your way. I don't care."

Mouse's heart was pounding. Did he mean... ? Sadao turned his head back to the pillow, closed his eyes and *holy mother-of-god*, parted his legs. If Mouse thought he'd been aroused earlier... the appearance of Sadao's dark naked pucker made him woozy with lust. Since day-fucking-one Mouse had wanted to mount this man like a rutting stud, but... he didn't think... fuck, he couldn't think at all... *want... ass... now... shit, don't wait for instructions... go for it!*

"Aauugngh, mmngh, mmmhm," Mouse moaned shamelessly as he gobbled his way south. Sadao's asshole was a hot bare ring of muscle under his tongue. He licked it and flicked his tongue all around the rim before he pushed in deep for a real taste. Guuh... so hot inside and delicious. He tasted even better than he smelled.

Mouse's mouth ran with saliva that he gathered and plunged up deep inside Sadao, easing him open – wanting to eat more and more of him. He swore he'd go cannibal for this guy in a minute. He was so hungry for the man's ass he forgot to check on him.

Mouse lifted his head, panting, his vision all blurred with arousal. Sadao opened an eye. "You need me for something?" he murmured all sexy, lying there spread open like a lazy dog with his hair tousled over his eyes. Mouse's cock throbbed so hard he couldn't take it.

"Please, rollover for me? I want to see your ass – all of it."

Sadao yawned and flipped, tucking his pillow under his head. He sighed and re-laxed.

"Ohhh... " Mouse whimpered. Sadao looked so good – just like the morning he woke next to him all sauced out. Muscular thighs and ass – the broadness of his shoulders and the line of his spine were all displayed under the magnificence of the Orochi tattoo. There was no way to take this slow. Mouse straddled him, grabbed the man's beautiful, firm ass cheeks and slid his poor suffering dribbling penis right into the cleft between. "Ahhhh! Ahh!" He was humping and moaning like a 16-year-old experiencing his first lay. He knew how stupid this must look to Sadao but he couldn't help it – he wanted it bad. And after five days apart, he was miles beyond his limit of control.

"Go ahead," Sadao said, watching him with one heavy-lidded eye. "Enter me if you want. I won't tell."

Mouse paused. *Tell... ? What the fuck... who would he... ? Oh, he's being a smart ass.*

That's it, get pissed at him so you don't come in under 20 seconds like a noob.

Mouse trembled in anticipation. "Do you want me to get... something... ?"

Sadao opened an eye and lifted his backside a little higher for Mouse's benefit. "What? Like coffee? Stop stalling and fuck me. I told you, I'm tired. For once I'd like to not have to do all the work."

"But... uh... "

"I'm no virgin," he snapped. "And neither are you. I'm assuming you know what to do."

Mouse threw all doubt to the wind and went for it – all the way. His dick made a bulls eye, popped the ring and slid in to the root in a series of quick desperate nudges.

Sadao made a snarling sound but didn't protest when he hit bottom. Good thing too, because the snug hot pressure assaulting his cock was overriding all other thought. Oh, *Christ*, he felt good. Too good. The first trickle of orgasm shot up his spine and Mouse screwed his eyes shut and fought to keep control. *Not now, not now...*

"Just come if you need to," Sadao whispered against the pillow, eyes closed. "Don't need to be a hero around me. Take what you need."

"Sorry... " Mouse gasped and pulled back, groaning. He could see all of Sadao laid out beneath him – muscles, skin, snakes, pearls and balls – it was all too much. He filled his eyes with it and thrust his hips instinctively, wildly, setting himself loose in that wet tight muscle. The rim of Sadao's asshole was darker than the inner flesh and it changed color as it rolled in and out, in and out, squeezing his dick so good.

"God... oh god... oh god... aaaaaaaghhh!"

"Nnngh... !" Sadao grunted under him. He gritted his teeth and tightened up to massage Mouse's cock and increase his pleasure, if that were possible. Mouse shuddered hard and emptied into him, making the fit even more hot, wet and amazing. He worked himself around in it, panting and moaning in the euphoria of release.

"Yes, do that some more," Sadao said softly, pushing up and back against him. It was hard for Mouse to keep going – his softening penis was so sensitive from the extreme arousal he'd just experienced. Mouse bit his lip, focused and fought through it.

"Ah... feels good," Sadao said, flexing and releasing his ass muscles, squeezing and milking Mouse's cock as it squished around in its new favorite place. His eyes were open now, alert and on Mouse's face which was still somewhat shocked by the whole situation.

"Does it surprise you I enjoy it like this?"

Mouse shook his head, no. But he was lying. "I didn't think you'd let me... oh, not so much... I'm trying... "

Sadao relaxed his ass and let Mouse adjust. "Sorry, we'll go slower."

"How... " Mouse panted, trying to get his head straight "... do you manage to still be the boss on, ahh... the fucking bottom?!"

Sadao laughed and bucked him off. Mouse's half-hard dick popped out with a trail of sticky gloop as he fell over onto him. "What was that for?"

"Want to kiss you," Sadao said, turning over and with hands under his arms, slid Mouse up his chest for a kiss. Mouse melted into his lips. Oh, he'd missed kissing. Their tongues moved in chorus – swirling, sucking, licking. Sadao's kisses always seemed to trigger Mouse's deepest emotional response – tugging at a place hidden in the center of his chest. *Love is what they call it, you know. Passionate love.* And that called for more passionate fucking. He'd show Sadao how he felt with his dick.

Mouse lifted his head, denying Sadao's tongue anymore contact. Sadao opened his eyes, questioning.

"Spread 'em, Cowboy. Time you were ridden hard and put away wet," Mouse said, gaining courage. His cock was standing proud and ready for action over Sadao's abdomen.

Sadao grinned and did as he was told. For once.

Mouse took it slow this time. Entering Sadao gradually, really getting a feel for him and letting Sadao get a good taste of the full of him as well. Nose to nose they kissed, eyes closed, sharing breaths, while their bodies moved together in slow waves.

Mouse found if he rounded his back just so and thrust just the right way he could make Sadao gasp – sudden releases of desire that made his eyes close and mouth part. He didn't scream like a slut – but the fact he let Mouse see him like this – open and vulnerable beneath him was far more demonstrative than any sounds he could make. For once, Sadao said, he didn't want to do all the work.

He's giving you this. Something he doesn't let the others see.

Mouse forgot himself – all focus was on his lover and tuning his movements to Sadao's responses and indications of need. His cock, although hard and flushed with the thrill of sex, was a distant concern. He lay over Sadao, running his hands up and down his body, kissing his mouth between gasps and sucking softly at his neck. Sadao tossed his head, murmuring shards of Japanese. *Dammit*, he needed to learn this man's language and soon.

"You want me to stroke you?" Mouse whispered in his ear, trailing his fingers down Sadao's chest. He could feel how hard his cock had gotten – propped between their sweaty bodies. He worked it gently, just milking him a bit, watching his face crumble in pleasure. God, he could fuck him all day like this.

Sadao's hands were loose around Mouse's waist, just following his movements, not forcing them. Sadao took a moment to respond as his breath came quicker. "Close... " he said, swallowing. "Just... " He took Mouse's hand in his and led his palm lower from his dick to the tightness of his balls. He was fighting it, the urge to come for as long as he could. This fact made Mouse aware of how close he was himself. He wanted them to get off together, and fingered Sadao's balls, rubbing them rhythmically with the slowly increasing pace of his thrusts.

Sadao's breaths sped up and he began to groan on each upstroke, forcing himself to relax on the down. God, he was so beautiful. Narrow almond eyes, sealed shut in pleasure, lips parted and wet from kisses, brow furrowed in concentration. Mouse rubbed and rubbed his tight straining balls, sliding a thumb down to feel himself surging in and out of him over and over.

Mouse kissed Sadao's parted lips and whispered. "I'm inside you... right here... "

Sadao groaned, tensed and bucked up. His lax grip became iron again and he thrust his ass up hard onto Mouse's cock as cum shot in hot spurts between their chests, tagging Mouse's chin. The feel of the heat of him coming on his skin triggered his own powerful orgasm and Mouse moaned loud enough for the both of them, releasing for the second time deep into the body of the man he loved.

It was around 3am when the whine of the radio woke Mouse up with a start. He sat up, and for a few moments he was confused as to where he was. Around him were the familiar walls of the upper level of the garage. He relaxed and reached a hand out to shut off the radio which had decided after weeks of static to pick up a signal – a really annoying one. Mouse lay back down on the cot and shut his eyes. He knew he should really get up and go finish the welding before dawn, and the persistently hot as all fuck salt desert weather, took over his productivity.

His internal time clock was all screwed up. At Dry Lakes he'd fallen easily in step with the afternoon siesta schedule – dropping dead asleep as along as he was lying someplace cool from 2-4pm like clockwork. Here, in the middle of baked white crust salt lake bed hell, his skin itched with dryness and his body, although well hydrated, fought to keep even a drop of sweat on his skin. Elevation, salt and dry air all combined to make this the worst wasteland living experience he'd ever had.

To make things even more sucktastic, he was on the opposite schedule of his lover. Sadao woke promptly at dawn, kissed his forehead and slipped out to join Shiratori and Tagata for racing planning meetings and route scouting as well as organizing training runs and managing the ongoing affairs of the camp. Or camps, Mouse should say – many of the arriving teams had spread out their trucks and vans a little too close to the Orochi's for comfort. This being an all-divisions race (Northwestern, Canadian, Eastern, Midwest and Central) meant there were a lot more bodies inhabiting the same general area. Sadao could be heard barking over his CB in more languages than Mouse could recognize. Although he had to admit, Sadao sounded sexy as fuck in French.

Still, it meant they were miles apart most days and when Mouse got back from another all-nighter in the garage at 5am to crash, he was lucky to get much more than a half-assed smooch and snuggle as they both lay under the blast of the air conditioner,

exhausted from the heat.

This was going on three weeks now and time was running out to finish the car. He'd taken care of most of the maintenance issues and replaced all moving parts that were replaceable – belts, valves, plugs... He'd even replaced the clutch just to hedge his bets. But he hadn't been able to tune the gearbox to his liking. The damn thing still stuck in 2nd on the transition to third whenever he test drove it over the garage rollers. The transmission had been the one aspect of the car they'd not been able to test in Laughing Elk's shed, and now he was regretting it. Soon Shiratori would be expecting results and a shift in priorities to the other vehicles' preparation – the sand car and the ATV. Tagata's Suzuki was already in tip-top shape from the Motocross and locked away safely in Tagata's personal trailer. The sand car was looking to require a technical overhaul of its onboard nav system. Sato as Shiratori predicted, had proven in training to be hopeless with a magnetic compass and maps.

Where it stood now, Mouse had to get the transmission to behave and secure the final welds in the seating and doors – something he'd saved for last in order to make the car more accessible during maintenance. The fact remained the errant transmission was currently sitting on the workbench in pieces as he tried to figure out what the fuck was sticking 2nd gear.

Mouse groaned and rubbed his temples, wondering if he should just give up for the night. He could slip back to Sadao's trailer, rouse the man and try to fuck away his problems, or just get off his ass and –

The sound of the side door opening stopped him cold. Nobody came in at this hour, not even Shiratori.

Mouse lay still. He heard whispered voices and snickers – more than two. The language sounded similar to Japanese but had differences in the consonants. He rolled over very slowly and peered down through the grating to the lower floor. Three dark forms with flashlights were sneaking in. *Fuck, we're being raided! Where are the guards?!*

In order to keep the stink of the heated salt flats out as much as possible, Mouse had insisted on working in the garage alone tonight with the ramps and side door locked up tight from the outside and the fans running full blast. The only people who could get in where the ones who had retina scan clearance – himself, Tagata, Sadao and Shiratori.

Mouse watched the men below him sneak about and dig through shelves and cupboards. They'd left a fourth man guarding the partially open side door. Mouse knew his only way out of this was to push the emergency escape release located on the lower floor by the utility sink which would lower all of the ramps and sound an alarm. There was no way he could reach it from where he sat. *Dammit! Who unlocked the side door?* They couldn't force it open without setting off even more alarms. The Orochi Team may have been fond of antique engines, but the garage security system was state of the art. Somebody was going to get a boot in their ass for this.

Crash! Rattle... rattle...

One of the idiots backed into a stack of pans and the others quickly chewed him out for it. They had packs with them, three of them did. They were stuffing parts or tools into them as fast as they could. It was nearly impossible for Mouse to see exactly what they were taking from his position in the dark above them. It took every effort he had not to jump down and start swinging. Odds were they were carrying knives or worse so he calmed himself and thought hard. If he could hit the emergency button, this whole caper would be blown.

Mouse rose from the cot slowly and stepped one foot at a time to the end of the upper floor grating over the utility sink area. From there he sat down slowly and slipped himself under the safety rail until he dangled over the lower floor. He'd thought he could get his foot onto the edge of the sink noiselessly, but curse his small stature; he couldn't quite reach the damn thing. He tried to swing for it and missed. He lost his grip and fell to the floor – Wham!

So much for a sneak escape – the men were on him before Mouse had a chance to regain his legs. He struggled but was no match for four pairs of arms and legs. They whisper-shouted in their language and twisted his arms back behind him, shining their flashlights in his face. "Aaagh! Let me go or I'll scream!" Mouse shouted. A gloved hand quickly came around his mouth and he bit it – but only got a mouthful of leather. Gnngh!

He was held down by the three men as the fourth scrambled around the garage for something, kicking over buckets. They didn't seem to be too terribly concerned about the racket they were making. They must have overtaken Shiratori's guards Mouse assumed. He hoped they weren't dead. Those morose thoughts were stopped by the sound of a chain being dragged across the floor. Oh shit, they'd found his leg tether from back when Sadao thought it was cute to chain him to his work. Not so cute now, as he was dragged backwards toward the center support post and quickly bound to the pole in tight loops of steel links. They fastened the cuff to the pole and replaced the leather glove he was chewing up with a strip of rag, gagging his mouth. More strips were used to efficiently bind his wrists back. Mouse struggled and screamed into the gag to no avail. Okay, this was really starting to piss him off.

Smack! Suddenly, and for no apparent reason he was smacked across the face. Mouse shouted into his gag and was hit again and again until his head spun and his jaw felt like it might come off. *What the fuck?* Stars lit up his eyes and he felt woozy as another blow hit him across the cheek. These weren't blows of attack, they were blows of punishment. Mouse heard more shouting and the men scrambled around the garage rummaging and gathering as fast as they could while his punisher kept his flashlight in his face. He was speaking to him now and in the haze of it Mouse realized it was Japanese. And a voice he recognized.

His eyes caught a glint that weren't stars. Although masked like his counterparts, his abuser was turning a knife blade about under his nose to get his attention before dragging the blade over his chains to point at his groin. He pulled off his mask with a wicked smile. Kinjo. *Fuck, here go my balls!*

He felt the knife press into the denim and begin to saw through the fabric right under his bulge. Mouse struggled at his bonds, but got nowhere. He was held fast as the sawing continued. The thick fabric of the Chairman's $400 designer jeans was no match for finely honed steel. The Japanese were anything but diligent about keeping their knives sharp and ready for battle. Or neutering, which this young man seemed to be obsessed with.

Pop! The fabric parted and Mouse's balls popped out with it. Kinjo laughed and poked at his sack hanging down in the safety net of his underpants. Mouse screamed profanities through his gag but all that came out was: "Mfmmdngnfgfm!"

"Ja! You not like me, eh?" he said in English suddenly. Mouse held very still as the knife resumed its sawing motion slowly against the fragile layer of cotton separating balls from blade. "I ask Shiratori-san why Sato? He lost. Lost all the time. He tell me. Mouse no like you. We lose, then! Shiratori-san will lose because of *baka* mechanic?"

Dammit! Shiratori told him?! Why??

Maybe that's who unlocked the door — have you not realized that yet?

Mouse's eyes went wide as the cotton tore open and the cool of the blade hit his sac and pain like a lick of flame shot up his groin. *Fuck, I'm cut!*

Mouse grit his teeth as the blade stilled just between his nuts. If it moved again he expected his scrotum to split and his balls to spill out onto the floor. He was dimly aware of shouting from the other men and their sudden scrambling to evacuate from the trailer. Kinjo glanced over his shoulder a moment, then back at Mouse. His eyes reflected uncertainty. Something was up. Was someone coming? He hoped to God someone was coming.

There was a shudder and a bang All ramps engaged at once. People were coming up the ramps calling his name. Kinjo gave a shout and retracted his blade and tried to run for the side door but was stopped by a thick black wall entering it – Sadao.

Wham! Kinjo hit the ground hard in one blow. The young man's bloody knife skittered across the floor and stopped at Mouse's knee. Sadao glanced once Mouse's way and his eyes went wide and filled with vengeance. He lifted the young man to his feet with one arm and beat him in the face with the other fist, sending splatters of blood all over the workbench. The blows came one after another, harder and harder. Mouse could hear the crack of Kinjo's nose breaking and the clatter of his teeth hitting the metal floor.

Someone was behind him undoing his gag and hand bonds – it was Tagata. As soon as the gag was dislodged Mouse shouted, "Sadao, stop! You'll kill him!"

Sadao didn't stop even as Kinjo fell again to the floor, motionless. Sadao kicked him hard where he lay, cracking ribs. "Sadao... !" As soon as Mouse's hands were free, he yanked at Tagata's braids. "Stop him for fuck's sake!!"

Tagata got to his feet and lunged at his Boss with all his height and weight – knocking them both to the ground. Fists were flying and both men were snarling at each other in Japanese, rolling about on the gory floor. Mouse tried to get out of his bonds but he was wrapped tight. The Tagata/Sadao ball of madness rolled slowly to a stop and both men helped each other up. Tagata, a bit bloodied, slapped Sadao's shoulder in forgiveness. Sadao nodded, calmer now and pointed to Kinjo's pummeled shape. He gave Tagata instruction as he came to Mouse and reached for his chain of keys with torn, trembling hands.

He knelt next to Mouse and unlocked the cuff from the pole, unwrapping Mouse as fast as he could. Mouse fell across his knees and Sadao picked him up, holding him to his chest and rocking him like a newborn. His lips were at his ear saying one word over and over. *Yurushite... Yurushite...*

Forgive me.

Chapter XVII

The Devil's Cartwheel

"Guys! Guys! Look, it's okay! I still have testicles!"

Mouse was lying on a futon in the medical tent with ice packs to his face and a bandage on his bloody head and balls. They'd been shaved a little too close this time. But in actuality, he hadn't received more than a scratch, though the cut had bled like a sonofabitch. It was his head and jaw that hurt the most. He got dizzy if he tried to lift his head, but if he didn't say something soon he was afraid the whole tent of wounded would soon be in grave danger from flying blows and blades.

Sadao saw him struggling and was at his side in an instant, forgetting for the moment his three-way shouting match with Shiratori and Tagata.

"You worry much about your *Okusama* and almost kill my Kinjo! Kinjo was Shiratori-clan, not Orochi! What good is he now?! All blood and broken bones!" Shiratori's voice was shrill from screaming. "I punish whitebird men, not Boss-sama!"

"He organized a raid, Shiratori-san! On your garage! He is dead to me!" Sadao argued as he eased Mouse back down and held the ice pack to his swollen and bruised jaw. "Even if he lives, he is dead!"

Kinjo, what was left of him, was being worked on in the surgery tent next door. Sensei reported three broken ribs, a cracked jaw, four missing teeth and a severely broken nose. They were working to restore his airway while they awaited chopper support from the Chairman to rush him to Utah University Medical Center.

"What proof you have?" Shiratori asked. "Boys are wild. Make stupid choices. Kinjo is mad. Sato has lead in sand race, not him. Not fair to him. So he take anger to garage. Stupid crime made by stupid boys – no thing important taken. Just big piss-off mess!"

"How did the garage open?" Tagata questioned, eyeing Shiratori. "Mouse says security system was armed."

Shiratori stared down at Mouse with disdain. "Mouse lies. Fell asleep with door open."

"I did not! And even if I had, where were your guards? Huh? Has anyone seen them?"

The three men looked at each other. No one had managed to answer this all-important question yet. As far as anyone knew, the two men posted that night had yet to be found.

"We are looking," Shiratori said, adjusting the pair of swords tucked into his belt. Mouse was beginning to understand why this man dressed for war everyday.

"They were Asian," Mouse added. "Not Japanese except for Kinjo. But... he knew their language. That's why I didn't recognize him at first in the dark. He wasn't speaking Japanese."

"Why you not say this before?" Tagata demanded, seemingly a little more convinced now by Shiratori's explanation.

"I... " Mouse looked pleadingly to Sadao who thankfully was still on his side. "I forgot. I'm sorry – a little brain damaged here, jeeze."

"Did they sound like this: *'zhè you huì jiang yīngyu de dàifu ma?'*" Sadao spoke in a foreign tongue.

Mouse shook his head. "No, less nasal. Lower in tone... "

Sadao tried another, *"Keopi shikgido jeone wonsyas ttaerineun sana-i."* It sounded similar in cadence to Japanese but the consonants were a little different.

"Yes, like that! That was it!" Mouse said.

Sadao looked up at his men. "Korean. Search their camp! Go! Now!"

Tagata and Shiratori locked eyes in solidarity and moved out.

Mouse looked up at Sadao and tugged at his sleeve. His shirt was still splattered with Kinjo's blood. He'd washed the mess from his fists and arms, but his knuckles were torn and swollen, leaving spots of red on the gauze Sensei had wrapped around them.

"You believe me, don't you? I did lock the outside doors like I always do. Then I ran up the rear ramp so it would arm behind me. I couldn't have fallen asleep, otherwise. Somebody had to clear the retina scan and I know it wasn't you."

Sadao was deep in thought a moment, then brushed Mouse's hair from his eyes. "I do believe you," he said quietly. "But did you see Shiratori's guards when you closed the ramps?"

"Yeah, they were right outside the side door like they always are, sitting on buckets playing dice."

Sadao's eyes narrowed. "They shouldn't be playing anything. They should be doing their job."

Mouse touched Sadao's wrist. "Does it hurt?"

Sadao shook his head.

"You scared me. I thought you were going to kill that kid."

"I scared myself. I saw you chained up and with the blood and the dim light... it looked to me as if he had taken his prize."

Mouse knew he shouldn't smile but it was sweet – his lethal gang boss boyfriend avenging his balls like a man possessed.

"And Kinjo is no child. He is 22. Young, but old enough to know the consequences of his actions. I mean what I say. He will never step foot under the Orochi banner again as long as I live. He's been a problem ever since our teams merged."

"Then what Shiratori said is true. Kinjo is one of his men. Do you think they could have planned this together?" To Mouse this seemed logical.

Sadao reacted strongly. "No! Impossible. Shiratori may not agree with me, but he would never betray me this way."

"But Sadao, someone had to open the side door with their eyeball. There's no other way. It was him. It had to be. Maybe he staged the raid to get me out of the way. Or Tagata... "

Sadao shook his head sharply. "No more talk of this. I know my men!"

"But you said yourself, Shiratori will do anything to win. Sadao, I've heard him call you his enemy!"

Sadao gave Mouse a cool look. "I said no more talk! You do not know Shiratori like I do. These are not his methods. You are injured. Rest."

The sound of a helicopter approaching soon caught their attention. Lights from the chopper passed over them, lighting up the white canvas.

"You'd better go meet him," Mouse said. "Try to explain this mess."

Sadao glanced toward the surgical tent. "They don't want me in there. Understandable. I explained the situation over the phone to the Chairman. He doesn't want any unnecessary drama."

The tent canvas began to flutter under the wind of the rotors. Shouting could be heard as men rushed about outside. Sadao stayed put at Mouse's bedside, eying the satellite phone attached to his belt. In a few minutes it rang and Sadao answered it, getting to his feet.

"Yes, I explained. Mouse was... I know. I apologize – " Sadao glanced down at Mouse as the Chairman chewed him out on the other end. He stepped away and took the rest of the call outside.

Mouse eased his thighs apart as Sadao left the tent. Damn balls were swelling and throbbing. He moved his jaw ice pack to his sac, applying it gently with a wince. Mouse was anxious to get back to the garage to see what was taken. He didn't trust Shiratori's statement that the pilfered items where "no thing important." He'd left a lot of crucial Mustang parts lying around. He was worried sick some of them might be stolen or damaged. But until he could walk...

"Mouse?! Mouse?"

Oh, joy with no end – the Chairman was coming. The man ran into the medic tent frantic, sweaty and out of breath.

"Where are the doctors?" he exclaimed, looking around.

"They're with Kinjo," Sadao said, lowering the antenna on his phone and stepping in behind him. Somehow they'd missed each other during their conversation.

The Chairman turned to Sadao and pointed at Mouse. "Why isn't he prepped for transport? We need to take off immediately!"

Sadao planted himself between the Chairman and Mouse's bedside. "He's not going to the hospital. He's fine here with us."

"But... that's absurd! He needs proper medical attention!" The Chairman looked at Mouse anxiously. "His head is bleeding! He needs a CT scan!"

"Sensei pronounced him well enough. Just cuts and bruises," Sadao stated, unmoving.

"I – I can't believe this! Mouse, don't you want proper medical help?"

Mouse sat up on his elbows. "The only place I want to go right now is back to the garage. I'm sure there's stuff missing that I need. Tired of all this bullshit keeping us behind!"

The Chairman stood at his full height and walked around Sadao to kneel at Mouse's side. His eyes were moist with concern. "If anything happens to you... " he said softly. "Please... " The man was crazy upset.

"I'm alright. Really. It's fine. I'm just sore. Sadao can look after me."

The Chairman jerked his head in Sadao's direction. "Will he look after you the way he looked after Kinjo?"

Sadao's eyes widened, but he kept his mouth tightly shut.

The Chairman got to his feet and stepped right up to Sadao in a way Mouse had never seen anyone else do but himself. Sadao had to look up at the man.

"If this camp is so well managed, then explain to me why I just had to put a 22-year-old man on a medevac chopper, fighting for his life?"

Sadao kept his stare cool. "He assaulted Mouse while conducting treasonous actions against this team. Not his first offense."

"If he was a threat, then perhaps you should have had the man removed sooner. Reported him to authorities where he would have been dealt with accordingly."

"You mean deported?" Sadao said, lead in his tone. "That is a sentence worse than death."

"That can not be helped. *Shou ga nai desu ne?* Be grateful you and your people have any kind of foothold in this country at all. Or actions will be considered."

"And were my people not present in this country, there would be little need for the Chairman's honorable position to exist to mandate such actions."

The Chairman stared at Sadao coldly and touched a piece of equipment attached to his ear. "Take off without me. I will be staying to monitor the situation on ground. The other patient will not be requiring transport, for now."

The Chairman gave Mouse one last worried glance, then moved past Sadao and out of the tent.

"Fuck... ! Fuck, fuck, *fuck!!*" Mouse slammed the tub of parts down on the workbench.

"Hey man, you need to chill," Lupe said, coming to Mouse's side. "Or I'll go get Boss to carry you back to the tent. You shouldn't be in here anyway. No pants."

Mouse didn't give a shit if his ass was hanging out or not. His important parts were all wrapped up anyway. He had managed a shirt over his bandaged head, but the persistent ballache had prevented him from being able to wear jeans. And the garage lockers weren't full of kilts.

Mouse had stayed put in the medic tent with ice on his nuts until he could see the sun beginning to rise through the tent flaps and he took a deep breath and rose with it. He slipped out and away before Sadao, who had been called away to help talk to the irritated Korean team, noticed him gone.

Mouse sighed and tried to calm himself. "Gear's gone," Mouse said, pointing to the tub. It was full of items he'd gathered up from what had been spilled around the floor. It contained parts of the Mustang's disassembled 5-speed manual transmission: gears, rods and fastenings. He'd been cleaning them, removing some corrosion that may have been the smoking gun in his shifting problem. Now second gear had become the problem in and of itself. It was missing.

Lupe peered into the tub. "No second gear, eh? *Mierda*, that's not good. How can you replace second gear? Maybe you tell Boss he's gotta drive a 4-speed now, eh?"

Mouse's throbbing jaw hurt too much to crack a smile at Lupe's joke. "Output shaft's missing too – and some of the disks are bent. I don't know what the fuck I'm gonna do. Can't just walk into an autoparts store and ask for gears to fit a 100-year-old transmission. Classic or not."

"Maybe... can you get somebody in the city to machine it?"

Mouse threw up his hands. "With what as a template? I didn't take tracings! I wasn't expecting half my shit to get stolen! *Fuck!*" Mouse threw a socket wrench kit to the floor, letting the two dozen or so pieces scatter.

"Hey! I just picked that up! Take your anger out on your own shit!"

Mouse leaned back against the workbench. "Sorry! I'm being a dick, I know. Fucking head and balls are killing me... "

Lupe sided up next to him and put an arm around him. Mouse leaned into him gratefully with a heavy sigh. "Shit day, but what can you do? Come with me, *vato*. I get you more comfortable."

Lupe had Mouse get on the lift with him and hauled them both up to the top floor. Mouse limped along with his help and didn't protest as his buddy pulled the cot down for him.

"Thanks," Mouse said, lying back slowly.

"I'll go get you some ice packs, okay?" Lupe said, about to leave.

Mouse grabbed his hand. Lupe stopped and gave his fingers a squeeze. "What is it?"

"How well do you know Shiratori and Tagata?"

Lupe looked puzzled a moment, then he seemed to understand where Mouse was going with this and shrugged. "As well as anybody, I guess. You want me to tell you who was behind this? I got no fucking clue. And that's an honest answer."

"You've told me about Shiratori, but I realize I don't know shit about Tagata. Was he one of Sadao's orphans?"

Lupe took a seat at the edge of the cot. "No, man. He was a trade."

Mouse was surprised. For as attached as Tagata was to Sadao – he'd assumed.

"Traded from another team?"

"Yeah, from another division. Tagata-san was with a mixed-race team in the Canadian Division. Big hotshot I guess, even then. Lots of teams put in a bid for him when he was offered up for trade."

"What was he traded for? Money?"

"I think so. It was five years ago, before I joined the Orochis so I don't know all the details. It's not unusual for young racers to be traded if another team wants them bad enough."

Mouse lowered his voice. "Do you think Tagata is motivated by money?"

Lupe shrugged. "I dunno. He's a quiet one. He doesn't talk too much, even in Japanese. So I don't know his story too well. Just what others tell me. But he's never done anything suspicious that I know about. You want me to put money on someone. I hate to say it... but I think maybe General Shiratori could have a motive."

Mouse blinked at this and sat up on his elbow so they could whisper. "Tell me," Mouse begged.

Lupe paused, unsure if he should voice his theories or not. "Nothing I know about but just that he's the one who lost his team. He's the one who used to be the Big Boss. Now he's – well, like a second-boss, you know? And Kinjo was his man, so... "

Mouse's eyes lit up. "I was thinking the same thing. You know what? Kinjo said something to me while he was cutting me up. He said Shiratori told him I didn't like him and that was why he wasn't chosen for the Overland."

Lupe looked concerned. "Why would Shiratori tell him that?"

"I don't know I –"

A bang and shuffling from below stopped them.

Mouse sat up. "Who's down there?"

Lupe peered over the rail. "Oh, it's Goro. Goro! You gotta leave now. Garage is big mess. *Kitanai zo! Ikinasai!*"

Mouse got to his feet in time to see Goro on the floor below setting the re-assembled socket wrench kit back on the workbench glumly. The kid looked up once, then turned to shuffle away.

Mouse gripped the railing. "Goro, wait! I'm coming down, give me a minute!" Despite the pain, Mouse took the ladder route and pulled his long t-shirt down over most of his groin area when he got to the bottom floor.

Goro looked nervous as Mouse approached. "It's okay, Goro. You're just trying to help, right?"

The kid looked at him shyly from under his long black bangs and nodded.

"Can you understand English?"

The kid nodded.

"Can you speak English?"

"... a little... "

"Did you put that whole kit back together just now? That fast?"

Goro looked uncertain, then nodded.

Mouse grinned. The kid was painfully shy, but cute in an oddball way. No wonder Sadao took 'extra care' with this one.

"Your boss tells me you want to be a mechanic, is that right?"

The kid lit up a 1000 volts. "*Hai!* – Yes!"

Mouse gestured to the mess around them. "We could use an extra pair of hands. I'm injured and can't crawl under stuff looking for missing bolts. You wanna help?"

The kid smiled. "Yes! Yes! I help good!"

Mouse looked over his shoulder at Lupe who was watching the whole exchange.

"Lupe, can you get him a bucket?"

"Sure thing, man. Goro, *kite kudasai.* I show you where stuff goes, okay?"

Goro nodded and bowed to Mouse. "Thank you very much, Mouse-san."

Mouse tousled Goro's hair as he came up from his bow. His first in the Orochi camp.

"*Douitashimashite,*" Mouse said and the kid trotted off after Lupe.

Mouse found his head didn't hurt quite so much anymore.

"This is what they found spilled across the flats between us and the Korean camp," Sadao said, dumping the contents of a rucksack out onto the workbench. Bolts, pins, hoses, wrenches, pliers, can of sealant, some spray oil – Shiratori was right about one thing for certain, the thievery was random.

Mouse sifted through it with a disappointed frown. "This can't be all of it, is it?"

Sadao sighed. "This is all Shiratori and Tagata were able to find. They tracked the thieves' prints in the salt crust as far as the Korean camp but there the footprints were too mixed to follow. The team leaders claim no knowledge of this raid, or of the missing guards. I don't suppose you could identify the men who jumped you?"

"No," Mouse said, dejectedly. "They kept their lights in my eyes most of the time. They were young. But the only one I knew was Kinjo."

Sadao ran an irritated hand through his hair. "The Koreans are not pleased. They don't believe some footprints and spilled maintenance items proves anything. They want names, faces. This is causing us a good deal of trouble. Rumors are spreading across the flats that the Orochi Team can't control its own men!"

"I'm sorry, Sadao. I couldn't say... "

"Enough pestering him!" the Chairman interjected. "Can't you see the man is injured and missing pants? Is this really the right time to be sifting through screws and bolts?"

Much to both Mouse and Sadao's chagrin, the Chairman was grounded with them for the time being until a relief chopper returned to claim him. The man had been shadowing Sadao all afternoon and was distressed to learn Mouse had discharged himself from the medical tent and had resumed his post in the garage, sans trousers.

"I'm fine," Mouse insisted. "Just a headache."

"You need proper care. Those bruises are not going to look good on camera." The Chairman paused when his clip phone buzzed and he held up a finger to take the call outside.

Mouse took the brief respite as a chance to have a real conversation with Sadao. He moved closer to him, keeping an eye on the Chairman.

"The problem is, when we were raided I was in the middle of taking apart the transmission and cleaning the gears. I had the cover off and all the rings laid out perfectly for me to put back together but... shit got knocked around and shoved in those packs so now two crucial components are missing!"

Sadao's eyes grew a size larger. He hadn't known. "What does that mean for the Obsidian?"

"It means she doesn't have a transmission, is what. And the race is next week!"

Sadao rubbed his temples. "We can't have that. You have to find a way to make it work."

"How? I'm a mechanic, not a magician."

"Improvise. It's what I hired your for, isn't it?" he argued, gesturing to Mouse's three-quarters assembled Ninja, tucked up into the far corner of the garage. God only knew when he'd get a chance to work on that project again.

"Sure, I could improvise if we were talking about the rear bumper or a wheel – I can weld like a rockstar, but this is different. These are finely honed pieces of fitted machinery. It has to be exact to a millimeter of precision or the car won't fucking shift!"

"You'll have to work from spare parts, it's all we have with the time that is left!" Sadao said, letting his frustration rise into anger.

"Fine, I'll try to make a output shaft out of junk metal. But meanwhile, you'd better send out your men to search every hole in this desert for my missing second gear and tell 'em I'll blow the guy who finds it and brings it back here!"

Sadao frowned. "That won't be necessary."

"Like hell it won't! This car is a mint antique! You could search a hundred junkyards and not find another like it. So either you get every man with a pair of eyeballs out in that desert now searching or show me who I gotta fuck to replace a 100 year-old Mustang 5-speed transmission!"

"Hey, what's all the shouting about? I could barely hear my call?" the Chairman said, walking back up the rear ramp.

Mouse and Sadao both caught each other's eyes in the same exact second.

Oh, god, no...

Two days later Mouse was back in jeans, pacing the length of Sadao's trailer while the man spoke in the privacy of his bedroom with the Chairman over satellite. After 48 hours of a team-wide, spare-part manhunt, the output rod had been located near another dropped pack a half-mile west of the Korean camp at the edge of the wetlands, tangled in the reeds and covered in duck shit. Best efforts had been made, but the plain truth was – second gear remained a goner. At last, despair had set in and Mouse with much reluctance, told Sadao not only about the Chairman's prize Mustang collection in Seattle but his creepy open-ended offer for "a favor with a price."

He'd expected Sadao to at least frown upon the idea, but instead he grabbed the satellite phone and shooed Mouse out of his bedroom to strike a bargain.

Please, God... I know I've been a sinner, but get me out of this one.

After fifteen minutes or so, Sadao beeped the phone off and opened the door exiting slowly. He came over to the table and sat on the edge.

"Well... ?"

Sadao looked Mouse over, thinking.

"What... ?! What did he say?!"

"He has a '68 T5 transmission for us, but it won't come cheap. He's not in the position, he says, to do charity work for the teams under his division. That wouldn't be what he calls 'fair.'"

"Well fuck him, then!"

"That appears to be our only possible option... "

"Huh?"

"Do I have to draw you a sketch? You know what he wants, *Konezumi*."

"Of course I know what he wants, but he ain't gonna get it! Offer him something else!"

Sadao reached for a pack of smokes. It was empty and he tossed it aside, shoving his hand in his pocket. "Don't think I didn't try. Problem is, the man has everything he could want already. Except one."

"And you told him to go blow a rattlesnake, I hope."

Sadao looked down at Mouse's crotch. "Not exactly. I told him I'd discuss it with you."

"Ah, fuck. You whored me out, didn't you?"

"No, I said I would discuss it with you. I did not make him an offer."

"Well it's simple. The answer is no. Fuck no! That's not how I roll."

"Are you telling me you have never had sex with a man to gain an advantage?"

"Sure, I've fucked lots of assholes – you, for example. But I won't fuck his."

"There are two reasons to fuck. One is for business; the other for pleasure," Sadao said, counting them on his fingers.

"Really?" Mouse said bitterly. "Which reason am I?"

Sadao sighed and reached out to Mouse, wrapping his arms around him. He held him a moment, rubbing his back.

"Forget I said anything, okay?"

Mouse felt adrift but clung to him anyway.

Sadao kissed his ear. "I won't ask you to do something against your nature."

"Are there only two reasons?" Mouse couldn't help to ask. He knew Sadao could hear the uncertainty in his voice.

"Of course not."

Love? Did the word mean anything to this man? Mouse wondered as he took in his kiss. It had to be, how else could he ask him to do such a thing? They kissed until Mouse reached up and took Sadao's face in his hands and pressed their foreheads together.

"Okay, I'll do it," he said.

"*Honto ni?*"

"Yeah, I'm serious. But there's a condition."

Sadao nodded carefully.

"I want you there."

Sadao blinked. "In the room?"

"In the bed."

Sadao smiled a little.

"Honestly, I don't think I could work up a boner for that guy otherwise."

Sadao kissed his forehead softly. "I'll ask him."

"I won't kiss him! Or put his dick in my mouth. Nothing of his goes in my mouth or it's getting bit off! He can have my ass but I don't have to like it. And no fucking way is he going to drop a load in there. If he does, I'll rip his nuts off and--"

"Okay, okay! Let me get a pen."

The Chairman cleared his schedule and Mouse and Sadao rode out over the flats to the Grand American Hotel in the Jeep the man had unwittingly paid for to meet him. The sun had just finished setting when they arrived at the penthouse top floor and rang the bell.

One of the Chairman's manservants answered. "Good evening, the Chairman has been expecting-"

"We know what he's expecting," Sadao said sharply, tugging Mouse in through the door by the hand. Mouse hated to admit it, he was nervous. He had no fucking clue if he could go through with this. He was just glad beyond measure Sadao was here with him – the presumed expert in this kind of business deal.

Can I fit both of them in my ass at once, or do they take turns?

Despite his ground rules, Mouse realized he didn't know what was expected of him. Or how the three of them planned to pull this off. He was a one-man-at-a-time kind of guy.

What if I can't get it up? What if I don't squirt? What if I laugh? Is the deal off?

"Welcome! Welcome!" The Chairman greeted them in his usual overly cheery manner. "Can I take your... vests? Gloves? Or something?"

"We're fine," Sadao said, removing his riding gloves and tossing them on the coffee table.

"Okay well, I took the liberty to have my chef prepare us a little late supp--"

"We didn't come to eat a polite dinner, Chairman. We came to fuck," Sadao said pointedly. "All that requires is a flat surface and some lubricant."

The Chairman looked pale. "Ah, yes. Of course, I did prepare the master bedroom... "

"Great," Sadao said, grabbing Mouse's arm. "Let's get started."

The Chairman did prepare the master bedroom. A bottle of champagne was resting in a bucket of ice with a trio of long fluted glasses. The lights were a bit dimmed, candles were burning and the bed was turned down neatly with a mint.

Who gets the mint? Mouse wanted to know.

Sadao knocked the silver wrapped candy to the floor as he tore off the coverlet and top sheet, bumping a fresh flower arrangement. The Chairman grabbed it just before it slid off the end of the table.

Satisfied the bed was prepared, Sadao shoved the light dimmer switch back up to full, stripped off his shirt and began to undo his pants. Which appeared to be bulging...

Holy shit?! Is he hard already?

"I uh... thought perhaps we could begin with a drink," the Chairman stammered as he set the rescued vase on the dresser at a safe distance and stared in amazement at Sadao who sat himself bare-assed on the bed to strip off his pants and boots.

Sadao grabbed the base of his nearly fully erect cock. "Only if you require alcohol to perform," he said, motioning Mouse to come to him with a finger.

Mouse balked. "I think I'll take you up on that drink, Chairman." He flashed Sadao a *what the fuck are you doing?* look and accepted a glass of Champagne from the Chairman's trembling hand and gulped it down, requesting a second over a loud burp. Fuck, he hated champagne.

Sadao grumbled and backed up against the headboard, stroking himself.

"Is that a... what is that he has?" The Chairman asked Mouse as he poured, looking in the direction of Sadao's erection.

"The pearls?" Mouse asked, wiping champagne off this chin. "Oh, he's pierced. It's a biker thing."

"They add stimulation to sex." Sadao said, impatiently. "Which is what I thought you invited us here to do."

Normally, the sight of Sadao's rod of steel would make Mouse's balls bounce with anticipation, but all it was doing for him in the presence of the red-cheeked Chairman was reducing his dick to the size of a button mushroom. *How can he just sit there and wiggle it like that!?*

"Mouse... I uh... "

Mouse nearly jumped out of his skin. The Chairman was trying to start conversation with him while the Orochi Team Boss was lying on the bed waving his tool around like a alpha male chimp.

"Sorry, I was going to say – I've already asked my head mechanic to remove the transmission from my '68 racing class Mustang. It was hardly ever driven so I think it will suit... "

"We know this already. The transmission will fit our needs," Sadao barked, leaning over to the nightstand and rummaging through the drawer. "We trust it will be delivered on time," he said, tossing out an LDS Bible.

"It will... um... what you're looking for is in the bathroom... I didn't know if... "

"We've had our shots, Chairman. And I trust you've had yours," Sadao said, getting up and walking into the attached bathroom, ass cheeks flexing, to inspect the medicine cabinet. "Unless you prefer to keep certain fluids from escaping. But Mouse is still recovering from injury, I'd prefer if he didn't have to pack in any more than necessary. Ah, this will do." He emerged and tossed a fat tube of lube on the bed along with a towel. "Well, that's settled. Can we get started now?"

The Chairman set his empty glass down on the table. "That's fine... whatever you prefer... I'm good," he said with a glance at Mouse. Then he lowered his head and began unbuttoning his pants – where a second bulge was brewing.

Mouse took a step back from them both. "Whoa, just a fucking second! I'm not a trained dog like you two! I don't... *do* this kind of thing every weekend!"

The Chairman raised his head and his pants dropped to the floor with a jangle. "Are we... going too fast?"

"No," Sadao said, taking Mouse's arm. "Mouse, stop stalling and come suck me."

Mouse panicked as he felt his cock retract up into his throat. *Great, penis just vanished for good. I'll need a surgeon to find it now.*

"I--I can't do this! I'm sorry... " Mouse said, shaking Sadao loose and moving toward the nearest exit. "You two can have fun! I'll just go watch TV or something... "

"But... !"

"Mouse! *Yamero!*"

Mouse stopped at Sadao's command with his hand on the doorframe. His heart was pounding. *I can't do this, I can't do this!*

The Chairman stood confused with his pants down around his socks and looked from one of them to the other. "Mouse, I didn't want to make you uncomfortable. I thought... "

"Chairman, give us a minute," Sadao said, pointing to the door.

The Chairman nodded, reached down to pull up his pants and shuffled out of the room. Sadao shut the bedroom door behind him and gathered Mouse up into his arms. Mouse could feel his breath warm on his neck and his dick, a heated pole of flesh up against his hip.

"Is this what you do?" Mouse whispered. "You just meet up with people and whip it out all set to go?"

Sadao chuckled in his ear. "I forget sometimes how innocent you are. To me this is as if we came to exchange business cards."

"I know that," Mouse said, looking up at him. "And you explained that to me, but I'm just not used to performing for an audience."

"I know," Sadao said, kissing his mouth, softly. "That's why I removed the audience

– for the time being. Come, let's go to the bed."

Mouse followed Sadao and watched as he sat back naked against the headboard, propping pillows behind him. "Get your clothes off and come sit in my lap," he said with a sly grin.

Mouse froze as his cheeks lit up. *How do I tell him I'm so nervous I swallowed my own dick?* "I can't... I'm not... "

"I don't mind. I like a challenge. And you're adorable when you're shy. Not a side of you I get to see normally."

Mouse couldn't help but smile. "I guess it's true. I'm usually biting your clothes off... "

Sadao patted his thigh. "Come, and let me put you in a better mood."

Mouse undressed completely and climbed up onto the bed, straddling Sadao's thighs. The man cupped his ass and gave it a welcoming squeeze. Mouse looked down at his frightened turtlehead and sighed dejectedly. "This has never happened to me before. And certainly never with *you*."

Sadao cupped his balls, weighing them in his palm, which felt deliciously warm. "Still sore?" he asked as he moved them around gently.

"It's okay. Doesn't really hurt anymore. But I'm a little... sensitive down there still... ah!"

Sadao nodded and reached for the tube of goo. He squeezed a few inches of the gel in his hand and slid his moistened fingers up under Mouse's balls to his asshole, slickening the whole area – back and forth – giving him a nice massage.

"Mmmm... " Mouse moaned a little, feeling Sadao's fingertips working around his rim. He was happy to find his cock did still exist and was beginning to peep out to get a look at who was doing such a delicious job of warming him up for sex.

"Move closer," Sadao said, sinking down lower onto the bed.

Mouse shimmied higher until he was straddling Sadao's chest. His mini-boner was hovering just above Sadao's chin now. The man smiled, looking up at him from his vantage point and began to plant soft kisses up the underside of his shaft.

"Ohhhh... " Mouse sighed. "That's so... it feels... mmmm... " Sadao had to move faster to keep up with the growing length of stiffening flesh. By the time he reached the head, Mouse was fully erect and eager to fuck the smug mouth that brought him so easily into this state.

But Sadao just kept kissing him, up and down his dick, making him start to surge with frustration. Sadao's beard tickled his balls while his asshole was being worked open with a pair of long wet fingers, going in deeper and coming back out, all the while just giving his cock the lightest of feathery kisses.

"Nnnnnghh!" Mouse gripped Sadao's shoulders in frustration and began to thrust back onto his cluster of fingers, which were now moving easily up inside him, working his asshole loose, making him feel crazy for it. They'd been abstaining due to his wounds, and three days without release was too much.

"Suck me," Mouse panted, squeezing his asscheeks around Sadao's fingers, trying to urge them in deeper. His cock was stiff as a board now, the tip wet and shining. And still Sadao just kissed and brushed his lips up against it. "Please... aaahhhhh!!" Sadao's probing fingers found his joy button and mushed up against it, making him cry out louder than he would have liked to with a pathetic piece of crap Romeo waiting in the next room.

Tap, tap, tap. "Can I come back in... ?"

Sadao eyed the door, then Mouse. "Listen, if we let him back in, I promise you can fuck my mouth, agreed?"

Mouse wiped the sweat beading on his upper lip and nodded. "Okay, just... don't make me look at him."

Sadao winked. "Chairman, I believe we are ready for you now!"

The door flew open and the Chairman zipped in wearing nothing but a pair of tented tight white underpants.

Ah, shit, I looked! Mouse thought and tried to refocus on Sadao's soft wet lips just a breath below his cockhead. Focus... focus on the hot one... Although the Chairman wasn't horrible to look at naked for a half second – he wasn't Mouse's idea of a hot lay by any stretch.

Mouse felt the added weight on the mattress behind him but couldn't see exactly what the Chairman was up to. Instead he gave all effort into just enjoying the feel of Sadao's hands and lips. Sadao was starting to lick him now, root to tip, in slow wet glides. It made Mouse shudder with delight and he closed his eyes to indulge it until...

boink! boink! Something warm and sticky was boinking his lower back. *The fuck?*

Mouse dared a glance over his shoulder. The Chairman had scooted up behind him and was starting to poke his lower spine with his schlong.

"Ouch!" Mouse protested. But it didn't actually hurt it was just... annoying.

"Hey!" Sadao barked. "Easy back there. Mouse has tender balls!"

Yeah, that's a turn on. Mouse angled himself forward and shut Sadao up with his cock.

Sadao relaxed his throat and took him in like he promised. Mouse wondered how much of him he could take and began to thrust forward, going deeper and a little deeper into the man's throat. It was incredibly exciting to give it to him this way – to watch Sadao's eyes close and his brow knit in concentration as his lips and tongue worked him. Being on top gave him the power to violate the man below him all he wished. But what he wished for more was for the body behind him to stop with the nervous poking and let him enjoy Sadao in peace.

The Chairman was making weird heavy breathing sounds while he ran his cold hands up and down Mouse's back and hips. Mouse could feel him brushing his chest up against his back while the man's boner bobbed around the general vicinity of his asshole, still occupied by Sadao's fingers.

"I'm good," Mouse gasped. "Let's do this."

Sadao, mouth full of Mouse bits, slid his fingers out and Mouse did his best to pretend the long bony object squirming up his crack was Sadao's, but the utter lack of any finesse proved to be a fantasy killer.

"Have you done this before, Chairman?" Mouse asked, giving Sadao a good thrust that made the man nip him a bit with his teeth in warning. Ooch!

"Certainly, I have special dinner parties up in Seattle of this sort. Now if you can hold still a moment Mouse, I will attempt to aim... "

Mouse sighed and arched for the idiot so he could work his way in, anxious to get this party over and done with.

"It's just... let me know if I hurt... ooooh! That is good. Uh... oh... very nice indeed... "

Sadao spit Mouse out. "A little less commentary and a little more fucking, Chairman. We don't have all night."

"Sorry, sorry, of course." Now that the Chairman was going for it, Sadao seemed more interested in keeping an eye on his boss' moves and less so on Mouse's erectile status.

"Hey, Cowboy. Remember me?" Mouse bounced his wet dick on Sadao's nose. Sadao grabbed it in his fist and jerked him instead, not looking pleased at all.

"What... ?" Mouse mouthed, but all he got was an irritated glance from the man prone beneath him. The Chairman continued to focus all his efforts in getting himself fully sheathed in asshole. He nudged his hips lamely at Mouse's backside as if he were trying to mount a skittish pony, not a man.

Maybe those are the kind of parties he's talking about. "Oh!! Aaaahh!" The Chairman didn't have Sadao's girth but he certainly had him on length – he was rooting in deeper than Mouse had grown accustomed to. It smarted his inner muscles in a way that was strangely pleasurable. Thank god, because Sadao appeared to have lost interest in his cock entertaining efforts.

"Ohhhh... that's so nice... Mouse, thank you, thank you... " The Chairman moaned as he began to lose control over himself and just hugged Mouse about the waist and began thrusting in full.

Mouse's head reeled. *Shit... shiiiiiit...* Instinct took over. He forgot who and where he was and just focused on the sensations building up deep inside him. Sadao was down there too somewhere squeezing his throbbing dick, but it wasn't nearly as enthralling as getting hit at this new depth. He moaned despite himself and backed his ass up against the Chairman's groin, anxious to come, feeling the taller man's pubes tickling his ass cheeks.

The Chairman was moaning too, really getting into it. He began to speed up a bit, tightening his arms around him. The Chairman stroked Mouse's belly and groin fur, breathing heavy against his neck. His lips were thin and hot. Mouse felt him start to mouth his neck, his very sensitive neck, and he turned his head a bit to allow him more.

"I want to kiss him," the Chairman breathed, his voice tight. The way he was starting to thrust hard into him now, he must be getting close. He touched Mouse's hair, stroked it sweetly back from his face. His lips were so close. "So beautiful. I want... "

"No!" Sadao shouted. Smack!

Mouse's eyes flew open expecting to feel a sting. *Who got hit?* The Chairman had backed away from his face and was gripping his hips tight, ramming himself home. Mouse collapsed onto Sadao's chest, rubbing his hot cockhead against his lover's dick in dire need while the Chairman – the goddamn *Chairman* – sent him to heaven.

"Aaaaaaghhh!!! Aaaaaaaahhh!" Mouse screamed in Sadao's face as he gushed out what felt like a half-gallon of jizz across his stomach.

The Chairman made some crazed animal sound himself and let loose a whopper of a load so deep up in his ass he was afraid it would shoot out his nose.

We did it! We did it! I did it! Oh thank Jesus... I didn't even laugh. Damn, that wasn't half bad.

"Whoa!! Hey, wait a sec – !"

Sadao lifted Mouse up and threw him off his chest. Mouse, lacking any real muscle power in that moment, slid off the bed onto the floor. "Ow!" Dazed, he righted himself in time to see Sadao wiping cum of his chest and legs with a scowl. He balled up the towel and tossed it at the Chairman who sat on his knees at the end of the bed, sweaty and stunned.

"I trust our delivery will come in as timely a manner as you have tonight, Chairman!" he said, leaving the bed and reaching for his clothes.

The Chairman blinked, looking down at his cock that was dripping onto the sticky towel thrown at his knees. He rubbed his arm idly where Sadao had slapped him. Five fingers were outlined in red on his pale skin.

He fucking hit his boss? What an idiot!

"I – I was hoping we... " the Chairman stammered, looking pleadingly at Mouse. "I thought... if Mouse wanted... "

"Mouse is coming home with me. Our... his business with you is concluded," Sadao said, packing his unused erection back in his jeans. "Get dressed!" he ordered Mouse, throwing him his pants. "We're leaving."

Still stunned and sticky from the whole ordeal, Mouse did as he was told and worked his clothes back on. Soon as he slid his shoes on, Sadao hauled him to his feet and began pushing him toward the door.

Mouse turned to look back. The Chairman still sat with his long sad cock hung over the towel, watching their – no *his* – exit mournfully.

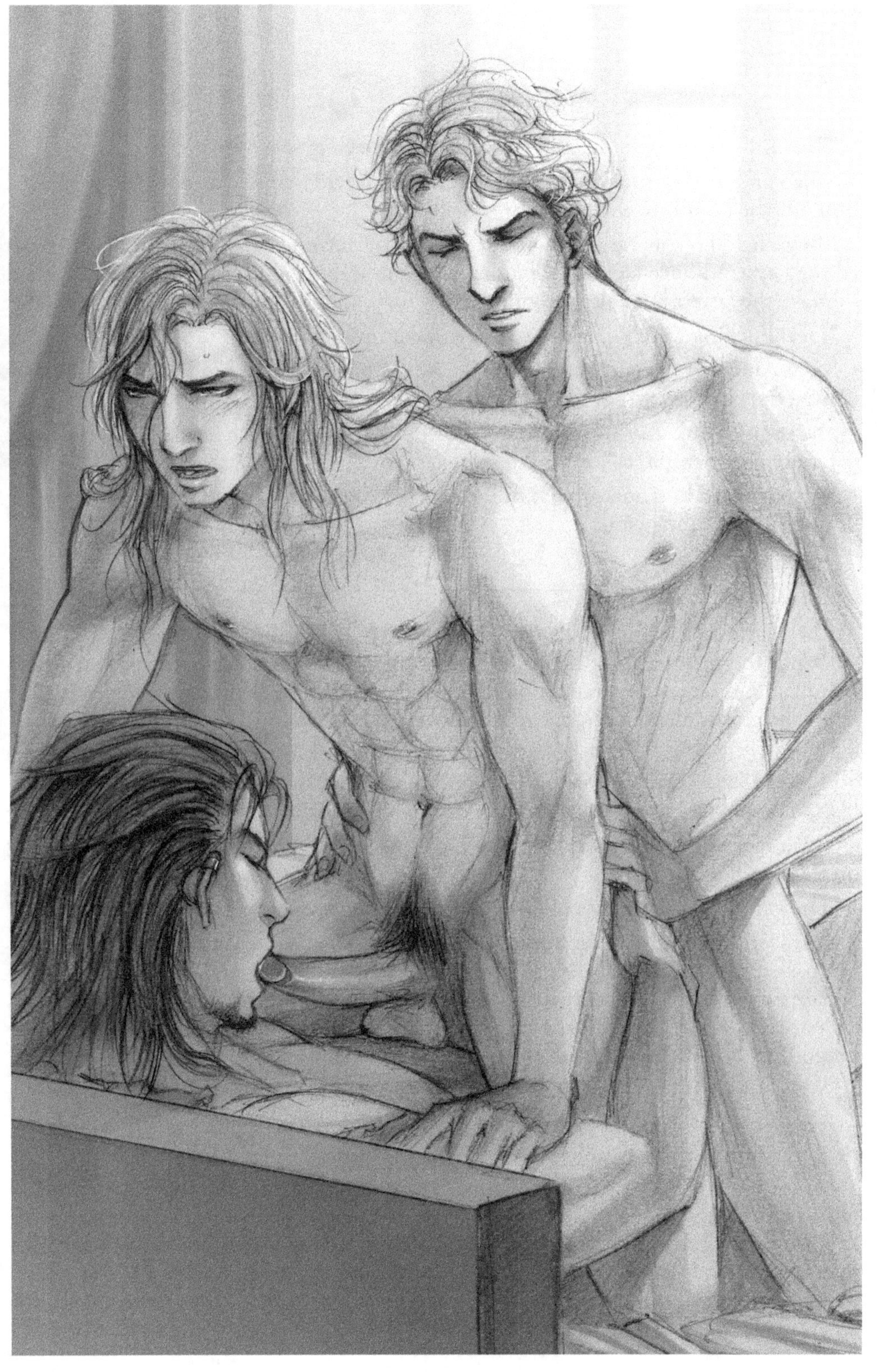

"Thanks!" Mouse said, for the first time really feeling sorry for the putz.

Sadao grabbed Mouse's arm. "I'm the one you should thank!" he growled and shoved him out the door into the hall.

Mouse held his tongue as they rode the elevator down to the garage. Sadao demanded the keys and once locked in, he slammed the Jeep into reverse and spun it around to make the fastest possible turn out of the garage and up onto the streets of Salt Lake.

"Hey! Fucking watch it! It's not your car, dammit! It's mine!"

Sadao, angered beyond speech, kept his eyes on the road ahead and soon as they cleared the city streets, floored it across the open desert.

The engine whined at its maximum rev. "I said fucking knock it off!! You'll burn out my clutch, you shithead!"

Sadao ignored him and pressed the accelerator to the floor, keeping a deadeye on the distant lights of their camp.

"What the fuck in hell's name is your problem?!" Mouse yelled as soon as Sadao slammed and locked the trailer door behind them. Without bothering to turn on any lights, he grabbed Mouse by the arm and ushered him toward the bedroom.

"Oh, hell no, I'm not sleeping with you tonight!" Mouse shouted, wrenching his arm loose. Sadao came at him and caught him around the hips. He threw Mouse over his shoulder, kicking and punching. "Fucking put me down!!"

Sadao kicked the bathroom door open and tossed Mouse into the shower, cranking on the water.

"Fuck are you doing?! It's cold! It's dark! I'm in my clothes!"

Sadao left him in there, shouting profanities and soon came back with a short knife. He pulled the sheath off with his teeth and got in the shower. He put a hand to Mouse's chest and slid the knife up under his belt. Mouse stood shocked and not a little frightened to see a knife once again so close to his jewels as Sadao cut off his new Hugo Boss belt with one firm yank of the knife.

"Wait. What?"

"He give you these too?" Sadao asked, voice cold as steel as he slipped the edge of the knife into the waistband of Mouse's $400 jeans.

Mouse just nodded, wide-eyed. Sadao's hand jerked down and out, cutting the fly right off. He set the blade in his teeth and knelt, ripping the crotch in half, tearing it down one leg to his knee. Between cuts of the knife and tears with his fists, Sadao managed to rend both legs of the jeans right off him. So much for Brand. The underpants came clear in one cut and rip, exposing Mouse to the full of the spray. Sadao threw the knife aside and yanked the shower head off its mount and shoved it between

Mouse's legs.

"Spread!" he ordered. Mouse did, gasping as the tepid water rained up into his balls and ass.

"What?"

"I want him off you," Sadao snarled. "All of him!" He reached up between Mouse's legs with his fingers and plunged them into his asshole, forcing it open for the water to get in.

"Ahhgh... stop! What the... " Water rushed up inside of him, cleaning him, draining out what the Chairman had deposited up in there. Mouse began to lose his fear as he looked down at Sadao on his knees in the spray, face tight with emotion so keen it was making the veins stand out on his face.

Mouse had never seen Sadao like this. Desperation blazed in his fixed gaze and it made Mouse want to swoon with desire. He tore at his own shirt, snapping buttons in a rush to get the foreign fabric off his skin.

"The only thing I want on me... is you... " he said.

At last, Sadao looked at him and threw the showerhead to the floor. He stood with lust in his eyes and tore open the fly of his own jeans, freeing his dick. He shoved his pants down to his ankles and lifted Mouse up into his arms and braced him against the shower wall, kissing him hungrily.

Mouse clung to his shoulders and hair, locking his ankles around his back. Sadao eased his ass down onto the heat of his rigid cock, thrusting hard up into his body. It stung from the fact the water had rinsed away most of the fluids, but Mouse cried out and took it, thrust after furious thrust. Sadao groaned loud as he fucked him, sucking at his mouth and throat. He slammed Mouse into the tiled wall in the effort to sate his need, biting and gripping Mouse's flesh like it was the last ledge that could save him from tumbling off the edge.

Chapter XVIII

Maiden Voyage

"*Yabai!*" Sadao exclaimed, entering the garage two nights before the start of the race to find Mouse working late at the workbench with his hand in a carburetor. "You will have to explain to me someday, *Konezumi*, what it is you have against pants."

"Well," Mouse said, glancing over his shoulder to grin at his lover as the man wisely shut the ramp behind him. "It's cooling, freeing, I get to feel more like a man, and it scares the shit out of camera drones."

"Eh?" Sadao came up behind him and rubbed his crotch against his ass affectionately. Mouse's cheeks were popping out of the back of the leather apron he wore when working with black sticky things. "What camera?"

Mouse, whose hands were coated in several layers of oil he was using to lube the ATV's four stroke carb, made a gesture with his elbow up at the corner of the ceiling.

Sadao's eyes followed his nudge. A basketball-sized shiny black floating drone hovered in the corner farthest from Mouse's full moon. It kept bonking itself against the roof as if it wanted to escape.

"How did that get in here?" Sadao asked, squeezing Mouse's ass a few more times before moving toward it for a closer look. The drone whirred and beeped at him and began to hover lower as if it were trying to determine friend from foe.

"Watch this," Mouse said and kicked the front of his work apron aside, flapping his junk at the lens. The machine shrieked, beeped and whirred back into its hiding place in the corner.

Sadao turned to Mouse. "I guess it doesn't agree with your wardrobe."

Mouse laughed as he reached deeper into the casing to lube a sticky interior valve. "Damn thing arrived today with one of the Chairman's tech geeks. It's been assigned to Murasaki's ATV here. They attached a tracer to the undercarriage so the camera can track it during the Overland. It's been buzzing my head all day."

"I thought you made it clear to the Chairman that he's not permitted to film inside our camp banners," Sadao said, annoyed. "Race footage only."

Mouse shrugged. "Your boss, not mine. Maybe you should go slap him."

Sadao frowned and came back over to Mouse to give him a smack on the backside.

"Ow! What was that for?"

Sadao resumed squeezing Mouse's globes. "That was for being so damned irresistible. What if someone else came in tonight and found you like this?"

"Working?" Mouse asked, dumbly.

"No," Sadao said, reaching down to fondle Mouse's free floating cock. It was beginning to rise despite their ongoing sex marathons. "Wearing only an apron and a sleeveless t-shirt will give racers the wrong idea."

"I think you mean the right idea... ahh! Really? Didn't you get enough today? I'm fisting this carburetor right now."

"That's something we haven't tried," Sadao said. He unzipped himself and pressed his burgeoning erection against Mouse's crack – hot dog and buns.

"I'm coated in oil up to my elbows!"

"You can keep working. I won't stop you," Sadao said, nuzzling his neck and kissing his bare shoulder.

Mouse moaned and leaned over the workbench to invite Sadao to hotdog him a little deeper. Ever since their disastrous sex-date with the Chairman, Mouse hadn't been able to keep Sadao off him for more than a few hours. Even though they were both busy as fuck, Sadao kept tracking him down and throwing him down in the most unlikely places and fucking him like his dick was about to explode. Today, they even managed to get off in the pantry of the mess tent during a 15-minute lunch break. Well, the floor looked like it needed a mop anyway.

Sadao spit in his hand and fed it to Mouse's eager asshole. Fingers went in easy as pie now. Mouse extracted his hands from the machinery and tried to get an oily grip on the table edge as Sadao entered him, slow and sure.

"Ahhh... Fuck that's nice... " Mouse purred, arching his spine in delight. Getting an assful of Sadao four times a day was a habit he could live with. "How are the change stations coming along?"

"We've finished setting up all but the last one – Park City. The elevation is keeping construction moving slow."

"How... oohhhh... yes... high is it?"

"About 9,600 feet. Air is thin," Sadao said, thrusting in and out slowly. "The workmen aren't used to it yet. I'm concerned about the Obsidian's performance at the peak. Low oxygen is death to acceleration. I want to test drive her as soon as possible. Speaking of, where is my special girl?"

"Mmmngh... she's with Lupe, he's putting the final touches of your insignia on her hood. The transmission went in like butter. Goro helped. You were right – he's a natural grease monkey. He'll be a great help during the … mmmnn… race."

"I'm glad you're putting him to work. The boy needs to feel useful. How did the Mustang take to the transmission?"

"I tested her on the rollers – she shifts like a whore now. You can have her back by tomorrow afternoon, Lupe promised. Ohh… God… fuck… do we really have to talk business right now?" Mouse spread his legs further and lowered his head, urging Sadao to go deeper.

"If we don't talk while we fuck we'll never accomplish anything. Move a bit more… ah… *umai*… "

"I saw more gas storage cans loaded into your trailer. Did your men find another stash?" Mouse asked over the smacking of their flesh.

"Yes, a good one outside of Provo. Another pumping station to nowhere. Your government isn't very bright. Gnngh, grip it like that… take it… good… "

"That will help overcome the low*ohhh*… oxygen mix," Mouse said and braced his hands against the edge of the table. He thrust back onto Sadao's cock as he sped up, letting the little jewels do their magic on him while the camera drone warbled in fright overhead.

He knew Sadao's jealousy toward the Chairman was the trigger that had put the extra lead in his pencil, but Mouse suspected fear was a co-conspirator. Sadao didn't want to risk losing his horny little ass to anyone within a 500-mile radius. The truth was, he had absolutely nothing to worry about. Mouse had craved a one-to-one dream relationship ever since he lost his virginity the summer of his 16th year to a hairy, burly tow truck driver.

"Aaaaaaaaaghhh!!! Oh fuck… yeah… Do it… nnnnghhh!!"

Sadao pulled out and jerked himself clean all over his back. Mouse gripped the workbench and panted, riding out the waves of his own release that splashed against the inside of the apron and down his leg. He could feel the cum cooling and dripping down his back as Sadao zipped up. The man planted a quick kiss on Mouse's cheek and smacked his ass one last time.

"See you back at the trailer."

Mouse laughed to himself as the ramps lowered. *He marks me like a fucking cat! Dream lover, my ass!*

The awful heat finally gave way to low clouds the following afternoon. For the first time in weeks the temperature hovered around a low 80. It felt almost like winter.

Mouse gave Lupe and Goro a hand putting the final wax shine on their dream machine. They had her gassed up and ready to ride as soon as Sadao returned from his morning training drills.

The four key Overland vehicles were polished, primed and ready to roll. As were the ever present drones whirling about their heads. Wherever their assigned vehicles went, so did the cameras.

Unless you dropped your pants.

Mouse was wearing his for once when Sadao arrived to take the Obsidian for her maiden spin. A large group of his men had gathered around the garage tent, excited to see their Boss take the stick officially for the first time in 10 years. A cheer went up when he arrived with Shiratori and Tagata to give her their blessing.

The three men dismounted their bikes and took their time walking around her. They leaned in to inspect the interior and asked Lupe to pop the hood so they could peer inside at the polished chrome intakes and engine block.

Mouse tossed the keys to Sadao who took them overhand and gave his shoulder a light brush before climbing in the drivers' side window. A helmet was waiting for him. He donned it and affixed the safety belts that crossed his chest.

Shiratori gave him a nod and Sadao turned the key. The old girl cleared her throat and roared, pistons pounding in her eight-valve heart. Shiratori lifted his arms and spoke a few words of Japanese. As the circle of racers answered him in unison, Mouse found himself filled with a powerful sense of fidelity to be a part if this ceremony.

Maybe now they consider you an Orochi.

Shiratori shut the hood and stepped aside. He brandished an actual sword that flashed in the sun and voiced his signature battle cry as Sadao put the car in first gear.

The Obsidian, resurrected from her retirement in Laughing Elk's shed, was reborn into the spirit she carried back in 1968 as the sun shone across her slick black coat. At her nose rose the joint body of the Orochi painted in brilliant red, purple and gold. The biting, hissing heads fanned and coiled out across her hood while the tails spread out from her grill, along both sides of the vehicle like Medusa's hair blowing in the wind. Lupe had pulled three all-nighters to make his Boss proud. Her number, 05, held a meaning only known to Sadao. He had chosen it upon his foray into the racing world back in 2056 when he stunned the world with his rookie win.

The men moved closer as Sadao drove slowly through them, allowing each a finger-tip touch of her slick black skin. At last the men moved apart to clear him to ride but Sadao did not immediately spin off into the salt flat haze. Instead, he pushed the brake and leaned out the window to gesture back at someone.

Mouse looked behind him to try and discern who. Lupe bopped him in the arm.

"He wants you, *Gringo pendejo!*"

Mouse jogged through the lines of men to catch up with the car. "What's wrong?" he gasped.

Sadao motioned him to stick his head in the driver's side window.

"Huh? The gauges... what? *Whoa!!*"

Sadao pulled him through the window by the back of his shirt. Mouse tumbled in and hit his head on the stick. "Ow! What?!"

Sadao yanked him across his lap and shoved him headfirst into a pile of limbs on the passenger's side.

"*Ganbarou!!*" he shouted and hit the gas.

Mouse, who was upside down, felt the engine's vibrations deep in his brain as he was thrown ass over head to the floor. The Obsidian was set loose, full throttle, screaming from first gear into the wail of second.

He's finally lost it. Mouse thought as he tumbled around, bouncing like a billiard ball between the door and seat and dash. *I'm going to die in the car I fucking built for him!*

Third hit hard and Mouse was temporarily airborne as they jumped a small dip in the salt crust. Bam!! He hit the seat again at more Gs than his stomach was properly designed for.

"Slow... fuck... down... assssshooooole – !"

All he could hear over the raging roar of the wind and the growl of the engine was Sadao hollering a whoop of pure joy.

"Strap in!" he shouted. "This bitch slows for no man!!"

Mouse's cranium survived the shift from third to fourth and the engine hit her stride, purring along at a full gallop. Mouse's sense of gravity returned and he was able to right himself. Hair was all over his eyes as he felt around for the damn belts and pulled them over his shoulders to lock in. Mouse pawed through his hair to glance at the speedometer – whoa, 0 to 92 in 40 seconds.

"What's her top?" Sadao yelled over the wind.

"I dunno! I clocked her at 103 in the garage. We had vibration and I didn't dare to go faster and catch a wheel."

"Let's find out! Hang on!"

Sadao threw his foot down and the Mustang took it like a stirrup to the belly. The engine roared, rising and rising – fighting to hold onto fourth. The speedometer needle rose with the RPM.

"Don't burn her up!" Mouse screamed.

"She was born to be a racer, wasn't she? She's been waiting a century for this!!"

Mouse watched the revs pass from yellow into red. *Fuck, he's gonna blow her and then I'll have to go blow the Chairman to replace the goddamn engine!*

"I didn't time her to carry two, you idiot!! Shift for fuck's sake!!"

Sadao kept his eye only on the horizon – a cold fire burned in his eyes. They had over 40 miles of flat open surface ahead of them with no end in sight.

"Shift goddamn you!!" The speedometer read 123...

Red went redder and still the engine climbed 125... 127...

"The tires are gonna fucking explode!"

128… 129… 130…

"Sadao!! I don't share your death wish!!"

His hand moved slowly from the wheel to the shift. 132 … 133… 135…

Bam! Fifth gear. The engine dropped from red to green and she sailed, absolutely sailed over the blurred flat of white salt forever.

From the flats Sadao took them up into the Wasatch on the main highway. Not yet closed for the race, the population of Salt Lake was significant enough to warrant some slow, sad solar traffic as they hit the 5,000 foot eight-mile grade to the summit peak at 9,800 feet. Even with two passengers, the Mustang soared past the local trucks and cars with ease. All efforts Mouse made to remind Sadao this wasn't a closed course fell on deaf ears. He slalomed around the other vehicles and hit the gas whenever the road was clear ahead, earning them a few middle fingers. Mouse was pleased to see that the rate of acceleration in the higher gears wasn't adversely affected by the decreasing oxygen levels. The higher octane in the government stash fuel would certainly give Sadao and his "special girl" an advantage.

Once they cleared the summit and headed downhill past the Park City checkpoint, Sadao turned out at a junction and steered them onto a much narrower, much curvier canyon two-lane highway that followed the Provo Canyon River ridge.

"Okay, so you saw that curves warning sign, right?" Mouse asked nervously as the visible land dropped away from his right window view. "I, uh… this lane is kind of narrow. You should brake into the – "

Sadao who had up until now not responded to his commentary, decided to. "Are you telling me how to drive?"

"Well, somebody has to! I just built this car, I don't want it going over a fucking cliff before tomorrow's gun and especially not with me in it!"

"What are your total years of open course racing experience?" Sadao snapped as they shaved a turn with only a tap to the brakes.

Mouse tore his eyes from the abyss deepening below him and scrambled for the "oh shit" handle – the very handle he'd not bothered to weld in, figuring Sadao would be riding solo whenever the urge to yell the handle's namesake came to mind. "Okay, I get it! But Lupe is gonna be pissed if you chip the paint!"

Sadao grinned and accelerated. "Fair enough!"

Should I mention I get carsick on mountain roads?

Once he decided to abandon all hope of controlling the situation, Mouse entrusted his life to the man at his left and focused on his shift work instead. Mouse was not trained in performance driving, but it was clear Sadao was. His line technique was effortless. For a road he had never driven on before with four wheels, Sadao had a second sense of the curves ahead and just how to cut it with minimal waste and maximum speed.

Mouse had heard of heel-toe shifting, but had never seen it in action. It tooks years of practice to work the clutch with the left foot while simultaneously working the brake and accelerator with the right to set the engine rev to match the downshift – all on the same turn. The man was truly awesome at the wheel – if not a little reckless – at least in Mouse's book of driving safety.

Just as Mouse was beginning to relax into the joyride, Sadao took a sudden turn to the right onto a dirt road, spinning out the rear wheels, apparently for 'fun.'

Mouse coughed through the cloud of dirt that blew in the windows as they kicked and bucked over a series of potholes to spin out to a stop on the wide flat shore of a small reservoir.

Sadao let out an ecstatic whoop and cut the engine. He unbelted and pulled himself out of the window before Mouse could finish brushing the dry weed bits from his hair.

Sadao was at his window. "Come here," he demanded and as soon as the belts were unhooked, Mouse was hauled out by his armpits.

"Hey, I can climb out myself--" Sadao picked him up and threw him face-up onto the Orochi-headed hood of the car. "What?"

"Shut up," Sadao commanded and pulled off his helmet. He tossed it aside and pinned Mouse down onto the warm polished metal. The man had a mad bulge going and his eyes were bright with excitement. His gloved hands tore at Mouse's belt and fly, yanked his jeans down to his ankles and folded his legs up over his head. Underpants in his face, Mouse heard Sadao's breathing go from 0-60 as the man's fly gave way and the solid heat of his dick pressed impatiently at his bewildered hole.

"Hey! Try a little spit at least – *fuuuuckkk!*" It stung, but he took it, pound for pound. He wasn't even hard, but somehow this sudden fuck went beyond a normal level of erotic. "Aaaagghh!!"

With his knees and jeans all bunched up, Mouse couldn't see Sadao very well but when he caught a glimpse, what he witnessed was a man making wild passionate love to a machine.

Sadao's eyes tracked the lines of the fender to the grill and up to the aerodynamic sweep of the hood – all the while giving it to Mouse like his ass was an integrated part of the engineering.

He's not even looking at me! He's using my asshole to fuck this car! Damn, that's hot -

Sadao fucked him hard for all of a minute and a half before he shouted and pulled out – squirting jizz all over the intake port. Sadao squeezed the final dribbles into his palm and rubbed them lovingly into the hood, cooing at it in Japanese.

Mouse unfolded himself and stared in perverse wonder at his autoerotic lover. Sadao, dick still out, dragged his fingertips all around the length of the car and back to the hood where he'd left Mouse half stripped. He smiled and grabbed Mouse's by the hair, kissing him solidly. When he withdrew, his eyes had regained some of their focus on reality.

"I take it... you like the car," Mouse said, catching his breath.

Sadao laughed and zipped up. He helped Mouse get to his feet and set him to rights – zipper and belt.

"I owe you," Sadao said with a wink. Mouse returned his smile. Amazing what a little taste of his glory years did for him – the man looked 10 years younger.

"You owe me for more than you know," Mouse said, pinching Sadao's beard.

Sadao kissed his forehead and wrapped an arm around him, walking them slowly to the water's edge. Mouse could hear the shallow waves racking at the wet gravel under their feet as they strolled. The sun was still high above the edge of the mountain peaks but for once the air was breezy and cool. He leaned into Sadao's body as they moved together. In the quiet of the reservoir, it felt like they were the last two men on earth.

Sadao was in no hurry to head back, which pleased Mouse immensely. So they took their time exploring the lake's edge and kissing under the oaks. Most of the lakes Mouse had grown up with were dry so Sadao showed him how to skip stones, which he sucked at. It seemed Sadao was skilled at many things, including stone-tossing physics.

When they got tired of walking they sat together on the hood of the Mustang and talked about Sadao's old racing days. And when they grew tired of sitting, Sadao laid back and Mouse snuggled up beside him to watch the clouds pass overhead.

At some point Mouse drifted off and awoke to Sadao nudging him. Mouse sat up, blinking. The sun was going down. "What time is it?" Mouse asked, yawning. His stomach growled. They'd passed a lot of time here – time he knew Sadao didn't really have. It was a rare pleasure to see him so relaxed.

"It's about time we headed back," Sadao said, fishing through his jacket for a cigarette. He found one and lit it, taking a puff and blowing it up into the sky.

Mouse lay back down on the hood, watching the curls from Sadao's cigarette mix with the clouds.

"Can I ask you about your number?" he said.

"Hmm? Oh, you mean my racing number?"

"Yeah. Heard it was a big secret."

Sadao smoked thoughtfully. "You are still looking to uncover a dark secret about me, aren't you?"

Mouse grinned back, trying to look devious. "I want knowledge no one else has."

Sadao regarded him a moment. "I don't think you need to seek anymore than you've uncovered all on your own. You live with me, after all."

Mouse stretched out lazily. "I know you sleep naked, have only one cup of green tea

05
05
NorthW
Divis

for breakfast, clean the trailer top to bottom every Thursday night with rubber gloves, get pissy when you run out of smokes, and get into messy drunken machismo matches with Shiratori."

"See, more than most. But the number really isn't a mystery. I was one of five brothers. The second youngest, and the only one to survive."

Mouse sat up cross-legged beside him so he could see his face. "Why only you?"

Sadao shook his head. "I honestly don't know. I wasn't the strongest or the brightest. I was lucky, I suppose. I found a way out they did not."

"Were they all murdered by rivals?"

"No, only the eldest two. My younger brother had died some years earlier at sea with my third brother before the war reached our village. My *Onisan* were already married and had children of their own. But they often brought their families to stay with us during harvest to help my parents. My father was an old man when he had me. I was a child of his second wife – my youngest brother was born to a mistress."

Mouse blinked. "Damn, your old man got around!"

Sadao laughed. "I suppose you could say that. But in old Japan, it was not so unusual."

"So they all died together? Your parents and your brothers' families?"

Sadao took a drag and stared out across the water, exhaling slowly. "The men were shot and the women tied together, left to die from fatal knife wounds and injuries resulting from rape. The children... a two-year old boy and an infant girl, were drowned in the *ofero*. Clan raids were never kind."

"And you? You weren't with them. Why?"

"I was staying with younger cousins at their rice farm in Ise. My mother's sister took me in while I took over lessons for an English teacher who had fallen ill at their middle school. I was the only member of my extended family who took well to language. I didn't know it at the time my interest in words would save me."

"Then, their father, your uncle, was the man that sold you... to that merchant from Chiba?"

Sadao lowered his eyes, and flicked his cigarette ash to the ground. "Yes." His eyes watched the sunlight playing over the ripples of the reservoir. "He did not have a passion for words."

Mouse waited patiently but when Sadao would speak no more on it, he interjected with a confession of his own. "I didn't know my mother. I actually have no idea who she was or what her name even was. My father never would talk about her. All he would say was that I had my mother's hair."

Sadao flicked his butt to the ground and eased back onto the hood of the car to touch the end of Mouse's tangles. "She must have been very beautiful," he said.

Mouse felt tears begin to sting the corners of his eyes and he wiped at them before they could gather steam. "Sucks I guess, how things turn out sometimes."

Sadao stroked his cheek. "It does," he agreed and bent to comfort him with a soft kiss.

"I don't want us to wind up that way," Mouse said, when their lips parted. "Some fucked-up modern-day tragedy. I've invested too much."

Sadao smiled. "So have I."

Mouse felt his heart skip a beat and a half. He looked deep into the eyes he loved so desperately, unable to say anything more.

"Come, *Konezumi*. I'll take us back. And I promise to drive the legal limit this time."

It was getting late when Mouse returned to Sadao's trailer for the night. He'd repolished, vacuumed and tucked Sadao's new mistress in his equipment trailer with the other three Overland vehicles. The equipment trailer would be hauled around to the proper change stations throughout the race. Gratefully, she hadn't a permanent scratch on her. Shiratori and Lupe would not sleep tonight in order to keep guard over the all-important vehicles, seeing as no one had been able to solve the mystery of the garage break-in. Once the race started, no further maintenance would be allowed anyway. The Overland was a test of endurance for both man and machine.

Sadao was busy at his carving table when Mouse came in. Mouse took off his shoes and came over for a closer look. Sadao was polishing a couple of silver objects in a rag under his maglamp. Mouse wrapped his arms around him and kissed his cheek.

"You need to come to bed. Big day tomorrow."

"Mnn," Sadao said in agreement.

"I saw Tagata was tanking up on extra fluid tonight. Weather report is threatening to make up for today's decent temperatures. That's gonna suck with the starting line out on the flats. No air or shade."

"Nmm... "

Mouse kissed Sadao's ear and moved to the bed, pulling off his jeans and lying back on the pillows. "You're a fountain of conversation tonight, aren't you?"

"I don't like to talk when I'm focused on something important."

"Whatcha got that's so important?"

Sadao clicked off his lamp and swiveled his chair around. On his forefinger were two silver rings, each fitted with a single black pearl.

Mouse sat up and crawled closer. "It's jewelry," he said. "Who are they for?"

"Us. Pick one," Sadao said, holding out his finger to Mouse.

Mouse was confused. *Us?* He reached out and took the one on the end. They both looked identical. The silver felt warm in his fingertips as he turned it around. There were tiny etchings on the loop of silver. Navajo design. "Hey! You bought these at the Trading Post. I didn't think... are they rings?"

Sadao lifted the second one off his finger and admired it. "Of a sort. They needed a little improvising."

Mouse looked at him. "Wait a sec. These aren't... are they?"

Sadao grinned. "Indeed."

"But, I'm not pierced there! I'm not pierced anywhere!"

"That will need to change," Sadao said, moving to sit beside Mouse on the bed.

Mouse shook his head vigorously. "I mean, I appreciate the gesture and all but, I can't handle anything sharp near my dick."

Sadao leaned into his ear. "That's not where yours is going."

"Huh? Where then, my nose?!"

"A bit lower where it will serve me as well as mine serves you."

Mouse's eyes got huge. "Oh, god no!"

Sadao only grinned at his distress and took his hand to admire his work. "When you wear my pearl, you will belong only to me. No one else can touch you – Orochi law."

"That's going to put a serious damper on my dating life."

Sadao cupped his chin and kissed him. Smooch. "Mine as well. We become a matched set."

Mouse felt a deep blush bloom from his neck up. "Does that mean you won't – ?" His heart was pounding progressively louder as he asked for clarification of Sadao's intentions.

"Yes. I'm 'retiring' from some of my after-hour duties as clan boss. It's time the younger ones took over all the fucking. I'm getting too old for that kind of thing."

Mouse didn't know what to say. He felt like his whole body was about to melt into a gooey puddle of Mouse joy.

Sadao nudged him with his shoulder. "You okay with this?"

"Oh hell, yeah! Get this fucker on me, now!"

"Did I say *now*? Because I'm thinking maybe we should wait until... I dunno, I don't actually have any feeling in the lower half of my body anymore? Or maybe when I'm really wasted or unconscious?"

"Hush. Stop fussing and keep the ice on it," Sadao said, holding his lighter under the longest thickest hollow needle Mouse had ever seen. And it was going where the sun didn't shine. "Stop watching if you don't want to pass out."

Mouse closed his eyes and pressed his face back into the pillow. He was bare-assed, bent over the end of the bed trembling while Sadao took forever to get the tools prepped. "You promise it doesn't hurt?" Mouse asked for the 12th time.

"I never promised it *wouldn't* hurt. I said it wouldn't hurt for long. Now relax, spread and show me your ass."

Mouse timidly set the icepack aside while Sadao poked at the extra ridge of skin just below his asshole on the balls-side. *Why are these Japanese guys always pointing sharp things at my nads?*

"Owww!"

"That's the pen. I told you I had to mark the spot first."

Mouse was shedding tears of pure fright into the pillow. "Hurry... "

"Need to do this right, or you'll regret it," he said, wiping the spot once more with antiseptic.

Mouse cringed at every touch. "Regret it how? Can we discuss the risks versus the benefits?"

"You'll thank me for the benefits. Now close your eyes and count back from ten."

"Okay... 10... 9... 8... *aaaaaiaiiiiiiaiaiaiaiaiiiiiiiiggghgggghghh!!* Take it out! Take it out! Take it out!"

"It's in. You're done. Not even a drop of blood."

"It huuuuuuurrrrrttttssss!!!!!!!!!!! Fuck you, it hurts!!!!!!!!!!!!"

"Looks good. Here, you want to see? Turn over."

Mouse slid over onto his back, cursing and took the hand mirror from Sadao and held it between his legs. Damn, there it was, right above his glory hole. Silver and black – kind of pretty. "Whoa. When can I take it out?"

"Never," Sadao said simply. "You belong to me now. You'll have to get used to that idea," he said, cleaning up. "Put the ice back on it if it hurts."

Mouse sat up gingerly and tucked the pack under his balls. The sting was beginning to abate somewhat – as long as he didn't move.

"What about you?"

"Huh, oh you want to do mine?"

Mouse nodded excitedly.

"Here," Sadao said and dropped trou, exposing himself. He was flaccid for once, but still impressive. Mouse held him eagerly. Squoosh-squoosh. "You'll need to pop that one out. It just pulls through."

"Really? This old one's a half-ring. Why did you change the shape?" Mouse asked as he slowly worked the dual pearls out.

"Have you ever caught a belt loop on a nail before?"

"Oh... that doesn't sound fun."

"It's not. Take my word on that."

The half ring came out smoothly through the hole, leaving a little extra bump of skin just under the head of his dick. Mouse bent and kissed it. Mmmm velvet baby skin.

"Before you get too involved, it's easier to put this in if I'm soft."

Mouse looked up at him and smiled. "Getting distracted, Cowboy?"

Sadao's cock gave a little jump, although his expression remained stoic. He held out the little ring to him. "Pearl unscrews," he said.

Mouse took the bit of silver from him and examined it. Sadao's jeweler's skills were impressive. He'd hollowed out a medium-sized black pearl and cemented a thin metal tube of threading inside. It unwound easily and a small gap between the ends opened up.

"Take the-"

"I got it!" Mouse said and pinched the ridge of skin, pulling it out a bit as Sadao held up the base of his cock for him to get underneath. He eased the non-pearled end into the little hole and relaxed the skin, wriggling the silver loop through and out. Easier than he thought. It didn't really go in that deep. He joined the pearl to the threads and rotated it carefully until it was snug. It looked nice. Really nice. Mouse pressed his lips to it and licked it with the tip of his tongue. Sadao's soft penis smelled wonderful.

Sniff sniff.

"I thought you wanted me to go to bed," Sadao said, amused by Mouse's actions. "Big day tomorrow, you said?"

Mouse grinned up at him and took a good long smell up his shaft, cupping Sadao's balls in his palm. "Don't we need to break them in or something? Consummate our marriage?"

Sadao laughed. "I suppose, but we have to let yours heal. You'll need to keep it very clean for a while."

"Mmmhmm," Mouse said, kissing and rubbing his nose all over Sadao's cock until it began to rise. "Doesn't look too tired to me."

"That's because you're playing with it," Sadao said and stepped out of his pants and stripped off his shirt.

Mouse, pain in his ass forgotten at the glorious sight of a nude Sadao, pulled his own shirt off and scooted back on the bed, leaving his ice pack behind.

Sadao laid down beside him and touched his chin for a kiss. Mouse hummed against his tongue and wrapped his arms around him, hugging him close while they smooched. "I don't mind the pain," Mouse said, when they paused for breath. His whole body felt warm and needy.

Sadao stroked his hair. "I mind. I'd rather give you pleasure another way."

Mouse pouted. "I want us both to feel it together. That's the point of consummation, isn't it?"

Sadao kissed him deeply, reaching down between them to stroke their erections together in his fist. Mouse moaned and thrust his hips in anticipation. Sadao kissed his way down his shoulder to a nipple and suckled him with little nips of his teeth.

"Ooohhh. More – " Mouse breathed, shivering.

Sadao sat up and swiveled around, presenting his new pearl to Mouse. He scooted his hips closer and teased the jewel against Mouse's lip, while he sank down on the bed to kiss the end of Mouse's waiting cock.

"Oh *that's* what you had in mind! You could have just said so!" Mouse grinned and opened wide to suck in a mouthful. Ooooh he loved tasting Sadao's thick juicy cock. He'd suck it all night long if it wouldn't eventually annoy the man.

Sadao groaned his approval and Mouse felt the man's warm wet tongue snake out and lick the length of his shaft. Sadao's mouth opened and he took Mouse into that warm wet place, careful not to bump his tender ass. The sight of Sadao's lips and throat moving over his shaft was unbearably exciting. Mouse had to distract himself if he didn't want this to end in the next few seconds.

Mouse drifted into a haze of pain-pleasure as he worked Sadao's new jewelry around his tongue. He licked and nibbled it, feeling him grow harder and thicker in his grip. He squeezed him at the base to make the veins bulge and the tip swell and redden. Oh, he was so beautiful and delicious. Lying up against him this way, feeling their muscles brushing up against each other, caressing asses and thighs, giving each other the same tender attention – it was perfection.

A matched set. Mouse had to keep replaying Sadao's words in his head, just to help him believe he'd really said them. Sadao had never made him any promises before and yet he'd felt so much for him. He couldn't begin to fathom the feelings rising in him now. So Mouse decided to tell someone about it:

God, I realize I'm deep-throating a guy's cock while I'm talking to you right now but... I just want to tell you, putting me through that fire and getting me lost in the desert and tying me up to the back of a motorcycle and bed and... later a table and... almost drowning me in a river... and getting my nuts and my hair cut... was the very best thing that's ever happened to me in my whole life because I belong to someone now and he belongs me and I can't fucking believe how good this feels and... I know I shouldn't have said fucking... I swear too much, I'll work on that. But, there's a big scary race coming up and I'll do my best to keep him safe but please, please don't take this man from me. I couldn't stand it. I can take anything but that. So please, please? God? Are you listening – ?

Hot tears dripped from the corners of Mouse's eyes as he drank down Sadao's shuddering climax and fed the man he loved more than anything else his own. But under this blanket of warm fuzzy happiness Mouse felt a cold chill creeping in.

Please – ?

Chapter XIX

Rabbit Down

In his dream, Mouse was up someplace high climbing a metal ladder. The air around him was filled with rain and smoke. The wind was blowing his hair all around as he reached up to grab the next rung. A red light blinked at the top of the structure, guiding him as he climbed steadily while a helicopter whirred somewhere nearby.

It's the radio tower, he realized, as he moved higher. The helicopter flew past again, nearly blowing him off. His limbs were wet and shivering from the rain that continued to fall. It made his hands slippery while the smoke of the fire clouded his eyes and stung his throat.

The helicopter made another pass just as he was nearing a small structure at the top of the tower. In the pilot's seat was Shiratori – sword in hand – screaming at him in Japanese. Mouse strained to hear him but couldn't decide if he was trying to kill him or warn him of something. Above, hanging from a wooden roof at the peak of the tower platform, was a dark heavy temple bell. It hung still and silent in the center of the storm. Mouse could see the silhouette of a man sitting under it, slumped against the tower structure as if he were exhausted. Sadao.

Mouse knew he had to rouse Sadao and get him out of there, but the clouds that spouted rain overhead weren't clouds after all but the complex threads of a spider's web. In the center sat a giant spider with a hundred shiny black eyes, watching him. The helicopter buzzed close again and Shiratori was pointing and shouting for him to look down. Mouse wanted to keep climbing to the top but Shiratori's gestures stopped him. Mouse clung to the rungs and looked down to see Tagata dressed in black, chopping the metal base of the tower with a diamond axe.

"Sadao!" Mouse shouted and woke himself up.

"Mngh?" The man who had been sleeping soundly next to him opened a heavy eye. "What's wrong?"

Mouse sat up and wiped the sweat from his forehead, trying to regain a grip on reality. "What time is it?" he mumbled.

Sadao rolled over and checked his watch. "4:45. Too early. Go back to sleep."

Sadao turned back over and shut his eyes. Mouse watched him in the darkness and shook. Fear was all he could feel. Sadao's eyes opened again. "Why are you up?"

Mouse shook his head. "I dunno. A nightmare, I guess."

Sadao reached out a warm hand and patted his trembling thigh. "You're just nervous. Get back in bed."

Mouse breathed shakily and lay back down, moving into the comfort of Sadao's body heat. Sadao rearranged the blanket and spooned him, kissing his neck. "Go back to sleep, *Konezumi*." Mouse closed his eyes and tried but the vision of the flames and the tower echoed in his mind and his eyes shot open again.

"Sadao... I'm worried."

"It's normal to be worried the night before a race."

"It is? But I feel like … something terrible is going to happen."

Sadao kissed his cheek. "Every race is a risk. All racers accept that. You needn't put that burden on yourself."

"But you're in this race," he whispered.

"I'm the last person you should worry about. I have the most experience."

Mouse gripped his arm. "I'm afraid someone is going to betray you."

"Someone nearly always is. That is why I never let my guard down."

"Even with those closest to you?"

"Hmn? You planning something?"

"No," Mouse said, pinching Sadao's elbow.

"If you are still concerned about Tagata and Shiratori – put your mind at ease. I have complete confidence in them. Now trust me for a moment and go back to sleep. We have to get up early enough as it is."

"Mkay," Mouse said closing his eyes, but felt no better for it.

"Still nervous?" Sadao asked much later that morning as they sat together in the lounge in the middle of the Chairman's giant helicopter-office. They were hovering a few hundred feet above the Overland starting line of bikes and cars stretched across the salt flats. Mouse gripped Sadao's arm and tried to breathe evenly. Panic kept rising and falling in his gut.

"Fucking hate helicopters," he said. "Why can't we set down? Doesn't look like this race is getting underway any time soon."

Sadao looked at his watch – 11:34am. The Overland gun was supposed to have gone off two hours ago. "Chairman!" Sadao barked, "It's nearing midday! If we don't start the race now you won't have racers left alive to delay!"

The Chairman was hovering over seven computer screens at his desk. He was busy with his head technician and arguing with a half dozen other voices on a conference call. He couldn't be bothered with Sadao's concerns for his one solitary man down on the ground, baking into the salt crust.

Sadao frowned and turned to Shiratori who was standing at the windows holding a long eyepiece to his good eye, watching the line below. "Shiratori-san," Sadao said, "What is Taga's condition?"

"Tagata-san is strong man. Prepared well for heat. He is still ready to begin. Others not so strong have left or are sitting under their bikes to find shade," he said, panning the desert below with his device. It looked like it came from the same manufacturer as his arm. "120 degrees. Very hot for such exposure. Men must move soon or die."

Sadao stood up. "Chairman, I insist!" The camera drone that was hovering about the helicopter's interior zoomed in for a close-up of his pissed-off face and Sadao whacked it aside. It shrieked and went flying off drunkenly.

"Hey! I haven't I told you a hundred times these cameras are highly sensitive pieces of equipment?! They can't be banged around like that!" The Chairman looked up from his clusterfuck of computers to chew-out Sadao. He was losing more patience with him every second. "What? No, not you, Chairman Davis, I'm dealing with clan people. But if you can just give me another 20 minutes to resolve this link-up issue... "

The Chairman had his hands full. His elaborate plan to revolutionize coverage of an anything goes 500-mile multi-terrain race was backfiring on him and now he had to explain his ongoing failure to the other division Chairmen and women. Whatever testing he had done during the Motocross with his camera broadcasting system was not performing as expected when attempting to sync up signals to tracers on over 200 vehicles baking in the desert heat.

"We have 75... no, 85% of racers covered. I assure you Chairmen, if we begin now before the other signals are locked in, we will lose critical footage. Yes, I know it's a warm day but... "

"Men are falling," Shiratori said from his vigilant post. "Medics are coming in."

Below, the sounds of sirens could be heard.

"Is this the kind of footage you were hoping for, Chairman?" Sadao continued. "Racers dying of heat exhaustion before the gun?"

The Chairman muted his conference call. "Do I need to remind you Koga-san that you are a guest onboard my craft? I can have you escorted off if these outbursts don't cease immediately!"

Sadao fixed the man in a cold stare until the Chairman blinked uncomfortably and resumed arguing with his tech.

Mouse tugged at his sleeve. "Sadao, don't. Yelling at him isn't going to help Tagata. Or you." Sadao made it no secret that he loathed this man. What tentative working relationship they may have had at the beginning had deteriorated into barely controlled malice in one another's presence. Not good, considering the man's position over Sadao. Mouse pressed his nose to his lover's shoulder. "Please, try to calm down."

The wobbly camera made a sudden return sweep to catch a clip of PDA between the two of them. Mouse gave the device the bird. It beeped its displeasure and flew up to the ceiling. *At least I found a way to keep my pants on.*

"Tagata-san has won many race before," Shiratori asserted, tucking his eyepiece under his remaining arm and adjusting his swords with his gauntleted hand. He was carrying the bokken as usual but the Chairman's guard insisted he leave his full mechanical arm checked with him in a security box when they'd boarded the craft. "He is young. He is Japanese. He can endure much. Not cry-baby like other men."

Mouse went to him. "Can I see?"

Shiratori bowed slightly and offered him the eyepiece. It extended like an old sea captain's scope and he scanned the row of suffering men until he found Tagata still astride his bike, poised for the gun. His braids were wet with sweat and his light riding jacket was hitched up over his head as a temporary sunblock. He wore a camelbak system that would allow him to rehydrate at need from a tube attached to his collar without moving his hands from the grips.

"Okay yes! We have 100% hook-up! Chairmen, the 2071 Overland Challenge can begin!"

A gun fired down below and Tagata, along with about 70 others who had not broken their focus, sprang out across the white flat plain. In the spyglass, Mouse could see the rest of the teams' racers scramble to get back in or on their vehicles and holy shit, go! It was comical in a way but soon soberingly clear that not everyone was fit to continue. Some men lay where they had fallen, others could not get up and some more soon wobbled off their bikes and hit the ground.

"It's a fucking disaster out there!" Mouse announced, handing the device back to Shiratori who passed it to Sadao.

"Taga looks good. He's moving fast, controlled. I think he'll be fine," Sadao said with audible relief. He turned to glare at the Chairman who answered him with the same disapproving look.

The Chairman's helicopter followed the leads across the Great Salt Lake Desert toward the wetlands. The Salt Lake, once an inland sea covering hundreds of miles, was now a wide labyrinth of pools and marshy wetlands choked with tall reeds and variable depths of mud. Mouse, Sadao and Shiratori followed the red and black insignia on Tagata's bike as it left a white cloud of dust fan-tailing behind it across the salt crust. He was among the lead pack moving between fifth and seventh place. For now, the leaders followed more or less the same direct line toward their first checkpoint at the edge of the wetlands. But once they crossed under the checkpoint banner, the riders fanned out to follow their own team-devised navigational strategy through the maze of muck.

They clocked Tagata at an average speed of 115 across the flatland. But now immersed in the mud lands, the speed slowed to 35 at best as he worked the bike in and out of the murky ponds and crumbling soil. Shiratori was watching his progress carefully.

"Is he staying on path?" Sadao asked.

"Tagata-san has good mind for direction. And good eye for land and water. He is making good progress. Not fastest but smartest. He knows route I design for him. He will not get caught in bog like some, see?"

Sadao took a look, scanning the wetlands below. "If he can keep his head in this heat he'll do well but we had hoped he would be on the highway by 2 pm. And now with the delay, he will not make the open road for some hours."

"Mouse... ? Mouse, you are needed on camera," the Chairman said, coming to break up their discussion. Sadao and Shiratori continued their conversation in Japanese and Mouse reluctantly followed the Chairman to a makeshift stage at the end of the helicopter's main chamber. He did his best to grin and answer a slough of inane questions from peek-a-boo tits about his opinion of the race so far. His opinion: the whole thing smelled rotten and he wasn't going to relax a muscle until it was over – 70 hours from now.

Tagata unscrambled the riddle of the boggy pools and hit the foothill dirt tracks by 1:15 pm – the fifth racer to clear the second checkpoint. Teams who had chosen auto for this section of the race were regretting it as the heavier vehicles took longer to spin out of the mud. Now on steep winding dirt roads, Tagata was able to shine. He out-maneuvered a number of competitors as he gained a better position by under-cutting several turns to gain advantage.

The hills became mountains and the roads grew increasingly steep. Soon, the helicopter lost sight of Tagata as they kept their craft on the tail of the lead bike winding upwards toward Lowe's Peak. From the peak checkpoint, the racers would wind back down the opposite side of the mountain range to Toole for one last checkpoint. From there, it was all hell bent for leather through the valley pass to the I-15, for an 80-mile highway race south to the first change station at Nephi.

Unable to track Tagata with their eyes, the Orochi team leaders turned to the Chairman's enormous digital glass display. The tracers affixed to each bike were represented as circles overlaying a real time satellite view of the Utah landscape. Each circle was marked with the proper team insignia and outlined in a color that represented the team's division. The Orochi head could be seen gaining steady progress up the mountains. It was the only blue-rimmed circle among the top ten leaders and the only Northwestern Division team to make it out of the bogs so far.

Mouse watched the panel anxiously, gripping the lounge armrest as the helicopter dipped right, left, aft and forward over the mountains like a ship at sea. Sadao and Shiratori were deep in hushed conversation by the windows, when the Chairman's head technician took this moment to leave his vigil at the broadcast monitors and rushed over to hand Mouse a small metallic object with a red blinking light.

"What's this?" Mouse asked.

"This is the tracer for the Orochi Mustang. My men weren't able to attach it earlier when they made their installments at your camp. The Chairman asked me to deliver it to you, so that you could affix it for us when you're reunited with your equipment tonight at Nephi."

Mouse shrugged. "Okay, sure." Sadao would be thrilled as a peach to have even more cameras on him, but Mouse felt he'd be less likely to jump out of his own skin with panic if he could at least watch Sadao's progress on this map display when it was his turn to take the wheel. Mouse thanked the man and slipped the tracer into his jeans pocket.

Mouse sat down and turned his eyes back to the map. He immediately noticed something odd. The Orochi head had stopped moving.

"Hey, uh... guys? Guys? I don't think Tagata's moving."

"Huh?

"*Nan da?*"

Both men came about to stare at the giant monitor. Sadao reached out a finger and tapped the Orochi head like it was a compass needle. The Orochi symbol didn't move.

"Don't touch the screen!" the Chairman yelled. "Don't touch anything! How many times -"

"Let me out," Sadao said. "I need to be on the ground. Now!"

The Chairman was taken aback. "We don't have parachutes!"

"Mouse and Shiratori-san can continue but if my man is down, I need to be on the ground."

"We don't have time to go around letting people out when it suits them. We will drop all of you off at Nephi as planned."

Sadao moved his hand closer to the glass screen, threatening to touch it again.

"Okay! Okay! Just stop touching my sensitive equipment! That screen cost more than what you earn in a year!"

Sadao was let out during a brief touchdown stop at Toole while the craft refueled. Tagata's insignia had failed to budge from its spot on the electronic map – ten or so miles north of Toole up in the mountains. Sadao had mapped the exact location and was tapping his actual compass as he backed his cruiser down the rear ramp of the Chairman's helicopter to the landing pad.

"I'll find him!" Sadao shouted up to Mouse and Shiratori on the main deck. "I'll be in contact!"

Mouse watched him back away and tried not to shout *Stop! Come back!* like an idiot, but every inch of his skin was crawling with worry. He shoved his hands in his pockets in frustration and felt the tracer tucked inside.

"Sadao! Wait! Take this!" Mouse ran down the ramp to him.

"What is it?"

"The tracer for your car. Take it. Please."

Sadao took his trembling hand in his own but not to accept the device. "Mouse, it will be okay. Tagata is strong."

Mouse fought back the urge to scream: *You don't understand! It's something terrible!*

"Just for my nerves please, put it on the cruiser for now. So I can track you. Please?"

Sadao looked at him with concern. "It's not like you to be this upset. But if you insist." He took the device, flicked it on and dropped it into his dashbox, closing it tight. "There, now you can find me," he said and squeezed Mouse's hand. Mouse squeezed back and let him go, watching him gun his engine and ride off toward the nearby mountains.

Mouse paced around the helicopter deck as they flew toward the main highway to catch up with the leaders again. He was now officially nervous as hell. He kept eyeing the Orochi dots on the map every five seconds. There wasn't any movement from Tagata's signal but Sadao's was drawing slowly closer.

"Mouse, why did you give Sadao an active tracer now? It's confusing the computers to have two Orochi men out on the map at once. It's causing camera transmission errors," the Chairman complained. He hovered over Mouse almost constantly now that Sadao had left. Shiratori was happy to just occupy himself with his eyepiece at the window and offered no interference.

"I'm not a computer geek," Mouse snapped. "I'm a mechanic. Give me grief about it later. Sadao's almost to him."

The Chairman watched the screen for a bit then snapped for his tech. "See if you can reactivate Tagata's camera."

Thanks, genius. That would have been useful about an hour ago.

A black square appeared over the map display. An image came through after a few blasts of static to reveal a shot of pretty much nothing. Tagata's camera was functioning, just aimed at the ground, filming weeds.

"Chairman, I don't think the camera is functioning properly--" the tech began.

The Chairman held up his hand to wait. Soon a bike engine could be heard approaching the camera.

"That's Sadao's!" Mouse said, ecstatically. The two Orochi symbols now overlapped. The engine shut off and steps could be heard. Sadao's boots were first to appear in frame. Then his riding glove grabbed the camera and turned it on his face.

"I don't know if you're seeing this," Sadao said. His face filled the screen, warped by proximity to the lens. "But it looks like your tracer system wasn't crash proof." He held up a cracked fender for the camera's eye. Underneath was the tracer, dead as a doornail. Sadao tossed it aside. "Tagata is long gone. His tire tracks continue on from here. It appears from the bits of wreckage here that he was sideswiped but recovered. If you want to find him, you should look to the highway." Sadao smirked for the camera before the thing gave a shriek and the picture displayed blurry tree branches for a moment before it made a popping sound and shut off.

"Did he throw it?" the Chairman asked in exasperation. "Did he just now throw one of my ICDs? Has the man no respect for technology?"

Mouse smiled to himself. He was relieved, but still not wholly at ease. Not with Sadao still out there without him.

The helicopter flew down the I-15 until it caught up with the southern-most blips on the map. The Koreans and Canadians were running a tight race on motorbikes but an auto from the Philippine team was burning up the road behind them. It gained on them steadily at 128 mph — faster than dirt bikes with knobby tires. With all the coverage focused on the drones buzzing above the leaders, no one caught the exact moment Tagata and his Suzuki cut onto the highway from a dirt side road to take the lead.

"Wait, how did he get that far ahead so fast?" the Chairman demanded to know.

Mouse shrugged. "He's resourceful, I guess."

"And unaccompanied! Who attached his tracer to a fender? I expressly requested that all tracers be welded to frames!" The Chairman's phone rang; and he had to cut his tirade short to go explain the lack of coverage to the rest of the Division heads, who had all heavily invested in his high-tech broadcasting system.

"Tagata-san too smart for dumb camera," Shiratori said proudly from his place at the window. "He probably ran bike into tree just to have excuse to ride unseen. His plan, sneak attack on highway. Very smart racer."

Mouse joined him. "Can I look again?" Shiratori lent him the eyepiece.

Mouse held it up to his eye and craned his neck to get a good look forward. The helicopter gained speed so it could hover over Tagata's head and get a down shot from the craft's onboard cameras. Tagata was holding a steady lead until the Philippine team's racecar outmaneuvered the runners-up to pull up alongside Tagata. The

Orochi Captain saw him and throttled up in order to gain on the car. But in a move almost too fast to see, the auto's driver reached out a hand through his open window and slammed down hard on Tagata's right handlebar. The Suzuki wobbled, lost all acceleration and although Tagata tried to fight it, he hit the asphalt on his side and was dragged under the bike for several hundred feet, skidding to a stop in a ditch.

"Oh my god!" Mouse exclaimed, jumping back from the view he just witnessed. "What the fuck just happened?"

Shiratori grabbed the eyepiece back while the helicopter hovered a moment, indecisive – continue with the leader or film the bloody mess in the ditch?

"Kill switch," Shiratori said.

"Huh?" Mouse asked.

"Auto driver hit Tagata-san's kill switch. Very bad to lose power at such speed."

"Is he okay? Is he alive?!" Mouse was desperate to know.

Shiratori adjusted the eyepiece. "Yes, he is alive. He is color of blood, but alive."

"Chairman! We have to land!" Mouse shouted as the helicopter made a decision to keep its camera on the leaders and flew off leaving Tagata to bleed alone.

"Mouse, that's not possible. We must keep up."

"I don't give a shit! Tagata is down and hurt! He needs our help, now!"

The Chairman sighed and put his hand on Mouse's shoulder. "I am not in a position to aid any of the team competitors, I'm afraid."

Mouse shrugged his hand off. "Don't give me that shit! He needs help! Where's your basic human decency?"

"Mouse, if we pick him up the Orochi Team will be disqualified from the rest of the race. He must either recover or surrender to medical assistance. Those are the rules."

"How can he surrender if he's unconscious? Fuck your rules! Land this goddamn flying penis extension and help him!"

"Perhaps if Tagata-san hadn't disabled his camera tracer, we'd be able to monitor his condition right now and make the best decision," the Chairman pointed out.

"Chairman is right," Shiratori said bluntly. "Tagata-san will have to choose."

Mouse looked at both men in disgust. "You both can go to hell! Where's a fucking camera? I've got something to say to the live audience right now!"

"Sir? Uh, Mr. Chairman, we have a camera feed on Tagata-san."

"How-?"

"Sir, when the ICD was damaged in the mountains, a new one fired off from central command and has just caught up with the other Orochi signal."

Mouse turned to the map. Sure enough, Sadao and his bike were nearing the spot Tagata went down. The Chairman had the feed patched in and as the distance closed between the two men, Tagata could be seen limping his bike out of the ditch and remounting. The left side of his body and face were all ripped to hell. Sadao pulled up behind him and shouted over the roar of the passing racers to him in Japanese. Tagata held up a hand to not come any closer. Blood dripped from open wounds on his left arm, but he started his engine successfully and pulled out onto the highway.

Shiratori beamed. "See, Tagata-san not cry-baby boy!"

"I'll be damned," the Chairman breathed.

Yes, you will be. If I have anything to say about it.

The lead racers were nearing the first change station as the sun began to set over Nephi. The helicopter touched down and as soon as the rear ramp dropped, Mouse ran down it and over the narrow highway to the Orochi makeshift camp.

Lupe, Goro, Kei and Sato were ready at their mark, ready for the Orochi banner to pass from Tagata to Sato who would take the sand car up over the open hills west of them and down into the sandy plains and high swept dunes of Little Sahara. They had hoped for a daylight start for Sato, who was directionally challenged, but the race starting gun delay now made this impossible.

"Lupe!" Mouse shouted, as he ran into camp. "Get the Mustang out now!"

"Why? What's going on?"

"Tagata's all fucked up. He's riding but he's fucked up and he'll need to get to the medical station immediately. I can take him in the Mustang."

Lupe nodded and ran to fetch the vehicle out of Sadao's equipment trailer. Mouse grabbed Goro and Kei and ran into the Orochi Team bivouac tent to grab first aid supplies and get clean rags ready. For all the moisture he'd lost waiting in the heat, the heavy bleeding would make Tagata's situation very serious. *Damn these pigheaded racers!*

Mouse waited by the window of the Mustang with the engine running, watching the racers go by one after another. Not that he cared, but it seemed the race for the Orochis was lost either way. He just wanted Tagata to be okay.

Dude almost killed you twice and now you're having a heart attack over this guy? Why?

Because Sadao, that's why, now shut up and focus!

Finally Tagata's bike came up over the hill, rattling the loose bodywork like all hell – but it made it across the line. What was left of Tagata's left hand passed the bloody Orochi banner he'd worn over his shoulder to Sato. The young man donned it with a bow and spun off in the sand car toward the dusty paths just beyond the camp stations.

Mouse and Lupe helped Tagata off the bike and both man and machine collapsed onto the ground. "Lupe, Goro, grab his legs! Kei, help me get him in the car!"

Working together, the four of them managed to insert a half-conscious Tagata in through the passenger's side window. Mouse climbed in the driver's side with his torn-up rags and tied them above what appeared to be the worst of Tagata's bleeding injuries. The man moaned in a haze of misery.

"We can't do much for him here," Lupe said. "You gotta get him to the med tent. They can radio choppers there!"

"I know!" Mouse said, putting the car in gear. "I'll be back as soon as he's safely in their hands. Watch for Sadao – he should be coming soon!" he said and drove as fast as he dared toward the medical tents.

When Mouse returned 30 minutes later, Sadao had just arrived.

"How is he?" he asked as soon as Mouse crawled out of the car's window.

"He's pretty badly injured on his left side – a lot of broken bones and deep scrapes and punctures. Fucking Philippine driver kill-switched him. How is that legal?"

"It's legal unless the cameras caught it," Sadao said grimly. "Or if the footage isn't conveniently lost."

"I can't believe you let him race like that!"

"Where's Shiratori?" Sadao asked, looking around.

"He's still with the Chairman, watching that big stupid map. I don't understand. Why didn't you at least radio a medevac?"

Sadao crossed his arms. "Believe me, I wanted to. But it was Taga's choice. He wanted to continue."

"His heartbeat is very fast, they say. He's lost a lot of blood. They're transfusing him and everything. Severe dehydration. He could fucking die, Sadao!"

Sadao laid a hand on Mouse's shoulder. "I know. Calm down. He's under the care he needs right now. There's nothing more we can do."

Mouse trembled and went into Sadao's arms as bikes and cars continued to roar past in the fading light.

"Better get your cruiser off the road before it gets hit," Mouse said.

Sadao agreed. "Goro-kun! Here, put my bike back in my trailer!" he said and tossed the boy the keys.

"Hai, Boss." Goro caught them and mounted Sadao's bike, turning it on and riding it toward the trailer. Mouse let himself be tucked under Sadao's arm as they walked back toward the camp tent. They had a skeleton crew at each station but in the wake of this latest disaster, Lupe and Kei had been hard at work preparing some kind of spicy Mexican stew. They even had the radio on, playing Mexican folk tunes to raise everyone's spirits.

There was a hum and a whirr and both Mouse and Sadao looked up as the partially damaged camera drone originally assigned to Tagata at last arrived in camp. It soared over Sadao and Mouse's heads before dipping to fly topsy-turvy into Sadao's equipment trailer after his cruiser.

Mouse groaned. "Oh for fuck's sake, I won't be able to get it out of there- *aaaagh!*"

A high-pitched whine from the radio made everyone cover their ears at once. The sound was followed by a hiss and a bang from the opposite direction.

Mouse uncovered his ears and looked to Sadao. The man's gaze was fixed back toward his trailer in shock. "Smoke," he said and started to run.

Mouse whipped around. Sadao's trailer was smoking and inside was can after can loaded with stolen fuel. "Sadao! Wait!"

He ran as if in slow motion after the man who was screaming Goro's name. Sadao had a few stride's lead on him. The trailer wasn't very far. There was no time to catch him. *Jump –* ! The word echoed in his head. *Jump, or he's dead.*

Mouse planted his foot and leapt forward for all he was worth. He dove through the air and connected with the back of Sadao's knees bringing the heavier man to the ground.

The explosion blasted over their heads as they slid to a stop in the dirt, Mouse atop Sadao's legs. Mouse put hands to his ears too late and a ringing pierced his brain as the sky lit up red and the air boiled with flaming smoke.

"Off!" Sadao yelled, kicking out from under Mouse. "Goro!" He got to his feet and attempted to run closer but stopped as fireballs of flame and black smoke continued to billow out of the trailer. Sadao winced and raised his arms to block the burning heat.

Mouse blinked the dirt from his eyes in time to see a form stumbling out of the red and black curling cloud of hell.

Goro. Oh fuck, oh fuck – ! His arms! Where are his arms?!

The clothes were burned off him, his hair – the hair that always fell over his eyes – was gone. His head was charred to the skull and his teeth were exposed from the absence of his lips. His arms – no more. Bones stuck out from his shoulders as he stumbled with one eye toward Sadao's screams.

Sadao inched forward into the heat and grabbed him. He dragged him back and away from the flames and subsequent explosions as the last of the cans lit up. Sadao's collar was on fire and Mouse tore off his own shirt and ran to beat at the flames. He could hear a terrible rasping, sucking sound.

Oh God, the kid's breathing? Why is he breathing?

Someone came up from behind the three of them and dumped the bowl of stew over Sadao's head to put out the flames. Sadao cried out but not for himself. He held the dying boy in his arms, hair steaming and dripping with rice and beans as he clutched the obliterated child to his chest. "*Goro!! Naze?! Naze?!*"

Mouse slapped the tears from his own face and looked around for help. Lupe and Kei, empty pot held between them, were struck numb. "Don't fucking stand there!

Call for help!" he yelled. "Lupe!!"

Lupe's eyes met his and he just shook his head slowly. Kei crumpled over and threw up. Mouse whirled around behind him to face the group of racers who had stopped to witness the explosion. The race for now, was forgotten.

"Why are you all just standing there?!" Mouse cried. Camera drones assigned to the stopped competitors whirred about, bumping into one another to get a shot of the carnage.

Mouse punched the first one he could reach and it knocked against two others. They bounced to the ground as two more whirred in to take their place to film a grief-stricken Sadao rocking a dead man. He kissed Goro's bloody burnt face over and over, sobbing his name.

Crying openly, Mouse came to his side slowly and knelt down close to Sadao. The boy was dead. Thank God.

"Sadao, please... they're watching you," he said, touching his arm.

Sadao sucked in a ragged breath and raised his eyes. His face was covered in stew, blood and crisp flakes of flesh. With a sudden hand he reached out and grabbed the closest camera, bringing it to his face.

"Did you see enough?!" he growled and smashed it into the ground at his side over and over until it was nothing but bits of sparking electrodes and wires. He hugged Goro's remains to his chest and stood up, facing the astonished crowd. He stepped toward them menacingly. "And you?! You want a better look?!" He held out Goro's bone-burnt limbs to the racer nearest to them, who jumped back in horror. "Do you?! What about you?!"

"Sadao! Please!" Mouse said. "Stop this! It's no good!"

Sadao turned slowly to him. His anger and grief twisted face looked like a demon's in the firelight. Mouse took a step back. *Shit, what do I do? What do I do?*

"*Sadao! Yamero!*" It was Shiratori, emerging through the smoke in his samurai armor. He held out his metal arms to Sadao. His voice was strict. "*Kaese, Sadao. Ima da!*"

Sadao blinked like he didn't recognize him. "Kyouji?" he said slowly as if waking from a dream.

"*Hai, ore da! Ima kaieshite kudasai,*" he said and at last Sadao broke from his trance and obeyed Shiratori's command. Shiratori took the body from him gently and bowed deeply to his rival. Sadao responded in kind and watched blankly as Shiratori turned and walked away with the corpse back into the darkness and smoke.

The ash from Sadao's cigarette had grown precariously long. Mouse, who was treat-

ing Sadao's neck and shoulder burns, nodded to Lupe to fetch the ashtray. The boy set it under Sadao's hands until the trembling in his fingers caused the long column to break and fall.

Sadao stared ahead at nothing, but his manner suggested he was seeing many things the rest of them could not. Mouse cut another piece of gauze and set it gently over a ripe red burn patch on Sadao's shoulder. He'd had to pick out the bits of material from Sadao's collar that had melted into his skin. Now that Mouse's fear levels had been justified, he felt himself moved into an odd calm as he tended Sadao's wounds.

Earlier, it had taken both himself and Lupe working together to get Sadao into the trailer and the shower. Mouse stripped the burned and bloodied clothes off him layer by layer, while Lupe waited outside the door patiently with a towel. Sadao's living quarters had survived the blast, having been separated and moved apart some hours earlier to suit the needs of the change station.

Meanwhile, Sato wandered the sand dunes blissfully unaware that Murasaki's ATV had gone up in smoke. Shiratori was ordering a new one sent down post-haste from their main camp in Salt Lake but Mouse found he had no fucks to give about whether or not the Orochi banners continued to change hands over the next day and a half. Behind them on Sadao's panel TV the race coverage continued with muted sound, but nobody was paying it any attention.

"I remember him when he came off the boats," Sadao said softly. "Ten years old – shy and frightened. Like a rabbit, I thought. I spoke to him and said, 'Why did you come to America?' He said, 'My mother is very sick. She will die soon. She brought me to the docks and left me. I had nowhere else to go.'"

Mouse tore off a piece of medical tape and fixed the gauze to Sadao's back. "Don't talk, baby. I need to finish this."

"I said to him, 'Do you want to come live with us? We will be your family. We will give you a new life, a better life than the one you've known.'"

Mouse exchanged a worried look with Lupe.

"He agreed but I don't think he believed me – that there could be something better waiting for him." Sadao paused and went to take a drag off the cigarette. It was already burnt down to nothing. He dropped it in the ashtray instead. "Wise kid."

"Sadao here, let me get this shirt on you." Sadao winced as the loose shirt went on over his neck and arms. To Mouse it seemed like the Mustang's fountain of youth had been sucked out of him by tonight's disaster and took a few more years along with it. At least the car itself had survived.

Lupe's eyes got big as something on the TV screen caught his attention. He went for the remote, turning the sound on. "Shit man, it's the fire coverage."

Sadao turned to look and Mouse gripped his hand. "Sadao, don't – "

On screen was an overhead shot of the fire blazing out of the doors of the equipment trailer as a hoard of racers and fans closed in to see the spectacle.

"Tonight, a shocking turn of events during the first leg of the Overland Challenge. An explosion in the Orochi Team camp sent flames shooting across the roadway and killed one young boy in its terrifying wake."

The footage immediately cut to Sadao holding the bloody torn body, screaming.

"The man you see here is Orochi Team Boss, Sadao Koga... "

Cut to Sadao yelling like a madman at the spectators, shoving Goro's corpse in their faces with the worst of the bloody mess blurred out. "Do you want to see? Do you?!"

"Apparently the Orochi Team had been hoarding a supply of stolen gasoline for sometime in Koga's personal trailer – the source of the blaze."

Mouse glanced nervously at Sadao. He was watching the report as if he was seeing the events for the first time and had no knowledge of who or what it was about.

"Koga has been Team Boss for over a decade, one of the longest running reigns in racing history. And yet some would say, a reign gone on too long."

Cut to Mouse: "Yeah Sadao's a real pain in the ass sometimes, but – "

Cut to the Chairman: "Koga-san has a rich and infamous racing heritage but many have said he's lost his edge in recent years. And that, naturally, is a concern to me."

"Northwest Division Chairman, Marcus Geddy has mentioned on several occasions a desire to clean up racing – to bring more wholesome traditions back to the sport."

Cut to an old man standing in front of the Iron Horse Saloon in Blythe: "Orochis yeah, we had Orochis. Those racer punks came through here, tore the place right up. Stole everything, burned half the town down."

Interviewer: "How old would you say those team members were?"

Old man: "Them Orochi kids? Dunno... 15, 16, maybe?"

Mouse gripped Sadao's arm. "That's not true. The racers were all legal age – that old fart doesn't know. And yeah, I said Sadao's a pain in the ass, but he has a big heart! They cut that! Fuck these editors!"

"Witnesses at the scene claim that the man killed by the blast was too far gone to determine age but as this footage will show, the Orochi Camp has an unusual number of young children far below legal racing age."

Clips followed of Sadao's little ones running around in the dirt, firing wooden carved guns at each other. They were dusty and some of them had taken off their shoes.

Cut to Chairman: "We have regulations and rules for a reason. No child under the age of 16 may be recruited for racing training. And none allowed to compete before age 17 upon completion of that all-important training. A racing team environment is no place for children."

"Some sources say these children were smuggled into the country illegally as part of a human trafficking ring aimed at kidnapping the youngsters from their native countries overseas and selling them as cheap labor to the highest bidder."

Cut back to Mouse: "Yeah, Sadao's a real sucker for kids. He collects them like stamps... "

Mouse paled and looked at his lover, who was still steeped in shock. "I – I didn't mean it like that! They are taking my statements out of context!"

"More disturbing is a report we have just received from Utah State University Medical Center. The man you see here, newly removed from life support, was one of the young racers under Koga's supervision. Witnesses say the victim has told doctors and local authorities his injuries, which include a severe concussion, broken ribs and a severely damaged nose, were the result of a beating he received as a disciplinary action from the Orochi Team leader."

Cut to Chairman: "No, no charges have been pressed at this time. But mark my words – I will be conducting an investigation upon the conclusion of this race. The safety and proper placement of those young kids is my number-one concern."

"Mr. Chairman, does this mean you will still allow Sadao Koga to compete in the final day of the race?"

"Of course," the Chairman said, smiling at the camera. "It would be unthinkable to deny the man his last chance at glory."

BAM!! Sadao had all at once come back into himself and proclaimed it by standing and smashing the surface of his much-abused dinette with his fists.

"Sadao, please... " Mouse began, reaching out to try and calm him. "You need to - *ohh!*"

Sadao grabbed Mouse by the belt and yanked him close, shoving a hand down his front pocket to retrieve the Mustang keys. Keys in hand, he turned away, wearing an expression so fixed and cold Mouse couldn't move for several seconds – not until Sadao had left the trailer and slammed the door behind him.

Oh, shit, Mouse thought as dread soaked into his bones. *Now the nightmare begins.*

Chapter XX

A Blind Eye

A storm was coming. Mouse could smell it in the heavy air as he rode, or attempted to ride, Tagata's busted-up Suzuki toward the landing pads. Sadao had driven off in this direction with the Mustang. Given the nature of the false broadcast they just witnessed, there was really only one possible destination for him – the Chairman's helicopter.

Please don't be a dumbass. Please don't fuck this all up, Sadao.

The dirtbike rattled and shook all over the road until the giant converted Chinooks came into sight at the base of the hill, glowing menacingly in the generator-powered landing area lights. All of the Division Chairmen and women were here, lording over their human zoo from their jewel-studded perches. The whole thing was a joke – this world was a joke. If you weren't lucky enough to sit at the top you were crushed underneath. Mouse had no doubts the Chairman had fully planned to destroy Sadao from day fucking one. He was only now beginning to show his true shape.

Mouse threw the damaged bike to the dirt, ran to the closed bay doors of the Northwest Division helicopter and pounded on them. The Mustang wasn't to be seen but that didn't mean it wasn't driven up into the craft itself.

"Let me in! Let me in, you motherfuckers! Sadao! Sadao, it's Mouse!"

Bang bang bang bang!

Mouse pounded until his knuckles swelled and rain began to fall from the sky. The clouds swirled and flashed and the approaching thunder growled.

"Let me in, damn you!" Mouse picked up stones and began throwing them at the craft's windows. Finally, a smaller door opened and an armed guard emerged. Mouse stopped throwing and went to him. "I need to see Sadao!" he begged. "Please!"

"He's with the Chairman right now. You'll have to wait outside his chamber. Quietly," the guard added.

"Fine, yes! I'll be quiet. I promise!" Mouse lied.

The guard lowered the stairs and allowed Mouse to step up into the main room.

Shouting could be heard from the Chairman's private office in the back. Mouse went toward the door, but the guard stopped him. So he paced the lounge area instead. On screen behind him was the ongoing race coverage. Competitors were passing through the hard-to-find checkpoints in the sandy desert 10 miles southwest of their current position. Sato's Orochi circle was among the 20 or so leaders. All was not immediately lost, it seemed.

Bang! Crash!

Something was being thrown inside the Chairman's office and the yelling escalated. Mouse exchanged a look with the guard and both of them went to the door together.

Wham! The door flew open, knocking Mouse over into the guard's arms as Sadao stormed out. Mouse watched him march toward the rear bay for the car. "Let me out!" he yelled at no one in particular.

Mouse scrambled to his feet. "Sadao! Wait!"

Sadao ignored him and kept walking toward the rear of the craft as the guard ran after him to facilitate his hasty exit.

The hell?

Mouse got to his feet, rubbing his bruised shoulder from the door slam. He peered into the Chairman's office. The man sat behind his big fancy smashed glass desktop, looking indignant. Mouse went in and shut the door behind him. Upon closer look, it appeared the chair Sadao had been sitting in had made a sudden impact with the side of the desk, shattering the finely crafted surface.

The Chairman sighed and rubbed his forehead. "Do you know the bills that man has racked up for me this month? Emergency medical services, pilot overtime, ICD transmitter circuitry repair – he's out of fucking control and I'm done with it."

Mouse grabbed the unsmashed end of the desk and leaned in. "Sadao has good reason to be upset with you and your technology! His man was killed tonight and another nearly died thanks to your innovations."

The Chairman sat back in his chair and sighed. "Mouse, I know you idolize him. Same as everyone under his rule it would seem; but he's a liability I cannot afford anymore."

"What do you mean by that?" Mouse wanted to know.

"I have relieved him of his command of the Orochi team."

"What?! You can't fucking do that!"

The Chairman folded his hands. "Actually, I can. And I have. The shareholders took a vote an hour ago. It was a joint decision."

Mouse shook his head. "No, that's not possible. You can't just remove him. He's the only one who holds that team together! They're not going to listen to you. You're going to have a mutiny on your hands. You don't even speak their language!"

"I know. That is why I have instated Ichiro Tagata in his place."

"Tagata's half-dead in a medical tent right now, no thanks to you!"

The Chairman held up a hand. "Tagata-san has been evacuated to the University Hospital. He's stable. My men are with him and will handle the paperwork as soon as he recovers."

Mouse was dumbstruck. *Did Tagata know about this? Was he part of it? Were both he and Shiratori part of it?*

"I don't believe this. This is how you're going to treat Sadao?! After all these years of hard work and determination to support and train those men who came from nothing so they can risk their lives to make you and your cronies stinking rich?! Shame on you!"

The Chairman cocked his head in challenge. "Does robbing your hometown blind follow your definition of 'hard work,' Mouse?"

Mouse opened his mouth and shut it soon after. *Fuck, he has a point.*

"We sent a camera crew out to the Arizona border to get a little backstory on you. As it turns out, your acquisition by the Orochi team wasn't exactly 'voluntary.' As I'm sure neither was the destruction of your homestead – your garage. Burned to the ground. Lots of folks back home thought you were dead."

Mouse frowned. *Fuck, fuck, fuck.*

"But, however you came to be with the Orochis aside, and whatever Koga-san did to convince you he was a righteous man, is ultimately not my concern. You are a consenting adult. To each his own. Unfortunately, not everyone under his shadow is of age to consent to such a lifestyle."

Mouse's heart skipped a beat. "What are you saying?"

"I'm saying what I said to Koga-san and to the public viewers – a racing team camp is no place to raise children. What happened to that unfortunate lad today I think serves as an excellent example."

"Goro is not Sadao's fault," Mouse said angrily. "Your camera flew in there all fucked up. It probably set off a spark."

"On an unregulated fuel supply, I might add."

"You told me you thought our fuel scheme was innovative or creative or some bullshit like that!"

"And highly risky – a risk children need not take part in anymore. Immigration authorities have been notified. The orphans belong back in their home country with their rightful families."

"They don't have families! They're refugees Sadao rescued from death and starvation in Mexico!"

"Rescued? Is that what he calls it? Did he tell you how much he paid for each of them?"

Mouse shook his head in disgust. "Don't even go there."

"It's men like Sadao that keep the human traffic market solvent, you know."

"You don't know anything – not one fucking thing that's true. I've walked a mile with that man. I know him."

The Chairman rocked in his chair a moment. "Did you know he's wanted for murder in three states?"

Mouse couldn't believe this. "What the fuck are you talking about?"

"Previous chairpersons have kept his arrest records off the books. And the sadly slipping provisional government of these so-called Wastelands has no real means for capturing or convicting him. He's an economical "untouchable" as they say. For a long time, he's been protected by people whose consciences have been ruled by financial gain. Mine however, is not. I meant it when I said I was here to clean up this sport and bring it back to the mainstream. My shareholders and fellow chairpersons agree with this vision. It's high time somebody cleaned house and sent these outlaws back to the shitholes they crawled out of!"

Mouse was sickened by all this to the point that all he could do was laugh. "So you're telling me you're going to deport every team member in five divisions with an arrest record? Good luck with that. You won't have any men left to race!"

"I'll have some. And I'll take my time with it. But first and foremost, the worst apples of the barrel have to go – starting with your lover!"

Mouse stared him down from across the broken table. "You disgusting piece of shit. I suppose fucking me in exchange for a transmission doesn't conveniently fall into your guidebook of sin. Neither does replacing one outlaw with another just so you can keep some semblance of control over the mobs. Do you really think the Orochis are going to strap happily into their vehicles and race their little hearts out for you after you've sent their idol packing back to Japan?!"

"Tagata-san is not an outlaw, nor is he an illegal. He's a Canadian citizen with a clean record. The men trust him. He will set a good example."

"Good example, huh? Let's make something clear. I'm done being your little spokesperson for your bullshit squeaky-clean agenda. My hands are just as dirty as the rest of the men out there turning circles in the dust for a buck. You've just made the worst decision of your life, mister. You have no idea the kind of people you're fucking with." Mouse turned to leave. "I almost feel sorry for you."

"I wouldn't walk out of here so fast with a threat like that hanging in the air. These walls are monitored. Anything happens to me, it will be on record, *Konezumi.*"

Mouse whipped around. "What did you just call me?"

The Chairman blinked. "*Konezumi.* It's your nickname, I thought. It means – "

"I know what it means! How did you know about it?"

"Koga-san calls you that all the time, I assumed."

Mouse shook his head. "No, he doesn't call me that all the time. In fact, he only calls me that when we're alone. Very alone."

"I must have just heard it once."

Webspinner has many eyes. Some that you can see and some that you cannot see.

Mouse took a step back toward the desk. "You didn't hear it once, it's a foreign phrase. To get it right you'd have to hear it a lot of times. Maybe during playback, rewind and play again and again. You sick sad sonofabitch, you've been watching us fuck. Over and over, holding your sad droopy cock, dreaming I was worshipping yours instead of his. That's what you've been after all this time, isn't it? That fantasy that someone would want you that much, do anything to get you hard and in their mouth and ass. When you had me that one time you came in me so fast it barely made it in!"

The Chairman flushed and jumped to his feet. "Enough! Get out of here! You want to go fuck that murder's cock – go right ahead! I have no use for either of you!"

Mouse smiled, slow and wide. "You think this is an easy victory, don't you? That you can just snap your fingers and change everything? Don't give me that crap that you have no love for money. Money is all you have. You could never be the kind of man Sadao is. You don't have half his balls. You destroy what you can't buy, but it doesn't work that way here in the desert. Never did and never will," he said and left the Chairman to his delusions.

Aside from the growing thunderstorm, when Mouse got back to camp everything was quiet. Sadao and the Mustang were nowhere to be seen. All he could guess for now was that Sadao didn't want to be found.

Mouse unlocked the trailer door and inside he found Kei and Lupe sleeping on the pullout sofa. Lupe opened an eye.

"Hey, what happened?" he asked sleepily.

Mouse took a heavy seat on the lounge chair. "Chairman threw Sadao out. He's called immigration to come collect him and the orphans. Anyone without a green card, I guess."

Lupe made a weird face. "He won't have any racers left!"

"That's what I told him. But as far as the little ones and Sadao are concerned, he's resolved."

"Fuck him, man. Boss won't let him get away with that bullshit. Those are his kids!"

"I know. I just wish I could find him right now. Talk to him. Anything."

Lupe sat up. "So you don't know where Boss is?"

Mouse shook his head dejectedly. "I need to talk to someone. Someone who knows him better than anyone... "

"Shiratori?"

Mouse nodded slowly.

"He came back alone about an hour ago. Got no clue what he did with Goro's body. Better take a knife with you, Gringo. We don't know how involved he is in all of this. You want me to go with you?"

"No, this is something I need to do alone."

Mouse slipped one of Sadao's carving knives into his pocket and headed out to meet the General in his nest. Shiratori's trailer was parked a few yards down the path. Similar to Sadao's in make and model, it was painted bright white with feathers here and there, blowing away in the wind. Mouse tried to peep in the windows but it was dark inside. Mouse knocked. No answer.

Mouse paced around the trailer a few times then went for the roof, climbing up the access ladder to the main air vent on the top.

Well, you've made it out of one of these before this way, might as well go in the same way. He can't ignore you that way.

Mouse used the end of the knife to unscrew the fasteners on the vent hood. It came off easily and soon he had the fan assembly popped out as well. He could see down into the main room. It was dark but he could make out the outline of Shiratori's armor lying on the pulled out sofa bed.

Does he fucking sleep in that shit?

Mouse stuck his legs in and lowered himself silently. His toe was able to reach the arm of the couch so he could shift his grip to drop himself the rest of the way in. Mouse stepped to the floor without a sound and let his eyes adjust. Shiratori's shape hadn't moved. He stood beside him, blinking until he could make out the details of the trailer. The interior was spartan compared to Sadao's. Weaponry and masks of war hung on the walls with little else. His armor – several different styles and colors – were set on stands around the room. It was eerie. It looked like he was surrounded by a small band of *ronin*.

Mouse eyed the sleeping man on the couch. His helmet hood was drawn and his metal arm lay limp beside him. He slept like the dead. Strange man, indeed. Wait... something was missing. The gauntlet. Mouse blinked. Shiratori's busted hand was nowhere to be – Gnnngh!!

Metal fingers came around from behind and bit into his neck squeezing him, threatening his next breath. *Oh, shit! Shit!*

"Like Mouse to cheese," Shiratori sneered in his ear as he held him with the missing gauntlet. "Did you think I did not expect you?"

Mouse couldn't breathe, but he could move so he threw his weight forward to shake the man off him. Shiratori moved with him like water and his grip only tightened. Mouse was starting to pass out and his legs gave as he hit the floor. The fingers released him. Mouse coughed and gasped for air as stars filled the air.

Shiratori put a bare foot to his chest and flicked on the light. Mouse lay there like a fish out of water. The man reached down and re-attached his arm and drew his wooden sword in two seconds. He held it at Mouse's throat as he reached down to relieve Mouse of his meager weapon.

Shiratori twirled the sheathed knife in the air and stuck it into the folds of his loin cloth – Japanese underwear thing – the only thing besides the arm and glove the man was currently wearing. His hair was unbound and hung long and black against his shoulders. It looked damp. He'd been showering.

"You look so surprise. Hahaha! Poor Mouse-san. Not so sneaky."

Mouse lay back on the floor to catch his breath while Shiratori laughed at him a moment then let him go.

"You're fucking insane!" Mouse said, when he could speak.

Shiratori looked down at him and smiled proudly. "Yes. This is correct. This is why no sane man can best me!"

Mouse sat up slowly and rubbed his throat. "Was it really necessary – all the theatrics? Why didn't you just open the goddamn door!"

Shiratori cocked his head curiously. "Because that is what sane man would do, ne?"

Mouse sighed and got slowly to his feet.

Shiratori extended an arm and helped him up with a pat to his shoulder. "We sit. Drink sake together, yes?"

"I don't want sake, I -" Mouse was struck dumb again as Shiratori turned to open his kitchen cupboards. His entire back was covered in a beautiful, highly detailed tattoo of a white bird of prey – like a bald eagle that was bald everywhere. Layers upon layers of feathers swirled and fanned across his shoulder blades and down his spine where two thick muscled talons reached forward in attack pose. The beak was solid black, the thin red tongue, screaming. The eye, Mouse was puzzled to see, was white. The bird-beast he chose to have indelibly marked on his skin, was blind.

Shiratori took down two small black lacquered boxes and pulled a large blue bottle, half-filled with white fluid from his fridge.

"Come," he said with a grin. "We sit and drink."

Mouse sat carefully across from the mostly-naked man and watched him pour the boxes with a critical eye. He wasn't too sure if he should drink anything this man offered.

"What did you do with Goro's body?" he asked suspiciously as Shiratori pushed the little drink box to him before pouring his own.

"You do not trust me," he said.

Mouse nodded.

"This is good thing. You are smart man, Mouse-san. This I know. When we first met I did not guess you were thinking man."

Mouse snorted disgustedly. "Thanks."

"But then I see you are man who can grow to his environment. Very quick to adapt. See everything. Know things very fast. This is man I like, I think. *Kanpai!*" he said and knocked his box back, drinking in a series of gulps.

Mouse picked up his box and sipped dubiously at the corner. The sake was cold and sweet. "You didn't answer my question."

"Ah, yes. Your question is good question. You should know that I took boy's body to quiet place up high. I lay him on rock and set his flesh to burn. This is how I release spirit. I do this for all our men who give their life for their brothers. I send spirit back to gods," he said with a wave of his hand.

"You think you're some kind of shaman for these poor bastards?"

Shiratori squinted at him with his good eye. "Not shaman. Priest. My *ojisan* tended important shrine in my village. I learn from him many things. He was wise man who knew way of the gods. He teach me to see many thing others do not."

"If you're so all-seeing, why is your back-tattoo blind?" Mouse asked bitterly. He couldn't help but notice how small and almost silly Shiratori looked without his coat of armor.

Shiratori laughed and refilled his square cup. "I tell you story, ne? You listen, then you understand maybe. I not tell this story to many," he said pointing at Mouse. "It is ancient secret only wise men can understand."

Mouse picked up his box and took another slow sip. It wasn't half bad actually, and a little alcohol was what his frazzled nerves begged for.

"Long, long ago in Japan lived old woman with big garden full of many good vegetable. Many food she grow for her village and family. Every night she come sit in her garden with broom to chase away *tanuki*. You know, *tanuki?*"

"No. What is it, a rat?"

"No. Bigger. Like American fox or raccoon. Raccoon dog they are called sometime."

"Sure," Mouse said, annoyed. He really wasn't in the mood for 'granny tales.' "So granny's got a yard full of raccoons, and... "

"Do not rush story," Shiratori warned, finishing his second cup. "You drink and listen or you miss point."

Mouse rolled his eyes and drank until his box was empty. This seemed to please Shiratori immensely and he soon poured them both another.

"Old woman sit in garden every night with broom to scare tanuki away from her food. One night she see tanuki with bad leg. Tanuki look sick and thin. Tanuki has bad fur and walk very slow on bad leg. Old woman feel sorry for tanuki-chan and she let him eat from her garden."

"This a story about being kind to others? Because I know the Golden Rule."

"Silent!" Shiratori hissed. "You smart man, but you no patient!"

"Okay! Okay!" Mouse zippered his mouth and let the crazy one continue.

"Many year go by and old woman become very old and sick. But now because of garden food, Tanuki-chan become big and fat on bad leg. He grow long pretty fur and bright eyes. One night old woman say to him: 'You must go. I am too old and sick to give you my food. I have only strength to grow for myself. You must go now, Tanuki-chan and find other place to eat. You are strong now, you can hunt.' But Tanuki-chan, refuse. He no leave this garden where he has grown fat. So old woman get broom and come to hit him. But she is old and sick and Tanuki-chan is fast and well. So he climb up broom to old woman shoulder and with sharp strong claws he take out her eyes and make her blind!"

Mouse jumped a bit. "That's fucked up! What wisdom am I supposed to gain from that story?"

Shiratori smiled at Mouse like he was a tanuki himself. "Old woman say same thing: 'Why, after many year you thank me this way?' Tanuki-chan say: 'Because you did not see with eye. Now I take eye and you learn to see. I do not have bad leg. I do not have bad fur. I always strong Tanuki. You always blind,' he say and walk away from old woman and eat last of her food on four good leg."

Mouse blinked. "So the little furry fucker was a con-artist. That still doesn't make him right. Why does the old woman get the shaft in this story? You Japanese are fucked up people, I gotta say if that's the kind of shit you tell your kids. And it doesn't explain your tattoo, either. Why a blind bird of prey?"

Shiratori studied Mouse's face carefully. "Do you know how I caught you tonight — come in from roof?"

"It was dark in here."

"No!" Shiratori said sharply. "You saw armor."

"Yeah, this place is kinda full of it."

"You saw armor on bed and make big mistake."

Mouse drank his cup and tapped the bottle for another. "Yeah, yeah, you got me there, I admit. But it was an easy mistake! You never go anywhere without all that shit on. Ridiculous. I assumed you slept in it too!"

"Not ridiculous," Shiratori said and obliged him, refilling his own again. "Smart. Smart like Tanuki-chan."

Mouse paused before he drank. Maybe it was the sake, but Shiratori was starting to make a little bit of sense to him. Mouse shook the notion off. "Both you and Sadao tell ridiculous stories. He's got one about a bell tower that's just as nuts."

Shiratori slammed his metal arm on the tabletop and laughed high and clear. "Sa--Sadao-sama, he tell you about bell tower?"

Mouse felt hurt. "Sadao told me no one knew that story. Not even you."

Shiratori made a small tower-shape with his metal fingers. "Poor little Sadao-kun, trapped in the tower... " he cooed. "He tell you why he not ring bell?"

"So that story was true?"

"Yes. Very famous boy, Sadao-kun and the bell. All children hear this story in my village. But I ask you again," he said, eyes narrowing. "Did he tell you why he not ring bell to save himself?"

From the way Shiratori was asking, it seemed he felt he knew the answer and that pissed Mouse off. "He didn't tell me. He said I should think about it. And I did and I still don't get it. I would have rung the damn bell. He said that's because I'm an American or some bullshit."

"Not just American way to think. Smart man way to think," Shiratori said, pointing at his own forehead. "I ring bell too, like you. Best way go down fast."

"So... Sadao's an idiot."

"No," Shiratori corrected. "I not follow stupid men. No, Sadao is smart man. I will tell you one more story, true story, and then I think you will understand bell tower riddle, too."

Mouse sighed, looking for a clock. "It's been a shit day. I need sleep... "

"I make quick story. True story about slave boy I once knew."

Mouse shrugged and took another sip of sake. "Go for it. As long as nobody loses an eye!"

Shiratori cackled, refilled their cups and began:

"In Japan during war I and my army brothers were sent to guard merchant road to Chiba. We need supply for our clan hiding from enemy in mountain. We have gun and knife and we hide in trees and wait for men to come. One day we see slave boy walking down mountain road alone with sake barrel on his back. Army brothers want to take sake, so we capture slave boy and tie him to tree. He no fight, no speak, just let my brothers do as they please. I see his face – thin and dirty and his back bloody from whip. I tell my brothers, 'Stop! I know this boy.' This boy is from Toba. He was student at my English school before the war. He was good student. Good fighter. Enemy clan, but good with sword. I want to know now, why is he slave?"

Oh my god, his scars. Mouse thought.

"So I watch him, feed him, give him drink. But his spirit is dead. He not speak. Not one word for two days. Then he look at me and he say: 'You must kill me. Kill me quick with knife.' I say to him: 'I do not kill the dead. There is no honor in it. Tell me, slave boy, who has stolen your spirit?' He tell me his master is very evil man. He beat him, he rape him, starve him. 'Why do you obey this master?' I ask. He no answer me.

"I tell him: 'You are warrior! You must take back your stolen spirit!' I cut him from tree and say: 'Go back to this master. Take knife. It is very sharp. When he come to beat you and show you his thing, you cut it off! Take his manhood and as he die, you eat his thing in front of him. This is how to regain your spirit he has stolen.' Slave boy took knife from me and went down mountain path without his burden.

"I do not see him for year. Then at harbor I see slave boy again. But he is not slave anymore. Tall, strong boy with clean skin. He is working at docks. He see me and tell me he is going to America. He will hide in boat and go over ocean to Mexico – be free man in America. I laugh at him. I say: 'Any place you can be free, if you have your spirit.'

"But I go back to camp in mountain and I think maybe I can be warrior too, in America. I sleep and dream of place with much land and clean sky and water. I think, slave boy has good idea. So I go back to docks and look for him, but he is already gone. Gone to America."

Shiratori stopped and shot back his sake, pouring another. Mouse looked at his dark little box and felt how dry his mouth had become and finished the lot of it. His head spun a little and his heart pounded. There was sweat on his forehead.

"You expect me to believe this story?" Mouse said quietly. "That Sadao ate his abuser's penis? That's disgusting. He wouldn't do that. If anything he cut the bastard's throat and escaped."

"Ask your boyfriend how he won back his spirit!" Shiratori said, angrily.

Mouse stood up. "You know what, I will!"

"You do not trust me." Shiratori said, looking up at him. "This is good. You should not trust me."

"That's because you know you're guilty," Mouse said, challenging him to confess.

"No. Because *I* trust no man," he said with a cold eye. He got to his feet to stand at equal height with Mouse. The white eye glared at him – the eye that had learned to see.

"What a sad and pathetic life you must have, General. To trust no one. Be close to no one. Care about no one but yourself."

"Ah, yes. But I am free. Free of everything that weigh down other man. I have none of it. I have perfect existence."

"You're probably incapable of feeling guilt or regret, aren't you? You've never spent one sleepless night worried sick about anyone but yourself. There's a lot of shit that's gone down these past weeks with no answers," Mouse said accusingly. "I want to know who let the raiders in the garage! And I want to know what happened to those guards! Somebody unlocked the seal on a can of gas in that equipment trailer tonight to set off that explosion! Somebody is to blame for all of this and I think it's you!"

"Is this what you will tell Sadao-sama tonight in his bed?" Shiratori said, without a flinch.

"I already told him. I told him he should question you. He should keep a better eye on you! You, who are his enemy. Your words, not mine!"

"Not all enemy should be defeated," Shiratori said simply. "When all enemy die, so must warrior. Without enemy there is no reason for warrior to exist."

Mouse stared at this enigma of a man in his underpants. Mouse realized he was no more knowledgeable of him or Sadao and his bell tower bullcrap or their deep dark monkey-jungle past than he was when he first entered the trailer tonight. Albeit a bit

more drunk, however.

He is a genius. You will see. One day he will impress you.

"I just want to speak to Sadao," Mouse said, pathetically, knowing he was no match for this man – guilty or innocent.

"Then sit and wait. Sadao-sama will come. He will come to me and say he want to talk."

Mouse eyed Shiratori carefully and sat back down across from him. "I'll wait. But no more sake and stories, okay? I don't want to wake up covered in udon."

Shiratori smiled, "No udon, I promise."

Twenty minutes later there was a knock at the door. Mouse answered it. As predicted it was Sadao. His hair and clothes were damp from the rain.

"Thank god," Mouse said and hugged him.

Sadao hugged him back and kissed his head. "Go back to the trailer and rest," he said. "I need to talk to Shiratori-san."

Mouse lay alone in Sadao's bed trying to sleep. Every time he closed his eyes and drifted off he saw the tower again – doused in fire and rain. He woke breathing fast, listening to the downpour outside. It was very late. Eventually the trailer shuddered as the door opened and shut quietly. Sadao was back. Mouse lay on his side, waiting for him to undress and climb into bed next to him. From his grunts he sounded exhausted.

Mouse rolled over to let him know he was still awake. "*Gomen, Konezumi,*" Sadao muttered. "We were talking late."

"I'm so sorry," Mouse said as Sadao's arms gathered him close. "Goro, the Chairman... it's not fair. He can't do this to you. None of this is your fault."

Sadao sighed into his hair. "We'll talk about this later. Now, I need sleep."

"You also need to take a stand. Stop this man before takes everything from you!"

Sadao's fingers stroked the hair back from Mouse's forehead where he planted a kiss. "In this I am powerless. But I am glad there are some things he cannot take from me."

Mouse looked up at him, at the softness there. "You were the one who told me you alone held this team together – no one else, not even Tagata can take your place."

Sadao caressed his face, calming him. "You do sound like an *Okusama.*"

Mouse leaned into his touch. "Don't tease me. I'm being serious. You have to stand up to him!"

Sadao looked sadly into his eyes. "Some battles are not meant to be fought."

"... and not all enemies are meant to be defeated? That's some shit Shiratori said to me too tonight. Sadao, I think Shiratori's behind this! He's the one who's been helping the Chairman set you up! He had access to the garage and your trailer. He's the lord of the damn keys! It would have been simple! If he wanted you out and Tagata in, then he's satisfied his goals. He only wants to win, you said that!"

"Tagata will be a good clan boss," Sadao said, ignoring Mouse's theory. "I always meant for him to succeed me. He has the right heart for it. The men respect him. It's his turn now."

Mouse couldn't believe what he was hearing. "And what about you? What will you do? You can't just lie here and wait. The Chairman wants to send you packing back to Japan!"

Sadao pulled Mouse close and kissed his mouth. "I made a promise to myself that I would never return to Japan as long as I was alive. And I don't intend to break that promise."

Mouse felt tears building in his eyes. "Fuck you, you're not going back dead, either. And you're *not* getting in that car tomorrow night!"

"I have to see this through," Sadao said resolutely. "Goro gave his life for this race. I won't dishonor his memory by not finishing it."

"Sadao, please," Mouse said, voice breaking. "I'm scared. If something happens to you... "

Sadao smiled sadly and taking hold of his chin, filled his mouth with a deep kiss that lasted a long, long time. Mouse was panting and wordless when the kiss ended and the man's teeth and tongue worked down his neck and across his chest. He squirmed with hopeless excitement as those hands slipped low, stripping him out of his underclothes.

Flesh to flesh they lay together – touching, kissing, tasting. Warmth and arousal rose deep in him. "I thought you needed sleep," Mouse said when he could find his breath. Sadao returned his smile. The hot damp head of his cock pressed eagerly against his thigh. "There are things I need more than sleep," he said. "Now, show me my jewel."

Outside the trailer windows, the rain fell hard and the thunder rumbled out across the wet sand dunes where buggies with lights and navigation systems struggled to continue to clear the final checkpoints on the course. Sometime after dawn the first of the sand racers would return to the highway and rumble on fat round tires south to the Canyonlands where their teammates waited with ATVs to enter the dicey labyrinth of slot canyons southern Utah was notorious for.

Mouse lay on his back, legs spread, drowsy with pleasure. Sadao had nuzzled his way between his thighs to slowly lick all around his cock, eating up the slippery juices they'd stirred up from their initial embrace. Mouse was still sore from the recent piercing, but he knew the little puncture was healing well. He begged Sadao to make love to him properly.

Tenderly, Sadao kissed the pearl ring. He took it into his mouth and sucked it gently, stirring up a wave of deep stimulation in Mouse's groin. Oh, he was right there were benefits – unexpected benefits to being claimed in this location. He spread his thighs wide and Sadao kissed his twitching hole, soothing it with his tongue. He held Mouse's balls in his palm, rolling them gently, taking his time. The tongue went deeper, tugging at his rim, urging the tight folds of muscle to open and relax.

Mouse moaned and ground his ass into Sadao's face, wanting to feel the prickling of his beard against his most sensitive skin. Sadao held his thigh back and ate him deeper, slipping a strong warm tongue in and out in a slow steady rhythm.

"Aaaaaaaah!" Mouse moaned. "More, please... "

"Shhh... " Sadao whispered. "The boys will hear."

Mouse had forgotten Lupe and Kei were on the other side of the locked bedroom door sleeping. Mouse opened his mouth and panted in frustration. Sadao's teasing tongue made him want to moan and writhe without reserve. His thighs shook as another wave of pleasure washed through him. He grabbed a pillow and bit into it. Sadao licked him as deep as he could go, for as long as Mouse could take it without screaming. Then with a kiss to his "jewel" the man raised his head. His lips were wet with juice.

"Sit up," he said devilishly. "I know how to keep you quiet."

Mouse spat the pillow out of his mouth. "Huh?"

Sadao sat back against the headboard and tucked a pillow behind him. He sat cross-legged, dick pointing due north. He made a motion with his finger. "Come here and sit in my lap."

Mouse swallowed a whimper and nodded, but first he needed a taste of his favorite hunk of flesh. "I want my pearl too," he said and dove for it.

"Mmmnnm, mmmm…" with his mouth full, Mouse was more muffled than normal. That was until Sadao reached forward and began rubbing his hole with his fingertips. "Gngngmmn!!" Mouse's hips bucked as he took Sadao deeper into his throat.

"Shhh... if you can't be quiet, we stop."

Pop! "Fuck you," Mouse whispered, licking the hell outta Sadao's big shaft while he tried to speak. "You tell me to be quiet and yet you keep doing... *that*... nnnngh!"

Sadao hissed as Mouse's teeth nipped him. "Enough of this, time to stop you up!" Sadao turned Mouse around so his back was against Sadao's chest, straddling his thighs. Mouse felt the tip of the man's dick nudging his ass.

Mouse bit his lip and shook with anticipation. Sadao tipped his head back and smothered his moan with a full kiss. "Ride me," he whispered to Mouse's lips. "Scream into my mouth if you must." Mouse swallowed Sadao's tongue while he worked his hips over Sadao's cock until his body had taken him all in.

"Aghmn!!" Mouse sobbed, feeling Sadao's tongue vibrating against his own. Sadao held Mouse's chin back, keeping their mouths together while they fucked. Mouse could feel Sadao's new pearl rolling over his nugget deep inside. The stimulation was not unlike the first pair, but the sensation was slightly different – new and exciting.

With his thighs and asshole stretched open so wide – Mouse's own pearled ring rolled and tumbled along the length of Sadao's shaft with every thrust and buck of his hips.

Sadao's fingers slid up his erection and formed a fist, holding Mouse's dripping cock, stroking and squeezing it as they moved and breathed each other in. Joined above and below, Mouse had never felt so completely filled. His mind was slipping. The world was falling away and fading until all that existed was this motion, this taste – this one body. He forgot utterly why he was supposed to be quiet and rode Sadao harder, unable to hold himself back. He felt no pain as he brought his hips down faster – grinding, working the jewels together – wanting to keep the pleasure building until they both exploded with it.

Sadao held his face firm, but in the end they both split apart, crying out in release, coming hard and breathing wet against each other's lips.

"Sorry," Mouse panted. "I couldn't… "

Sadao's breath was hot on his cheek. "It's okay, neither could I."

"Mmmn… " Mouse rose and let Sadao slide out of him. He turned and put his arms around his love, peppering his face with soft kisses. Sadao closed his eyes and pressed his lips to his shoulder. His strong arms wrapped him up so tight, Mouse felt the air leaving his chest. "Haahhh… "

Mouse went limp and let Sadao hold him for as long and as tightly as he needed to. They were so close, Mouse could hear their heartbeats slowing in unison. But as happy as this intimacy made him, Mouse somehow knew this was Sadao's way of saying goodbye.

Chapter XXI

Static

Mouse stood in an inky black puddle in the middle of Sadao's burnt out equipment trailer holding his nose. He wasn't sure why he was there. The putrid stench of cooked metal and flesh hung thick in the air, making him want to retch. What was left of Sadao's collection of fine street bikes was melted to the floor in Daliesque forms. Mouse was glad he'd had the mind to move his still uncompleted Ninja to the Orochi garage, even if no one had been able to foresee this tragic turn of events. It nagged at the back of his mind, *Why? What happened in here?*

"Hey, man! Hurry it up in there — we gotta go! We gotta make it down to Canyonlands today!"

"I know," Mouse replied. "Just give me another minute." Lupe was anxious to get Sadao's trailer rolling to the next change point 200 miles southeast to the start of the canyon leg. Since losing their helicopter support after yesterday's hullabaloo with the Chairman, the Team had to split up and drive the remaining vehicles out themselves. Shiratori left early with Kei in his trailer to intercept a hauler bringing down the replacement ATV from base camp. Sadao left soon after with the Mustang. Since they no longer had an equipment truck to haul it in, the car had to be relocated to the last change station at the south end of the canyon route on its own wheels. Mouse and Lupe would send off Murasaki into the north end of the canyons, then haul ass south to meet up with Sadao before he took off for the final highway leg of this insanity.

Mouse kicked at the soggy debris underfoot and sighed. He didn't like having to spend the last night of the race apart. It felt wrong to him — another evil omen in a long list of portents that had haunted him ever since he was pierced by his lover.

Maybe the pearls connect us more than we thought, Mouse mused, pausing to pick up a chip of plastic. The ring threaded through his flesh ached every time he sat or crouched, reminding him of the one that was missing. He pushed the little chip of plastic around in his palm — it was translucent. He didn't recall any part of Sadao's bikes having that color or texture.

Ah fuck me, it's part of the missing camera! The part that flew in wobbling right before the boom. Where's the rest of it?

By all appearances, the remains of the camera drone were blown to oblivion. Curious, Mouse tossed the chip aside and headed out of the back of the burnt truck to fresher air.

"'Bout time, Gringo! You were the one who wanted us to get to Boss before his start of the race! We gotta move!"

"I'm only riding with you to the north end of the Canyonlands," Mouse said, bending to look under the trailer. When he didn't see what he was looking for he kept strolling around, eyes to the ground.

"Wait, what? You gone *loco*? How are you getting there without the truck? You gonna walk, man?"

"No... " Mouse said, pausing to look in some bushes. "I'm taking Tagata's Suzuki."

"Eh? That shit won't roll. I saw you walking it back last night in the rain."

"I just need to hammer out the kinks," Mouse answered, looking up the road. "Oh there's where those fuckers went!"

"Where who – huh?"

Mouse trotted up the road a few paces and bent to pick up the two black translucent shiny objects that had rolled into the curve of the road.

"What you doing with those drones?" Lupe asked. "You want them to spy on us?"

Mouse shook his head as he carried them toward Sadao's trailer. "Nope. These are shutdown. When a camera is damaged or stops working properly another flies out from central command in its place. I knocked these two down last night when I got pissed at the media spectacle. Two others must have been sent to replace them once the racers remembered they were supposed to be racing and continued on," he said and stepped up into the cab. He set them on Sadao's couch, blocking them with pillows so they wouldn't roll off.

"What are you going to do with them?"

Mouse nibbled on his thumb, eyeing the dead drones. "I dunno yet. I gotta get Tagata's bike working first and there's not much time. Help me get his ride up in here and my tools. I'll get busy while you drive us out of here."

"Sure thing, but I'm confused. If Sadao damaged Tagata's camera when he threw it at the site near Toole and another one came in to cover the rest of Tagata's race, why did the damaged one show up all fucked up and trigger the explosion?"

Mouse looked at his little buddy and frowned. "That's the mystery I need to figure out in the next six hours. So do me a favor and cue up some race footage for me from yesterday will ya? Before we roll out?"

Lupe shrugged. "Sure, man."

"And teach me how to use this damn remote!"

●——————○——————●

Six hours later, they rolled into the change station camp just as evening began to set over the maze of canyons stretching out below them to the south. The Suzuki was in reasonably decent working condition, but the drones – Mouse had tried everything he could think of to get one open, bouncing around on Sadao's kitchen floor, but there weren't any seams in the devices' outer shell. He tried a hammer and chisel at where a seam should be, but that proved to only make a series of cracks travel across the globe. He'd watched Sadao destroy one with his bare hands but the idea here was to take one apart intact so he could study the insides. He figured at this point he was only damaging it.

Lupe pulled the trailer up alongside Shiratori's by the Orochi banner. As soon as the parking brakes were set, Shiratori was at the entry door banging.

Mouse opened it and Shiratori stomped his way in, surveyed the array of tools and bike parts on Sadao's kitchen floor and pointed at Mouse's nose, eye flashing.

"You late! Very very late! Race already go past quick."

"Huh? Murasaki's already started? What time is it?" Mouse whipped his head around to find a clock as Lupe stepped in from the cab to take his share of the General's tirade.

"Kei must take sand car back with Sato. I make repair to ATV. I attach tracer to frame. No mechanic! No painter! ATV has no *Orochi kishi!*" he said, barking at Lupe. "You drive too slow! Watch too much TV!" Shiratori made a grab for the remote, but Lupe beat him to it and held up his palms.

"Whoa, whoa... Shiratori-san. *Sumimasen*, Mouse was fixing up the Suzuki and checking footage for coverage of the fire last night during the whole drive. We didn't stop rolling even to pee!"

Shiratori's eyes narrowed. "Maybe if Mouse-san kept cap on gas can no explosion happen at all!"

"Hey! For your information, General. I was watching coverage to see if anyone entered the equipment trailer last night other than Lupe and Kei – neither of whom smelled gas!"

"Humph! And what did you see? You think you find your smoking gun, eh?"

Mouse sighed and gestured to the TV, which was still running footage from random cameras of the prior 12 hours. "I didn't see anything unusual," he said and sat down heavily at the table, rubbing his head. "Trust me, I watched hours of this shit."

Shiratori pointed to the remote with his metal hand. "Show me explosion," he said to Lupe. "Maybe Mouse-san have good idea."

Mouse looked up. "Wait? What?"

Lupe rolled the footage back. "I don't know which camera you want to watch but...
"

"Why is sound off?" Shiratori asked.

"I don't like having to listen to myself, okay?" Mouse said, embarrassed. Various points in the broadcast were interspersed with his interview sound bites shot before and during the Overland before the big blow out. Creative editing made it sound as if he was talking about the explosion itself.

"With no sound, you are using only half your thinking mind," Shiratori said, stepping closer to the screen, motioning to Lupe to turn it up.

The camera footage shown was one of the closer and clearer shots. It was taken from the drone feed of one of the passing racers who had the misfortune to turn the corner of the track just as the event happened.

All three of them stood and watched with their eyes and ears. The roar of the racer's bike engine could be heard, then the tiny sound of the Mexican music station playing as he approached the Orochi camp. The explosion flared out from the back ramp of the equipment trailer followed by the deafening blam. Then the camera feed went dead.

"I've watched this a hundred times," Mouse said. "If you zoom in close you can see poor Goro running Sadao's bike up the ramp just as the camp comes into sight. Then there's the flash as the camera gets right alongside the trailer and boom! Dead camera."

"Play again, slow frame," Shiratori said. Lupe did and Mouse watched the little man's one working eye dart about the image. Then he leaned forward as if he saw something he was unsure of. "Play other view," he said. Lupe cued up another clip of footage, this one was shot right over the handlebars of a bike racing past just ahead of the explosion. You could clearly see both Goro and the wobbly fatal camera enter the trailer separately. Then the boom sounded from behind the racer after they passed the point of the accident.

"See, that," Lupe said. "The camera set it off. That much is obvious."

"Show me second view, slow," Shiratori said, narrowing his eye. Lupe did so and just as the bike passed the trailer, Shiratori shouted for him to pause the playback.

"Huh... ? What do you see?" Mouse asked the General.

Shiratori stepped back, looking proud of himself. "There are two explosion! Run back recording. Look at chrome handlebar and tell me what you see."

Lupe and Mouse both moved closer to the screen as Lupe played it back frame by frame. Sure as shit, there was a flash of light reflected in the polish just before the big boom.

"Holy shit! Why didn't I see that?" Mouse asked himself. "That little drone exploded first! It set everything off! Fuck! How? Was it being controlled by remote?" He looked back to Shiratori for answers.

"Only one man can order offline camera to come back online," Shiratori said pointedly.

Mouse's brain jumped back to the previous day when they were flying with the Chairman. "You're right. Shiratori's right, Lupe! When we were trying to figure out what happened to Tagata that bastard asked his tech to start up the shutdown camera.

They were able to get two feeds at once but only if they set it up manually. A double feed screws up their tracking otherwise. Shit, are those things little bombs?"

Shiratori looked to the couch behind them where the two drones sat snug in the cushions. "Get rifle," Shiratori said to Mouse, picking up the cracked, dead drone. "Meet quick outside."

Outside it was growing dark as the three men marched to the top of a rocky rise. Shiratori held the mini bomb in the crook of his metal arm. Mouse had the rifle loaded and slung over his shoulder. Once they reached the top, Shiratori turned to him. "Are you good shot with rifle at bird?"

Mouse nodded. "Reasonably, yes."

"Then ready weapon and shoot on my word."

Mouse unlatched the safety on the loaded gun and positioned his eye on the site. "Okay, go!"

Shiratori used the power of his mechanical limb to toss the device high in the air. Daylight was dimming but Mouse caught it in his sight and followed it.

"Fire!" Shiratori shouted and Mouse did.

Bang! Blam!!

The little fucker blew up mid-air, sending trails of sparks down around them like it was the Fourth of July.

"Holy shit!" Lupe exclaimed. "You were banging all day on that thing, Gringo! Could have blown us sky-high! Then we would have been really late."

"No," Mouse said. "I don't think that's how it works. They need to be safe enough to handle am I right, Shiratori?"

Shiratori watched the cloud of smoke from the blast blow away in the breeze. "Chairman is not stupid man. If he want to make secret bomb, then bomb must be safe for normal use."

"Yes, but he got nervous every time Sadao batted them around, did you notice that?" Mouse asked.

Shiratori nodded. "Yes, because he knows what others do not. He no like to have big boom in his helicopter. Bomb must have special trigger. Special signal. Signal only he can send."

"That would explain why it didn't go boom when I chiseled at it. Or when Sadao smashed up one with his bare hands! Jesus! I can't believe he did that. Oh, fuck! I need to talk to Sadao! Now!"

"Yes," Shiratori agreed. "Sadao-sama should know not to smash bomb with hand. Come, we will use my radio."

Huddled around Shiratori's dinette, each of them tried to raise Sadao on his CB but there was no reply – only empty static. Mouse paced the floor of the trailer nervously. Rain was beginning to fall again and it was dark. Odds were Sadao was snug up in a bunk somewhere 50 miles south of them, resting before his leg of the race at first light. He had no chance of hearing the CB on his dash barking for someone to come answer.

"So Murasaki has a tracer and a camera right now, right?"

Shiratori nodded. "Yes, he drive into canyon with camera hovering above like black wingless bird."

"And when Sadao starts his race tomorrow, the ATV tracer will switch off and his will switch on so his assigned camera knows how to find him, right?"

Shiratori agreed. "Yes, that is how vehicle change works."

"But Sadao doesn't have a tracer welded to his frame yet. There was no time to attach it and the tracer meant for the Mustang blew up in the trailer blast. So there's still time!"

"Time for what? It's dark and raining outside!" Lupe interjected. "We will have to reach Boss by CB in the morning."

"And what then?" Mouse said, voice rising in panic. "They'll have a tracer on that car for certain by sunrise! We have to go now!"

"No!" Shiratori said, stopping him. "We do not go. Cannot drive truck fast enough around canyon. No big roads. Take Tagata-san bike. Ride fast, alone. Then you make it to camp by sunrise."

Mouse clasped Shiratori's metal arm in agreement. "I trust you," he said with a nod of his head.

Shiratori smiled. "Ride fast. Ride smart. I tell you path you should take."

Mouse took off into the rain 20 minutes later dressed in racing rain gear with a full tank of gas, a compass, a flashlight, the rifle and a map with Shiratori's navigational instructions on it in a waterproof sleeve. The remaining drone was strapped to the rear fender of the bike in his pack. He wasn't sure why, but he was insistent on carrying the device off with him. No one other than Shiratori and Lupe knew he had it and it was best he had one with him in the event he needed to prove to some thick-headed person what the cameras were capable of.

Thick-headed as in Sadao? Yes! As in Sadao! Do heads come any thicker? Now shut up and ride!

He sped off in a southern direction, keeping the tree line about a half-mile off to his right. There weren't many trees this far south in Utah and those that did grow here were stunted and small, set apart in small clumps. It was important he didn't stray too far west of their guideline in the dark or he'd tumble ass over handlebars into a slot canyon. The area was riddled with them, about six feet across at their narrowest. Some you couldn't see at all until you were in them.

Mouse rode hard for about an hour when the trees started to thin out. Shiratori had warned him about this and told him to choose a marker off to the east instead – a line of high rocks, but he just wasn't finding it in the darkness. Even the occasional thunderbolt wasn't enough to light up the far vistas. He paused, engine idling, for a map check. The CB crackled to life.

"Mouse, this is Coyote 5, come in?"

Mouse lifted the bagged receiver to his ear to listen through the plastic in the downpour.

"Yeah, this is Mouse. Lupe, what's up?"

"You sound muffled, but listen up. There's been a change in plans. Rain's flooded the lower canyons. I repeat, rain has flooded the lower canyons. They are diverting the racecourse. Can you hear me? There's a diversion!"

"Yeah, I can hear you!" Mouse yelled over the drops hitting himself and the plastic covered everything he was riding with. "Where to?"

"They're gonna pull them all out at Moab and take them up north on the 191 to the 50 east back to Green River and change vehicles there."

The fuck?

"Hang on, I'm trying to find this shit on the map!"

"Don't worry, just listen to me – I have new directions for you. Shiratori says you should be near the end of the tree line, is that right?"

"Yeah, I am. But where am I going?"

"You won't be able to catch Boss in time at the south Canyonlands station. That whole area's been evacuated due to mudslides, they're showing that here on the broadcast! You gotta head back north and west to meet him at Green River!"

"Fucking wonderful! Doesn't this bring the race closer to you?"

"Yeah, but we're already blocked off at the 191 junction. Only small traffic is being allowed through due to the race and the weather! Shiratori says if you head northeast now as fast as you can you'll catch Boss at Green River for sure!"

"I assume you haven't been able to hail him yet?"

"We tried earlier tonight but he's still out of range most likely. He's probably been on the move for a few hours now."

"Okay, I'm turning around but, how the hell do I find Green River?"

"Hang on… okay. I'm going to repeat the directions…"

Follow the tree line on your left and pass through it about halfway back. Then cross an open valley to the farthest ridge in a line of three. From there, turn north until you see the highway.

Mouse ran the instructions over and over in his mind as he rode into the weather. Rain was coming down hard and pelted his helmet so loudly there was no way he could have heard a call come in on the CB unless he managed to see the light flash. He'd been out in this shit for four or more hours now and daylight wasn't too far off. He only hoped the movement he saw up ahead were headlights passing along the highway and not a hallucination.

At last there were some trees so he paused under them to lift his shield and check his bearings. The compass read north by northwest – dead on what Shiratori ordered. Squinting through the rain, Mouse could just detect a small red light and another white one passing each other in the distance. It had to be the 28, which would take him north to the 50 east to the improvised Green River change station. He hoped he would be in time.

Once on an actual road, Mouse was able to make better time and cranked the throttle as fast as the still somewhat wobbly Suzuki could manage without skidding out on the wet asphalt. The rain thinned some by the time he turned onto the 50 East, where Mouse was unnerved to see racers already soaring past him in the opposite lanes. They were heading back toward the 1-15 and the highway course north – 250 miles back up to the Wasatch Mountain loop climb before descending into the finish line on the salt flats.

Shit, I'm late again!

Four minutes later he was pulling into the change station and the flurry of confusion therein. Racers, Team leads and race officials all looked to be on the edge of blows over the change in course. Not everyone had gotten the message in time to relocate their final vehicles and were now facing delays with highway closures due to rockfalls and landslides. Banners and vehicles were parked half-assed all over the turnout as 100 plus racers tried to get their grievances heard.

Mouse secured the bike, grabbed his pack and rifle off the rear rack, and worked his way through the crowds to read the posted rosters. Radios were blaring reports, as it seemed nobody in this haphazard camp had thought to bring a satellite dish. Mouse tried to make sense of it all as racers pushed and sloshed their way around him in the mud.

"Excuse me! Excuse me!! Where are the Northwestern results? Excuse me!" Mouse wasn't getting anyone's attention, so he did what Shiratori would do and took out his rifle and fired a shot over everyone's heads.

Bang!

The echoing shot stopped everyone cold. "I'm trying to find the location and position of the Orochi Team!" he shouted at the stunned crowd. "Can anyone tell me if Sadao Koga, number 05, left this checkpoint yet!?"

"Are you out of your fucking mind?" someone bellowed as the pushing and shoving resumed. Mouse was soon thrown up against a post with a hand-written statement nailed to it.

The race official pointed a muddy finger at it. "Can't you read?"

Mouse read the roster as fast as his eyes could move. The third man down on the Northwestern Division list was "Koga, Sadao – 05 : 4:45 am."

Mouse tugged at the race official's arm. "Did he have a tracer? Hey, can you tell me, did he have a tracer on the car?"

"Of course, everyone must have a tracer before they can clear the station! Are you stupid? It's a requirement! We had to affix Koga's – his idiot mechanic forgot to put it on! Now, bug off with that gun before you kill someone!"

Shit shit shit!

Mouse ran back to the bike and hailed Lupe.

"Coyote five! Can you read me?"

"Yeah man, you find Boss?"

"No, fuck, he got past me. They gave him a tracer when he cleared the station at 4:45 am. What time is it? I don't have a fucking watch!"

"Oh shit man, it's after five. Uh, hang on I was kinda asleep... let me … turn on… "

"Huh? Lupe?"

Mouse heard a whoop of joy on the other end.

"Lupe?"

"Holy tamales! Boss is in the lead!"

For those fortunate enough to have TV screens, it was obvious where the Orochi Team leader was. His snake symbol was leading the pack out the 50 toward the I-15 at speeds in excess of 125 mph – in the rain.

Mouse was on a muddy dirt track heading northwest for the I-15 in hopes that leaving the wandering highway would be the trick to catching Sadao.

"Boss just blew through Salina on the TV!" Lupe reported over the CB, giving Mouse periodic updates and navigational changes via Shiratori. "Take the next trail road at the fork and go north!"

"I already passed the fork!"

"Did you go north?"

"I-I think so! I'm gonna try Sadao again!"

"Okay, over and out."

From Salina the racecourse ran south for a few miles on the 70 before catching the I-15 and heading back north. Mouse's plan was to cut over to the I-15 twenty miles ahead, while Sadao caught the checkpoint on the loop.

"Big Snake, this is Little Mouse, come in?"

Nothing. Sadao had to be in range now. So the Mustang's CB was either non-operational or Sadao was ignoring him, for an hour or more now.

"Big Snake, this is Little Mouse, pick up please!"

This was getting tiresome. Trying to ride top speed on a dirt road one-handed in the rain on a busted bike with a bomb attached to it sucked.

"Sadao, you pig-headed piece of shit! Answer me!"

There was a crackle. *Yeah, you've been hearing me the whole time, haven't you, asshole?*

"*Nan da?!* I'm driving!!"

"I know, I know... so just listen! You have a bomb following you! Those little black round fuckers are bombs, do you hear me? The Chairman triggered that explosion that killed Goro! He was trying to kill you!"

"I know that already!"

He knew?

"Shiratori predicted it! The man has had a target on my back ever since he was voted in!"

"Then why did you let them re-attach a tracer?!"

"Can we discuss this later? I have this bakayaro Korean on my ass!"

"Let him pass! Sadao, throw the race! Get out of that car, now!"

"No!"

"No?! What the fuck is wrong with you?! You want to die behind the wheel that badly?!"

…….. ... . signal went dead.

Fuck this! Fuck him! Fuck the Chairman! Fuck this whole fucked up world!

But even as he bitched out everything and everybody in his mind, Mouse had an idea.

Mouse lay in the grass above the I-15 on a knoll, rifle perfectly balanced on a log, aimed at a long stretch of highway with his finger on the trigger. The CB was locked in receive mode.

"Okay, man. Boss just passed the 117 junction, you should see him soon."

Mouse couldn't respond to Lupe and hold his aim, so he thanked his little buddy in his head and waited. The sounds came first – the fwap of rotor blades and the thunderous roar of bike and car engines as the lead pack drew closer. Three enormous Chinook helicopters came up over the rise first, carrying the heads of various divisions. The Chairman's craft was among them. It occurred to Mouse he could just shoot the bastard right out of the sky and he would have, if it didn't mean possibly killing all the crew and guests as well in the crash. Mouse didn't have the type of soul that could live with that.

The first helicopter flew over his head just as Sadao's Mustang caught air over the short rise and slammed back onto the asphalt, leaving a trail of sparks bouncing off the windscreens of the racers hard on his tail. But Mouse couldn't spare Sadao another glance, his target was smaller and faster and hovering a good 100 feet above and behind him. Mouse tracked it in his sight, took aim and fired. Missed, *shit!* He cleared the chamber and dove to the dirt on his belly to catch a retreating shot. The freeway was long and straight here so there was more time to focus his aim.

3... 2... 1... BANG! BOOM!!!!

"I got it! I got it!!"

The little black ball of evil that had been filming Sadao's progress exploded mid-air – directly in the path of the two rear helicopters. Bits of pulverized translucent plastic splattered all over their windows along with a thick cloud of smoke. Both helicopters pulled up and out of the debris to regain their bearings. Only the Chairman's helicopter kept on the leaders.

"Hah! That's right! Everybody saw that, motherfuckers! Yes, I so rock!"

A whoop of joy came over the CB – two of them. Was Shiratori whooping for him? Mouse hit the dirt and grabbed the CB.

"Didja see that?"

"Fuck me, Gringo can shoot! Every channel we got here filmed that! People gonna be askin' some questions, you know! Like maybe that camera that flew in Boss' trailer was a hit!"

"That's what I'm hoping," Mouse said, catching his breath. But his joy was short lived. What if the Chairman knew he was cornered? What if he decided to strike anyway? Mouse knew it was only a matter of time before a replacement camera came around to take this one's place. And he couldn't take short cuts and shoot cameras down all day long. If only Sadao would listen to him and stop -

Shit, what is the trigger? What is it? Why can't I be smart like Shiratori says I am?

Mouse put his head on his knees and closed his eyes. He'd only had about four hours of sleep in the past two days and it was beginning to affect him.

"Hey Gringo, you okay? You better move from that spot before they come looking around."

"I hear you, I'm out."

Mouse shut off the CB and packed up. He rode Tagata's bike back down the hill away from the I-15 into the shaded gullies out of sight.

Mouse shut off the engine and lay in the grass with his arms over his eyes to think. *Think like Shiratori... no not even Shiratori's figured this one out. Think... like the Chairman? No, maybe... think like Mouse. After all, you were there during every incident.*

Mouse let his mind drift back to the night of the garage raid. Somehow the doors had opened and he was as convinced as Sadao now it was neither of his devoted men. But that time there were no explosions or cameras involved – just an unlocked door and two missing guardsmen, who were still missing. Then came the explosion in the equipment trailer. The defunct camera bomb associated with Sadao's tracer had exploded the moment it made contact with the gas supply. To assure maximum damage? No, to make it look accidental. That's his goal – to make everything look like an accident. He's no different from the Chairmen and women before him, buying out mechanics to make faulty welds in the racer's vehicles to manipulate outcomes and win big dollars. Only Chairman Marcus Getty was more high tech than the others and the current mechanic on the Orochi Team couldn't be bought for a handful of green – though he had certainly tried!

Yeah okay, the technology. It controls everything. Controls the cameras, etc. But unless Mouse could morph into one of the Chairman's tech crew and beam aboard the helicopter and push the right buttons... *Ugh!*

Mouse lay with his eyes closed and tried to calm his nerves enough to reach a deeper level of consciousness to dredge up the missing piece. It would be nice, he thought, to listen to radio static for a bit to calm himself and sat up to reach for the CB. Radio... radio static! That's it! *Fuck me! I can figure shit out after all! The radio's the key!*

Mouse bounced to his feet and donned his gear to ride. He flipped on the CB.

"Lupe! I need you ask Shiratori to give me the fastest route possible to the Salt Lake Basin Radio Tower."

"What you talking now? Radio tower?"

"Yes! That's right, the fucking Radio Tower! Get me there now!"

Chapter XXII

Fallen Bird

Two hours and a frantic ride 130 miles north later, Mouse was crouched behind the miniature oaks at the base of the Chairman's enormous radio tower. Sadao would be coming into CB range again soon as he rode up the I-80 grade he'd test driven with Mouse just a few days earlier. Mouse wanted to warn him if he could about what was going to happen. He removed the CB console from the Suzuki and strapped it to the pack on his back with the dead camera inside it and the rifle over his arm.

There was a high fence at the base of the tower and a pair of armed watchmen were pacing the perimeter. He'd watched them for 30 minutes now trying to think of a way past them. He could climb the fence, that was no problem. But once on the tower ladder climbing toward the transmitter, he'd certainly be seen. The guards had to go. The rifle was loaded with six shots, but Mouse still could not bring himself to shoot another human being.

This mess isn't their fault. They don't deserve to lose kneecaps so I can save my stubborn asshead boyfriend from blowing himself up in a race-related "accident."

Mouse's heart beat loudly as he struggled with what to do. In his nightmare, the sky had been filled with rain and fire as he climbed the rungs to rescue Sadao from the top. Shiratori was trying to warn him of something from a helicopter and Tagata was trying to chop it down. But Sadao wasn't trapped in this tower, he was trapped in the Mustang and the race. Trapped in his obligation?! Is that what Shiratori wanted him to understand? Is that why Sadao didn't ring the bell? Because he felt obligated to suffer and bear everyone's weight?

Ah, fuck parables! They didn't make sense when he read the Bible to those old ladies as a kid and they didn't make any sense to him now, either. Straight talk was what worked for him.

Hold on... what's this?

The guards were changing shift. Two men came up to replace the two leaving duty. Mouse grabbed his rifle and watched them through the gunsight. Oh my god. Now it all made sense. Straight talk was what was needed, so he grabbed the CB and hailed Shiratori.

Mouse, with a pack of bomb on his back and the rifle slung over his shoulder, strolled out from the brush. He cleared the fence without being seen and marched right up to the two armed uniformed men after their counterparts had left the area.

"Hey guys!" he said and waved.

The guards stood stone silent and watched him approach, dumbfounded.

"You know," Mouse continued as he sauntered up to them. "There sure are a lot of people who've been looking for you two. I got one of them on the CB right now."

Mouse clicked the CB speaker and Shiratori, their former boss, proceeded to bitch out the two missing guardsmen from the night of the raid in a typhoon of Japanese. Their skin went almost as pale as Mouse's as they looked at one another in panic.

"I'd suggest you two go now and get a head start on the General. He'll be catching up with you shortly to discuss your severance."

The two men squealed like schoolgirls and ran past Mouse, leapfrogging the fence and dashing into the cover of the hills. Mouse clicked off the CB and smiled. *Too easy.*

The rain began to fall again in sheets as Mouse climbed the emergency maintenance ladder up the side of the tower on the leeward side. The tower's designer had that much sense at least to keep the workmen and would-be saboteurs out of the worst of the wind, which blew out through the valley between the 12,000-foot Wasatch peaks. Why did his dream have to be so accurate about the damn rain? Clouds had been collecting and breaking all day. He could use a break about now as he chanced a quick look down.

Nope... nope... don't do that, bad idea. Looking down, not inspirational!

Instead he set the CB mic into "speak mode" and let it dangle from his neck as he hailed Sadao.

"Hey Cowboy, it's me. You don't have to talk. I know you're busy, but I want you to know I wouldn't go risking my stupid neck like this for just any guy. Though, I will say the view up here is amazing!" Mouse kept his eyes ahead and reached for the next rung. One hand, one foot; one hand, one foot.

"You see, I figured it out. Maybe Shiratori was right, maybe I am smart, or maybe my creature comforts aren't just a random pain in the ass. I've loved radios ever since I was a little kid. I liked taking them apart and putting them back together. I built little antenna you know, out of coat hangers and shit trying to get a signal. I'd tear the radio out of any car in the junkyard if it looked like it might work a little better.

"I sat up on that hot tin roof and cooked my skull trying to build a bigger and better receiving grid. But aside from some crappy Country Western and occasional evangelical broadcasts, all I ever got was static. And as I grew older, I got to love that static. Like this might sound crazy, but there were almost whispers in it. I could imagine someone was sending me a message.

"That's why I gotta sleep with the radio on, you see. I know you get annoyed when you come back to the trailer and I've left it on, but it puts me right out. Doesn't matter where I am or what I'm doing or what kind of trouble I'm in, I love that static. Okay, I'm gonna pause here. I think I'm high enough. I can see the main transmitter. Wind's really bad up here and I don't want the pack to blow off before I can climb down."

Mouse paused his ramblings and slowly, removed the strap from his shoulder and unclipped the binding. He tossed the free end of the strap over the support post and reconnected it before slipping the bag off his other arm. He unzipped the compartment and peeped in. The translucent dead eye of the camera stared back at him. Mouse showed it his middle finger and zipped it back up. Then he unzipped the smaller compartment and took out the CB console and shoved it into his racing jacket pocket and zipped it closed. Done. Now the hard part, getting down.

"So that's how I figured it out, you see," Mouse continued into the open CB as he descended the rungs toward the ground and his waiting rifle. "The trigger, it's in the radio signal. The night of the raid it woke me up with that piercing screech. I've never heard anything like it. It came right through the speakers and shot me awake. The Chairman used it to bypass the retina scan and open the door for Kinjo and his punks. I was stupid enough to tell that sonofabitch at dinner during our filming that I was having issues with a kid named "Kinjo" in the camp. If he couldn't buy me out, he could buy someone else out with a bone to pick, or a couple of bored guards interested in a career change.

"But the other night we both heard it, right? I'm not crazy – Lupe and Kei were making that stew and had the Mexican oldies on, remember? The radio went nuts a second right before the explosion. Shiratori caught that too – not the signal, it didn't make it into the broadcast, too much engine noise – but he caught the flash in the reflection of a racer's handlebars. We have that all on playback. Lupe recorded all of it, including the broadcast of the camera I shot down over your car. Lupe says the networks are scrambling now to make sense of that explosion and are making the connection to Goro's accident.

"It's all coming together, Sadao. You don't have to finish this race just to spite the man who tried to take you out. We've done it for you. Now have some sense and drop out now! You hear me?! If I'm willing to get myself killed falling off this 200-foot tower for you, you can at least return the favor!! Are you listening?!" Mouse clicked off the speaker and got an immediate reply.

"Mouse! Shut up and listen! I'm trying to tell you the drone is in the car! The new one just caught up and flew in the window! It's bouncing around in the back!"

Mouse looked down. He had reached the lower rungs. He slipped past the ladder and slid down the central support pole 30 feet to the ground like a fireman.

"Shit, Sadao! Get out of that car!!"

"Can't, the Korean is trying to rear-end me! He's not even pretending to pass. He wants me to spin-off! He keeps tagging my bumper! *Kuso!*"

Mouse's heart pounded as he ran for his gun. "Just hang on, okay?! Don't slow down! If he tags you and you hit the ditch, the camera will go off. The Chairman wants to take you out in a fireball! I've got the rifle now, this bitch is going down!"

Mouse dropped the CB and shouldered the gun. Despite the rainfall he was able to aim precisely on the backpack left hanging in the breeze 200 feet up.

Bam! Bam!! Boom!!!

One of the shots hit and Mouse dove for cover as the dead camera drone released its hidden weapon in a stunning explosion, bringing down the top five feet of the tower with it.

Shit, run!!!

Without time to think, Mouse ran as fast as his legs could carry him. The rain fell down around him mixed with a hail of smoking, fiery bits of metal and plastic as the tower top crashed into the hilltop behind him in a tangled mess of melting steel.

The next time Mouse would hear from Sadao was when the 100-year-old Obsidian Mustang he'd rebuilt for him roared across the finish-line 30 minutes later in a fantail of muddy salt, splattering an enormous crowd of cheering fans. Mouse pushed and shoved as fast as he could to the winner's circle, crossing ropes and leaping over the blockades to run up and give that man the biggest hug he'd ever felt in his 21 years of racing.

"Uumph," Sadao said in his ear, hugging him back. "I thought we were trying to avoid a collision."

"Fuck you," Mouse laughed and kissed his neck. "Where's that goddamn camera?"

Sadao pointed behind him as bouquets of flowers pelted them both. Mouse let go of Sadao long enough to peek in the window. The camera drone was dead as a billiard ball, rolling around on the floor. *Haha. Got you, bastard.*

When Mouse popped his head back out, Sadao was already being escorted away by security. They were taking him up toward the stage platform through the throng of news reporters with microphones and flashing cameras.

"Hey, wait!" Mouse tried to follow but was stopped by a security officer who put a gun barrel in his side.

"Back off!" the guard ordered. "Winners only!"

Mouse was soon pushed aside by reporters rushing to greet the Korean and Taiwanese drivers who had now pulled up into the circle to take second and third. "Ow! Fuck, wait! Sadao!"

Sometimes being small really sucked.

Mouse stepped back and retreated to an area under a flagpole where he was able to climb up a few feet and stand on a pair of rungs to see around. On the far side of the stage, he could see a glint of gold flashing off the polished armor of the one and only General Shiratori. Security guards were removing his arms and whooping his outfit, only to give up and waive him through, with the ceremonial bokken intact.

Down below, Mouse spotted Lupe getting pushed around in the mass of excitement and put his hands over his mouth to shout down to him.

"Lupe! Lupe! Look up!"

Lupe eyes tracked to him and the young man smiled, bouncing his way excitedly through the audience toward the line of flags. He climbed the pole next to Mouse and high-fived him mid-air.

"Good job, Gringo! We just pulled in! Did you see Boss cross the checkered banner?"

"I sure did, smug sonofabitch! Probably thinks he did it all by himself."

"Hah! We'll teach him better, yeah?"

Mouse smiled and watched his lover take the stage next to a comically armless but regal-looking Shiratori, as well as a hapless looking Chairman and other division Chairpersons represented in the winner's circle.

Mouse's eyes stayed only on Sadao, who looked exceptionally reserved on this occasion. Mouse had to imagine this event would be bittersweet for him, especially given what potentially tough roads the Chairman had laid out before him. As the webspinner approached the microphone, Mouse wondered if he would retract any of his threats, given Sadao's clearly uncontested win and the controversy with the cameras.

"First ladies and gentlemen, fans of this amazing sport – I want to thank you for joining us in the concluding ceremony of the 2071 Overland Multi-Division Challenge!"

A cheer went up and shouts of Orochi! Orochi! could be heard among them.

"And second of all, I'd like to apologize for the technical difficulties we encountered trying to bring everyone closer to this highly challenging race."

A chorus of boos went up. But for once it was nice to not see a dozen drones flying about overhead. Only local news cameras were covering the ceremony at present. The Chairman would have a lot of explaining to do to the networks as to why the last 30 minutes of the race went black.

"We regret that our main broadcast tower suffered what we believe was a freak lightning strike during the final minutes of the race, rendering our mobile systems inactive."

Another chorus of boos went up and someone threw a dead camera drone up onto the stage. The Chairman leapt away from it and pointed to one of his guards to remove it at once.

If my rifle wasn't buried under two tons of tower right now, I'd have shot it clean off the stage for you, bastard.

"Anyhow, without any further adieu, I'd like to award our winners... "

The crowd went nuts as the Taiwanese driver and his Team Leader graciously accepted their wreaths and cups. Then came the Koreans – the driver and his Team Leader received their awards for having no trouble throwing the race just to attempt to blow Sadao off the road. The fans didn't know any better and screamed for them anyway. *Idiots.*

"Now, may I confess it gives me great personal joy to present the first place award to a team I followed throughout most of my youth. From the day a young rookie placed first in a race very much like the one today using nothing but his cunning and skills as a fine racing champion. Sadao Koga of the Orochi Team, it gives me great pleasure to present to you and General Shiratori this winners' cup and all the glory that it embodies."

The words slipped off his tongue like honey as he passed the four-foot tall beast of a cup to Sadao. Sadao took it and smiling, raised his arm to the crowd as the flashbulbs went off and fans threw desert flowers into the air.

It was only when the Chairman and Sadao exchanged a handshake and bow that Mouse at last looked toward Shiratori and noticed something odd. In his *obi* belt he wore the short bokken as usual but underneath it, the hilt of the long blade was mismatched. It was unlike Shiratori to make such a wardrobe mistake.

Sadao waved to the crowd one last time and passed the trophy to Shiratori, who armless, was only able to grasp it against his chest with the forearm of his three fingered hand. Sadao stepped toward him to steady the trophy. But as he pulled back to allow the cameras to take the shot of his decorated General, Sadao reached for the mismatched katana and drew the very real, very sharp blade from its scabbard.

"Nooooooo!!" Mouse screamed, but nothing could stop the sweep of steel as it swung out from left to right in a full circular thrust to slice clean through the Chairman's neck.

Bonk!

The sound it made when the curly-haired skull hit the stage was almost comical. At first all anyone could do was laugh nervously. Clearly, this was a joke. The Chairman's head couldn't really be sitting there plopped awkwardly, looking down on them with its ever-present grin. The six-foot body, in a tailored tie-less suit – now made five-foot and some change – stiffened and fell forward with a splat, raining pulsating spurts of red gore down upon the packed mass of reporters and fans.

Someone screamed – it was Shiratori, ponytail flying as he ran forward into the line of stunned armed guardsmen with the heavy trophy tucked under his arm like a shogun playing football.

Sadao went for the remaining guards to their right – and hacked at their arms and legs before guns could be drawn.

"Fire! Fire, you idiots!" Someone shouted onstage and bullets hit the air in nearly every direction at once. That was all it took to set the crowd to panicking.

Mouse exchanged a terrified look with Lupe. Their poles were being knocked about precariously by the fleeing, screaming mob all running at once in ten different directions.

Mouse was the first to snap out of it. "Lupe, take the jeep! Go find Tagata! He's at Utah University Medical Center!"

Lupe nodded, still stunned. "What about you?"

"I have to go rescue these idiots!"

Lupe had tears of fright in his eyes. "Don't get shot, okay?"

"Not planning on it," Mouse said with an ironic smile and jumped down into the mass of moving spectators.

Mouse was pummeled and knocked about left and right as the panic wave blew past him. He steeled himself and headed upstream one step at a time toward the dwindling sounds of gunshots.

Damn them! Damn these Japanese fools and their samurai bullshit! This is 2071 not 1702!

Bodies began to appear as Mouse fought his way up to the rim of the stage. The Chairman's guards had been so trigger happy they'd shot up part of the crowd and stage crew as well as their apparent targets. Mouse could hear moans and screams coming from the stage as he climbed up a short ladder and peered over the lip to check the scene.

Two hapless guards were standing amidst the carnage turning about in a panic, weapons drawn, ready to shoot anything that moved. There were bodies all over the stage – some alive, some not so alive. Mouse fought back his bile and waited until the two remaining guards just gave up and ran.

Mouse crawled up onto the black flooring and scanned the casualties. The Korean driver who'd tried to run Sadao down was shot dead through the throat. Two stage-hands who were shot in the legs and arms, were trying to help each other get away. Hacked up parts of fingers and flesh filleted from shoulders and calves littered the stage under their bleeding moaning victims. And through it all near the far upper end, Mouse saw a glint of armor. Shiratori! He ducked his head and ran to him.

"Shiratori! Shiratori! Where's Sadao?"

Shiratori lay on his back, grinning up blankly at the sky, which now at this very late moment was beginning to clear and let the sun come out. The General's glimmering, golden armor was littered with bullet holes, as was the very bent and blood-smeared trophy that still lay clasped under his left arm. It looked like he was trying to speak. Mouse leaned in closer to his lips. A spurt of blood came out along with a single word of Japanese.

"Kachimashita!"

Red bubbles followed and the proud eye, the remaining eye, went sightless. Mouse panicked as tears fell down his face. He laid a hand on Shiratori's chest and shook him.

"Shiratori! Shiratori!"

"I win," groaned a voice behind him – so weak and pained he'd barely recognized it.

"Sadao!!" Mouse cried, kicking aside the heavy stage curtain that had fallen over him, keeping him from view. Sadao too was on his back not far from the General, reaching out toward the golden man as if to take his hand.

Mouse grasped it instead and leaned over Sadao's face, checking his head for wounds. He was coated in layers of blood – who knew whose. "Sadao... why? Why did you do this? Why?" Hot tears of anger flowed over the ones of sorrow.

Sadao's eyes were still on Shiratori. "*Kachimashita*, he said. 'I win.' So he is gone. *Sayonara, ore no tomodachi...* "

Sadao's eyes closed and he let out a long breath.

"No... No – ! No!!" Smack!

Mouse hit him across the face. Sadao's eyes fluttered open. "You open your eyes and look at me, you sonofabitch!"

"*Konezumi?* You do not belong here among the dead... "

"And neither do you, you piece of shit! Now tell me which puddle of blood is yours!"

"Leg," Sadao gasped weakly.

Mouse pushed the curtain aside further and found what was left of Sadao's hip and upper leg blown open. The bones were shattered by bullet holes and a very large artery was bleeding freely into the brushed black velvet.

Oh shit! Oh, shit... no... no... this isn't happening! Yes it is and you'd better find a way to deal with it fast before he bleeds out!

Mouse brushed his tears aside and gathered up a wad of curtain. With everything he had, he pressed it down into the gushing wound with both hands. "Help us!" he screamed, looking around. "Somebody help!"

"Phone... " Sadao sighed, motioning with a limp arm.

"Huh?" Not far from Sadao lay his satellite phone – coated in blood too, but still flashing. It had power. Mouse lunged for it, still holding Sadao's leg and dialed with his free hand.

"911. What is your emergency?"

"We have a shooting! People are bleeding all over the place!"

"Your location?"

"Um, salt flats. We're on the grandstand stage just north of Saltair. There's been a massacre! Send choppers now! Please! Men and women too I think have been shot and stabbed!"

"'I'm sorry sir, did you say you were shot or stabbed?"

"Neither, I'm okay ... my ... boyfriend, he's hurt! He was shot in the leg. It's bad, really bad. Please, I'm begging, send a chopper, as many as you have!"

"Sir, choppers are already being sent. They are in route... "

Oh God. Thank god, thank god!

Mouse dropped the phone and let the emergency operator talk to air while he tended to Sadao with both hands. Every time the man tried to close his eyes, Mouse would scream and smack at him to stay awake.

"Sadao! Baby, please!" He pressed as hard as he could on the wound but the velvet wadded in his hands was only growing thicker and stickier with Sadao's blood.

"Please don't go! Please – !" Mouse sobbed, kissing the man's cold cheek with trembling lips. "Please stay with me, the choppers are coming!"

He could hear them now thwap thwap in the distance. Mouse pressed his forehead to Sadao's and begged God to hear him. *Take whatever's good in me and save this man! Please! I can't be in this world if he's not in it! Take my soul and leave his. Please, God!*

"Your God never made a purer or more stubborn soul."

Mouse raised his head. Sadao had spoken. Had he heard the words inside his mind?

"'Find us a man who cannot be bought,' Shiratori said. 'Find us an American.'"

"What... ? Baby, don't try to talk, okay?"

Sadao's eyes had gained some focus and his hand rose to touch Mouse's cheek to wipe at his tears.

"Don't cry, *Konezumi*. A warrior must sacrifice whatever he can to protect his people. My little ones... they will be safe now." Sadao smiled wistfully. "Taga has gathered them. He will lead them to a better home than I could ever give... "

"Sadao, Tagata is in the hospital. You'll see him there soon."

Sadao shook his head slowly. "I am sorry I couldn't tell you our plans. Why I could not stop the race, even as you begged me to. Your words were hard to hear but I could not bring myself to shut off the radio. I heard you, my sweet Mouse – every mile, every turn, I listened to your voice, thinking I would never hear it again."

"W-what... ? What are you saying?"

Sadao motioned him closer and pressed his dry lips to Mouse's that were wet with tears. "*Gomen, Konezumi* – I did not want to be the one to break you... "

Sadao's eyes closed and his chest fell, releasing breath as the wind of the landing helicopters blew Mouse's hair across his face and wet cheeks. And for Mouse, who had never missed a chance to embrace life as it swirled and shifted around him, felt this world he'd held onto so tightly, rend in two.

Mouse sat on the stage alone, surrounded by the dead. The ones who could be saved or that the paramedics deemed possible to save, had been lifted out – their retreating wings now only an echo across the clearing blue skies. He was too numb for sorrow or pain and just sat in the stench of blood as the recurring futile vision of the paddles zapping his lover's chest over and over filled his sightless eyes until he saw something small and white fluttering across the surface of the stage. *A bird*, he thought, as he watched it hop and dive in the breeze. It came closer and flapped its one long wing against the golden carapace of Shiratori's armor.

Mouse stumbled to it on stiff limbs and lifted it up. It was a torn scrap of the Orochi Banner, rolling about blithely in the aftermath of armageddon. He rolled it up and tucked it into the back pocket of his bloodied riding pants. Looking down he could see the reflection of his distorted face in Shiratori's armor. The man still lay dead within this golden self-imposed coffin. Something wasn't right and Mouse bent to untie the cords that held the General's breastplate in place, pulling it loose and away. Underneath, Shiratori wore only a thin cotton white yukata. It was so thin you could see the color of his skin underneath – now greyed by death.

Mouse reached in and whispered '*Gomen*' to the body as he undid the sash. He took both flaps of blood-stained cloth in his hands and redressed the man properly for his condition – right over left. Then he re-tied the *obi* and replaced the breast plate.

You were wearing it the way we bury the dead!

Mouse stood up and admired his work. To him it seemed as if the General was smiling up at the sky – seemingly as at peace with the world the day he was born as the day he left it. Mouse kicked around the stage until he found Sadao's missing racing jacket. He picked it up, and sure enough, inside the pockets he found a pack of cigarettes and a lighter.

He took the lighter and pulled out the rolled-up Orochi Banner from his pocket. He walked back to the glinting body and tucked one end into the folds of the layered metal feathers, and lighting the opposite end of the banner, let it fall and burn. Using his teeth, Mouse bit the end of the plastic striking head off of the lighter's base and dribbled the fluid over Shiratori's body. The skin and cloth lit up in red-orange flames.

"I set his spirit free," Mouse proclaimed to no one in particular walked away without a backward glance.

Chapter XXIII

The Open Road

One month later.

"Welcome to the Utah State Prison. Voice recognition required to proceed. If you have voice recognition clearance, please speak your first and last name into the microphone."

"Mouse."

…..… "Unable to verify. Please speak your first and last name clearly into the microphone."

"I said, it's Mouse."

…....… "The name, 'Mouse' is not a valid entry. You must speak both your first and last name into the microphone to proceed."

"Mouse… Mouse."

…....… "Unable to verify. Please speak your first and last name clearly into the microphone."

"I don't have a last name you piece of shit speaker phone! The name is Mouse. Just Mouse. M-O-U-S-E!"

"Voice recognition successful. Please proceed… Mouse."

The heavy metal door rolled back. Before him was a small overlit room with plain white walls with a small white desk and two chairs. The room was divided in half, floor to ceiling, by a thick plate of plexiglass.

Mouse sat in the chair and waited nervously for the opposite door to open. He could see his face reflected in the glass and fiddled with his bun. *Does the hair look okay?*

There was a robotic beep and the opposite door opened. Mouse stood up.

Sadao.

He was dressed in yellow – terrible color – and so pale and drawn. He shuffled forward painfully, leaning heavily on a crutch. Mouse knew those bastards had released him too early from the hospital. But every protest he'd filed through the Public Defender's Office fell on deaf ears. He was lucky to get these ten minutes.

Mouse sat and slowly put his hand up to the glass, hoping he could somehow magically pass through it and brush aside the unkempt bangs that fell over his lover's eyes. The beard was long and uneven, too.

"Sadao?"

Sadao raised a finger toward the left of the window. Speakerphone, yes. Mouse clicked it on. Sadao raked his bangs back and did the same. The com hissed and came to life.

"Hey, Cowboy... " Mouse said, trying to smile. "How you doin'?"

Sadao coughed and returned the smile. "Been better."

His cheekbones stood out more than normal. Mouse hadn't seen him since the chopper lifted him away dead. Just the fact he was breathing was a miracle to him.

"They been feeding you okay in here?"

Sadao shrugged. "About as well as Cook-san."

Mouse laughed as tears fell from his eyes. "That good, huh?"

"Don't cry, *Konezumi*," he said and put his hand up to the window to mirror Mouse's.

Mouse pushed his forehead to the glass to get closer. "Want to take care of you," he said, licking the salty drops from his lips. "I want you to come home. It's lonely in that big ass trailer."

Sadao reached out to stroke his cheek where it lay against the glass. "Might be awhile, I'm afraid. Lupe keeping you company?"

"Yeah, he's been great. Pissed as hell at you, though. He told me to tell you that. 'Tell Boss he's a *bakamono* for ditching our asses!'"

Sadao nodded. "Tell him I'm sorry, but I wanted someone to stick around and keep an eye on this guy I know. Gets into trouble a lot. Has a thing for older men with tattoos."

Mouse sniffled in agreement. "Yeah, maybe I do need a babysitter. Maybe we both do. It was a cruel trick to leave us abandoned in the desert with nothing but tire tracks leading away from the camp in all directions."

"I'm sorry about that. But out of the whole team you two were the only natural born citizens. Are you both okay? Is the media circus leaving you alone now?"

"Yeah, they've moved on to juicer stories. The whole world of racing is on trial – no thanks to you. Investigations into the various Division heads are bringing out all kinds of skeletons. Did you know Chairwoman Baker was once a man?"

Sadao raised his brows. "Do you really want me to answer that?"

"Okay, no! No... that's fine!" Mouse said, fending him off.

"Made you smile, though. A real smile. That's all I wanted to see."

Mouse let the smile linger on his lips a moment longer. "Oh, I brought them for you, the books you asked for." Mouse pulled the two small worn paperbacks from his jacket pocket and set them into the sliding tray in front of the glass. He shut the lid, which allowed Sadao to pull the tray towards himself and lift the lid on his side to retrieve them.

Sadao held them up to his nose and sniffed. A smile came over him. Mouse had no idea what books they were – they were both in Japanese.

"I was glad I could bring you something. They won't let me pass you carving knives or tobacco. Sorry."

Sadao tucked the books lovingly into his jumpsuit pocket. "It's okay, I've been told I need to quit."

"Really? Big bad snake is going to give up his vices?"

"Not all of them," Sadao said with a wicked grin.

A buzzer rang. "Five minutes remaining …"

Mouse felt his heart drop back into his gut. "Sadao – !"

"It's okay, *Konezumi*. It'll be okay."

"It's not okay! You don't deserve to be in here! You need to post bail! Call whoever you need to call – wherever you sent the clan off to – and come home to me!"

"I won't ask my children to pay for their father's crimes."

"Damn you, Sadao! I need you and I miss you. They're going to send you away and the idea I'll never be with you again is terrifying me!"

Sadao didn't answer, but closed the lid on the tray and passed it back to Mouse.

"Put your hair in it," he said.

"Huh… ?" Mouse sniffled.

"Put your head down and let your hair fall into it."

Mouse pressed his cheek to the cool desktop and undid his bun, letting his tangles fall in a messy puddle into the tray, and shut the lid over it. "Don't pull it!" he said like a child.

Sadao chuckled and dragged the tray toward him slowly and lifted the lid, drawing out Mouse's hair strand by strand like he was handling fine silk. He wound the longer hairs around his fingers and palm, dipping his nose to inhale their scent.

The gentle pull of Sadao's fingers and the softness of his expression as he indulged in the smell of him made Mouse's cheeks flush and his belly melt. *How does he do that?*

Buzzzz! "Time is up. Remove contents from tray and retreat from viewing area. You have 20 seconds to comply… 19… 18… "

Sadao raised his head and kissed the wad of Mouse he held lovingly in his hand. He folded it gently and set it back into the tray, shutting the lid. Mouse pulled it back to him numbly and just stared. His heart pounded, as Sadao struggled to a standing position, fitting the crutch back under his arm. The man smiled warmly at him. He didn't look as haggard as when he first limped in.

"You're going to be fine, *itoshii Konezumi*. Just, take care with your hair," he said, pointing to the tray.

Buzzz!!! The lights shut off.

"Sadao?! Sadao?!"

"Your scheduled visitation time has expired."

"Fuck you and your idea of time! I wanted a lifetime with that man! Do you hear me? Sadao?!"

Mouse stood up and a wad of his hair ripped out where it was caught on the tray lid. "Fucking stupid hunk of... " He felt around in the dark blindly to pull himself loose and was startled to feel a small slip of paper wound up in with the tangles. He palmed it quickly and exited.

Outside Lupe stood in the sunlight in a pair of shades, leaning up against Sadao's trailer, waiting for Mouse to come out.

"You okay, Gringo? You see Boss?"

Mouse nodded briskly. "Yeah, I saw him. Get inside."

Lupe opened the cab and they both hopped up into the main compartment. Mouse motioned him to come away from all the windows as he unfolded the tiny scrap of paper in his hand.

"What is it?" Lupe asked.

"Something Sadao passed to me. It's numbers... "

Mouse blinked confusedly while Lupe flipped up his sunglasses and took a look. When his eyes rose from the scrap, they were bright with excitement.

"Not numbers, Gringo *pendejo* – coordinates! Map coordinates!"

Mouse grinned. Maybe Sadao, for the first time in his life had at last decided to ring that fucking bell.

"Feel like a road trip, little buddy?" he asked.

"I sure do!"

"I call shotgun!"

"Fuck no, you can't call shotgun. You can haul this big ass motherfucker around for once."

"I called it, too late!" Mouse said, jumping into the passenger's seat.

"Ah, shit," Lupe said, crawling into the driver's seat in defeat. "Why'd Boss ever pick your lazy gringo ass to fix his damn bikes?"

Mouse laughed as he pulled a heap of maps out of the glove compartment and let them spill out onto the floor.

"Because he told me the night we met that he was looking for a mechanic he could trust."

The Orochi novel series continues in:

Orochi no Yaiba
Orochi no Saido

by Itoshi

with novel illustrations
by Aldaria

Visit: yaoi-revolution.com

by Chris B

Orochi no kishi

by Itoshi

Cover Art by Aldaria
Interiors by Lehanan Aida & Aldaria

The Hourglass comic
by Aldaria | story by Itoshi

Publisher/Typesetting: Sharon Barela
Associate Publisher: Emie Butcher
Editor: Mujani Sowell
Marketing Assistant: Nicole Le
Additional Artwork: Chris Barela
Special thanks to: Kimina & Cindy!

Fourth Edition: August 2016
ISBN: 978-0-9889111-9-2

©2013/2016 Yaoi Revolution /A Saguaro Media Company - All Rights Reserved

All characters and situations contained in this novel and comic are fictional.
Any resemblance to people/characters living, non-living or fictional is coincidental.
No portion of this book, text or images may be reproduced in digital or print formats
by ANYONE without the written permission of Yaoi Revolution.
Scanlators - THIS MEANS YOU!

**This doujinshi is to be read left to right!
Please go to the end of the book, and read
in the opposite direction of the novel. -->**

**Thank you for experiencing the first 12 pages of our
52 page Orochi doujinshi, *The Hourglass*.
For ordering information, please visit:
www.yaoi-revolution.com/hourglass
and follow us on Facebook:
www.facebook.com/YaoiRevolution**

www.yaoi-revolution.com   yaoirevolutionnow@gmail.com

HA
HA
LICK
MMN...
SQUEEZE
FEEL BETTER?
GET DRESSED. WE'RE LEAVING!
YOU KNOW, IF IT'S A FLAT YOU NEED FIXED, THERE'S ALWAYS THE 'HAND PUMP.'
?
NOT AS EFFICIENT!
TO BE CONTINUED ...

YEAH, RIGHT! YOU MET YOUR GARAGE MANAGER? TOTAL PRICK!
THUD
MAYBE YOU NEED A NIGHT OFF?
DON'T EVEN THINK ABOUT IT! YOU'RE HALF THE REASON I DON'T GET ANY SLEEP ANYMORE. THIS ASS IS OFF LIMITS UNTIL THIS RACE IS OVER, OR I GET A NEW CAREER!!
I'LL DEAL WITH SHIRATORI-SAN IN THE MORNING.
RIGHT NOW I NEED A MECHANIC!
GRAB

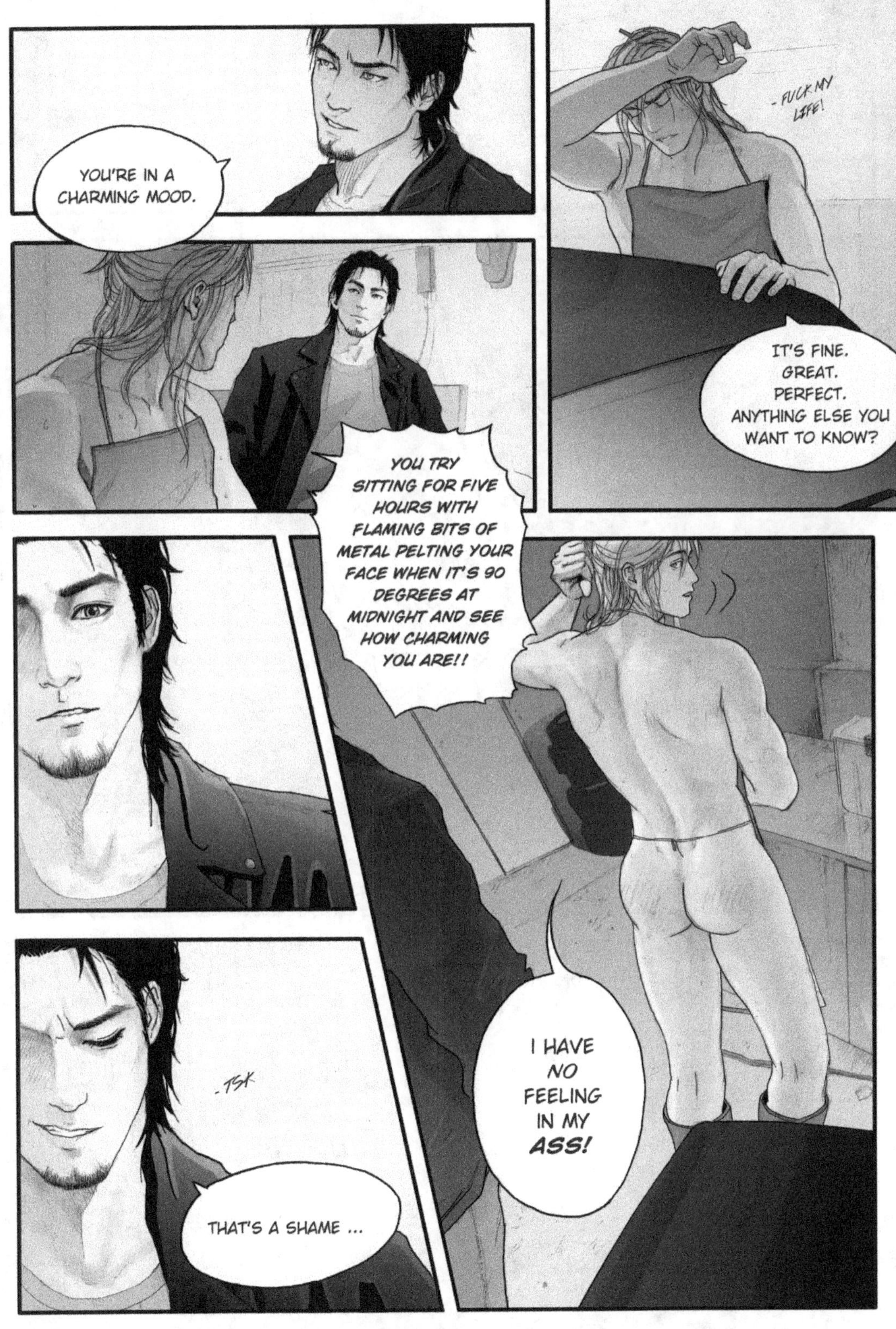

YOU'RE IN A CHARMING MOOD.
- FUCK MY LIFE!
IT'S FINE. GREAT. PERFECT. ANYTHING ELSE YOU WANT TO KNOW?
YOU TRY SITTING FOR FIVE HOURS WITH FLAMING BITS OF METAL PELTING YOUR FACE WHEN IT'S 90 DEGREES AT MIDNIGHT AND SEE HOW CHARMING YOU ARE!!
I HAVE NO FEELING IN MY ASS!
- TSK
THAT'S A SHAME ...

SADAO?

SO CUTE WHEN HE'S PISSED

FUCK!!
WOULD IT KILL YOU TO RADIO FIRST?!

NO TIME. I JUST CAME DOWN FROM THE SUMMIT STATION.

THOUGHT I WOULD STOP IN AND SEE HOW YOU'RE COMING ALONG WITH THE MUSTANG.
!!

TZZDT!
NUDE... AGAIN?

KNOCK!
KNOCK!
ZZZZZ

POP!
GAAH!!

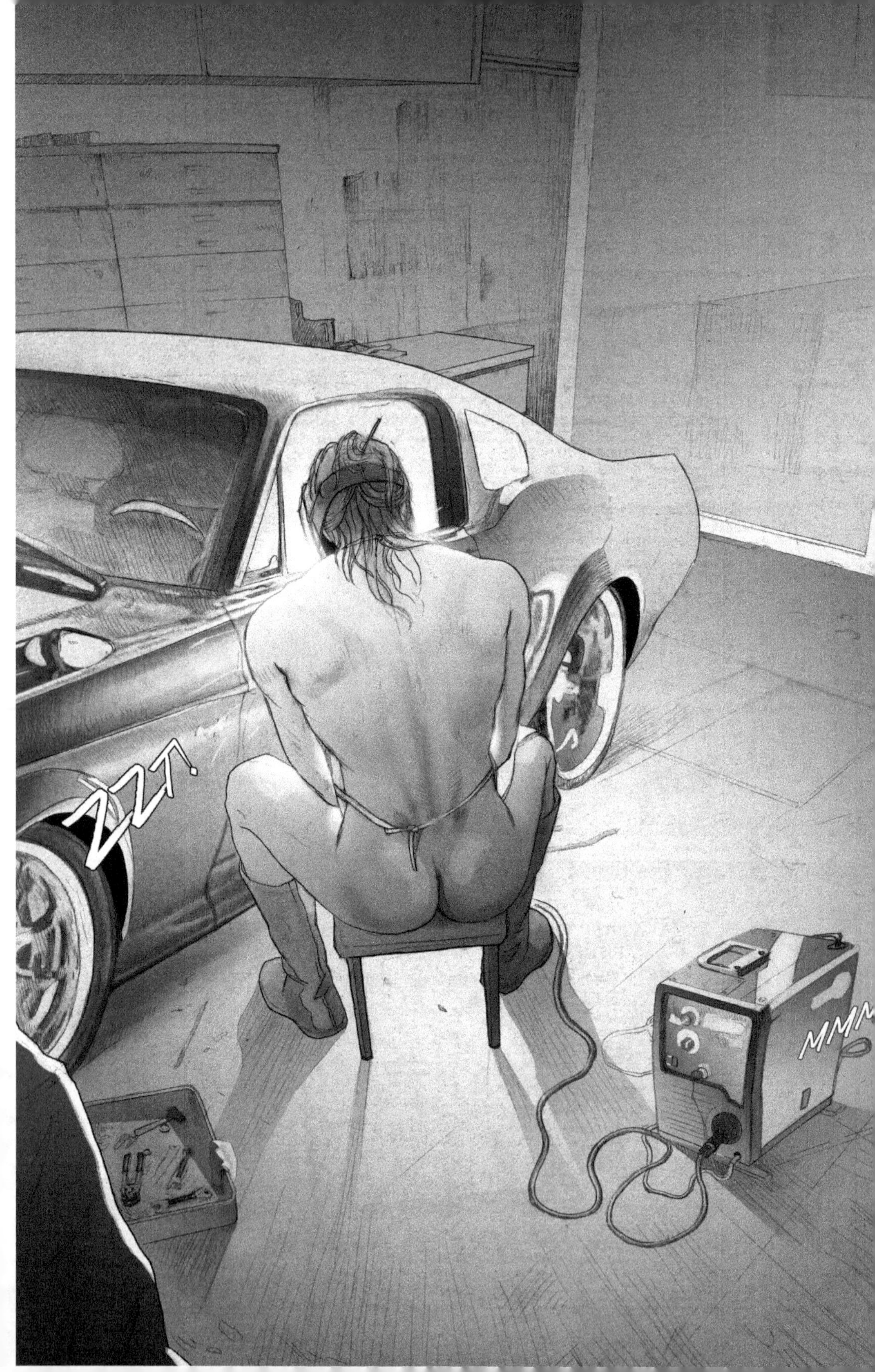

ZZT.
MMM

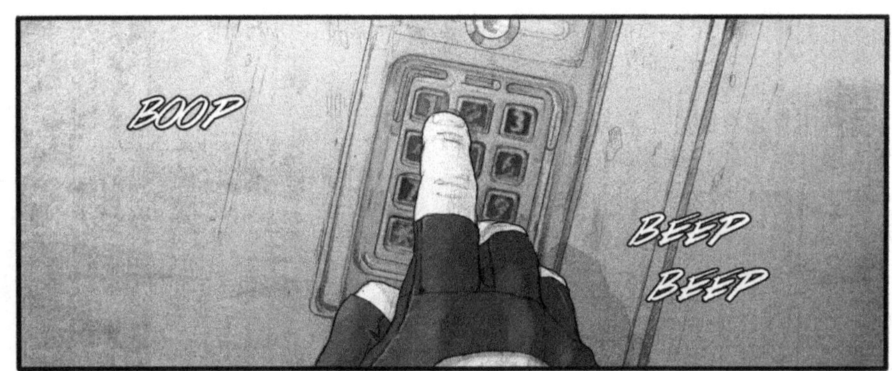

BOOP
BEEP
BEEP

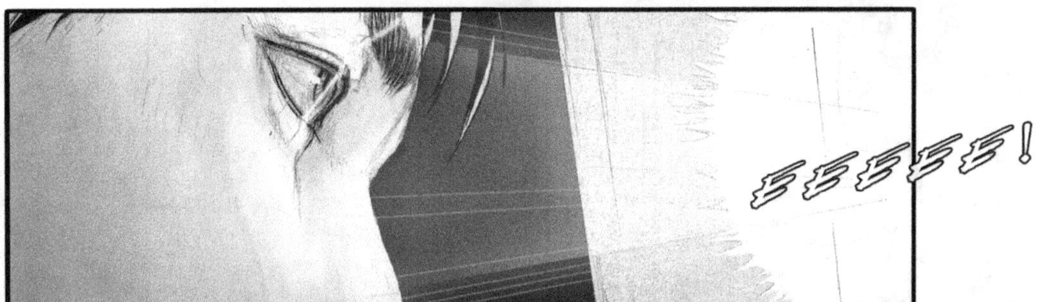

EEEEE!

BAM!
SLIDE!

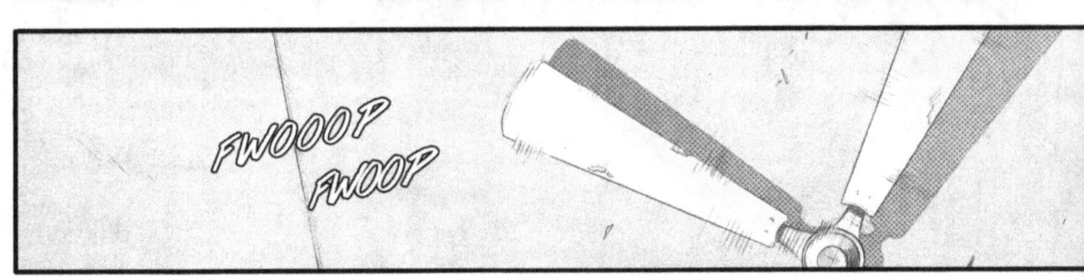

FWOOOP
FWOOP

- DOKO KARA?
SLAM!
OTSUKARE...
NOD
BOW
BOW
- SUIMASEN BOSS!!

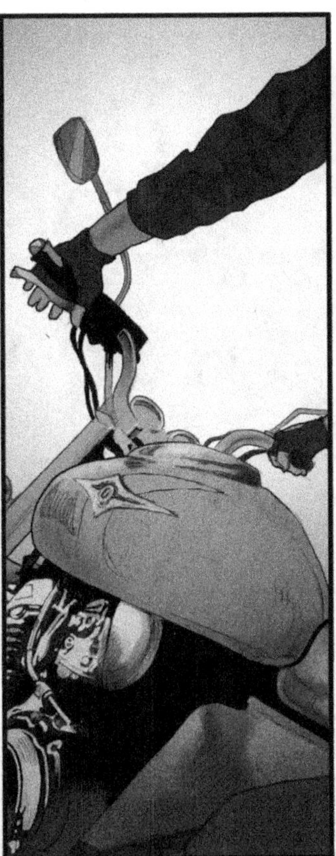
CRUNCH

SWIPE

CRUNCH

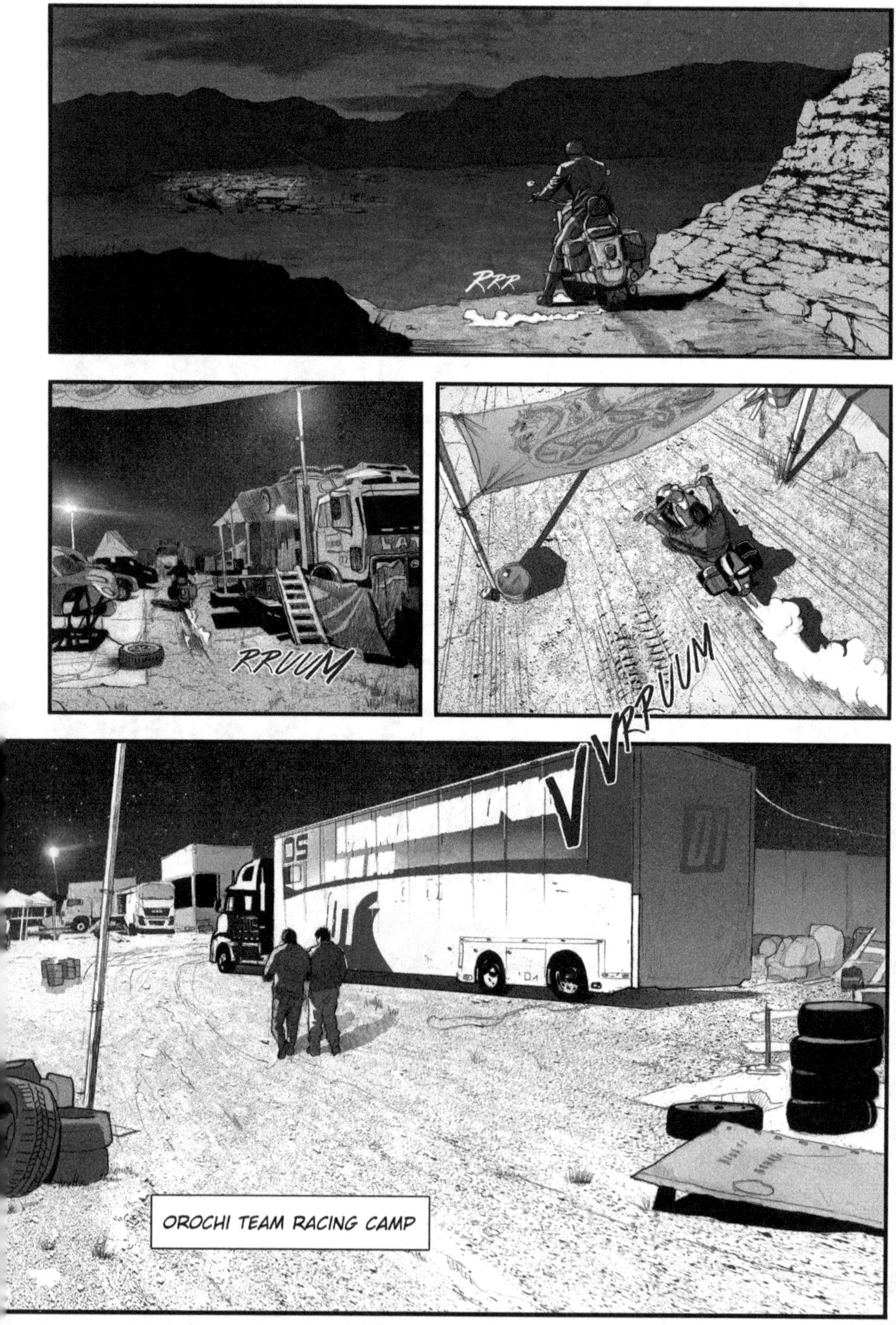

OROCHI TEAM RACING CAMP

POP!
VROOMMM!
RUUMMMM!!

THE GREAT SALT DESERT
UTAH WASTELANDS - 2071

The Hourglass

by Aldaria

story by Itoshi

The Orochi Series
by Itoshi

Orochi no Kishi

The Hourglass

Orochi no Yaiba

Orochi no Saido

Visit: yaoi-revolution.com
for ordering information

The Hourglass

Special
12 Page
Preview

Art
by Aldania
Story by Itoshi

12 New Artists – Fantasy Artbook Collection
SAMURAI 2.0

YAOI REVOLUTION
www.yaoi-revolution

www.ingramcontent.com/pod-product-compliance
Lightning Source LLC
Chambersburg PA
CBHW060944120726

47910CB00002B/488